"Tom Berger is a great writer. No doubt about it."
—*The Los Angeles Times*

"Hilarious . . . Reinhart may be a fool, but he is not a joke; he is simply human . . . REINHART IN LOVE gives [Berger] a solid place in contemporary fiction."
—Granville Hicks, *Saturday Review*

"An Adam-like innocent, trusting and open-eyed, Reinhart sometimes pretends to be a tough-minded and knowing conniver. The results are the same, however, he does not gain the whole world, but does manage to lose his soul. Mr. Berger's world (the American Midwest) is an enormous confidence game. Political graft, industrial fraud, false social facades, venal love, phony intellects, pastel-colored liberals are the ingredients of this contemporary morality. The forms of American life evoke in Mr. Berger a sardonic, if not always silent mirth . . . Reinhart . . . an oaf with blinding periods of intelligence . . . keeps the reader off balance."
—Thomas Lask, *The New York Times*

THE REINHART TRILOGY
by Thomas Berger
published by Ballantine Books:

CRAZY IN BERLIN

REINHART IN LOVE

VITAL PARTS

REINHART
IN LOVE

Thomas Berger

BALLANTINE BOOKS • NEW YORK

Certain portions of this book, in somewhat different form, were published in the following magazines and under the titles indicated:

Chapter 6 as "Reinhart Goes to Work," in *The Dial*, No. 2, 1960; Chapters 3, 4, 7, and 8 as "In Lieu of Dr. Goodykuntz," in *Esquire*, June 1961; and Chapter 9 as "Feeling the Squeeze," in *Mademoiselle*, October 1961.

Library of Congress Catalog Card Number: 62-9631

ISBN 0-345-27174-2

This edition published by arrangement with the Richard W. Baron Publishing Co., Inc.

Manufactured in the United States of America

First Ballantine Books Edition: April 1978

To my father and mother

REINHART
IN LOVE

Chapter 1

In a shed of unpainted boards, a kind of swollen privy, on a compound of like structures in a field of dirty snow somewhere in Indiana, an anonymous major after an eleventh-hour pitch for the Regular Army or at least the Reserve, bade goodbye to thirty-odd soldiers—among whom was Corporal Carlo Reinhart, 15302320, the oddest of the lot, take it as you would: clinically: his last six months' service had been as patient in the neuropsychiatric wards of sundry military hospitals abroad and at home; emotionally: as near as he could tell, he was the only man ever released from the U.S. Army who was sorry to go; legally: the official typist had printed an error on his discharge certificate. Instead of having been born in 1924 as he had always assumed, he was but four years old; according to the War Department he had been sprung from that first imprisonment in 1942, and there were all manner of officers' signatures to prove it and perhaps even to confine him in Leavenworth if two months hence he applied for some deserved privilege in his authentic person of twenty-one.

So, although now a civilian, he reported his problem to the major with nostalgic military courtesy, and got for these pains a rather wry direction to the typing building. The other jokers all rushed out towards the camp gate and the waiting bus, not having a minute to lose in getting back to brown-nose their civilian bosses. Reinhart was unfair because he didn't know any of them; the shitty thing about a separation center was that you were there for only three days of signing papers (which were sometimes faulty!), and everybody arrived slightly hostile to one another, already halfway back to civil society.

In the typing building a skinny T/4 looked as if he would spit in one's face.

"What's eating you?" Reinhart asked forcefully, using his new technique of the direct approach, learned from Europeans though perhaps ruder than theirs. But when challenged in a genial yet tough manner, your average man sheathes his fangs.

So did the T/4, who was suffering a bad case of dandruff, which allowed him some leeway in Reinhart's judgment. With a none too careful eraser—one that looked like a pencil, with rubber where the lead should be; Reinhart at first thought the jerk clerk was sabotaging him by merely blacking out the offending entry—he obliterated the wrong date and asked the right one. The finished job looked very fishy.

"Don't I need an officer to initial this, or something? Aren't you going to make a memorandum about it? Isn't there a duplicate that will read otherwise?"

The T/4 scratched his head, causing a minor blizzard. "You're out. What do you care?"

"Oh," said Reinhart. *"That's* what's eating you!" He prided himself on his understanding of people.

Of course by then the Indianapolis bus had left, and the paper schedule pasted on the board that marked the stop was illegible, having been defaced by the elements and the kind of malefactor who delights in dirty deeds towards the world at large. The ground was flecked with cigarette butts and frozen sputum. Two girls from the PX waited five minutes alongside him for the local. Naturally the fan-toothed one had a friendly mien and the pretty one not, though he haughtily turned away from both, preserving the exaggerated dignity by means of which he had at last got free of the nut ward. Actually, he was sane enough and had been so all the while except for a few weeks at the beginning of the therapy, when furthermore the temporary goofiness owed rather to a head wound sustained in a fight than to any natural predilection for mania—that is, any more than average. Which was no more than to say he knew right and wrong or anyway the theory of it subscribed to by civilized people in the Western Hemisphere: everyone who exalts himself shall be abased, while he who abases himself will be exalted.

At the moment he was sane with a vengeance: lonely, bereft, cold—because he was twice as large as your typical Homo sapiens, there was more to freeze—hungry, and utterly hopeless. It was just sheer luck he had remembered to pee before leaving the discharge building, or in addition to everything else he would have been shifting from one foot to the other like a schoolboy: you had to join a club to find a public toilet in America.

He waited forty-seven and a half minutes. A peculiarity of the Army overcoat was that it weighed like chain mail while deflecting the wind like gauze. Two civilian cars stopped and offered him rides: the first, a maroon Grotesque, apparently new though automobile production had been halted in 1942, was driven by a dark man who grinned like a dog rubbing its ass on the carpet. Reinhart had been warned by the Army against confidence men who lay in wait for veterans wadded with mustering-out money. The driver of the second, a chattering old heap that burned oil, was a fat, morose queer who had no real hopes that Reinhart would accept his offer, some stricken 4-F traveling salesman with his own irony on the myth. A sergeant, alone in his jeep, spun onto the highway without a look. On the other hand, a paternal colonel in his chauffeur-driven staff car did stop, but he was going the wrong way.

At last the bus arrived, slaying every living thing for a hundred yards with its mustard-gas exhaust. Reinhart paid the outrageous fare and went down the aisle to the back, where he would find room for his yards of leg; over his shoulder was the barracks bag of free clothing from Supply. He inadvertently clobbered the hat of some middle-aged woman and there ensued a demonstration from which he retreated. No unaccompanied girls, no other GI's—but through the window he saw the newest wave of dischargees hurtling down the camp road like hyenas who have sighted a cadaver. And so did the driver, and made haste to pull away before they could reach him.

Reinhart attempted to put into action his device for surviving civil life, cynicism, but it was especially difficult in the rear of a bus, where, he now remembered, he was as liable to car sickness as a Girl Scout. Not even his great strength sufficed to open the window sealed years ago by some Detroit assembly-line sadist. So he went to sleep.

He went to sleep again on the train going towards Ohio, having an entire seat to himself after the girl, who had gathered tightly against the window so that it was impossible to play sneaky leg with her, got off at a place called Rushville without a backward glance. He snoozed fitfully. Leaving the Army! He was still twenty-one and had never had another profession; he feared America, people, and life—not really but poetically, which was worse.

He awoke as a rat-faced vendor swayed through the car hawking sandwiches, and tried to see himself in the window

11

montage of moonlit corny cornfield and fat-faced ex-corporal: for so he had become in six hospital months, unfortunately not enough of them on the light diet. Neither had he shaved that morning; however, his beard did not reproduce well upon the glass. But he had spilled coffee on his suntan shirt and that did, so long as the ETO jacket hung open; which, too bad, was necessary because one jacket button was broken and wouldn't hold and another had disappeared.

Vanity. It was clear to Reinhart that Reinhart had none. His unkempt ghost, imposed on the passing countryside, grinned back peevishly. Some rain began to slobber the window. Masochistically he bought for twice the standard rate—at least it was in a paper envelope, for the vendor's fingernails were in severe mourning—a sandwich of gristle, Vaseline, and unidentified vegetable garbage. He drank a leaking cup of tepid water from the tap at the end of the car; the overflow served to wash his hand, which he wiped dry on his rump. His cigarettes had been crushed; the one he lighted looked like a twist of crepe paper and tasted ill in his mouth, which had been open while he slept.

Reinhart saw half his rumpled self, clear, in the toilet mirror; unseen beneath the Army shirt was the life preserver of useless flesh about his waist. The last time he had bathed, now a dim memory, he had soaped arms the color and consistency of uncooked bratwurst, and his pectorals had sagged like a woman's.

The figure he cut nowadays was unusual for a man who until six months before had been blond and pink and muscled as Hitler's prescription for the *Herrenmensch*. Reinhart was no longer even blond; what sprang from an untended crewcut grew snot-mottled and here and there dark with grease. To get away from the psychiatrists he had been forced to replace one kind of pride with another; thus his honorable discharge, which breathed no hint of how his service had ended; and thus his will, which was nonexistent. For example, if he had not been able to get a seat, he had just as soon have rolled up on the washroom floor between sink and W.C. Or if someone had encountered him and said: "Stay on the train till Newport, Kentucky, I'll get you a job there making beds in a cat house," why, Reinhart would have answered O.K. He cared as little about women, or money, or esteem as he cared about—his fingernails, which he noticed would give the sandwich seller's a run for the Filth Cup.

On the other hand, he could be a bright man again almost instantly: bath, shave, clean clothes, haircut being a matter of hours; and regular work with the dumbbells would sculpture

12

the old Reinhart from the flab in a mere month. If he so chose. For his will had not really been destroyed but just lay dormant. He delighted in his capacity for alteration, believing that it made him more human than your ordinary *homme moyen sensual* who stayed the same from cradle to grave. Not to mention that it gave some point to freedom of choice: he knew the differences between options, had experienced being a fop, then a slob. He had also been exposed to a host of other things in the British Isles and occupation Germany, and was certain he had at least dreamt of most philosophies. In his time he had been both sane and mad. The only trouble at the moment was in what he wanted to *be*. But he might decide that as early as the morrow.

With an open mind and the everpresent barracks bag, he detrained at the grandiose station in the Ohio city nearest his town, and wandered about under the mosaic murals of heroic pioneers and workingmen, in search of his father, whom he had requested by wire to appear with transportation. At the central newsstand leaned an elegant old person in gray homburg with cane. A great bald vulgar man and a small gracious woman annexed a skinny son at the gate of Track 3, and Reinhart was shocked and then touched to see that Dad kiss his PFC on the cheek, and the soldier wearing the Indian Head patch and Purple Heart, no pansy he. A swarthy gangster type swaggered at the side of a larger replica of himself home from the paratroops, where he had no doubt got invaluable experience in mayhem. One attractive lady—seeing whom stand alone Reinhart had to admit he considered moving in on: she was a touch old but had conniving green eyes and make-up laid on with a trowel; and lucky he didn't make his move, for out of the men's room shining from a shave stalked a young lieutenant and kissed her like a lover. A May-November liaison in the French style? The horny aunt of legend? Reinhart the rubberneck lurked behind their linkage and heard the officer murmur into her hennaed hair: "Momma! There's nobody like you." In retreat Reinhart struck and floored a man shorter but fatter than he; anyway, knocked off the old fellow's hat, picked it up, ran its nap along his arm like a haberdashery huckster, gave it back, and voided the area.

I have scanned the rotunda with my telescope but no father did I see, Reinhart said ironically to himself over his whiskey in the bar. Since in a handful of civilian hours no other suggestion had been offered, he supposed he would return to college, which anyhow was free to veterans—he had a premonition that every civil possibility was in lieu of the real, i.e., the imaginary thing—and no sooner had he submitted to that supposition than he began to perceive events through the filter of

13

various old quotations: "I have scanned the heavens with my telescope but no God did I see," to which the devout had made some rejoinder which naturally he had forgotten; "the white-faced onanists of cities," who seemed to be as numerous as ever; "put out the light and then put out the light"; etc., the detritus of a year and a half of university, three years before.

Lieutenant Oedipus and Jocasta were also in the bar, at a little round table, drinking from squat glasses clogged with fruit. Reinhart passed them on the way to the cigarette machine, where he applied for king-sized Whelps; he got Blackguards with a cork tip and no matchbook at all. He bruised the machine's multicolored façade until the manager threatened litigation.

When Reinhart returned to the bar stool he had a new neighbor: the distinguished gray-haired gentleman he had last seen at the newsstand, a New York or London type, *very* friendly, who offered to fire his cigarette with an expensive lighter of the kind called "engine-turned," whatever that was, and advertised in the low-pressure manner with the price spelled out, for example, Eighteen dollars and fifty cents, in snotty magazines—Reinhart concentrated on the lighter to avoid the gentleman's lean face, for such elegance conjoined with such geniality, in America, could only mean much inversion. He decently accepted the light, though, but having got it looked very vague and, collecting his coat, drifted to and waited for the unspinning of the revolving door, which was stuffed with a heavy, dark-clothed man in a crushed hat.

Again in the great marble hall, a kind of Reichstag as yet not burned or bombed, Reinhart lurched toward the main portal and soon found himself outside taking night air and a vista of the automobile approaches to the terminal, between which lay a lighted concrete esplanade leading to the slums and, above, dead fountains on several levels. "Where every prospect pleases and only man is vile." From his point of view every car, in the line like cartridges in a bandoleer, looked to be a 1938 Chevrolet, and driving it in or out was his father, who had missed or would miss him; and he, Reinhart *fils*, was alone in the great world. He suddenly wearied of the inevitable childishness of his fancies and decided to take a streetcar—home? Anyhow, in lieu of. So far as he knew, since his parents seldom wrote and he returned the favor in kind, a defense worker, spawned in some estaminet of Kentucky, still occupied his old room.

To take the trolley meant he must walk some incredible distance—somehow with each inch of modern progress came another mile of inconvenience: in the good old days everything

14

you needed was in sight of your cave—and he started down the middle of the ramp, prepared to bluff automobiles: if a car hits a moose, the animal is killed, but, so is the vehicle. Notwithstanding that he now weighed 221, and was sensitive, authoritative, sanguine, and would receive a pleasant surprise in the near future—all this assured by a little ticket, stamped in violet, ejected from the men's-room scale in answer to his penny, while an Uncle Tom dressed like a physician waited behind with obsequious towel—notwithstanding this full cargo, Reinhart felt almost light and very wieldy as he sauntered along, and his spirit kept pace, a certain sign something was missing. Opposite one of the dry fountains, now a big candy dish of cigarette ends, Kleenex balls, and dog turds, he was conscious that his barracks bag was no longer a constant companion. Probably the old fairy in the bar retained it as hostage.

He had got back as far as the station entrance when he saw coming through the door the fat nameless type who infests public places—except that this fellow he was seeing for the third time: hat knocked off, coming into bar, and now; and now the man was carrying his, Reinhart's, bag: and furthermore had a kind of license to do so, having become increasingly familiar to him. Indeed, Reinhart literally could not have got started without this person and as much as acknowledged it in his greeting.

"Dad!"

Immediately his father disappeared into the collar of his heavy coat; like a turtle, his reappearing hinged on how badly he had been scared. His voice issued feebly from under the carapace.

"I recognized your sack before I recognized you—because it has your name on it." His cucumber nose inched over the collar. Pretending distant acquaintance, Reinhart quitely searched for the cigar he had purchased for the occasion, and found it in the right breast pocket, of course busted like a little whiskbroom. Which was no more than just, for he remembered his father did not smoke.

But, ah!, by this time his old man had partially emerged.

Taking care, Reinhart said wanly: "I'm sorry, Dad, I didn't know you at first. I—" He flipped the cigar fragments into the icy wind, which reversed itself at once and blew them like ape hair across the front of his ETO jacket.

Dad hastened to claim the onus: "Well I didn't know *you*, either, uh, Corporal—"

"The name's Carlo, Dad."

"You're discharged now, is that it?" His father's hat was still crumpled, despite Reinhart's earlier having put it to rights

15

after he knocked it off; retroactively he saw the gold initials on the sweatband: his father always found a haberdashery with a stamping service. The point was, though, that Dad was a natty fellow—or had been. Now he seemed altogether down at the heels. For example, in addition to the seedy hat, there were his lapels, from which the nap had worn; and his shirt collar was one size loose about a chicken-veined neck and puckered all the way round under the tie. His father was an old man. Terrible, and more so than in Europe where they were born ancient and when they died, did it instantly. In an American railway station, in the evening, during the obsequies for the old year, it is always the dark night of the soul; and the lighter, the darker: above them in the entryway marquee shone a fluorescent tube under which passersby appeared green-faced, ambulatory corpses.

"Have a lozenge?" asked Dad, producing a white paper bag.

No, it was too horible. Reinhart seized the olive-drab bag instead and hurried his pop down the ramp toward the car park. Lozenges! What could be more telling? In the old days Dad habitually chewed caramels; obviously now his teeth were done with the vanished years 1942—45. Reinhart had distinctly heard a hideous clicking, and nothing around the station front was loose. Reinhart was grateful for his own lack of condition and tried to look even fatter, weaker, whiter, and more slovenly as he ambled slowly so his puffing father could keep stride.

Nevertheless they had gone but halfway when Dad seized his arm and failingly groaned: "I can't walk too fast, being not as young as arsewhile—on guard, here comes a taxi!" He sprang in terror upon the curb and almost collapsed on the footwalk. In the little things which menaced no one else he was a great coward. As a boy Reinhart could never hold a pocketknife, even closed, without hearing his father's augury of accidental bloodshed; had never ejected a pea through a shooter without a warning of punctured eyeballs. Preparing to go to the corner letterbox, his father issued a formal farewell; in the hundred yards between here and there were possibilities of lightning, drunken drivers who might leap the curb, hydrophobic Airedales, and that legendary staple of quiet neighborhoods, the ordinary householder who suddenly goes mad as an elephant in must, ignites his window curtains, and attacks passersby with a Stillson wrench. If you cross your eyes in horseplay, they might lock so. Sitting on concrete will give you piles. A jovial backslap will dislocate a spine. He who lifts stacked newspapers is a ruptured man. Never drink milk while eating fish: your bowels will worm. One drink of champagne

16

makes you reckless; a second and you're out like a light, and someone will rifle your pockets. Remove the screens by the first frost, or a burglar will assume you're on a late vacation and make violent entry. Never lower your guard before the relatives or they will apply for a loan.

Walking in the deep gutter as compromise, Reinhart said to his father, up on the walk—they were now the same height— "I never did find Granpa's family in Germany."

Immediately his dad recovered from the fright, and indeed Reinhart had only mentioned it as therapy.

"Guess you lost no sleep over that." The son of a native Berliner, his father knew as much German as he did Patagonian. He also had about as much in common with his own son as he had with F. D. Roosevelt, whom he had voted against four times. Yet walking there both below him and on his level —the complexities of physics having some reference to the moral order—Reinhart realized his fundamental feeling towards his father was not contempt, as it had seemingly been from roughly the age of sixteen to approximately five minutes ago. He did not much like him, but he probably loved him.

"Dad?"

"Huh?" His father warily edged towards the spiked winter shrubbery on the far side of the pavement. Another fluorescent lamp, the usual undertaker, jutted from a high post like an opening straight razor; good old right angles had been everywhere outmoded since Reinhart donned the knapsack and marched away.

"Dad, do you mind? We haven't shaken hands yet." Reinhart put out his large right, with the dirty nails.

"Is that the thing to do?"

"Who gives a damn?

"I wish you wouldn't stand in the street—*here comes another cab!*" He referred to a vehicle at the entrance to the esplanade, a good quarter mile away.

"O.K.," answered Reinhart. "I wouldn't want to hurt it." He climbed to the sidewalk and took his dad's hand and squeezed it until the taxi passed them. Whether his father returned the emotion he didn't know—for Reinhart's fist was bigger than everybody else's and perforce commanded every shaking—but the old chap's head came entirely out of his coat collar for the first time. He had not shaved well, and some of his whiskers were white. He smelled of Aqua Velva, as of yore.

"Dad, you know what David Copperfield's aunt once said to him? 'Never be mean, never be false, never be cruel.' You never have been and I guess that makes you unique."

They had arrived at a point where they had no option but to cross the roadway to the parking lot.

"That's very considerable of you, Carlo," said Dad, "but in this place, look out that a car don't back over you without a signal."

Reinhart's father drove the gray sedan slow as a hearse; otherwise it bore no resemblance to your typical funeral wagon, being drab and small. The man who in life drives a Chevrolet, in death is chauffeured in a splendid Cadillac like a South American dictator. Reinhart could not shake off the mortuary suggestions, for which he blamed the Stygian approaches to his bailiwick. He only wished he had got a little jar of instant Golden Bough. Certainly they passed enough delicatessens, even a supermarket or two burning bright in the forests of the night; here people trapped particolored containers and pushed them around in wire cages on wheels.

They passed taverns full of testy men glowering into tumblers served up by morally enervate bartenders. The waitress in a chili parlor wore a nurse's white cap and a butcher's apron gory with catsup. Some strange howling unruly animals under a streetlamp proved to be pubescent males. From the public-library door sidled a small, bug-eyed man, clutching his guide to poisons. At one corner an inebriate confessed down the slot of a postal box to a midget priest within, but before they got the green and Dad shuddered into low, the drunk finished his *peccavi* and prepared to sin again, hooting obscenities at their rear tires, which smooth as eggs habitually lost traction on the streetcar rails.

"How many miles on your heap now?" asked Reinhart.

Wincing at a boor's bright headlights, which violated a law never enforced—his father said: "Whatever you see on the speedometer, plus a hundred thousand." And then swallowing and blinking, sprang his surprise: he waited on the list for a new convertible.

"You're kidding."

"Yes I am," Dad admitted smugly, then had to shy the car from a suicidal dog, missing it but almost killing the vehicle: a piece of metal, probably the motor, clattered behind on the trolley-car rails. Reinhart decarred and went to fetch the part, only a hubcap; even Dad's accidents, like his humor, were innocuous. Declining to squat upon the blacktop and fit it to the wheel while passing autos singed his posterior cheeks, Reinhart tossed it onto the rear seat and got back in in time to hear the end of what he assumed to be the comments Dad had started earlier, for his old man was habitually oblivious to whether or not anyone heard him, being utterly without ambi-

18

tion. ". . . a standard two-door is good enough for me."

His tone reminded Reinhart of a second parent, the woman of their threesome, who whenever he had brought home a college friend stated across the dinner table: "Start right in. We're just plain folks here," seeing it as something to brag about.

They had come to the colored ghetto west of town and as they waited for another light a slender Negress minced diagonally across corners, articulating in the midsection of the best ball bearings extant since the Eighth Air Force razed the factories at Schweinfurt. She was all girl.

"Look at those coons," wistfully noted Dad, being plural because he meant a group of male hangers-on in front of a drugstore, digging each other's ribs, yacking and saying *Man!* twelve times a minute. "They sure have fun." But just as well nothing fell from the car in that district, for he would have been scared to let Carlo get out and retrieve it; even more fun for a black man than standing before a windowful of trusses and Lifebuoy, was to assault lone Caucasians.

So much for the old man, who was free, white, and past fifty. As they neared home, Reinhart's concern was his mother, a person who could be rather formidable if she caught you in the uncalloused places.

"How's Maw?"

"About time," answered his male progenitor. This was the only theme upon which he was capable of even a minor remonstrance. "She's thought of nothing but you for the past three years. You know you're all she's got."

"Poor woman," said Reinhart sarcastically. "What about you?"

"Ah, what am I?" Dad paused a moment to strip the gears. "But a very old geezer."

They turned left at the Presbyterian church which looked like a firehouse; passed the high school, which looked like a church, and a pencil factory that resembled Christ's College, the alma mater of many old poets, in some textbook illustration; and finally the town hall, looking by God like what it was, the air cigar-blue in the lighted upstairs windows. Reinhart suddenly chose now as the time to wonder what he was doing here at all, at this precise moment in late February 1946, at 9:31 P.M., alongside an inappropriate father, bumping over streets not germane to his idea of his own identity, approaching an irrelevant home. Every atom of the human substance has been renewed in the course of seven years: a hundred of Reinhart's pounds were of another meat than he had carried away, and this change was little beside that of the spirit. In the school yard he saw his grammar-school self in dunsel cap and leather boots waterproofed with neat's-foot oil smelling like a wet hound; he toted an oilcloth bookbag in the depths of which a banana was turning black. From a candy-store doorway slouched Reinhart the adolescent, who suffered from unprovoked hard-ons and blotches of the forehead, and wore a fake press card in the ribbon of his hat. Through the last three blocks, residential, level as a bowling alley, deserted now except for an impatient man roped to a pet doing its business, walked an apparition of College Carlo, hitchhiked home for the weekend, supercilious, penniless, flunking;

They pulled into the driveway on parallel tracks of concrete, divided by a strip of grass Reinhart had once been commissioned to trim weekly. He stared at a vision of the squatting boy in merciless sunshine. Art thou there yet, truepenny? The lad thumbed his nose. Night returned, and Reinhart, fat, twenty-one, a veteran, was Home.

His father was all for slinking around to the back door like a felon, his usual mode of entry, but ceremonious Reinhart demanded the front. On the way around, they saw under the nearest streetlamp the man walking the spaniel, which was the inevitable neurasthenic quaking with emotional ague. In great disgust Reinhart recalled them both: Claude Humbold, a realtor with whom his father was in some kind of cahoots, writing insurance for the houses Humbold peddled, and Popover, the dog.

The latter salivated over Reinhart's combat boots while the former, who wore a red balloon for a face and had painted on it a hairline mustache, shouted in the timbre of a washtub being kicked, though coming so close he clipped Reinhart's gut with an elbow: "Hiya Georgie."

"I'll be a son of a bitch," said Reinhart as Humbold managed at the same time both to walk through him and ignore him. But as of yore he went unheard, Humbold's rubber soles sucking the pavement and letting go in a series of deafening belches. This man was his old nightmare, and he should have known that small things like a war, reaching manhood, going halfway around the world, etc., were like taking aspirin for syphilis.

"I must say," said Dad, "that next to your mother there goes the human being who thinks more of you than anybody."

"Yeah?" asked Reinhart on the porch steps. "What about you?"

"Ah," said Dad, "you'll be buried in pauper's field if you got no more assets than me." He fished beneath his overcoat for a key with which to free the door he locked against wandering brigands—poor cutthroat who would break in and face Maw!

"Wipe your shoes!" commanded a martial, metallic voice as they crossed the threshold. Its source then receded, taking with it his father, into the blackness of the living room—no sense in paying the electric company for needless lights. An overstuffed chair, with pelt of mohair, attacked Reinhart in the thighs while a footstool bit his shins. When a wrought-iron bridge lamp joined the fray he surrendered and ignited his cigarette lighter. No folks, much furniture. On the radio, a photo of his maternal uncle in lodge fez, looking vicious as a Cairo procurer. In the bookshelves above the secretary desk, ninety of the *World's Hundred Best Short Stories;* Volume Seven had not yet been found. Nor had the spot on the rug where the dog had once puked ever quite gone. A real kerosene lamp wired for electricity, and a fake one fitted down to a mock wick which could be elevated, flanked one another on an end table so giddy it quaked when a truck went by, to which as if castanets the windows joined with their clatter. Plastic acorns terminating the shade pulls. One shade showed a stain where it had been rained on in 1939. New shade on the bridge lamp, which had an adjustable transverse member that you could clutch and turn and play tommy gun with at an enemy behind the hassock-fortress.

All the while Reinhart took inventory he was conscious of being stared at by a photographic image within a golden frame on the drum table behind him. If he did not face it down now, he might have to in a nightmare, where things like that always begin with the upper hand. It was the likeness of a perfect idiot of twelve, wearing hair grooved in the middle of the scalp and a degenerate grin that claimed the entire terrain south of the part. He preferred to think his visions of himself from the car were sounder than the camera's, but unfortunately could not, being bluffed by any kind of science. Choosing the only mode of rebuke the little swine would understand, he counseled the picture: "Siss on you, pister; you ain't so muckin fuch," and moved into the hall, at the end of which was a glow signifying the kitchen and perhaps life.

Dad stood behind the refrigerator, arranging for the woman known as Maw to upstage him. She held a hot iron as if she might force Reinhart to accept it in handshake, then dangled it from her pinky, for she was terribly strong. Yet Reinhart was of course larger, and perhaps threatened by that fact as he filled the doorframe, she cocked her pugnacious jaw and snarled: "Here comes six more shirts per week."

"Welcome home," said Reinhart.

Maw answered: "You should be mighty grateful you got such a lovely home to come back to."

He said he was, and eventually she thawed to the degree that she catalogued for him a number of catastrophes having as their principals nobody he knew. At last, too, he ascertained that his old room was still occupied by the defense worker, and Supply Sergeant Maw issued him 2 blankets and 1 pillow. He was assigned a billet on the living-room couch, to which he repaired when permitted and where, his head on one doily, socks on another, and being goosed by a loose spring, he immediately fell asleep and dreamed of love and criminality in an exotic *mise en sène.*

Chapter 2

For the next two weeks Reinhart made wan attempts to tell his European reminiscences to the folks, doing this from a sense of obligation, since as yet nobody had mentioned a word about board payment, and while he didn't really have a room and ate only moderately (for him) of his mother's insipid cuisine, which agreed with his intent to diet, he was certain he owed them something, though he wasn't certain what.

To these accounts, from which of course all sex and violence were stricken, leaving almost nothing, Dad's reaction, or lack of it, was polite boredom and Maw's a rude interest. Dad, with his head—now snow-capped!—in the *Intelligencer's* sports pages, was privy to the personal lives of ballplayers, knew what songs they sang in the showers, when their children had scarlatina, where their wives were birthmarked. Nevertheless he said the right things at the right places: "Well, I'll be!" "Is that right!" And even repeated the dénouement—"So Marsala gave his candy ration to the German kid"—while all the while he was actually down in Florida with Chuck Rafferty, who had reported to spring training with hemorrhoids.

On the other hand, Maw resisted an anecdote from start to finish, no device being too extreme: stew onto tablecloth, coffee into Dad's lap, counterstories about neighbor lads introduced just before Reinhart's punchline, the boiling kettle with its whistle; once she caught a fork in the cloth and pulled the whole table setting to disaster, to kill a pretty meager thing

23

about a taxi-tour of London. Yet, having taken the field, with Reinhart in total rout, she might dramatize Churchill's In Victory, Magnanimity: dishes done, the scene removed to the living room, glaring at him in a kind of bellicose affinity (he being both repugnant and hers) she would demand: "Go on, what about Wallis Warfield Simpson's house? I got to drag your stories out word for word. My, I expected when you came back from the war we could never stop you talking. Looks like the other way around!" And here, one of her rare laughs, the sound of steel wool against rust, showing strong sarcastic canines.

That she was in many ways an impossible woman went without saying and actually suited Reinhart's sense of himself as a highborn orphan. On the other hand, he did respect her grievance. As a girl she had showed a gift for sketching, which Philistine time and circumstance had gone on to deny her as a vocation. Art is short and life is long. No girl of her class and place became an artist. It was probable that she had yearned to be a man, and the evidence of her failure was Reinhart. Thus he, Exhibit A, could hardly condemn her, and concentrated instead on defending himself. From time to time she still drew fine-penciled heads of old-fashioned ladies with Gibson coiffures. He occasionally came across one in the margin of a woman's magazine—these first days he spent much time sunk in apathy and overstuffed chairs, reading whatever he could reach without getting up—a gracious, shaded, high-haired head of circa 1910 hovered wraithlike above the fatuous pink housewife of a 1946 ad making an instant roast beef that hubby would never distinguish from the authentic.

The olden time before Reinhart was born—Reinhart too was nostalgic for it when one day he realized that all Maw's sketches were self-portraits. For a time he backslid to an earlier conviction which six months' therapy was supposed to have obliterated: namely, that his purpose on earth was to rectify life's dirty deals. Damn, damn, damn, his head reeled and his heart overpumped, and he lost his place in "Frost on the Hyacinths," A Novelette Complete in This Issue, by Persephone Claxon, about a young woman named Jennifer married to a genial accountant who soon after the nuptials turns bilious, cynical, and cryptic owing to (concealed from Jennifer) the reappearance of an old flame with whom he thought it had been finis when she fled to the Virgin Islands the year before and cabled one word: "Adios." When Jennifer finds. . . .

It stood to reason, if not to the nervous system, that the genuine injustices could be amended only by discovering how to outwit clock and calendar. Reinhart wondered why Einstein, up at Princeton, did not put away spatial time and take

24

up mortal—the time that was numbered for him, too, poor old Albert: minute by minute, the forward gears working famously but the reverse *kaputt*. A movie film run backwards, the diver undiving, the blasted mountainside imploding, were mere pathetic images of light: the diver may already be dead, and the mountainside is proven so.

At any rate, from his regrets Reinhart derived nothing but an urge to escape, by any means less final than the Dutch act—"If life and death are just the same, why don't you commit suicide?" "Because they are just the same," said his favorite philosopher, whose name he didn't know, which was probably why he was his favorite.

Civilian life had more terrors than even he, who seldom knew a sanguine anticipation, dreamed of. Add to this the distinct impression he had that in America it wasn't serious, either—because all tragedies here seemed to be specific rather than generic; mad little private hopelessnesses—and you had his dilemma. Which need not be permanent, however, because he would go back to college in June, when the next term started, in a year or so get a crash-program BA majoring in Vagueness, be instantly hired for the young-executive training by Whirlpool Inc., the great detergents empire of southern Ohio, and issued a wife, sedan, and six-room cottage from their stockroom and whatever the quota in kids. Living to a smooth old age, and a clean one owing to the employes' discount on soap, in time retiring to a dotage of home-workshop puttering and a bland diet for his ulcers, he would finally and unobtrusively turn up his toes, leaving behind the means for his delinquents to accept the obligations of maturity and in their time follow suit.

Who did he think *he* was? as Maw always asked.

A fat man, for one. He hadn't yet got around to using his weights, which he couldn't locate; he suspected they had been sold during the iron shortage.

After a time of this turbulence within and utter quiet without—Reinhart yet always had a feeling that something would turn up, from nowhere would come money or women or adventure and even an old friend, that, is an *opportunity;* Christ, it was the richest and most powerful country in the world, and you every day read about vagrants picked off park benches and made movie stars and John T. Nobody whose name was pulled from a hopper to win radio lotteries worth thousands— after a time during which the remarkable failed to happen, Reinhart issued forth on foot, though Dad offered the car, to seek out people. For several weeks he had been with Maw & Dad but hadn't seen a *person* since he returned.

25

He was at some disadvantage, having had in high school five years before three real friends and one girl, all of whom by now were as altered as he or had vanished. A pudgy little woman with bird's-nest hair, trailed along Market Street by two slum urchins, turned out to be Bettysue English, once so merry and reckless. Mortimer Bother, though built like a water buffalo, had been tubercularly disqualified from the draft and did well at the bank, working up from third teller's cage to first from the door. When he cashed Reinhart's mustering-out check he coughed into a blue handkerchief, said "Hi fella," and quickly affixed the sign reading: GO TO NEXT WINDOW.

From Hepworth Bax, whom he ran into coming from work at the pencil factory, smelling of wood shavings and graphite, carrying a lunchbox stenciled with someone else's initials, he heard that "Doc" Joyce, who had always dreamed of West Point, was in fact still wanted as a deserter from the Coast Guard.

"In my opinion," said Bax, who had developed an eccentric stride, "he couldn't stand that uniform. No pockets."

Bax had been tolerated in the foursome only because he admired the other three, being himself but a poor uncoordinated boob who did nothing well, running like a crab, showing too much tongue when he laughed too loudly at others' wit, having none of his own, and still in 1941 wearing a jacket belted in the rear. *He* at least had not changed, and with his encouragement Reinhart, still in a uniform showing the Good Conduct ribbon and three more decorations issued to everybody who ever spent a month under arms, found it easy to brag about his European service.

"Gee," interjected Bax at points in the narrative, and later offered his friend a lift home in a specially equipped car the Veterans Administration gave him in exchange for the ankle he had lost at Utah Beach. When Reinhart, looking for a cat to give his tongue to, declined, Hepworth shook with the left hand—his right being aluminum—and saying don't call me, I'll call you, bluffed a hole in the traffic and shot off through it.

Although his father kept pressing the Chevy keys on him, especially on weekdays when Dad needed the car for business, Reinhart wouldn't take them. He knew his old man would travel the miles of collection-rounds on foot, and he disapproved morally of this demonic kind of martyrdom, having at last understood that Dad was much subtler with the needle than Maw.

However, one Tuesday morning when Dad announced a

dead battery and walked away—almost ran—down the block, Reinhart believed he might put himself into a feasible relationship with the car. His rump against the forward garage wall, hands on grille, he inflated his great chest and shoved. He was fat but not weak or stupid—he had remembered to open the doors, thus the car did not burst through them, only rolled at a speed not exceeding ten mph over the threshold, along the driveway, across the street, over the curb, and encountering on the bias an old elm belonging to Mrs. Bangor, sideswiped a shallow dent in the rear right fender.

But when he sought to start the engine, he succeeded instantly, and pulled across her front lawn in two muddy furrows and was round the corner before Mrs. B. emerged screaming.

At Joe Laidlaw's All-in-One Service Station & Body Shop he approached the pop-cooler hangers-on, whom he remembered from before the war: Willard Millan, Hector Hoff, and "Pup" Agnew, all apparently 4-F from poor posture; they said little, moved only when the iceman dumped a twenty-pound block into the tepid water surrounding the Dr. Pepper, and chewed up in the aggregate perhaps two hundred toothpicks a day.

"Joe around?" asked Reinhart.

Willard looked at Hector, who dug "Pup" in the ribs, who swallowed a mouthful of Coke and belched like distant thunder.

"What's that?" asked Reinhart.

"I never chew my cabbage twice," said "Pup."

Willard, who wore a felt hat on the back of his head, explained between snorts: "He went to crap and the hogs ate him."

"Hey," said Hector, who had been staring at Reinhart while getting after a neckful of blackheads. "This here guy is old Carlo."

Willard wiped his face with his hat. "Sorry, Carlo, I took you for a rube from upstate. They stomp in here smelling of cowshit. Why are you wearing that getup?"

"I've been away in the war," answered Reinhart.

"I be damn," Hector exclaimed, cleaning his teeth with his tongue. "Thought you was in cawllege."

"That was before the war."

"I be damn."

"Overseas, too," said "Pup," intelligent flushes permeating the overcast of his acne. "Only a dumb sonbitch like Heck wouldn't of seen them ribbons."

"Me!" Heck said. "It was me who made him out, you sonbitch."

Willard shook his hat. "You old sonbitch of a Carlo, over-

27

seas. I never. What's it like to slip it in a gook girl?"

"I don't know," said Reinhart, drifting toward the rear of the garage, which was intermittently illumined by the eerie blue light of welding. "I was in Germany."

"Thought he said he was overseas," Hector noted to Willard, and "Pup" spat Coke-brown upon the floor and streaked it with his foot.

"Joe!" cried Reinhart, over the sputter, to the Martian in the welding mask, who turned off the torch and uncovered. Years over a hot flame had changed his race, as working in a hormone factory was said to change your sex. He was burned black as a Negro. As Reinhart realized that he *was* a Negro, and not Joe, he got pretty sick of this annoying habit of misidentifying people, and believed he could hardly be considered well so long as it continued. But he was soon diverted—as he always was; which explained why he *never* improved his character—by going on from the specific to the particular. Not merely a Negro, the welder was a known Negro—a considerable difference and one which might, if Reinhart thought long enough about it, being a lump to his throat. For here had been a Negro with remarkable gifts. They had gone to high school, if not together, at least at the same time.

"Splendor Mainwaring!" said Reinhart with such hearty force that the welder lowered his mask as if in self-defense and kept it so. This was progressively more unnerving as the interview continued; through the square window, made of dark-blue glass, came not even a glint from Mainwaring's great lemur eyes; yet you felt his surveillance, as in jungle movies the hero knows that when he sees least, his enemies see most.

Reinhart tried to put his apprehensions aside, which were ridiculous in a Midwestern garage when fifteen feet away Hector had just goosed "Pup," who squealed like a pig and put Willard in stitches.

"Don't you remember me?" he asked the window.

"I don't blame you," he went on, lowering himself onto a stack of tires. "All the while you were breaking records on the track, winning rhetoric contests, and getting A's in class, I was doing nothing. I was—" A certain slipperiness under his fundament told him the top tire, smeared with grease, was printing a great target round his ass. A clucking issued from the mask, rather metallic and more statistical than laughlike.

"Well anyway," said Reinhart, rising from the nasty seat, "I had a little accident with the car. It's outside." He backed slowly toward the door, wagging his hand at Splendor every so many steps, who would move only upon this signal and stop in between. In this strange fashion they passed the three clowns,

28

who occupied within their own glass bell of mock farts, real belches, and mucul clearances, paid them no mind.

"See, a dent!" Reinhart for some reason said triumphantly when they reached the Chevy, and Splendor, kneeling, passed his hands lightly over the bruised body, just like a witch doctor in his motions and his mask, though now Reinhart got a more scientific perspective of the latter, for it was turned away from him and he could see the close-cropped back of the head that wore it.

"What are you doing here, anyway? he asked instantly and, he regretted, cruelly.

Splendor inserted a clamped fist under the fender and with the other hand struck thrice upon the superior surface of the depression while pressing from beneath, as the vibrating cords in his left forearm testified. His right arm, power for the aggressive hand, was almost lax; and never more so than when upon the third blow, for which the first two had been exploratory, the dent sprang out along its entire length, leaving behind no memory but superficial scratchings in the paint—which he went on to eradicate with sputum and an oily rag.

Splendor removed the welding shield and squinted in the reflection from a show windowful of chromium accessories, but didn't smile. He was not too colored except in his color, that being darker than most, approaching the blue serge with a sheen of use. But his nose had a long Caesarean figure and overshadowed thin lips which, if anything, sank in rather than protruded over his teeth. What he suggested was a Calvinist in blackface—at this point, a weary one who had seen his code everywhere defied.

But from looking at Reinhart he seemed to derive an energy, and he suddenly asked: "Why are you so anxious?"

"I honestly don't know," Reinhart confessed. "I have everything to look forward to." He leaned against the restored fender, feeling very immobile.

"Yet you have the most excruciating doubts," said Splendor, "and carry awful burdens. You yearn to prevail, but will at most times settle for survival. Unsure of persons, you are at ease with things, which of their inanimate nature are incapable of betrayal."

"That's what you think," said Reinhart, trying to resist, but he was so tired. "It's the other way around—"

"Silence!" ordered Splendor, though more in understanding than in anger. "Do not seek to fight it." He clasped Reinhart's shoulder and stared him in the Adam's apple, which was how tall he stood, about the middle height.

"Fight what?" Nevertheless, Reinhart knew a growing serenity. He had always been on the Negroes' side, a position in

29

which he had to deny their being reservoirs of primitive wisdom, because everybody who believed that was perforce Jim Crow. They were just like everybody else, except that in high school Splendor had been better.

"Nor question it." Splendor hung his head in the area of Reinhart's heart. "You're not with me. The force is congested somewhere between us, cannot reach the vital organs." He rapped furtively upon Reinhart's chest as if it were a brothel door, and remarkably enough Reinhart did feel a certain vitalization, though not enough yet to rise, which was what Splendor now commanded him to do.

Being so large, Reinhart always worried inordinately about how he looked to passersby, especially here in his home town; for, because she had no friends, his mother had ever used strangers as control, as if there were a host of people who prowled about making judgments—and as a matter of fact, there were; his mother was one, and he another. Had Reinhart seen a Negro poking a white man in the chest, he would have believed it the preliminary to a race riot, though this was not the South. That is to say, he realized that snobbery, and even more negative sentiments, was holding him down.

"Ah," Splendor intoned, flexing his eyes, "you are anchored by the leaden humors." He struck Reinhart's forehead with the flat of his hand, saying: "Rise."

That really got Reinhart's goat and made him smart all the way to both temples, besides. Still sitting, he punched out with his right, which Splendor nimbly avoided.

"Are you nuts?" cried Reinhart.

Splendor slapped him again, same place, not hard but most penetrating. In a second the vibration reached the soles of Reinhart's feet, and they danced in wrath. He leaped up, ready to give the fellow what for. Still grave as ever, his tormentor, who now had to reach high to do so, gave him another between the eyes. Now Reinhart grievously wished to take this witch doctor's life. Forgetting service-station decorum, he chased him cursing round the concrete apron, among cars. He fell over a motorcycle with dual foxtails and was gored by a horned device for adjusting headlight beams. Meanwhile Splendor, recordholder in the 220 and high hurdles, trotted effortlessly by, or easily vaulted, the obstacles, his features still inhospitable to any kind of violent feeling; certainly he was not frightened. At one point, having run up a lead of perhaps fifty yards—for Reinhart, whose anger had in the exertion gradually altered to something else, followed his opponent's precise route, that is, instead of dashing across the radius to intercept him, doggedly kept to the circumference and its barriers—with this lead, Splendor entered the garage, got himself

30

a bottle of Dr. Pepper, emerged and, drinking, resumed the race, running so steadily that the liquid did not foam.

What a garage! Reinhart groaned as he fell winded on the hood of Dad's car. I've never seen the equal in all my life long. It's not in the least realistic. Nevertheless, along with air, he received an authoritative access of well-being. Strange that this should result from defeat! He opened his eyes to see Splendor advancing on him with the pop bottle.

"I'm finished, you understand," he cried. "Just let me alone. I don't like to fight. I killed a man once overseas. I don't know my own strength. Besides, I don't have anything against you and I think you're nuts."

Splendor couldn't have been more delighted. He made a weird smile that broke his face; his upper teeth made an arch, the center ones being shorter than his molars; rather imbecilic; Reinhart now didn't blame him for being most of the time grave.

Splendor said benevolently: "Fighting back now, eh? Your pride restored. Well done! That will be one dollar."

Well, it certainly wasn't exorbitant, considering the fender was as good as ever. Since Splendor was a maniac, though, Reinhart checked the car once more to make sure. He then paid him, still breathing strenuously and then couldn't resist saying with obvious spleen: "You're not charging me for the race? Oh thanks." He climbed into the car and slammed the door.

Splendor looked in through the window. "You'll sleep tonight as you haven't in months, and you'll rise tomorrow purged of the grievous need to stuff yourself with carbohydrates—" Reinhart ran the glass up against him and swiftly backed off the apron, but Splendor, trotting alongside, suddenly struck *himself* on the forehead and began to make desperate signals. This time Reinhart was sure he could, with the Chevy's help, outrun him, but since the chase was reversed, his pride—which he reluctantly admitted, had been stimulated by Splendor's shenanigans, nuts or not—wouldn't let him. He braked and having reached under the seat for a monkey wrench or other weapon, and typical of Dad's car, found only a little whiskbroom, defenselessly lowered the window.

"Sorry," said Splendor, his eyes sad as cold fried eggs. "I better collect something for the fender, otherwise Joe will think you paid me and I stole it. He is an unsympathetic individual."

"So am I most decidedly," Reinhart answered. "What do you believe the dollar was for?" But even as he asked he knew he had been hoist with his own petard. He joined his voice to Splendor's, and in chorus they said: *"For the treatment."*

31

At supper Reinhart asked for either Maw or Dad, "Do you recall a boy went to high school with me named Splendor Mainwaring?"

By now Maw had got into the habit of looking derisively at Dad whenever Carlo spoke. That done, she speared a piece of pork chop and masticated violently. Dad imitated the ceramic French cook's head on the kitchen wall above him—a cavity behind the Frog's distended cheeks hid a ball of twine, the end of which issued through his pursed lips—through Dad's a string of spaghetti went the other way. While he swallowed, his eyes crossed briefly.

"I see you got the car off the Fritz, Carlo, and thank you. Be sure and remind me to reimburst you." He pursued a rolling Brussels sprout across the plate, onto the table, and—it bounced soggily upon the floor. "Ah, the jig is up."

Maw fled choking into her two hands. "Oh haha. George, had you only been a Jew you'd of made your bundle as a network comedian."

Dad smiled modestly, having no idea of what she meant and not lusting for any. Suspense moved him not. He would pad off to the toilet just at the climax of radio mysteries, and never opened his Xmas packages until badgered by the giver. The old Chinese would have run out of water before he screamed for the next drop to fall.

Reinhart, however, blessed or cursed by the affinity with his mother, which is why he never missed her when away, changed the subject with no hope of success. "I notice you still have—"

"Splendor Mainwaring's a jig, you goof!" she chortled at Dad.

Dad smiled at the wonder of it and addressed the milk bottle: well, he was going to say something but opening his mouth had trouble with his upper plate, readjusted it with thumb and forefinger, turned a long gout of milk into his cup of Sanka and drank it down, getting after the molten sugar in the bottom with a prehensile tongue.

"Jigaboo," explained Maw.

Reinhart was laboriously preparing the protest which his superego insisted upon; actually he had always thought these epithets harmless, but had read that the people to whom they were applied did not; besides, as a college man an enlightened attitude was expected of him. But it was a complex business, for his parents, who were of German extraction, not only did not bridle at someone else's saying "Kraut," but thinking it cute habitually used it themselves.

Before he spoke, Maw proceeded to confuse the issue: "Poor niggers, personally I always stick up for them. You can

32

imagine how popular that makes me!" Her delight in having no friends never waned.

"Anyway," said Reinhart, "I ran into Splendor Mainwaring at the garage."

"Remind me to reimburst you at the earliest convenience," said Dad, with a spoon examining his canned pears for foreign matter.

"But," continued Maw, "I won't stand for noise, sex, and enthusiasm, like what used to happen every single night after Joe Louis won a fight. They would shoot off a cannon on the West Side, making windows rattle this far away. Then if somebody would of been lynched, they would of griped. One thing you can say about a coon: he's never satisfied."

"Del-Ponte," said Dad, happily munching his fruit. "First pick of the crop. You never get a tinge of yellow towards the end of a Del-Ponte pear. Inspectors follow every inch of the canning process. They find a bit of the core on *one* pear, they disauthorize the lot—and I don't mean your one can but your whole carload. Because of this their product costs a few pennies more, but is well worth it to discriminating consumers."

Reinhart momentarily forgot his subject to swell with pleasure about Dad, who so loved life. "Have one?" he asked, passing a box of Lorna Goons.

"I'll have two," Dad joked. Having chosen his cookies, he closed the box according to the little diagram printed on its wrapper, a complicated mode of closure guaranteed to seal the contents against moisture: *Twist waxpaper inner liner, folding end upon itself; insert flap A of outer cover in slit B; shake container vigorously so contents will settle; rush out and buy more when cookie level falls below danger mark on See-Thru© index window.* Dad read the instructions aloud, and in due time came upon the recipes which followed. "Listen to this, Maw. 'Turnip Casserole a la Grand Hotel': two pounds turnips, pint oysters, white of an egg, leaf sweet basil, whatever that is, box Lorna Goons, oregano to taste, dash Angostura bitters, teaspoon cooking sherry—or could that be a mixprint for 'cherry'—pinch allspice—"

"Now George," interrupted Maw, "how a man as brilliant as you—whom I have always insisted could have known no end to his accomplishments had you not liked the Good Life too much; and I'm not criticizing but merely noting—how you can believe everything in black and white is beyond me. Could you keep your wits about you you'd recall I made that very dish one time in January, 1943, and no sooner did it go down your hatch than you rushed to the john, where it came right up again. The remainder of the bowl I put out for the Schiller cat, who up and died three days later, I shouldn't be sure

33

whether or not from that, but have my suspicions. So while I guess it wouldn't bother this two-hundred-pound lout who came back to me from the Army, and prefers talking to anybody else—including members of the dusky race who so I heard were dishonorably discharged from the service for impersonating officers—you and I got too tender stomachs for either."

"Aw," groaned Reinhart. "The poor guy!"

"Aha!" screamed Maw. "So you're another! I wondered how you could have got to Berlin as just a corporal. Probably were caught and dishonorably discharged as well. You snuck home in a suspicious way, I'll say that much."

You could imagine how Maw might receive the true account of Reinhart's last days under arms, which was probably what she now fished for, suspecting something though he had always been prudent. Because he had served on the staff of a military hospital, there had been no change of address when he entered its psycho ward as patient; besides, he seldom wrote anyway. It came in handy now that he recalled his old wish to be a spy.

"Say whatever you will, Maw. I got strict instructions never to speak even to my own family about Intelligence work, till ten years after."

Holding her fork like a screwdriver—she still worked on seconds of the main course, never ate desserts, spurning the soft and sweet—Maw slitted her mouth towards his father and asked: "Kindly explain, George."

"Sarbotage, Maw, S.P.-onage, clock-and-digger stuff. Behind enemy lines in the dead of night. 'Who goes there?' 'Colonel Schultz of the German Imperial Guard.' 'Pass, friend.' When really it is old Carlo here, wearing a fake mustache and speaking Kraut like a native." He spooned up the last drop of pear juice, tilting the bowl.

"Oh they could *tell*," Maw insisted, but dropped that line.

"Did they," asked Dad, "give you one of those teeny little cameras that fit into the head of a ring, or a gun disguised as a cigar, or a sword in a umbrella?"

"Never," said Reinhart, preoccupied. "Tell me more about Splendor, Maw. Can't you see why a fellow like that would impersonate an officer? Can't you see? You know what he's doing now? Working in that crummy garage, is what he's doing. Why he was valedictorian."

"You're a mighty snob," answered Maw. "Your cousin Turner has worked in a garage his livelong days and is white besides. Besides, it was salutatorian, if you want your facts. That's second. First was that skinny little thing"—she picked up her third pork chop and cropped it with her teeth to the bone, flung it onto the plate, *clunk!*—"Angelica Slimp, whose father sold homemade horseradish door to door in the Depression—"

"Yeah. Why, Splendor was offered three college scholarships!" said Reinhart, who was getting all worked up and feeling just great, getting back to his old self, feeling morally superior to just about everybody, including Splendor, in a world where a gifted Negro got the dirty end of the stick—and took it, apparently unprotesting.

Of course Maw refused to say more when she found Reinhart was interested, and Dad had actually gone to sleep right at the table. Later Reinhart hunted up his high-school yearbook, *The Specter,* and looked first at his own picture, near the end, face like a balled athletic sock—he had determined not to smile, but the *buffo* photographer, whistling, farting, etc., soon succeeded in breaking him up and snapped the shot just as he exploded. Then there was Splendor, in the high white collar and black suit Negroes always wore for ceremonies, no doubt owing to their noted respect for the cloth. His middle name was "Gallant," his nickname nonexistent, for nobody apparently had known him that well, including the other Negroes, who all had them: "Fox," "Sport," "Jellyman," etc. There followed a list of academic clubs, Latin, Spanish, Drama—of course, drama: Splendor had once played the magistrate in Lady Gregory's *Spreading the News,* in which the actors, even he, were obliged to simulate Irish brogues. Reinhart supposed he should find this recollection humorous, but decided instead it was singular.

The Class Will, written in a spirit of levity: "S. Mainwaring bequeaths his track shoes to Bob Ball" (a white sophomore, so obese he could hardly walk). The Class Prophecy: "Splendor M. in 1961 was elected Mayor of Harlem, New York City, where he had long operated one of the better known nite spots for jazz devotees." A piece of malice that, though probably well intentioned at the time. Reinhart somewhat peevishly remembered as he put the book aside and settled on the couch for the night, that he himself had been omitted from both Will and Prophecy, which on the other hand signified that both his past and future were open.

Reinhart did sleep well, as Splendor predicted, and next day, on foot, he returned to the garage prepared to chaff the Negro about it as prelude to an explanation, on both sides, of the, when you thought about it, hilarious error of the day before. But no sooner had he entered and run the gantlet of Willard, *et al.,* who wheezed and sucked their teeth at him, than Splendor looked up from the tire he was battering off a wheel with a ballpeen hammer, and reproached: "Wasn't that an unsympathetic thing you did yesterday!" His lower lip had come out like a camel's. Through the door to an adjoining wing labeled "Lube Dept," Reinhart saw Joe Laidlaw, the garage owner, raise a car on the grease rack and assault its rusty private parts with a wrench. Splendor beat his hammer on the wheel. Someone howled up outside with a ruined muffler. Hector and "Pup" began mindlessly to strike pop bottles together, and Willard, to test his strength, intermittently lifted the entire cooler an inch and dropped it shatteringly to the floor. A customer entered and seeing nobody to attend him, tested his spark plugs himself, on a sand-blasting device. Joe kept dropping tools, then gave an enema to the car on the rack, using a monstrous squirtgun powered by a compressor whose noise prevailed over the various rhythm sections, until outside, the jealous virtuoso with the bad muffler opened his throttle to the extreme, producing a maniacal blast of sound at which Reinhart's socks fell to his ankles and a fly dropped stone-dead out of the air.

What a place for a sensitive man to work! Reinhart noticed, as he had not the day before, that all manner obscene advices were posted through the garage: GARFAC! LUBELOC! KULAKIZE YOUR KAR! WHEN IN DOUBT, FRAG IT! BUDGAR YOUR TAILPIPE! FROKK YOUR VALVES! WHEN YOU THINK OF BRAKEBANDS, ASK FOR HUMP. On a 1939 calendar representing the good will of D'Amato Brothers, inner-tube jobbers, a big blonde wearing glassine panties and otherwise her birthday suit supported barrage-balloon tits in webbed fingers while chiding a tortoise-shell cat. This photo was entitled: "Naughty Pussy." On another called "Dog's Life," a Scottie had got his leash entwined between a redhead's legs, pulling high her skirt and slip to show frothy underwear and long garters; red tongue out, he stared up glassily at her Y, on which the joker who traveled from garage to garage to provide that service had sketched with a black pencil.

By the time Reinhart had got up his wind to shout, all noises ceased at once, as it is their wont to do, and when he cried to Splendor: "Hey, let's talk!" he alone broke the stillness and out in the lube room Joe twitched his grease gun in annoyance.

"Is it your purpose to get me in trouble?" Splendor asked quietly. He had freed the tire from the rim, and now trundled it out a side door into an areaway which, because the sun was on it, stank worse of oil than did the interior. Indeed, Reinhart felt as if his nasal passages had been Garfacked.

"Listen," he told the Negro, "I am interested in what you did yesterday." While in reality he was far more intrigued with what Splendor was doing at this moment: writing, in chalk, "Recap" on the tire's sidewall, though the tread was almost new in a time when rubber was still scarce.

Splendor sullenly straightened up. "I'll return your dollar, okay? Hector told me you weren't a hick from upstate but the son of Mr. Reinhart the insuranceman. I don't hurt anyone, so don't act as if I do. One day a rube came in here with a headache and was ready to take a couple of aspirins with a Coke. I said not to take that combination which as everybody knows will make you drunk. He answered with an offensive remark and I had to strike him. It so happened he reeled back with a smile. You did it, he said. What? asked I. My headache's gone! He gave me a dollar and from time to time thereafter other individuals come in with sundry complaints. Most ills are of the feelings. Change the feeling, the trouble's gone. What harm is there in that?" He kept frowning at Reinhart, obviously mistaking him for a foe.

"You still don't remember me from high school?" Reinhart asked. "I was one of the crowd of Irish peasants in *Spreading the News*. I wore a pair of rubber hip boots and carried a pitchfork. Harry Wales accidentally backed into it and Miss Atkinson had to find a replacement for him within two days of the performance."

Splendor snapped his jaws together. "And please don't look at that tire as if you think I'm going to profit from it. Joe gives the orders here. After dark he'll shellac this, wind it in paper, and put it with the new ones on the shelf. He'll send an old skin to be recapped, and thus get paid twice."

"She threw me out of the play," said Reinhart, getting woozy from the oil fumes. "Well, it wasn't much of a part, anyway."

Splendor kicked the tire in chagrin. "My truck ran over a mine in Normandy. The explosion ripped the shirt off my back, though strangely enough didn't damage me except for shock. The lieutenant gave me his blouse while he went for the medics. Before he got back some MP's came up and arrested me for impersonating an officer in a combat zone. The lieutenant was killed before he could make a deposition. Hence I was condemned by the court-martial. . . . But I don't suppose that will touch your heart when you write your report."

"Nevertheless," Reinhart went on, "I certainly wanted to be in that play, and to be thrown out in such a humiliating manner! Well, I'll tell you, Bettysue English, whom you have probably forgotten too, who was my girl friend at the time, she wouldn't speak to me for a week—what report?"

"I suppose you're some kind of inspector," said Splendor.

37

"Once bitten, twice shy. I'm not so naïve as to get fooled again."

"Awwww . . ." Reinhart threw up his hands. "I've been trying to tell you, but what's the use? You've got some kind of phobia. Too bad there's not another Splendor to cure you of it." He made as if to leave.

"Wait a minute," said the Negro. "I think I've got a recollection. . . . Hip boots, eh?" he asked, scratching his ear, the great ball jumping in his biceps.

"And pitchfork."

"Pitchfork, eh?"

"And hip boots."

"You were lighter then, of course."

Reinhart said: "Though not for a moment to be compared with your difficulties, I had a trouble or two in the Army and ended up in the hospital where there was little to do but eat. I probably used food as a substitute for something."

"For what?" Splendor asked, suspicious again. "It's perfectly normal to take one's sustenance."

"Well . . ."

"I see you still wear your uniform."

"Yes," said Reinhart. "I can explain that. It is a symbol of my loneliness in civilian society, but the fact that I don't keep it neat shows I don't want to go back to the service, either."

Splendor authoritatively shook his head. "Forget all those theories if you want to be my friend. The truth of life is that things are exactly as they appear, and symbols are the bunk. You are either too lazy to change your clothes or too parsimonious to buy new ones."

"All right, have it your own way," said Reinhart, delighted he had roused Splendor's interest and wary of denying him. "But you have to admit a lot of people would disagree."

"And as for you, you agree because I am a Negro. Which is also why you remember me so well from high school."

Now Reinhart was at first embarrassed by this unrelenting naturalism, but then he saw that Splendor, who after all implied they were to be friends, was smiling fraternally upon him.

"Then I'll tell you, since you're being so frank," he said. "Why are you, with all your intelligence, working in a garage? How are the Negroes ever going to get anywhere when a gifted person like you refuses to better himself?" Reinhart had really meant this to be affectionately offensive, since he had been somewhat offended by everything Splendor said, while liking him all the more for it, for he had long understood that a real friend invariably draws blood. But he was surprised when Splendor did not thrust back, but rather gulped, bagged his eyes, and muttered: "Man, you're ruthless."

"Around crums like Hector and Willard," Reinhart went on, to confirm Splendor's judgment of him. "And the boss is a crook. Haven't you any pride?"

"Go on," said Splendor, collapsing on top of the tire, "That's what I need."

"Why, there's all sorts of opportunities around," cried Reinhart.

Splendor extended a cautionary finger, on which the color began very dark at the joint with a palm and shaded to fawn at the tip. "With a D.D. I can't qualify for the GI Bill."

"Balls to that. And stand up when I'm talking to you!" A kind of fiend in Reinhart provoked him to provoke Splendor, but his friend leaped up without cavil and maintained a military attention. "For Christ's sake, man, pride, pride, pride!"

"Which is a Christian sin." Splendor noted mildly, yet keeping his eyes front and fingers at the seams of his trousers.

"That's typical," said Reinhart derisively. He realized only now that he should have gone in seriously for officer's training during his Army career, or better yet, posed as a lieutenant; unlike Splendor he would have succeeded, for he had real command presence. Thinking about which he grew so pleased with himself that he lost authority—which should have been a lesson to him.

Splendor relaxed from attention, though not from pride. "I needed that," he said. "A good bracing now and again puts a man into a relationship with the high powers."

Reinhart now himself fell upon the tire and gazed dreamily into a nearby pool of grease, which gave a thick, sort of Negroid cast to everything it turgidly reflected. He threw an old bolt into it and waited forever for the viscid splash to subside.

"I don't know," said Splendor, "when I ever met a man before of whom I could say he, as has been pointed out by some thinker or other in reference to the quality which should be sought in prose, is so characterized by *justice*, a term I infinitely prefer to *reason*."

"That's most kind of you," Reinhard replied. "But in all fairness, I spent my last six months of service in the booby hatch."

"Doesn't it figure!" Splendor neighed in exasperation and rippled his body skin like a horse. "What I'm getting around to, though, is—"

Joe stuck his head through the doorway and whined from a mouth distorted with grease and grievance: "Customer! I got to do everything?"

Splendor rolled his eyes at Reinhart. "Joe is really what you call a good guy. He commands with pathos. What's become of the good old-fashioned tyranny that made you feel like a man? Anyhow, I got to go now, without having a chance to tell you you were wrong: I have my plans, which I only needed you to come along and crystallize."

"Glad to have been of service," said Reinhart, rising slowly like a mountain coming through a cloud.

Splendor seized his hand and shook it; he was one of the persons who try to damage you thereby, avoiding the palm and catching the fingers down near their ends where they are resourceless. Now fat, contrary to popular supposition, has no deleterious effect on strength; and despite Splendor's conspicuous musculature, Reinhart could have seized any part of him and squeezed it lifeless. For just that reason, he did not, and accepted his brief suffering, even taking some satisfaction in it since it was unnecessary.

"But," said Splendor, releasing him, "your obligation is only beginning. I want you to have dinner at my house tonight, and shall look for you about eight. *Don't let me down.*"

His profound stare, all expanding iris, elicited an assent from Reinhart before the ex-corporal understood what inconoclasm he was in for. Though they did not live on Rebel ground, nobody in Reinhart's suburb ever broke bread with, or talked to a person of the opposite sex who was a, though you might walk down the street with, give a ride to, take a school shower near, and slap on the back someone of your own sex identified as a: *Negro*.

Reinhart muttered expletives as he slunk through the areaway and into a back alley, where a small woolly dog instantly harassed him. He could foresee being spat upon by the drugstore-corner sentinels, perhaps even pursued through back yards of washlines and rotting fences and howling curs, and at last ensnared in some Aunt Jemima's circus-tent bloomers, getting his lumps from a gantlet of furious natives.

The dog at his feet presently locked its teeth in his pants cuff. His mind as usual on troubles to come, Reinhart plucked it off by the scruff of the neck and flung it yelping way up on the roof of the garage, where it sat for a long time barking at a whirling ventilator and at last made water on it—something to see.

Chapter 3

When Reinhart informed Maw of his dinner appointment, of course withholding his host's identity, she shut off the wash-machine for her question, prepared to turn it on again to kill his answer, and asked abrasively: "Dinner?" She wore a bandanna headdress, being suspicious of the basement's clemency, although this cellar—Reinhart's first since the home of subterranean friends in Berlin—was paved, painted, calked, drained, weatherstripped, and the little windows were curtained in dotted Swiss. Screens were stacked in the beams. It was all very nice and sound, and brighter than the upstairs living room. They had put in an oil burner just before Pearl Harbor: the ex-coalroom was Maw's laundry and colored in green like a marine cavern.

"Thank *you*," Maw went on. "And I been bothering all morning about your dinner, putting on galoshes and tramping to the groshery to get smear cheese and ham sausage and real rye and sweet jerkins for Mr. Big, because he's home from the Army." She peered malevolently through the washer's porthole, like a shipboard husband spying on his wife and the steward, then opened the airlock and removed a cocoon of damp sheets. Although, once she came out of the laundry, Reinhart was the only obstruction in a basement of wide vistas, she steered towards, and managed to collide with, him; ordering, "Clear the way, *Lump*." Which, though the English that it sounded like also applied—he was indeed something of

41

a lump—was really a kind of German, meaning "bum."

"Ah," said Reinhart, clasping the clammy end-of-sheet she thrust to him, "I got it, Maw. We're using different lingoes! I mean *evening* dinner—"

"You mean 'sthupper,' ith what *you* mean." Maw took one clothespin from a series of them, like split cigars, in her mouth and stabbed it over sheet-end and ceiling line. "And it isn't evening, but five-thirty, which is when *we* eat, and if it isn't good enough for you, you can lump it." Here of course she meant the American colloquialism, but the German also made sense: you can bum it—which in a sense was what he was going to do. An eloquent woman, and rather proud of him in her own way, for although his invisible claque had ears too poor to hear it, he had already detected within her symphony of negation a piccolo note of acquiescence.

And surely enough, when he had secured his end of the sopping percale she disapproved of the job, resituated the clothespin, yet said: "'Spose you're going to shave? And don't think Dad'll let you use the car, because he's going to Lodge and you can just walk. Put that in your pipe and smoke it, my fine feathered friend."

FFF, who saw the moment as hardly propitious for revealing the name of his host, let alone the race, wiped his damp hands on his olive-drab behind and steered upstairs, calling back: "Look forward to the gherkins, Maw. See you at lunch."

"*Dinner*, you galoot!" yelled Maw. "And stay out of the living room once." The washer began its idiot tumble.

Later, circa 5:25 P.M., after an inconvenient afternoon—denied the living room, and wherever else he tried to go Maw found good reason for his exclusion, Reinhart took refuge in the garage, very cold with its concrete floor, and threw an old sheath knife at a knothole on the wall—at about 5:25, without taking off his shirt, he shaved. He defied the house rule of open-bathroom-door-except-when-crapping-or-full-immersion-bathing. A rule observed even by the defense worker, whose name was Emmet Swain, except that Swain seldom used the bath, by reason of seldom being around; he owned an old fat Hudson of the kind usually parked in platoons before blatant roadhouses, and was presumed to be generally out in it when not working on the swing shift. Reinhart had met him but twice in rapid passage: he was small, hairy, and saturnine.

Lathering with the old GI-issue brush, Reinhart heard a sound outside the door not unlike what he supposed obsolete novelists meant by "a scratching in [or *on* or *at*] the wainscot," whatever that was. Couldn't be Maw, who would have

42

split the wood. He asked Dad in, thinking it would please him to be recognized unseen.

And surely it did; yet the old fellow showed worry behind his good manners, saying "Thank you, Carlo, I don't want to intrude, but . . ."

"Be my guest." Reinhart indicated the toilet seat in its green chenille envelope, and Dad went there and sat.

"Carlo, I was wondering—look here, why don't you use my gear? Seen it?" He rose and in the linen closet found an enormous giftbox of men's toiletries, matched: powder and lotion and scalp-goo, a blade for corns, nailclippers, rotary mower for nose-hair, and a paste to allay underarm offending. "Your aunt's Xmas idea for me. Pearls in front of swine. I wish you would use it. I don't."

Pointing to his own porcine face in the mirror, Reinhart asked: "Why then cast it in front of me?"

"Good-looking fellow like you?" His father in embarrassment leaned against the toilet tank behind, agitating its heavy lid, and the Epsom-salts and bicarbonate jars thereon made their clinking remarks. "Fellow with all the advantages?"

"Going out to dinner," said Reinhart, trying to get a new blade out of its many wrappings without cutting his thumb, and as usual failing. With all his liberalism he rejected a negative worry about going into a Negro district with an open wound: all those germs.

"I knew you'd make swell friends in no time," said Dad. "If I'd known, would have given you a dollar to go to the while-you-wait cleaner's and have your uniform done."

At least Reinhart hadn't cut his face so far. His cheeks emerged bright pink from the shearing; in the colored section he would shine like a dime among pennies. The white race was screwed when it came to camouflage.

"They give you a barrel to stand in," his father went on, a man who could sit forever without adjustments to the life force: nose-picking, scratching, etc.; he had never even chewed gum. "No they don't, Carlo, but you have seen those cartoons, I imagine. Have you caught up again on the funnies?" Had Dad found a profession that could be conducted in, or from, a bathroom, he would have made his fortune; he took ease there and even wore a faint smile; and taken as bowels and epidermis, Caesar, Napoleon, *et al.*, were hardly more than he.

"Tell you what was on my mind," he apprehensively changed the subject. "Now, no criticism intended, it goes without saying, but I was contemplating what you figure on doing till school starts. Because I know you'll be taking ad-

43

vantage of the GI Bill, full tuition paid and in addition this generous emmolient per the month of expenses. A *wonderful opportunity*, and one never before vouchfaced to the American veteran. . . . You *will* take advantage of this wonderful opportunity?"

Dad attended patiently on Reinhart's deliberate opening of the tap—the son refused to assent before the plumbing did; at last scalding his finger, Carlo nodded.

"Righto," agreed Dad. "But till the onset of the summer session, if I have sized you up, with all your pep you can't stand laying around the house. Mentioned my calculation to Claude Humbold today, and as you might expect, that good-hearted man—who thinks almost as much of you as your mother—well, to put it in a word, he's ready to make you an offer."

Reinhart left the Nirvana of the hot washrag and asked, with open pores: "For what, Dad?"

"A job, Carlo. Or rather, if I know him, a position. Till college starts and even then, maybe, for late-afternoon and Saturday morning, ess etera, ess etera."

It sounded like a gangland killing up the hall towards the kitchen, double-barreled shotguns and Italian venom, but it was rather Maw's announcement: *"Fine time to pick for going on the throne, George. I slave for hours over this supper to see it turn to cold grease on account of your bullheadedness. Well I can tell you, one minute more and you eat it out the garbage can."*

"Coming, Maw," called Dad, rising warily to the thin ground between him and Carlo, who realized by that movement that his own silent malevolence was stronger than Maw's noise—and that Dad *was* bullheaded and most formidable, despite his disguise. Reinhart had never concealed his distaste for Humbold, having nothing particular against the man but everything in general.

"Ah, Dad, you never give up. You've been throwing that bastard at me all my life. I cut his grass and washed his car, and he beat my price down ten cents less than I got from anybody else. I walked the rotten dog he had before Popover, which tore my cuff, and Humbold simply laughed when I told him. Before I left for college you had me go see Humbold, I'll never know why, because he left school in the eighth grade and is, so he told me, an enemy of higher education who could buy up the entire faculty of the Municipal University from his petty cash." Reinhart milked the water from his shaving brush and tossed it into the medicine cabinet between tincture of Merthiolate and cocoa-butter suppositories, feeling a pain the latter could never assuage. "You are the Mahatma

44

Gandhi to my British Empire, Dad, and I see your strength but don't get the moral behind it."

Dad showed him a back of rumpled shirt and baggy seat, handkerchief three-quarters out of the rear left pocket, cuffs scouring the floor and frayed where the shoe heels bit them.

"Okay, okay, okay." Dad's voice issued from the little end of a megaphone, and his expiration seemed imminent. He would never reach Maw's overcooked repast, but die like a dog in the hall.

On the way out, Reinhart dropped by the kitchen, where his parents sat forlorn over their coffeecups—surely not because of his absence, but rather owing to a habitual postprandial *tristitia*: belly full, what was left?

At least Maw got some fun from his intrusion. "Oh great!" she chortled. "Late for your first *dinner* invite. That'll go over big! Everything cold with the grease congealed, your hosts sitting around ravenous. You know other people work all day and need their food. You'll get punched right in the mush, and never think you'll come waltzing back here to get your grub. You'll have to go that boogie joint on the West Side and order ptomaine goulash."

Could she suspect his destination? While his back was turned, Dad slipped out to the living room.

Reinhart took the load off his feet, on Dad's empty chair. "I might take some of your coffee."

"Pretty egotistical, eh? Half-hour late is not enough, make it an hour. To heck with the next fellow." She seized the pot from the adjacent stove and filled a cup which was already waiting at his tableplace. This cup was of course decorated with Chinese (?) birds, summerhouses, etc., in blue and had a chip where your lips would go if you drank it right-handed. Before he could catch her, Maw turned the coffee blue to match with a great flood from the milk bottle.

"Don't have to be there till seven," said Reinhart.

"Aren't we grand?" sneered Maw. "Their nigger chauffeur picking you up?"

Again he was startled by the relevance of her images, but laid it to the psychic sympathy between mother and son—even such an unlikely Mutter and Sohn as those having coffee at this moment, once had used a common bloodstream, and Reinhart was but a maverick projection of Maw's essence. Thinking this over, he seemed to recall certain tendernesses tendered him when he was but a babe, the last time he had been satisfactory, even to himself, and he now put a hand on Maw's forearm irregular with tendons.

"Ah, Maw, don't fight it."

She shook him off, rose, and began a brutal clatter in the

sink. Sometimes the gall gathered in her throat in a kind of tumor, as at present. She sought to hum some private Horst Wessel Song and choked.

"You all right?" asked Reinhart, making a treaty with the rancid coffee, i.e., leaving it.

"Sure, it's only my cancer. Now git!" She shooed her apron, which had dual pockets for potholders, at him; and held a copper-bottomed pan as if it were a missile.

"Oh, is *that* all?" He fled, having as a child served many times for her target practice. She rated Expert with all the kitchen implements, and what with age and weight he had lost the old agility.

When he reached the front door Dad crept from behind a bookcase and tried to press the car keys on him.

"What about Lodge?" asked Reinhart, patting his father's spongy shoulder.

"I'll walk," whispered Dad. He kept advancing the key case, which had a little replica of a Chevrolet embossed in its leather as well as the incised address of the dealer, to whom it could be mailed if lost and found.

"No, *I'll* walk," said Reinhart, and they Alphonsed and Gastoned for a time, but being very quiet about it, and heard the kitchen clatter testify to their success.

Finally pointing to the waist flap of his ETO jacket, which missed closure by a half inch, Reinhart established the fact that he could use the exercise and escaped, though not without suffering a folded dollar bill from Dad, who advised: "Be sure to take along some candy or flowers. That's the way to make a hit with swell people."

The evening was falling rather shabbily as Reinhart set out on the two miles to the West Side, a murky cloud or two melting like old dumplings into the stew of the sky. He sniffed for rain, and got the bouquet of some neighbor's fried haddock. On the main East-West axis, three-quarters of the journey behind him, he bought several cheap cigars from a tobacconist who himself represented the transition: he was white, but gradually darkening from the ills of aging man and the cares of storekeepers. For example, he assured Reinhart that the people who had mobbed him for black-market cigarettes during the war, with the same zeal avoided his place of business now that smokes were plentiful.

"Your typical customer is a louse, I must say," he must have said, though Reinhart, choking on the El Ropo, heard him imperfectly. "You servicemen got yours for a nickel a pack, I know, and sent loads home, but I don't complain of that."

"You don't?" asked Reinhart sympathetically, lighting the

cigar again at the little blue gas flame which sprang pistil-like from a kind of metal tulip planted on the counter.

"Nah? Where you think I got my extras to peddle? A son in the Navy, hoho. But you can bet I never sold any to the boogies."

It seemed the whole white world knew where Reinhart was going for dinner and tried to make him feel guilty about it, no great job with a person of his temperament, but shortly he was at the frontier. Just as he feared, the hour was not too early for the drugstore guard. They stood with their striped shirts and keychains and cuffs choking their ankles and hair in their necks, and one fellow, whose skin was navy-blue, wore a great white fedora banded in alligator. As Reinhart approached, nobody looked directly at him, yet he was under a keen surveillance. He walked with his eyes tight and his hams followed suit, and he bumped right into the man with the white fedora.

"Oh excuse me!" said Reinhart. As unobtrusively as you could when you were his size, he tried to slip by.

The navy-blue man, however, hung on, his great hat riding at Reinhart's right shoulder. "Say Captain," he said, "you looking for action?"

Disingenuously, Reinhart made a naïve smile. "I come in peace," he asserted, believing that the affected utterance was what might go over.

Beneath the alligator band his companion chuckled with the sound of frying butter and said: "Well after the services, then, maybe a little action for the Blessed Lord?"

It appeared to Reinhart that his companion—who was quite small, anyway—was not suggesting violence, but rather some sport. Besides which the other colored fellows had dematerialized as evil spirits might at the appearance of a shaman, or more likely vice versa, for he had seen the noted rolling of their eyes in apprehension and even the shill at his elbow suddenly asked: "You sure you ain't The Man?"

Calmer now, Reinhart looked down at him and said: "Frankly, sir, I don't know what you are talking about."

"The Man, Captain, the bulls, the po-lice. I guess you ain't cause you wearing Army." He tipped back his hat. Oddly, he wore no gold teeth, and the others were not startlingly white, that is, the others that could be seen, for the front ones were gone and he guarded what was left with his massive lips, speaking from the smallest possible aperture, as if he would rather whistle. "And 'action,' that's *action*, which tonight is craps in the second-floor front over Honey Dove's Turkish Lounge, which is two doors from Daddy Small's Blessed Angel of Peace Church, which you already made an announcement you was in motion towards. Now if you *is* The Man, it will be *you* word only against mine that I be scout for said action, as you can appreciate by realizing potential witnesses to the otherwise has gone up the spout, as is said among our English cousins."

"England?" asked Reinhart. "Were you ever in England?"

"England?" the man repeated. "I tell you, Ducks, I as English as George Rex! You make my action in Bridgwater? I was with the Army," he added. "Ours."

"Never," Reinhart answered. He would so have liked to give some assent to the man and call back the potential witnesses, but he feared that such a move would be exactly what they expected of a disguised policeman. "And I'm sorry I can't make it here, but could you direct me to Mohawk Street?"

The scout turned suspicious. "You collecting on in-surance or overdue liberry books?" He reconcealed himself under the hat. "See, I don't live hereabout but come in on the commute, familiarizing only with this here corner."

"Now *you* don't understand," said Reinhart. "There's nothing devious or illegitimate about my present endeavor. My purpose is essentially—"

"Man, you do talk up a sirocco," said the scout. "And verily I don't pick up your pip on my radar *a*-tall. But being you change the motion of you de-sires, I am always available for consultation. My card." He passed it on, a square of cream-colored cardboard, much thumbed, embossed: THE MAKER.

Reinhart thanked him kindly and went to put it away.

"You can't *keep* it," said the Maker. "I only got one." He reclaimed the card, inserting it within a wonderful old fake-alligator wallet that matched his hatband but was somewhat older, several of the scales having come loose at one margin, like so many little trapdoors.

Regretfully, Reinhart saw he must, for the present, make his way without the Maker's help, and was about to move on when a potential witness filtered between them saying: "Maker, here come a john," and returned to the fourth dimension. A lone white man ranged the far sidewalk and lit a new cigarette at every store window, in which he was terribly interested though they were each one dark.

"Now I was wrong about maybe you," said the Maker, with a jerk of his hat and a flash of his many rings and a whiff of his breath smelling of lavender and a tug at his camel's-hair coat almost as white as his hat, "but if I ever saw a mortal ready to do business, it's our slinky friend yonder."

"Action?" asked Reinhart.

"Jelly roll," answered the Maker. "I got me a stable of

cows." He waved goodbye. "Bridgwater, I see you around, hear?"

A half hour of Limbolike wanders ensued. The passersby in Splendor's quarter were, to a man, deaf and dumb, though all very polite. When he at last found it by chance, Mohawk Street turned out to be what elsewhere would have been called an alley, its entrance posted with a platoon of trashcans captained by a broken beer bottle. Here a very large rat or a very small cat served as scout, and badly, for it deserted at Reinhart's approach. As he climbed over the cans he smelled caraway seed, creosote, wet fur, hay, oilcloth, coal dust, linseed oil or putty, burned rubber, moldy literature, ink, some sweet animal filth—but no food except banana, although that may have been rather the oil of the fruit, good for sundry purposes.

No illumination, and little on the adjacent street, where the nearest lamp was shattered. But while Reinhart groped for the trusty Zippo that had lighted him through Berlin, a spark flashed at the end of the alley, became a flame and then a burning automobile. It was something to see as a small man, presumably an enemy of the owner, seemed to be throwing combustible materials into the back seat, though that was probably a mirage.

"Say there," called Reinhart, fifty feet away and already taking the heat on his face. But by now the combustion was nicely under way and noisy. What the newspapers, and no one else, called a "holocaust" filled the interior of the car, swirling behind the windows like a scarlet shirt in a Bendix.

Reinhart was still calling, blinded by the flames, when he felt a touch on his arm. It was undoubtedly the man he had seen a moment earlier in silhouette, a version easier to discern than the present state of the fellow: a disembodied white shirt, for he was of a like blackness with the surrounding night or had been made so by soot from the conflagration.

So Reinhart, with his big fat glowing face, was at a visual disadvantage; as if the moral one were not enough, for there he stood still holding the open cigarette lighter, precisely as a pyromaniac might when caught in the act.

"Yes sir," he said guiltily to the white shirt, "may I help?"

Gleeful gleaming teeth appeared about three and a half inches above the collar, which was buttoned and tieless. Weird but benevolent. "Hep?" answered the teeth. "Thank you no. No hep will hep now. When, ah, it is hopeless. Car is gone, too bad, but in-surance will buy another. . . . Am I correct, you are Army and not the bulls?"

"Oh cut it out," said Reinhart, irked. He put away the Zippo. "Why do you people always expose yourselves first and then worry about the police? It's self-destructive. I speak as a friend." He thrust his white hand forward into the void, where it was not taken. "My name is Reinhart. For an hour I've been looking for a man named Splendor Gallant Mainwaring, who I'm supposed to have dinner with. He lives on Mohawk Street, which the sign says this is, but I see only a burning car, some rubbish cans, two sheds, and a fence full of dirty words in chalk. If you know Splendor, you can tell him I sure tried."

Reinhart reclaimed his unused hand and started toward the cans at the alley entrance. The animal had come back, and was neither a cat nor a rat, but an old sad possum. This time it was too weary to retreat again, and just closed its eyes, rolled over, and feigned sudden death. "Oh cut it out," said Reinhart. Avoiding the bald tail, he collided with a can and made a fearful racket.

A window came alight in a building he had hitherto not know was there, and a fuzzy head poked out screaming in dramatic soprano: "I see you, Henry Bligh, you goddamned dirty son of a bitch. You are a m——,—f—, is what you are and don't say me nay." And so on, becoming more immoderate by the second. Assuming White Teeth had now got a habitation and a name, as well as a profession, Reinhart did not stop to hear an essay on it, for he had given up on Negroes. They were simply one more line on a long roster that nobody could do anything about, and he remembered—perhaps because of the possum—that a man is rich in proportion to the number of things he can afford to let alone.

But still clattering among the cans and under the shower of abuse, he felt a poking at his back, like a goose aimed too high, and the voice of White Teeth shouted: "Just refrain up there, Seneca Bligh! Your man is not present, I guarantee."

Reinhart's elbow crook was now caught in a little fist strong with authority and good intentions. The ex-corporal supposed he was soon to be lynched for arson, without trial. Overhead, Mrs. Bligh answered: "Thank you, Mr. Mainwaring. You are indeed a gentleman, as I always say," and closed her window.

To his captive, Splendor's father apologized, while guiding him into the sidewalk. "Them boys turned that sign around. Mohawk is the street and can't be the alley." He pointed his shirt cuff toward a murky frame house, where a porchlight had been burning all the while, a light consisting of a bare yellow bulb, whose outer globe had been knocked away to a mere scimitar of milk glass.

That last fragment was dislodged by Reinhart's vibration on the porch boards, Reinhart's alone, for Mr. Mainwaring returned to the glowing car with an admonition from his guest:

"Look out for the gas tank!" To which he replied: "All drained, thank you," turned, and became invisible: he must have been wearing a dark jacket or sweater which, opened, showed the white shirt before but not behind.

The screen door, with torn mesh and splintered frame, allowed no signal to be made upon it; neither could it be pried away to get to the door inside, which was hardly better, its knocking surface studded with protruding nailheads, around each a triangle of torn paper: the Mainwarings were given to posting notices, and also to tearing them away when no longer current. Reinhart had not discarded the notion that he might be the victim of a hoax, and derived from it—while looking for a place to knock—certain intimations of unreality of the kind known to people who are awakened at 3 A.M. by the secret police, or, in America, to folks whose full bladders are a wee-hours Gestapo.

Then the inner door suddenly opened and within the rectangle of rusty screening he saw the most beautiful girl on the planet. She was made of amber and, when the car exploded in the alley, for an instant turned to gold.

What had happened was that though Mr. Mainwaring had drained the gasoline from the tank, enough vapor remained to blow up—fortunately injuring nobody and nothing except a shed belonging to the Blighs, and Mrs. Seneca B. appeared, wrapped in an Indian blanket, cursing her absent husband, and pardoned Mr. Mainwaring the gentleman, who promised to hand her a certain percentage of his auto insurance when that sum was paid him, which would surely occur in the nearest future. And of course a window or two in both houses dissolved in the blast, but everybody agreed that they had already been broken, either absolute or half, and there was no point in striving in this world unless you were willing to risk what you had to get more.

As to Reinhart, his soul had fused with that of the amber girl, albeit unbeknownst to her, and he sat paralyzed on one of the trashcans, playing with his overcoat button, not helping one whit to extinguish the fire in the shed, although the girl herself was in action with a garden hose that leaked a fine spray in every particular, soaking the exquisite serpent of her body. She wore a beige woolen tube, cinctured with a belt of great copper seals joined one to another. Reinhart yearned to sweep her up and sprint off with the wind to a barbarian country of blood rituals, fig-eating, and bronze utensils, where it would be a capital crime to wear clothing or sneer at certain jealous gods.

Eventually he did get into the Mainwaring house, as unlikely as that once had seemed—all fires, except his own, quenched and the cinder of the auto left steaming in the alley —and at last Splendor, in a maroon smoking jacket thin at the elbows, had descended from the upper reaches, untouched by the brouhaha, given his sooty father a snooty disregard, made Reinhart welcome, and with evidence of distaste introduced his sister. Her name was Loretta. They, he and she, did not shake. Wet through, she had put her back near a kerosene heater and trembled ever so lightly in the negation of cold. She acknowledged Reinhart with a mock death of her large eyes, the steep lids shining. He had an awful, though rather beautiful, suspicion she was dumb, that a malignant neighbor tribe had excised her tongue in some bestial, though sacred, rite, then lashed her to an altar for King Kong to ravage, defying the tradition that the victim be a Caucasian blonde with scarlet nipples and otherwsie fair as cottage cheese.

"Father," ordered Splendor, "fetch the wine to the table. Carlo, if you move slowly towards the dining room, I shall have the bisque piping hot when you reach your place." He strode through a curtain of jet beads depending from an archway above which showed a ticktacktoe of bare lath and missing plaster. Mainwaring Senior, whose contrasts were less radical indoors—for one thing, he was really burnt umber of skin, and for another, his splendid teeth clicked constantly like the escapement of an alarm clock, indicating they were as false as Reinhart's father's—Mr. Mainwaring respectfully slunk through the other exit, into the hallway of spavined hatrack, cracked umbrella jar, and ten-foot Victorian mirror with yellow silvering.

Despite the cooking odors, which were unpleasant, suggesting burning hair, Reinhart smelled the bouquet of Loretta's wet wool. At first he thought she slept on her feet, but then caught a distant sparkle from her lowered lashes. Rumpled, fat, hideous, he deserved her amused contempt, but even a stable-knave with his feet in horse manure can look upon a lady. And look he did, so forcefully that the power of his eyes opened hers in fright, and no longer his own master, he crossed the threadbare carpet, trapped the fluttering thrush of her hand, and kissed it, saying: "Excuse me, I love you."

Chapter 4

"Soup's on!" was what Splendor must have shouted from the kitchen, but since it was a rather vulgar call from his friend, Reinhart heard it as "soupçon," a French word of which he could never quite recall the meaning, but the *c* had a little tail like the lower extremity of the figure 5. A little tail . . . lower extremity. In shame, he dropped Loretta's hand, although he had not looked at her below the high ridges of her clavicles, which the dress was cut to display. It was well known that a man of the dominant race could take a woman of the recessive at his pleasure, and he deplored the sullying of love by power politics.

The ludicrous aspect of his situation, however, was that Loretta had again closed her eyes when he took her hand and if she attended on either his passion or his loving-kindness, she did it in the most subtle way imaginable, which a volatile man might have taken for total indifference.

"Excuse me," said Reinhart, moving away. "Things like that just come over me." The kerosene heater sat in the fireplace niche below a mantelpiece where stood sundry photographs of dark people, some curled, one technicolored, several of marriages with solemn brides in white lace and all the men looking like ministers. "I didn't mean to offend, that's certain," Reinhart went on.

This time Splendor yelled: "Come and get it or I'll throw it out," and there was unfortunately no other interpretation:

53

when other than face to face, he became rather coarse, if not corny.

"Coming!" said Reinhart, and then to Loretta: "Won't you speak?"

She thought about it for a second, the lobes of her small nose shining and choosing the negative, soughed through the bead curtain into the dining room, where he followed and was directed by Mr. Mainwaring to the foot of the table.

Well, Reinhart was probably no gourmet, but the soup—or "bisque," as Splendor, vis-à-vis, again called it—was pretty ghastly, with what purported to be clams being rather little snippets of inner tube.

"Fust rate," said Mr. Mainwaring to his son, but Reinhart detected the fundamental horror with which the older man brought his dentures into play.

With each mouthful from his own spoon, Splendor grew more expansive and self-approving, and there was no doubt that he made a genteel decoration at the head of the board. The velvet smoking jacket, for one, with its braided trim of gold, frayed here and there; inside it he wore a white turtleneck jersey, very clean in the light of the chandelier, though four of the six bulbs in the latter were cold and one was winking.

"Ah," said he, "how nice to see a friend across the comestibles! I've always regretted, Carlo, that we were never closer in high school."

"That's true," Reinhart responded, taking a soda cracker and eating it dry, causing a blizzard of crumbs. And Mr. Mainwaring and Loretta regarded him in courteous awe, which after a moment of resentment—if a white man eat, doth he not chew?—he took as flattery. Though he knew he did not eat well; for example, noticing Splendor's technique, he remembered that he had forgotten to push the spoon to the far side of the soup bowl instead of in toward the body. Then too, he supposed he should have broken the saltine rather than shove it whole into his mouth.

When Splendor spoke again, Loretta picked up her bowl and drank directly from it, as an Etruscan must have imbibed wine from one of those marvelous handled vessels glazed in black and red, and it was the most graceful thing Reinhart had ever seen, she with her red lips shining. Her hair was high, in short black curls, and lay soft as mink.

Reinhart decided at once that he must finally establish himself, become mover rather than the moved he had been for two hours past: such a decision was always difficult for him who awakened as if from death each morning, never sure he would be able even to walk (but Maw would come banging

54

into the living room, fetch the paper from the porch, and clout him on the bare feet which extended over the arm of the couch; and he had to). So he said to Mr. Mainwaring, who had sneakily given up on the soup and lighted an old pipe with much smoke and a beating of small black hands to dissipate it: "This wine is really excellent. I'll bet it's Burgundy, or something, and you made it yourself."

"Now," said Mr. Mainwaring, "I'll tell you. Now that will be pure grape, Mr. Hart—"

Splendor peevishly tapped a fork against his own glass. "Reinhart, Father."

"Now I tell you I *am* in the wrong," Mr. Mainwaring said to the guest; "Now I never call a man out of his name."

"Father," said Splendor, "I'm sure that Carlo Reinhart is wondering, as am I, why you must start every sentence with the word 'now.' When do you think these remarks take place if not in the present, namely *now?*"

Embarrassed, Reinhart said: "Go on, Mr. Mainwaring. I don't mind the 'now's.' Without them I'd think maybe you meant last year, wouldn't you, Loretta?"

She looked at her brother and said—

Her long-awaited speech had been at the very point of utterance when Splendor, who would not be denied at his own table, arose in a clatter and a huff, and removed to the kitchen.

"Grape, Mr. Mainwaring? How nice," was Reinhart's banal attempt to step into the breach. His original plan had been to ascertain whether Loretta had trod them with her little umber feet, which however, as she too now got up, to collect the soup bowls, he noticed were not small but rather long and wearing high, crooked heels.

Nor was Mr. Mainwaring to be encouraged to sedition, though he put down his pipe, seized a cracker, and demolished it à la mode de Reinhart, a kind of allegiance, but with never a sound except those issuing from his dentures which could be termed independent of his essence.

The meat course was thin strips of beef reduced to charcoal. Splendor called it "London broil," no doubt something he had got onto in the British Isles, though Reinhart could not confirm it, having himself eaten only fish & chips in England, from a folded newspaper. In accompaniment were peas, once frozen, green as poison, hard as jade; french-fried potatoes, still frozen more or less; and a dessert of butterscotch pudding all air, over a circle of sponge cake to which no exception was just. Namely, Reinhart liked it, having a sweet tooth. Thus he ended the meal with a good taste in his mouth—until the coffee came in a midget cup, from which it oozed onto his palate in its own excruciatingly good time, being thick, bitter, and heavy, a sort of molasses distilled from bile.

For the coffee they went into the living room. Splendor called the formidable decoction "Turkish," and Reinhart shaped his grimace into a resemblance of approval and praised it, though no more than the rest of the meal. Splendor lighted like a marquee and, taking the queer pot he had brought along to the chairside table, refilled his guest's cup. That was the unhappy reward for hypocritical charity—yet it wasn't, for Splendor began to talk with such enthusiasm that Reinhart saw he wouldn't have to drink it.

"Carlo Reinhart," said Splendor, "Carlo, Carlo Reinhart. In *Spreading the News*. Extraordinary. Ah, to have such a memory! Wonderful. How nice to have you as guest." He had lost completely the hint of haunt that characterized him at the garage. "So you liked our humble fare? Loretta is the routine cook, I take over on special occasions, Mother is gone."

Reinhart knew not how to look, since he understood the statement to mean Mother is dead—and everybody hereabouts, apparently now including the West Side, pretended death was merely an absence—but Splendor suggested no bereavement. Loretta and Mr. Mainwaring: one looked at the rug, the other at the ceiling. Reinhart was conscious of the fundamental gutlessness of the overstuffed chair into which in deference to its sorry state he had lowered, rather than dumped, himself.

Splendor elevated his own thimble, drained it, placed it smartly upon a chipped china tray of the same substance as the cup, and Loretta humbly took the coffee things and vanished.

Mr. Mainwaring rose. "Will you be wanting me further, Son?"

"Have you finished your Turkish, Father?"

"All the way to the sludge, Son. Now I never do with that, cause it's all grainy like dust done got into the pot." He shuffled to the hall door—strange, for he had been most nimble in the alley—and got out the old pipe. "Begging your pardon."

"Exasperating man!" Splendor blurted when his father had gone. "I understand he arranged things so that you would be a witness to his arson. Don't worry, the insurance company knows him of yore and will simply ignore the claim. You can assure your own father of that."

"My dad," said Reinhart, "insures persons, not things; he would be interested only if you set fire to a man." Immediately he regretted the bad taste of his joke, and compensated for it by lighting one of his cheap cigars and, seeing Splendor's nose go up at the first expulsion of smoke, realized that it was

56

hardly better. "But how awful! Now he hasn't got a car or the money either."

"Believe me, Carlo, that vehicle—" Splendor coughed dramatically into a fist—"hasn't run since last year. Had it been in operating order, the owner would never have sold it to Father." With his habitual gesture he struck himself in the forehead, where Reinhart noticed for the first time there was a vertical groove from his hairline to the upper root of the nose, as if years of similar batterings, begun as an infant when the skull was still plastic, had impressed it.

Reinhart hastened to snub out the offending cigar, choosing as receptacle a complex *objet de rebut* made of oyster shells, pipe cleaners, turquoise paint, and shellac, commemorating Atlantic City. Here as elsewhere these days you couldn't tell an ashtray without a scorecard, and he had made a terrible mistake. For Splendor dashed across the room as if he would high jump through the window, seized the object, and yelled for his sister. Reinhart expected momentarily to be assulted for violating a sacred fetish.

Loretta appeared through the bead curtain by half, forever in emergence, forever suspended, a warm nucleus to the cold sun from the dining room, the jet beads washing over her inferior shoulder like black rain. Splendor thrust the souvenir at her, crushing it in his fist, which took no great strength, for it was a sorry little thing of no stability or craftsmanship—and yet it was suddenly very dear and beautiful to Reinhart.

"I told you to destroy that monstrosity!" said Splendor. His hand eluded hers outstretched to take it, and dropped the shells upon the floor, where they did not break but rather rolled, crazy yet living, beneath the couch.

"Get it!" ordered Splendor. Loretta raised her dress above the knees and knelt upon the carpet. Reinhart thought he would die when he saw three inches of her bare thighs. Before he knew what he was doing, he ejaculated "No, no, no," and crawled there beside her. He found time to be astonished that his hand under the couch encountered none of the balled-and-feathered filth that was standard under-furniture landscape in his own home. Splendor, overwrought, seemed to have left the room. Reinhart's free hand, which sought to push Loretta up, was suddenly bitten by her beautiful pearl teeth; she socked him, as well, with considerable force, in the shoulder. He took these aggressions with a leaping heart: she was not indifferent to him. His hand smarted with love pangs; he withdrew it to rub it with the other and saw her little red brand forming: the Clenched Teeth Ranch, where never was heard an encouraging word. Free of his obstruction, she wriggled head and shoulders beneath the couch, and her skirt worked up. . . .

Reinhart rose, fat and old, and went away, because lust was always being a spendthrift with his spirit. What a silly thing to do, to fall in love with a Negress. He sought out the hassock and fell upon it, it squirting sawdust, and deplored everything, including his vocabulary: the female suffix made her sound like an animal and he Clyde Beatty, whereas the reverse was the true state of affairs. His great difficulty lay in reconciling superficial desire, which was stirred in him by almost any member of the recessive sex, with this holy yearning, which he could not recall having felt for anyone before, toward Loretta. She was so pure, so whole, so simple, as well as so mistreated. He could have beaten Splendor to a pulp for it, but that would have confused the issue.

When Loretta emerged from under the sofa and gave him a dirty look, he interpreted her ill will as anyone else's *tendresse* and smiled sadly, sweetly.

He beseeched her: "May I have that to keep?"

She took stock of his hulk, considered the shells in one hand and then threw the other across her face and giggled behind it till tears coursed shining across her cheekbones: pretty, pretty, pretty, insane. She melted through the beads, as does butter into a waffle, leaving behind the same sheen.

Splendor returned through the hall door, carrying a bottle of brandy the color of Loretta and two glasses. "Courvoisier," he said as if he had never been other than dispassionate. "I drink nothing else in the way of cognac. And you?"

Reinhart nodded vigorously, wondering whether these alternations of mood were generally Negroid or peculiarly Splendroid.

The host decanted two inches of brandy into each glass, which looked to be ex-jam: Splendor would spend a fin or so for the Courvoisier, which once drunk was gone forever, yet not a dime for a real wine glass at Woolworth's; this to Reinhart was curious.

"The same with clothing," Splendor went on illogically. "You buy something of good quality, it will never wear out or go out of style. These silly people who buy cheap and soon discard!"

"Not me," said Reinhart, still on his hassock. "I buy cheap and wear it forever." He accepted the brandy from his friend and waited for a toast, not being the sort of fellow who would suggest one on his own.

"Well, that's another way," said Splendor in tolerant good humor. He took the wingback chair that, being the piece with most gravity, was manifestly his, conspicuously inhaled the bouquet from his jam glass and then without drinking placed it alongside him on an end table that swayed at the contact.

Just above his head on the wall behind was the framed picture of a cockeyed fat rogue in red, the size of a full page in *Life* magazine, which in fact it had once been: Raphael's portrait of Cardinal Tomasso Somebody, according to the caption, which slightly nearsighted Reinhart, who had impatiently glutted some brandy as if it were the grape wine of recent memory and thus developed a sudden telescopic sight, remarkably could read from where he sat. Botticelli's Venus on the Half Shell, which hung on another wall, he of course recognized. The brandy went down like a whole loaf of bread.

"You are interested in pictures?" asked Splendor. "Art? I suppose it goes without saying, considering your devotion to the drama."

"Oh yes," said Reinhart, who had felt drunk on arrival and now, with mixed alcohols in his belly, was sobering and therefore assumed his host's inconsistencies, disjunctions, and non sequiturs to be rather his own. "But I haven't applied myself with anywhere near the proper—uh, application."

"And music, no doubt, as well. Sound." Splendor imbibed some brandy and circulated it throughout his mouth, swallowing it finally as a giraffe might a cantaloupe, with bugged eyes and an agonized chin putting traction on his neck. Indeed he was the most ingenious caricature, the question was of what? "I could put on a record, *André Kostelanez Plays the Waltzes of Johann Strauss* or Ferde Grofé's *Grand Canyon Suite*—"

"You wouldn't have any jazz?" asked Reinhart, to put him at ease.

"I wouldn't permit that trash in the house," Splendor said. "And I take it you make mention only in jest. Filthy stuff. The very name signifies sexual coition, and the lyrics to every song are Negro code for more of the same. This is what love has degenerated to. Your average fellow nowadays turns with a sneer from something beautiful, gracious, and solemn like the Lord's Prayer as sung by Igor Gorin, which might provide an access to supernal realms, soaring above earthly shackles which bind us here below to animal pursuits which fittingly are termed by the ancients 'the beast with two backs.' I think that can be found in *Droll Stories,* by Honoré de Balzac."

Reinhart shrugged.

"That is to say, real love," Splendor explained, "and freedom, which are one and the same. As to sex, that is no more than a foul captivity, as Count Leo Tolstoy has pointed out in the *Crootzer Sonata.*"

All this while the initially faraway sound of a radio had been creeping closer. A sudden increase of volume established it as directly overhead; its program was apparently *Gangbusters*: there sounded sirens, whistles, and simulated machine-gun fire, and among these a portentous voice. Splendor found a cane beneath his chair and with it pounded furiously upon the ceiling. The din diminished gradually, decibel by decibel.

"Father," Splendor said, and pointed with his cane, which was banded in a metal foil commemorating the Great Lakes Exposition of 1937. "But to go on. Here we have what is established as the conditions of existence, and here"—he had indicated two articles of furniture, Reinhart's hassock and his own chair, the first being the conditions of existence and the other—"man standing naked in his loneliness, and the 'standing' is significant. The best science believes it is a mistake that he arose from all four to the two back feet; apparently the internal organs are affected thereby adversely, hanging along the line of the body rather than the vice versa for which they were intended by Nature, namely, at right angles to the longitudinal axis of the body, in the fashion of animals; hence your heart trouble, intestinal malfunctions, and even corns of the feet, since they bear twice the load for which they were designed."

To humor him Reinhart asked: "You then advocate going on all fours?"

"Not in the least!" said Splendor, listening with cocked ear to the last strain of dying sound overhead. "How you catch me up on my general observations! We'll make a great team."

"For what?" demanded Reinhart, worried, and quickly drank his remaining brandy.

"Have you," asked Splendor, who had taken his seat again under Cardinal Tomasso's eyes looking in two directions—his own bulged beneath narrow-slit lids, rather crocodilian— "have you ever longed to Break Through?"

Now Reinhart began to suspect, my God, that the man was a fairy; he knew that queers habitually believed themselves prisoners in a Dachau of heterosexuality operated by the Amazon SS.

"I mean," Splendor went on, "to soar."

That did it. Reinhart rose and moved toward the hallway exit.

"Notice," said Splendor, "in your demonstration, how gravity impedes locomotion. Do you realize how many pounds of air we carry on our shoulders? No wonder arthritis, rheumatics, and assorted diseases of the bone."

Not only did Reinhart realize he had been wrong, but also Mr. Mainwaring suddenly crept in from the hall, apparently in search of his tobacco. He looked up at Reinhart with the most touching sympathy.

60

"Rheumatic in a man you size! Ah, misery! Pity ain't in Jawgia. Some blue clay like they done got in Jawgia and rep you in it like a feesh, lay you bake in the sun, poison come outn the bones, that clay come hard as stone, got to chip you out with a sledge, you be just fine except you was hit by that sledge in the taking out, but I tell you this, you ain't got the rheumatic no more. That be all you could do this side of the witch woman, say my old granddaddy." Mr. Mainwaring stooped to a little bookcase alongside the sofa and from between Papini's *Life of Christ* and a bright copy of *Mein Kampf*, by Adolf Hitler, got a tobacco can, filled his old pouch, and from the pouch loaded his pipe.

"*Vox populace,*" sneered Splendor when he had gone. "*Populace wult dessippi.* 'The people yearn to be deceived.' In this district there are, at quick count, ten evangelists, five voodoo centers, and more palmists and phrenologists than groceries."

Mr. Mainwaring poked his sleek little head back into the room. "You boys done miss a good show on the *Gingbuster*. Man done drive up and down a street shooting a masheegun inside ever house. Dint know none of them people inside, just wanted to do bad. Just a bad man is all he was, couldn't hep it, just shot that masheegun laughin' like a fien'."

Ignoring him, Splendor said: "Some explain this by the cheap pseudo philosophy of the malcontent, namely the writer Karl Marx, who you should always remember suffered from carbuncles and rectal hemorrhoids and because of these discomforts was led to sell his birthright for a mess of potash. But there occasionally emerges an individual who is peculiarly gifted, call it science or sacred as you will— Father, you can stand there all night, but you won't get a drop of brandy from me."

"Just believed I'd take a try, Son," said the elder Mainwaring and withdrew for good.

Splendor went on: "Who breaks through. Who strikes through the mask of appearances to the underlying reality. Such a man is Lorenz T. Goodykuntz of Pocatello, Idaho, and had further written about it in a series of books published by himself at a dollar seventy-five per copy, as well as a monthly journal entitled *Enlight*, as well as operating a noted college."

"Such a man," said Reinhart, reseating himself, "is, I suppose, not known to anybody but a handful of devoted followers."

"To the contrary, he has world-wide renown, with honorary degrees from Harvard, Princeton, and has been decorated, among others, by the sovereign of Andorra. And I can explain your not having heard of him only by a brief mention of his powerful enemies—the American Medical Association, the Methodist Episcopal Church, General Motors Company, and the State Health Commissioner of Delaware—who have sworn to run him off the face of the earth, for such a man cannot swing a sword without leaving scars. I mean to lend you his literature."

"I look forward to it," said Reinhart, who was dying of thirst and had hoped Mr. Mainwaring would get some brandy so that he might be offered another drink of it himself.

"Well," said Splendor, looking sheepishly pleased, "since I see you're sympathetic, I can reveal that my story of this morning was at a salient point false. I did not just come by this art of healing—that's the kind of thing an ignorant Negro like Father would believe. I took a correspondence course from Dr. Goodykuntz which cost 225 dollars and consumed the major part of a year, a lesson arriving every Saturday, and having completed my final examinations last week, am expecting any day a certificate for the degree of D.N.M., which is to say, Doctor of Nonchemical Medicine."

"Splen—" Reinhart began, meaning gently to remonstrate with him, something like 'Splendor, how could you, who were devoted to reason in high school, be so taken in?' But what was the point, now that he had paid the 225 dollars, done the work, and got his degree? Anyway, he *had* cured numerous headaches, if one believed him; and one must, since it was a principle of life that dupes were never liars. So instead of saying "Splendor," Reinhart muttered "Splendid" as his host fetched from the bookcase, from the shelf below *Mein Kampf*, a black, looseleaf notebook and presented it to him.

Inside were clamped, to three rings, the fifty-two weekly lessons, mimeographed on a crude paper the early leaves of which had already turned purplish-brown. On the first page were certain vital facts: "UNIVERSAL COLLEGE OF META-PHYSICAL KNOWLEDGE, PO Box 1000, Pocatello, Idaho. Lorenz T. Goodykuntz, President. Beatrice Spain Goodykuntz, Registar, L. Goodykuntz, Dean of Men. B. S. Goodykuntz, Dean of Humanities; G. Lorenz, Dean of Science. G. Beatrice, Chancellor."

"Turn overleaf," advised Splendor, hanging over Reinhart's shoulder though careful not to touch him; he smelled of the toothpaste which contained Irium.

On the following page, no doubt to save paper, the title was crowded toward the top—"*Comprehensive Nonchemical Medicine,* Degree Course, by Dr. Lorenz T. Goodykuntz, M.D. (Harvard School of Naturepathy), Sc.D. (Princeton Institute of Creative Dynamism), Ph.D. (Akademie der Naturwissenschaft, Stuttgart, Germany), Former Medical Advisor to the Sovereign of Andorra." The course started hard after.

GENERAL ANATOMY

When the Prime Mover (whom some call God, others Allah, Jehovah, Yaweh, Manitou, etc.) created Man, It (which some call He) constructed the human body to make it a integral yet diffuse structure embodying the three principal life energies, Reason, Sympathy, and Passion. Reason= Head, Sympathy=Heart, Passions=the Reins. Reason governs the body structure to the point of the ingathering of veins, muscles, and ducts in the little hollow below the neck. (You can see a pulse beating there if you look in the mirror.) Sympathy rules from that point downwards, including chest, shoulders, the lactatory glands if the subject is female, lungs, belly, and all the internal organs therein: heart, stomach, duodenum, jejunum, spleen, pancreas, Alimentary Canal, appendicts, viz., viz., & i.e. At the crucial junction of the limbs to trunk, including the generational organs, we enter the domain of the passions, thighs, hams, calves, falling to the pedal appendages.

GENERAL OSTEOLOGY

Meaning bone structure. The Humerous (vulgarly called the funnybone)' is in the arm; the navicular, in both hand and foot. (Wait for next lesson.)

"Well," said Splendor, moving away, "I don't want you to ruin your eyes reading in this bad light. Take the lessons home with you. Oh no"—he fought off Reinhart's negative gestures and tapped himself on what Reinhart knew, without Dr. Goodykuntz's help, was the frontal bone. "I've got them all up here."

The ex-corporal was glad to seize that opportunity for leaving. Splendor's gullibility was about to break his heart. He had sworn never to feel sorry again for another person, having become convinced of the fundamental immorality of sympathy. But this poor devil!

"Now I think you begin to get the idea," said Splendor. "When I saw by your lapel insignia you were an Army doctor, and by your manner, which was forlorn, that what you needed most was another fellow with something in common, well, it is self-evident."

"What is? I was only a corporal in the medics. I had a first-aid course and then worked in an office until the end of the war."

Splendor shook his smiling face. "Now don't tell me the United States Army would put a caduceus insignia—the historical symbol of the healer, dating to the time of Hippocrates

—on a fellow unless they believed he was equipped for the job. See here." He brought forth his wallet, from which he withdrew an identification card showing his name and role: *Interne, Nonchemical Medicine, Universal College of Metaphysical Knowledge*—an institutional title which since he had first heard it reminded Reinhart of something else, an old radio quiz show operated by an orchestra leader noted for a kind of cretin enthusiasm, the name escaped him.

"What's your idea?" he asked sarcastically. "To go into practice?"

"Yes, let's!" Splendor replied, putting away his little card. "You for the chemical therapy, I for nonchemical."

"I don't understand this stuff about chemistry," said Reinhart, beginning to stride around the room, hoping Loretta would come out again.

"My persuasion employs no drugs or fluids, introduces no alien substances into the life stream, but that doesn't mean we aren't tolerant of other schools, despite the great evidence that the orthodox practitioners are every day poisoning thousands of our countrymen. You see we believe that if the Prime Mover approved of aspirin, say, He would have built into the human body a gland secreting same. Which he did not. Therefore in treatment of a headache we employ instead the laying on of hands, the introduction of rather the life force from the physician's body into that of the afflicted, to liberate the congested channels of the latter."

Seeing Splendor approach him, Reihart threw up a guardian hand, saying: "Yes, I remember your other demonstration."

"But live and let die, is our motto—a little joke Dr. Goodykuntz is fond of making," said Splendor with a professional smirk.

Man, is this crazy, is what Reinhart was aching to say, but such a statement is not advisable, we all know, to someone of whom it is literally true.

"Anyway," Splendor said, with gloomy glee, "what have you got to lose? What else are you going to do? Has it ever suddenly come over you that all at once you are tired of everything: one piece of self-indulgence is like the last; gorge three times a day without relish; one dental cavity after another, hair ineluctably turns gray, clothes wear through, make more money to pay more taxes, politics with its ritual resentments, routine religions with their rivalries, and we all know what education is in this country: tasteless. And one's own face! Why can't we wake up one morning with green eyes, lantern chin, and red hair, instead of the old predictable us we have seen everyday since children."

Reinhart waited for an opportunity, found it, and said: "That's true."

"It figures in what I say about Breaking Through the Barrier. Through what barrier? Why, through the Is!" Splendor shook his fist at the old hassock, which was an excellent focus for his threat, being even more conspicuously sick of the Is than Reinhart. "We could use a little triumph!" Splendor shouted, his ears vibrating like hummingbirds buzzing each side of his head.

Reinhart felt a suggestion of invigoration but found, through his contempt for fake science, that he could handle it.

"Now, be cautious," he said, patting his friend's shoulder. "There are laws against qua—irregular medical practices. I'm afraid the state of Ohio, perhaps unjustly, doesn't recognize your college, eminent though it may be. Why don't you take a course in something else that the law considers harmless, like philosophy or Latin, or Spanish, which will qualify you for a job among our neighbors to the South in the vigorous young republics of Latin America?" He had just that noontime read such an ad and rejected it for himself on the ground that he didn't like food fried in oil.

"You know why they won't let me practice," Splendor answered sullenly. "You know why, and the only reason." He made himself look so Negroid, so much the projection of other men's vileness that Reinhart, insulted to the core, was almost moved to strike him.

Instead he replied: "Use your head." Which Splendor did, to illustrate his refusal to conform; he pulled his eyebrows toward his mouth, and his lips in the direction of his eyebrows; between, his nostrils rose to the perpendicular.

Reinhart soon surrendered, paternalism being his Achilles' heel. "Oh for Christ's sake all right. Open your dispensary and if I get syphilis you can cure me by a knock on the scalp."

Splendor relaxed from his scowl. "I'm not so naïve as you seem to think. I know you can't practice in the regular way without A.M.A. authorization, who are poisonously hostile to natural therapy. But that is just the point. We are talking here of the union of science and religion. Anybody can open a church. Anybody can rent an empty store and make devotional addresses, and if the Prime Mover sees fit to heal the afflicted in the audience, who paid no admission charge, all contributions voluntary, no ordinance is defied."

"I think you've got your project nicely worked out," wryly said Reinhart, with a wistful glance at the brandy bottle so richly transmuting the light that fell on the table doily. "But I'm not going to be your co-sky pilot."

"My dear friend, I ask nothing more of you than that you attend the first meeting and sit conspicuously in the front row of seats. You might, if it's not too corny, interject certain phrases from time to time in my remarks, such as 'Ah, Lord!' or 'Bless Him,' or even just 'Amen.' Okay, okay! It was just an idea." He had followed his guest to the hallway, where Reinhart got into the Army overcoat unassisted and at this point was wincing.

"Is that all?" Reinhart asked. "I guess I can manage that, the sitting there, I mean—but what good will it do?"

"You have no idea," Splendor replied, taking the crook of his arm and applying pressure toward the front door, "how beneficial a white man, a white man with fair hair and blue eyes, of the king-size, if you don't mind my saying it, would be to my humble efforts."

Suddenly Reinhart was out on the porch with the medical course under his arm instead of Splendor's hand, and his host could be seen only as an obstruction within a rapidly diminishing rectangle of light. "Wait a minute!" he cried, thrusting back the screen and getting his fingers inside the inner door. With superior weight he could have forced Splendor back, but chose rather to offer him the alternative of letting his guest re-enter or maiming him.

"Yes?" asked the interne when he again came into full view.

"Remember me?" Reinhart said in snotty humor. "I'm collecting money for the Old Soldier's Retirement Fund."

Unsmiling, Splendor wanted wanly to know if he had forgotten something.

"Yes, but I've forgotten what." He remembered when he saw Loretta prowling quietly down the passage from the kitchen, all great soft eyes and tender mouth and long tan legs.

"Miss Mainwaring, it's been more pleasure than I can say."

Her brother said: "Don't try then, Carlo. There are people with whom the amenities are useless." With a sigh, a promise soon to get in touch, and an adjuration to learn his Goodykuntz from the lessons, Splendor tirelessly applied himself for the second time to Reinhart's departure and succeeded unconditionally.

Feeling his overcoat pockets, Reinhart discovered that Mr. Mainwaring had indeed confiscated the last cigar.

Chapter 5

Now Reinhart needed no urging to look at Dr. Goodykuntz's text. He wanted to find a particularly glaring piece of quackery that, when contrasted with established medical practice—of which he remembered a modicum from his Army first aid—would convince even Splendor Mainwaring that his mentor was not only a fake but a criminal; something like treating polio with the Dutch rub, was what Reinhart sought. But as it happened, stretched on the rack of the couch later that night, holding in one hand the Zippo's blue-and-yellow flicker—he dare not illuminate the table lamp, honoring Maw's claim that it could miraculously negotiate fifteen feet of hall and two right angles to murder her sleep—and in the other the three-ring notebook, he read precisely one sentence of the second lesson, "General Osteology continued: the Fibia and the Tibula constitute the bonal structure of the calve of the leg," when he heard Maw bound from the bedroom on naked soles and be sick in the bath. Even when under the weather, she was athletic, and came running out again, screaming over the toilet's Niagara: "Douse that light, you dirty dog," and vaulted bedwards, presumably kneeing the lump of Dad, who let out air.

In the succeeding hour, she repeated the performance thrice, while Reinhart listened in the darkness, cramped with the general guilt which comprehends all specific ones from the dawn of man: but for the grace of God, there vomit I. He wished he were capable of some other emotion than regret. For all his added flesh and veteran memories, and the seams of heart that, like the fabric of an auto tire, show from travel, it was if he had never, three years ago, marched away. Maw suffered, or enjoyed, one of her spells, and it seemed queer to him that she had waited so long to institute it; he was home two weeks, and she never had needed time to work up to anything, being able to fall ill on the instant the world, or a son, did not go her way.

Along towards dawn, all crumpled at the middle from being repeatedly vaulted over, Dad stumbled through the living room to the secretary desk just beyond Carlo's head and clutched the telephone, grunting till Dr. Perse agreed to come. Obviously the doctor then returned to bed, for he did not arrive at the house before ten A.M. and when he did was still snorting from the night's phlegm. The doctor knew Maw of yore, not to mention Carlo whose navel in fact he had knotted more than two decades earlier. He had not bought a suit of clothes since, if one went by the salt-and-pepper jacket, back-belted, he wore as he entered now and headed straight for Reinhart, who though dressed was yet snoozing in the living room, the nearest recumbent figure to the door.

Quick as a wink, Dr. Perse had Reinhart's shirt up and an ancient stethoscope, of which the hard-rubber cup was chipped like the rim of a bottlecap, applying suction to his stomach.

"Gee," said the doc through his white mustache. "Oh my, you're in trouble. Sounds like a crowd of elves are in there, eating popcorn. Lay off bananas, herring, egg-drop soup, mutton, and shirred eggs."

Reinhart protested, striving to rise.

"Don't fight me, Ralph. I know the history of your system since you were small enough to swim in a teacup. Still got the sneezes, too, I'll warrant. Therefore lay off all raw meats."

Reinhart struggled, but the old doc was incredibly strong and held him down with the stethoscope as you might pin a beetle to a cork.

"Don't fight me, Paul. I pulled you wet and hairless into this world and you weren't much then, nor will be unless you get off your back and play more with other kids."

At length the ex-corporal managed to explain to Perse the proper state of affairs—though not without promising to eat wheat germ, charcoal, etc., and eschew cumquats, mussels, and guava jelly—"If you ever go to Cuba, take your own food along," said Doc—and got him down the hall to the right patient.

If anything, Maw looked healthier than ever, there in her

bed of illness, both HIS and HER pillows propped behind her Psyche knot, flannel nightgown arms rolled up to where her big biceps stopped them. With her fair hair and muscles, Maw might have been Holland's entry in the Olympic high hurdles. However, the whites of her eyes were pinked with self-sorrow and when she saw the doctor she gasped and began to slide beneath the covers as if they were water and she an amphibian.

"Not *her!*" blurted the doc in stage astonishment. "Oh, never! That girl's built of steel tungsten." He stepped to the bed, cupped his hands, and shouted down, but as if from a distance. "Hallooo there! I say Miz Reinhart, you can't fool Powell Perse, M.D. Come out, you strapping wench, I see youuuuuu."

With showing her face, Maw extended a coquette wrist from the blankets, and Doc, creaking at many of his articulations, sat beside and felt its pulse while eying his dollar watch on a chain of braided hair with dependent Elk's tooth, and humming what Reinhart was at the point of identifying as "Lady of Spain" when it ceased at an arbitrary note.

Doc chided: "You young girls are alike, your giddy heads filled only with parties and proms and beaux."

Maw emerged from the purdah of the sheet as a gigglish maiden, mouth curved like a barrel-stave ski, eyes like jacks: grotesque, and looking ten years older.

Reinhart refused to witness any more of this; he could never understand why his mother would not like everyone else use a mixture of pleasure and pain instead of taking them singly. Either she was a charwoman for fourteen hours a day, or an invalid for twenty-four. Who knew how long her current recumbency would last? With Dad doing the chores and creeping around as if he had piles and couldn't sit, and chiding Carlo for indifference.

Carlo now went into the kitchen and indifferently stuffed himself with a second breakfast, two more eggs, a slice of fried boiled ham large as your shoe sole, and two and a half pecan rolls from the familiar cellophane package which made its contents sweat: the icing was all sticky. Yes, he grew fatter and fatter, and knew not what to do about it. Demonically he gouged out cavities in the center of the rolls and pushed into them stout bullets of butter. He could hear Maw and Doc in some push-pull gaiety over the purple-pills-or-the-red-ones. Maw shrilled: "Now Doc!" Doc boomed: "Now Miz!"

Reinhart drank a cup of coffee with sugar, and then in a spasm of swinishness made himself some hot chocolate, so sweet he gagged. He swore he could feel the molecules of starch and sugar being translated into pounds of lard at his midsection, like the lead waist-weights of a diver. He was going down, down, down in the quicksand of suburban faeces: your only real horror, making concentration camps and secret police a sport. What an ass he was not to have stayed in Middle Europe, joined some ruthless movement, and maltreated small-businessmen.

On the other hand, he expected a summons at any moment, from an unexpected quarter: some slight acquaintance come suddenly into power and wealth, would cable; or he would be chosen, by chance, as sole heir to an aging tycoon, whose bibliomancy was potent enough to find him in the phone book, where he wasn't listed.

Paradoxically, the telephone did ring at that point, and he fell over several articles of furniture, breaking one, a Louis Krantz chair from the matching suite of same, in his haste to answer: "I accept!"

The voice that wheedled through the coils in the black earpiece was old, all right, far enough away to have its origin in Manhattan, and spoke of a splendid opportunity—to work for Humbold. It was Dad.

"But first, how's Maw?" Dad sneezed directly into the phone; it sounded like some crank had blown up the Bell System's main transformer. "I'm coming down with something, myself. Likely the flu."

"Where are you, Dad? Out of state?"

"Just at the corner drugstore, Carlo, and on my way home. I nearly collapsed while on the rounds collecting my premiums. Thought I'd better stop here first and load up on Vicks, Rem, Analgesic Balm, Ex-Lax, Kleenex, and a Benzedrine Inhaler or two. Will you just check a minute on our atomizer—the bulb may be rotten. Also the toilet-paper supply—Maw uses the Kleenex, but t.p.'s good enough for me to blow my nose in."

Reinhart laid down the receiver alongside a Dresden shepherdess, product of Japan, and went to the bathroom, feeling very giddy, as if, indeed, he must *go to the bathroom*. He saw Doc depressing Maw's tongue with a stick as he passed her room; in one second she would bark in Doc's face, which was averted to avoid just that.

When he opened the medicine chest above the washstand, the coiled copperhead of an enema hose sprang out and struck Reinhart at the jugular. He wrung its neck just back of the shiny black head. Ah, the atomizer! Just there behind a cartridge clip of cocoabutter suppositories. He reached for it, but the heebie-jeebies split his vision and he saw two hands where but one was extended. The rectal bullets began to fire at him like dumdums. He seized the atomizer and, crouching below

70

the washbowl, down by the gurgling gooseneck, in which was stuffed a wet rag, sent up a burst or two of ephedrine spray.

An ominous quiet reigned on the middle shelf as his head rose slowly to its level. Then hell broke loose. A red hot-water bag slapped him to the floor, and Argyrol made brown water on his chest. Gauze wound him in cerements, assisted by Adhesive Tape, who paid out white binding as it traversed his trunk on its unicycle. He fought back, crushing Merthiolate, who died in a pool of gore. Under an enfilading fire of codfish-oil pellets, he crawled to the linen closet and pried open the door, seeking asylum as if in a church, never suspecting the ambush that lay in wait. Down sprang the bath brush, the boa constrictor of the rubber spray with its evil pimpled mouth, the toilet swab, bath salts and bubble bath, a reserve phalanx of Lifebuoy, washcloths and Cannon towels, pillow cases, shave stuff, Epsom salts, bicarbonate, Dr. Scholl's, Lydia Pinkham's, rubbing alcohol, camphor ice, hair tonic, Nervine, Stanback, Empirin, Anacin, and Bayer's, the bath mat, rubber gloves, hair clippers, corn trimmers, mustard plasters and a thing for cuticles; floor mop and dust rags, Sani-Flush, Drano, Bon-Ami, Lysol, Listerine, Windex, and the bottles, capsules, tubes, boxes, canisters, jars, casks, decanters, canteens, buckets, tubs, carboys, firkins, and demijohns of outmoded prescriptions. Down came the footbath, leg splints, back braces, and a crutch; an eyepatch, an enamel basin, a portable urinal shaped like a duck; a doughnut cushion for the rump, a cane for the gout, a truss, elastic stockings, finger stalls, oral, anal, and axillary thermometers; depilatories, deodorants, dental floss, Vaseline, Noxema, Iodex, suntan lotion, zinc oxide, and manicure equipment; wrist straps and bellybands, an athletic supporter, an insulin set; compresses, traction bandages, and tourniquets; a fever chart and a blood-pressure gauge; an ice bag and nose drops, eyewash, forceps, scalpels, tweezers, throat swabs; Absorbine Jr., Vitalis, Pepsodent, Mexican Heat Powder, Unguentine, Castoria, Alka-Seltzer, Bromo-Seltzer, and Eno Effervescent Salts; Sal-Hepatica, Pond's Honey and Almond Cream, Zymol Troches, and creosote shampoo. . . . A final avalanche of Waldorf Tissue buried Reinhart beneath scores, hundreds, thousands of rolls, carrying tens, nay, hundreds of thousands of thirsty-fiber sheets.

And everything in the linen closet was but a duplicate of that more quickly to hand in the medicine chest and on the top-of-toilet. When, beaten, Reinhart ceased to struggle, it grew very quiet under the mélange, except for certain siftings when he breathed; a kind of existence might have been feasible there, with instant nourishment from the vitamin capsules and instant embalming in Lysol if one died. And Dr. Goody-kuntz talked of nonchemistry.

No, they did *not* need ass-wipe in the Reinhart house-hold—thus did responsibility at last rear its uncomfortable head from the burial mound, and in answer Carlo must needs struggle up and go inform his father. Who by the time he reached the phone had desperately rung off and bought a regi-ment-sized carton of the item in question, along with the other medicaments promised, and indeed was already on the front porch with them, struggling at the door.

"Ah-oof," groaned Dad when he was in, dropping the pack-ages every whichway. "I'm in bad shape, Carlo. Might as well face it. I'm on the way out. The job devalves on you now." He wore his hat like a clown, down so far on the back of his head that it fanned his ears. He grasped the hog's thigh of Rein-hart's upper arm. "How you feeling? Looked a bit peaked. What's that dried blood on your chest?"

"Not blood but Argyrol," said Reinhart. "I had an accident in the bathroom."

In anguish Dad crumpled his hat and wiped his face with it like Wallace Beery. "Owowowowowow," he cried. *"Argyrol?* You're going blind!" He staggered down the hall in a stupor of despair and presumably crashed to the floor of the bed-room, for there was a great soggy noise, Maw cried out in ecstasy, and Doc Perse, who had only one patient other than the Reinharts—a seventy-year-old woman who believed the King of Siam was poisoning her through thought waves—be-gan to chortle and clap hands.

Reinhart decided then and there to flee for parts unkown, having a conviction that nothing but his departure would bring his parents out of bed, where for as long as he could re-member they had threatened permanently to retire, to wane a while in agony, and then to die. As a naughty child he had al-ways received this threat rather than whipping, for they were very modern in their methods. *Make the next guy feel it's his fault,* rather than *An eye for an eye.*

But being a practical as well as impulsive fellow, first he had to count his money. He owned ninety-four dollars, thirty-two cents, and a five franc piece made of zinc; all of it in his wallet, bills in the paper pocket, coins in the little compart-ment fastened by a snap; where his identification documents had been before he discarded them as obsolete, was a contra-ceptive in a tin-foil wrapper, the way the Army issued them. Staring at it through the glassine window, Reinhart was almost overcome with nostalgia: how lusty he had been as a youth! Since he had sailed under the Statue of Liberty two months earlier he had had no great zest for tail, he couldn't say why.

He grew old, he kept his rubbers rolled. He had, however, acquired a taste for cultivation and begun to look forward to college again. He thought he might take off for New York and enter one of the many universities in that metropolis, living the while in a seedy furnished room illuminated by a candle in a bottle, eating a bit of spaghetti now and then for the inner man, and perhaps finding a girl with a brain and celebrating with her the magnificent legacy of Western Civilization rather than merely fornicating mindlessly night and day.

Unfortunately, his civilian clothing, from which he had taken a white shirt and gabardine trousers just that morning, was stored in a basement trunk, and to get there by the usual route he must pass his parents' bedroom. His plan was to get his gear and cut out before the doc left, for otherwise he would feel grossly guilty of abandonment, even though the whole project was in great part, he felt, to their interests. They had never much liked him, was the bare fact, and who could blame them? he asked quite objectively as he crept out the front door, around the house, and into the outside entrance to the basement.

He shared his skin with an enemy. For example now, when he had every reason to hurry, he was helplessly fascinated by the closet next to the trunk, where, between the hoarded canned goods, were a number of valuable old possessions: an unstrung bow with rubber-tipped arrows; a fishing reel, put there years ago after undergoing an inextricable backlash—nor could he still undo the snarl; a game of tiddley-winks—which, notwithstanding the anxiety like a burr at his sacroiliac, he took down and started to play upon the cement floor! Tiddley . . . *wink*. There was also a jigsawed map of the U.S., with Fla. looking like a water pistol and the western border of Montana a kind of face peering into the back of Idaho's head. Precisely above him on the first floor, the toilet flushed incessantly. He was mad as a hatter, for in reality his childhood had been morose.

At last however he knocked off the silly crap, which had been a mere access of cowardice, put away the toys, marveled at the approximately 200 cans his parents had laid away against, originally, an invasion of the Japanese and no doubt kept for the next war—they had a rather touching faith that Ohio was a prime target for whatever enemy—and fished from the trunk, smelling of mildew but unfortunately not of insecticide, his favorite tweed suit of 1941, now like a seine from moth holes. A trenchcoat in sorry condition. One leather glove. Deep in the corner, a ball of neckties like a nest of snakes making mass love: who did what to whom?, like the queer who brought a Lesbian to his room. Everywhere he saw analogies, and thought he might at heart be a poet.

The interior of the trunk was the cellar's only refuge for disorderliness and unpredictability, like the Gothic ruin in a formal garden. All else was arranged, stacked, whitewashed, and policed. He dug deeper and came up with a pair of pegged pants, cuffless; a clump of new pencils bound in a rubber band, which gave off a pleasant odor; and an old college notebook in zoology, on the first page of which in his childish handscript he read some forgotten data on the amoeba, to the effect that it reproduced by binary fission. Life was most colorful on the lower microscopic levels, and chiefly liquid and thronged, exactly the opposite of your macrocosms with their untenanted interstellar space and inhuman distances all cold air.

He realized he was interested in depth, not expanse: what he would have liked to do was take a cubic inch of matter and spend his life watching what went on in it, molecule by molecule. He might stay here if only he didn't have to be nurse to his folks. He put on the tweed jacket, notwithstanding its air conditioning and its girth too meager for his, and pulled a plain blue necktie from the embrace of its fellows. From the closet he brought his Army duffel bag, and put into it the pegged pants and—no more outer clothes because, beyond the trenchcoat which he would wear, there weren't any; he accepted the possibility that the rest he had left behind in '42 were ripped into cleaning rags. He packed the pencils and the notebook, on the chance that this idea that he was basically a poet might arise once again, and went into the ex-coal bin, now laundry, in quest of his Army underwear which Maw had presumably washed. He rooted through the wicker basket, and trying to get his spirits up, sang a robust ditty.

Five pairs of undershorts and -shirts, and wearing one; all olive drab, they were exempt from urine's insidious dye. A couple of socks, and he was ready, fastening the ingenious grommets, staples, and hooks that secured the bag, which was now so light and lifeless: civil life for him was an immediate retrenchment. He invariably started on voyages with a hopeless heart, an anti-Ulysses fleeing from his Ithaca.

Had he stayed he might, by fair means or foul, have persuaded Maw to give him the laundry as his room. It was private; it was under ground; it had poor light—all of which he held most attractive: a good place to scheme, and also to study minor nature at close quarters, for the single little window opened onto the level of the earth. To ascertain exactly what he was leaving, he slid back the curtains and peered out upon the roots of certain bushes, on one of which a tribe of aphids were in convoy, dedicated little beasts. A sleek black beetle trotted along, gauging things with his aerials. From the damp turf of early March, which would take forever to dry in a feeble sun that hardly reached the ground, an earthworm made his deliberate egress for a breath of air, so near the glass that Reinhart could see the workings of the primitive blue entrails within its translucent tube: *there* was a little creature who embraced reality as close as it could get; a moot point whether it moved through the earth or the earth through it. Reinhart believed some lesson was being dramatized as the worm lay in the sparse winter grass and simply breathed; its wants were few. But he saw the great flying monster of a blackbird alight nearby and begin an evil, nosey stalking which would soon have led it to his invertebrate friend and murder, had he not waved his hand behind the glass. The bird flew off in a bursting, messy manner. Meanwhile the worm knew nothing of these larger incidents. How small an event must be to fit into *its* ken!

Convinced that the humble beast had a message for him, if one could only find its idiom, Reinhart pulled a straw from an old broom in the corner. He meant to reach out and tickle the worm, and opened the window towards that purpose. Because the job, being benevolent, must be done with caution yet firmness, he would rest his wrist on the brown rock near the outer sill—a dull, quotidian object with yet a precious jewel in its head, which vanished as his hand descended. He withdrew. At once the jewel reappeared, and the rock—which was actually a toad—spat out an incredibly long tongue, snatched up the earthworm, and ingested it whole.

Well! The old fellow must have come from hibernation. Reinhart tickled him with the straw, on the quivering goiter, *very* gently. The toad opened his mouth slightly, showing a blob of tongue, but didn't throw it because he couldn't see a target; toadlike, he had only one perspective. He ran down the shutter over his gemmed eye, as if in satisfaction rather than fear; anyway, he kept sitting there with his warts and the little behind that ended in a point, which Reinhart now suddenly goosed, uttering the traditional goosing call with pursed lips. The toad's eye shot open and he flexed his front fingers. His dignity in question, he might move on, like a Republican taunted by a radical, any moment now.

Reinhart's straw was relentless. The toad prepared the muscles of his thigh; he was giving Reinhart every opportunity to desist, and the ex-corporal admired the pluck and integrity that the amphibian stood for: a better lesson than the earthworm could have demonstrated, who, unlike Reinhart and the toad, had no central dorsal spine ending in a rump that could

75

be goosed. Reinhart felt his link with animate Nature and received intimations of immortality. Meanwhile he kept his straw at work: he had determined the quality of the toad's response; now for the quantity. He looked for a great, splendid leap beyond the bushes, freedom in a single spring, and then a bounding series of celebrations across March's gray lawn, high arcs separated by instants of invisibility. The toad gathered himself, looking desperate at the nostrils—I'm telling you, *just once more and*—he got it and jumped . . . about a quarter of an inch. A hard character to provoke.

A lesser man would have made a pet, but Reinhart had the greatest moral objections to domesticating animals. Midget imitation men in fur coats and long ears turned his stomach; as a boy he kept his dog outside and fed it raw meat, but once when he was ill, Maw brought Spot into the house and put it on the canned crud, and before long its teeth went bad, it whimpered at loud noises, and it would screw your leg till you kicked it loose.

Reinhart said a grateful *wiedesehn* to the toad and closed the window, determined to stay home but on his own terms. He proceeded to make the laundry his quarters, and brought from the closet a folding canvas cot and assembled it. The Rinso, blueing, etc., he removed from the shelf above the wash machine to a corner of the outer basement, along with the clothespins, ball of rope, and wicker basket. On the shelf he placed his zoology notebook and pencils, and underneath drove in a few nails for garment hooks. In his old room were several items which would make life down here considerably cozier—radio, mounted pike's head, pencil sharpener, the portrait of a stallion, and a rug his aunt had braided from discarded neckties—but Emmet Swain, the roomer, no doubt would be reluctant to part with them and had a legal right to be so.

Having at last heard Doc's departure overhead and the flatulence of his ancient Ford in the street, Reinhart went upstairs to his parents' chamber and its loaded bed. At the collar of his father's pajamas he spied a fringe of woolen underwear, and before he could utter a word Dad said through chattering dentures: "Just run me my muffler from the chiffonier, Carlo, and then we'll talk about your eyes. Can you make it out? Here, get against the wall there and grope your way around."

"Ha," said Maw, balling her big fists, "watch out he doesn't throttle you with it now you're down."

Dad mildly disagreed with her while pulling the blanket up to his nose, but when Reinhart came toward him with the scarf he nervously met it at arm's length and put it on himself.

Reinhart asked ritually: "How'd Doc say you were?"

"Look at him!" snarled Maw. "Already starting to gloat over the goods we'll leave behind. Can't wait till we cash in our chips. All we worked and strived for, in one instant will be nought when Mr. Big takes over. Streetwalkers will sweat in this very Simmons Innerspring. My beautiful kitchen will be knee-deep in booze.

Reinhart sank onto the top of the cedar chest. "I don't know why you're taking on so. All you have is the grippe."

"Why you—why you—why you dirty—" Maw rolled over and blasted wily Dad, who in anticipation had wadded the muffler round his ears. "George, you going to lie there like a gourd and let me take that?"

"Why won't we all alm wown," groaned Dad, inside his swaddled. "Provolone ill bet us mohair."

"There you are," said Maw to Reinhart as she settled back, immediately drained of spite. She had an erratic but authentic respect for Dad and relied on him for certain interpretations, on others not; when sick more than well though now he was ill too the lines of motive were complicated, and her acquiescence probably owed to her true woman's sense that his message required translation. " 'Calm down,' says your father, 'and don't provoke, which won't get you anywhere.' " She smiled; like anyone else, she was pleased to have met a responsibility and, if she did say it herself, well.

"Sorry I flew off the handle," said Reinahrt.

"Do you mind moving your big *arsch* off my hope chest?" asked his mother. "The last time you sat on it—which was in February 1941 when you hitchhiked home from college having three days between exams and then decided our home wasn't good enough for you to study in and went back to that broom closet the authorities swindled you into taking as a room, for which your poor father had to pay through the nose —waiting for me to darn a blue-and-red Argyle wool sock that cost one dollar fifty per pair just that past Christmas time, when cotton at sixty-five cents is good enough for the other boys, while you sat on that hope chest you sprang the lid and it took me years to pry it open, for long as I remember you been disgustingly overweight."

"That's all true enough," said Reinhart, rising. "Except I was never fat before six months ago. However, what I want to say is only: I think I ought to have my own room again. I feel like a punk sleeping in the living room, and it is beneath my station to do so when I am a returned veteran and after all had a room to myself since I was five. Therefore—"

"Silence!" thundered Maw. "If you were half the man our roomer Emmet Swain is, you'd of got a defense job and made

77

the shekels rather than running off to the Army like a sneak. Emmet Swain leaves here over my dead body."

A shattering howl issued from the pupa that was Dad, who had heard imperfectly. "Emmet bread, Carlo rind, you and me fast frying . . ."

Maw called time out to her spleen and shouted into his muffler: "George no! Emmet has never passed on. It was a figure of speech on my part referring to what will happen to *me, me, me* if your son keeps tormenting, who by the way I wish you would stop saying he's blind. He sees his way clear enough to the grub, for that is his sole feeling in all the world."

"Therefore," Reinhart continued, with the aplomb of his friend the toad, "I have decided to make a room for myself out of your laundry, have already in fact moved some things of mine in, and am now on my way to call the plumber, who will install new water outlets for the wash machine in the northwest corner of the basement, and I will pay him from my own funds. I must request that from now on if you have any business in the cellar, you conduct it quietly, for I have under consideration the proposition of an influential friend, which I must study in peace. Naturally, I shall give you a fair rent— say ten dollars a week—and if this idea goes through, who knows? I may require an address of my own."

Dad's eyeballs swiftly rolled up to the white and the lids slowly descended as he fainted dead away. Maw put her nose into a Kleenex and stertorously breathed, her wide forehead so shiny Carlo could have seen his reflection there, a face within a face that was already his.

Dry-crying—she had never his life long produced tears, just as she had never laughed in amusement, yet her life was pure emotion—Maw stretched forth an arm that would not have reached him had he been in range, for it was meant to demonstrate the ultimately empty hands of parents.

"Boy," she cried. "Not that, boy, oh not that. We don't want rent. Just stay by me, now you've long last come home from far away. Have the warshing room, if you will, or expel Emmet Swain if you must. Just don't forsake your old mother or you'll break her heart."

Now the strange thing was, in the degree to which Reinhart believed this plea to be hypocrisy he was sincerely moved by it, because behind false feeling it stands to reason somewhere there exists authentic. It was a great sorrow and difficulty to him that human beings cannot regularly be candid with one another especially in matters of love. On the other hand, he could recognize the delight which deviousness made possible by affording suspense. His personal folly was that he liked almost everybody; this temper allowed nothing for the next person to work against; he could neither be won nor lost, like the last noodle which eludes the fork but remains glued to the plate. Though true, he was a clump of resentments, all of them were very shallow-rooted, waiting to be instantly eradicated by a kind word. He could not explain his weak character on the basis of either of his parents'.

"Well?" said Maw, getting fierce again as he stood there to all appearances vacantly studying the inverted bowl of the ceiling light fixture, a cemetery of flies.

"Shame on you, Maw," he answered, "for equating money with feeling. Sure I'll stay and sure I'll pay rent. But right now I'm going to make you some toast and a soft-boiled egg."

"You just boil it long enough, brother. If the white comes all snotty, I'll throw it at you."

Before he escaped to the kitchen, Dad revived and ordered: "Campbell's chicken-and-rice soup, Carlo, and three crackers with butter. A cup of tea if you don't mind. And maybe an extra piece of toast for me and you might smear some marmalade on it. I might also try one of your eggs, but poached. No, make it two and please put them on that piece of toast and make another if you will for the marmalade. Also a glass of milk, chocolate milk, stir in a little Hershey's syrup—excuse me, malted milk, rather, if there's some Horlick's around, and beat a raw egg in it—"

"And don't," added Maw, "stir it with your finger and then lick it. I know you won't do my egg right and can just see it swimming in goo like the eye of a cow. No thank you, I'll just have a cut of that cold roast beef, and not too thin, either, and one of those baked potatoes you'll find wrapped in wax paper in the back of the fridge. Alongside I'll have a dill pickle, and you slice me a tomato and a bit of onion and splash on a little Thousand Island—"

"Got to get the phone," interrupted Reinhart, for its bell was tolling in annunciation of money, power, and beauty at the far end of the line, and he knew it rang for him.

Indeed it did. A throaty female voice asked his name and gasped in ardor. "Mr. *Reinhart*, oh!"

Which was consistent: a rich man would have his secretary call. There was a rustle as if she were removing her clothes.

"Mr. Reinhart, my name is Constance Fluellen, and I'm positively mad to meet you. Yes. I am building you in front of me on the basis of your virile voice. Have you time for me or do I go forlorn?"

"Oh don't go," cried Reinhart through constricted passages.

"You want me?"

"I do, I do!"

"Sight unseen? But I am forty-nine, myopic, and portly."

"Please don't joke."

"Teehee, well then. Sure? Dear, you must act now," said Constance, whose velvet murmur had begun subtly to recede. It came closer again. "Say 'I will.' "

"I will."

" 'I will buy.' "

"I will buy."

" 'A set of the *Cyclopedia Rusticana.*' "

"I'll be damned!" said Reinhart.

"Don't swear at me!" Constance ordered, suddenly acid, and a man's voice whispered *Give me that phone you horse's ass* and came on with maniacal vigor.

"Congrats, sir! King-size vol one reaches you in Friday's mail. Three cheers for joining the march on ignorance. You can pay your hundred eighty-five ninety-nine in easy daily payments. We are delirious to have your pledge." The last was nasty with threat.

"I'm reporting this call to the FBI," said Reinhart dully. The line went dead as his heart, and he walked into the kitchen and began to break eggs.

Chapter 6

Reinhart got all moved into the laundry, where it was hardly as comfortable as he had imagined, being very damp. No matter how many blankets he used, the scene of every dream was the floor of some Norwegian fiord, on which he lay naked and paralyzed; and until noon of each day he went about trembling to the core, as if an ice cube were lodged in his stern tubes.

Dad got worse while Maw flourished; both stayed in bed and had many wants, particularly in the direction of food. Twice a day Reinhart fetched comestibles from the grocery; in between he cooked: custards and consommé for Dad, but Maw's requirements were heartier, robust meats cooked to a cinder and boiled potatoes taken only with a bit of salt, and cake or pie to follow. Yet she stayed sinewy, while Dad grew plumper and Reinhart worried about him: Dad had loosed his engagement with the animal cycle and was preparing for hibernation at the wrong season; outdoors, spring crept surely into every vital passage, the toad now jumped five-eights inch when goosed, a soviet of ants instituted a splendid new penal colony beneath the hydrangea bush, and the bush itself seemed to be in labor.

On one of Doc Perse's visits, Reinhart waylaid him and communicated his concern.

"Fortunately," said the doctor, beadily inventorying the living room as if it were to become his after he buried his patients, "your father's case is simple. In three words: he is dying." Jerking at his mustache, he dashed out the front door and sped away in his gasping Ford.

Reinhart spent a fearful day and night wondering how to make Dad quickly understand he loved him, notwithstanding the foregoing years that may have given the other impression. Along towards dawn, down in his room, at the little card table under the bare ceiling bulb, he began to write him a note, and for "Dear Dad" inadvertently wrote "Dead Dad." He scratched his cheek in agony, tearing out a bloody furrow, and had to go up to the bathroom, get the styptic pencil, and inscribe a false scab. Naturally he had trouble at the cabinet and made a clatter that awakened Maw, who had instantly to come throw up. While she was occupied he stole into the dark bedroom. Not hearing his father's breath, in panic he groped for Dad's face on the pillow. The forehead felt waxen. He traced the large nose and found the nostrils, which were quite still and cold. God!

Suddenly, Dad's voice, stronger than usual, vibrated through his hand: "Do you mind taking your fingers out from my nose, whoever you are? Take my money but give me my life."

No sooner had Reinhart withdrawn than he received a ferocious blow to the face that sent him reeling against the dresser. Dad, out of bed, dealt him several more; old, fat, dying, his pop was strong as a rhino. He had Rinehart floored now, sat on his chest, and beat him about the noggin. For all his phantom fears, Dad showed lion courage in what he supposed to be the extremity. Swelling with relief and with contusions from his old man's blows, Reinhart at last managed to make himself known.

Meanwhile Maw had returned and snorting "What a time to wrestle, you jerks," plunged into sleep.

"Carlo," Dad acknowledged. "Oh my, I must have had a nightmare. I thought an unknown assolvent had come to slay me, hahaha. Imagine what a brute like you would do to old pooped-out me." And Carlo, whom he had just been beating the piss out of, had almost to carry him back to bed.

"Dad, I just came to see if you were O.K.," he chided, adjusting the blankets.

"Thank you kindly," said his father. "Easy there, not so tight around the neck."

Next day Reinhart related the incident to Perse as a confutation of the doctor's diagnosis.

"Naturally, Gordon, any fool knows a man begins to die the day he's born," said Doc, getting after a profound itch under his vest, which set his watch chain and its ornaments a-jiggle. "So you see a baby crying and say 'Poor thing, his days are numbered,' and you're right, as you would be if he was even laughing. That is Nature's Law, red in tooth and claw. Bad diet only brings it on quicker. Howsomever, there are at least two times when a man knows this about himself: pooberty and another crisis called climat-eric, not as marked as in the woman but indisputably occurring when the individual knows himself as eventually a goner. He may feel this as soon as the early fifties and then live another fifty. *Blurt!*" Doc coughed dry, yet wiped his mouth on a tweed lapel. "Or somebody who doesn't feel it might go out like a candle in a tornado: a young boy like yourself, who looks habitually so peaked." He coughed again and averted his bleary eyes. "I want to say a word to you about self-abuse, John: it can make you weak-minded." He picked up his bag, which had a hole in the corner and was leaking tongue-depressors, and loped to his patients' room.

Now Reinhart, with his overdeveloped sympathies, felt at once both worse and better about Dad, having apparently suffered a climacteric recently himself, with no immediate signs of coming out of it. Now that there was hope, why couldn't he once do something for the old man? The something was of course nothing other than applying to Claude Humbold for that job, which, gritting his teeth, he could probably survive in till June and the beginning of the summer term at the university. He had to trust that Dad would understand the sacrifice being made for him. He also believed it might do him, Reinhart, good by doing him bad, which was a principle he had worked out some time before and told to a friend in Germany on the night they got into a certain trouble resulting in the death of two men, including the friend, and his own psychoneurotic difficulties. It had taken him until this moment to really get well, which he did now at once when he realized—as how few people do! hence the widespread disaffection—that the mere formulation of a principle has absolutely no effect on existence *in re*; which, for example, is why you'll look forever to find a good Christian.

He went to the phone book, found the realtor's number, dialed it, and soon heard a competent female voice in his ear. He asked for his enemy and was icily resisted, the secretary being one of those persons who confuse intermediary with principal positions. He had to invent a house he wished to buy; even then, in ignorance he put the price too low: five thousand dollars, what he recalled his parents had paid for their bungalow years ago; one forgot that inflation grew by leaps and bounders like Humbold.

"Five?" sneered the secretary. "Say, who is this? All our listings are in restricted neighborhoods—"

To his own delighted surprise, Reinhart heard himself answer harshly: "Madam, I suggest you let me talk to someone in authority. I am Conrad Fluellen, regional director of the Federal Bureau of Investigation and I said *twenty*-five."

Soon a man who must have been Humbold came upon the wire, though Reinhart hardly recognized the voice, so wheedling had it gone. He decided he had begun on the wrong foot, and quietly hung up. He would report personally to the office.

The least he could do was travel in dignity. He phoned for a taxi—in an impulse of Bohemianism, the Negro one. When at length it appeared—an aged Chrysler with a yellow roof and body of asymmetrical checkers, belching blue smoke and making odd groans at the tailpipe—in the driver's seat sat none other than the Maker. He wore semi-official cab clothes: cap with a sweatband of wicker, his jacket had epaulets and the pocket was compartmented for pencils; but Reinhart knew him well enough. The reverse, however, was not true: see one Caucasian, see them all.

The Maker hopped out and opened the rear door, which was more than a white taximan would have, but then he proceeded to do another peculiar thing: cheat on the distance by taking the longest way, up around the end of the suburbs, where a sallow woman scratched the start of a garden; down to the other extremity, where some Slav with an enormous family all boys sold waste paper and rusty iron: then plunged to the eastern limits and its railroad of abandoned boxcars.

Now Reinhart never said a word until they finally stopped before the mock fieldstone exterior of Humbold's one-story office at the edge of the business district. Over the years he had never learned how to remonstrate with a malefactor face to face; between his indignation and its expression always rose the specter of his own corrupt person; he feared damaging countercharges.

Thus now he could only say with veiled sarcasm: "Thanks for the tour."

The Maker answered: "We aim to please." He left the taxi, slipped between its forward bumper and the rear one of a bloated auto parked ahead, probably Humbold's, and opened Reinhart's door. He announced the fare as thirty-five cents. It slowly became apparent to Reinhart, who tipped him the remainder of a half-dollar, that the Maker's cab like all suburban taxis went by zone charges rather than meters. The ride had cost him under five cents a mile, and he just wished he had been intelligent enough to enjoy it.

To boot, the Maker returned the tip, explaining that he was owner-driver, not wage-slave, and Reinhart thanked him, and the Maker rejoined "Yours truly," and drove away.

Expecting the resistance of a compressed-air device, Reinhart thrust too hard against the glass door to the office. It swept back, hit some hidden elastic stop, and came forward with great velocity. Was he struck? No, deft fellow, he performed a neat evasion, but the door's wind raised the papers from the secretary's desk and whirled them to the floor.

"I'm terribly sorry," he said, secretly resentful. Since the inconvenience must occur repeatedly, he supposed it was artfully arranged to happen, to put the caller at an immediate disadvantage. On the other hand, he was thrilled he understood it, that within his first moment on the premises he had divined one of the subtleties of modern business.

"Not at all," the secretary answered malignantly. "You're not sorry at all. Neither are you really the regional director of the FBI." She was actually as young as he, but in her clothing and make-up pretended not to be, wearing the tight under-armor and pungent perfume of a middle-aged woman simulating youth, as well as conspicuous junk jewelry. She stared so caustically at Reinhart as he crept about fetching papers that he believed his fly must be open. Coughing as a cover, he checked it, and it wasn't; but he regretted not having bought a new suit, for at his right hip was a considerable moth hole through which protruded a corner of his olive-drab drawers.

"You don't want to do anything for *us*," the secretary charged. "You want *us* to do something for *you*." She wet on her tongue the end of a purple-taloned finger and pressed it upon her glossy knee.

"Got a runner?" Reinhart asked sympathetically, trying to ingratiate himself, for he foresaw that working with or near this girl would be abrasive unless he could, metaphorically speaking, refasten her brassiere strap from the tighest to the loosest connection.

She swung her legs into the cavity provided for them below the desk. "You don't look like an Italian, but you have Roman eyes." She bit her lips, which were small but full and permanently drooped in exigence. Every so often she widened her gray eyes and then squinted, at which times the point of her little nose was depressed and the back of her brown bob seemed to lift like the behind of a chicken in flight.

She was really kind of cute, and Reinhart turned on for her his winning grin. He fundamentally liked all girls, especially those who worked in an office and took it seriously; a woman's life being ever threatened with disorder—for example, at least once a month—he found both delightful and touching a secretary's illusion she had hers arranged.

"How did you know it was me?" he asked, meaning the counterfeit Fed, and she understood. He also liked clever people, or tried to.

"I remember voices like a sensitive person remembers slights." This was perhaps too clever, and she meant it to be, and flipped both her pretty, insolent head and the switch of an intercom, reporting: "Mr. Humbold, a person to see you." Dirty with static, a reply was metallically audible: *"Hen or rooster?"* Miss X answered: "Rooster," and superciliously pointed coxcomb Reinhart to the private door.

Humbold, sitting behind a blond desk, next to a rubber plant in a bamboo-wrapped urn, lost no time in demonstrating his disappointment; nor could the gravel in his voice be blamed on static any longer; he had a throatful of saliva and was too lazy or arrogant to clear it. Frankly, Reinhart would never understand such a person, and thus at a moment which called for strength had only weakness to offer. On the other hand, perhaps the weakness was just as good, since Humbold would not permit the offering of anything. It was *his* office, *his* secretary, and shortly Reinhart discovered that he himself was owned by Humbold, having hypnotically assented to an oral indenture which he failed to hear properly except for the wage terms, which were extraordinarily generous: sixty-five dollars a week.

Reinhart was suddenly rich; at the same time, he felt distinctly deprived of something he had with him when he entered the office. He studied his employer, to see if he had taken it.

Humbold wore his trousers very high to cover his wide belly; the end of his gaudy necktie was secured under the waistband of his pants, and a golden safety pin fastened his tie to his shirt, which was white with a white figure, looking at which you were sure your vision was failing. He wore a pin at the collar as well: conspicuous consumption, for the collar was also button-down. In his shirt pocket, fastened to an isinglass liner bearing on its fold an advertisement for his own business, he carried a matched pen and pencil of silver with onyx topknots, though no cigars. His face was smooth as a bladder and as fat, but harder. He had unusually long and loose earlobes; like a turkey's wattles, they continued to move when he did no more than stare. His eyes were smaller than the muzzles of his shotgun nose.

"O.K., bud," said Humbold, "never had a job? You ain't paid for gawking."

"Excuse me." Reinhart collected himself—which was what

had turned out to be missing—and asked: "Mr. Humbold—"

"Call me Claude," said the boss.

"I just wanted to be sure you knew who I was."

"No danger of that," jeered Humbold. "You just flush when I pull the chain. Your daddy called me every day. I done a lot for your old man, and I'll do more, though ten years younger. than him. I'm *making* this job for you, bud, there being no opening. Everything I got, I built for myself." He touched the knot of his tie with a hand wearing two rings, a watch, a manicure, and hair fine as a baby's. "Now get to your work."

"Just what would that be?" Reinhart asked, choosing this moment to sit upon a chair of metal tubing.

"Well it ain't sitzing!" cried Humbold. "Bud, you ain't one to appreciate opportunity. A man give me a opportunity like this and I'd have his bidniss inside a year." He rose, impudently rejecting the swivel chair with his large hams. His face grew so amiable as to appear imbecilic: his eyes vanished, his ears grew, his teeth showed, and his tongue dangled. Rubelike, he sauntered to Reinhart and squeezed his hand as if it were a cow's udder. He doffed an imaginary straw hat and droned: "Take a piece of propitty off muh hans? You an me'll mosey later to take a look at whut I got fuh sale, but fust we drink a bourbon and branch water?"

Humbold came out of his role and explained: "That technique is for the city type, contrary to what you might think. You always be different from the client. What a man buying a property *don't* want is for the salesman to be no more than him. Now if you get a hick, you act hoity-toity and then show a property near a exclusive golf club, tell him everybody in the neighborhood eats supper in a Tuxedo and set their dogs on Baptist. Get the point? You always work *against the grain*."

Humbold returned to the other side of the room, where two different kinds of his own calendars were hung, turned, put a twist on his hip, and waltzed back like a fruit.

"The mosth darling little place," he lisped, "that you'll *dearly* love! . . . The approach for a crude, physical type with a mousey wife. You have to watch he don't belt you, but you'll make a real hit with the little woman. On the other hand, you get a sissy, you lay on the threat: you start by hurting his hand when you shake. You belch, sneeze, spit, and pee in a deserted hallway. You pull him inta some tough saloon and show only slum properties near a factory where the air stinks."

It had taken Reinhart all this while to understand that he was being hired as a real-estate man, and he was very gloomy about it, disliking nothing more than houses and lots, dreaming invariably of palaces in parks on the one hand and urban apartments on the other. For a moment he hated Dad for having had to do him this favor.

"Never," said Humbold, "sell a man what he wants!"

"Why?" Reinhart asked. "Why are people like that?" For if Humbold said they were, they were; he did not challenge his employer, the one man hereabouts who had made an unqualified success and was worth, they said, six figures, and continued to live in the same neighborhood as Reinhart's parents only because he had the biggest house there.

Contrary to what his employe expected, Humbold looked pleased at the query and answered ecstatically: "Because that's not what they want!" He plunged into a closet and brought out the jacket to his pin-striped suit, a fawn-colored topcoat, and a kind of Confederate cavalry hat of light gray with a narrow black band. From the lapel of his jacket sprouted a crimson feather-duster boutonniere, apropos of the predominant color, in a mélange of others, in his necktie. An Alp of white handkerchief rose from his breast pocket. He cocked his hat and cried to Reinhart: "Let's move out, bud!"

Struggling into his old trenchcoat, Reinhart followed Humbold through the outer office and past the secretary. Their air swept her correspondence to the floor again. She shook her little fist at Reinhart, and he stopped to make things right. "Bud!" shouted Humbold, half through the street door, admitting a March wind that mocked any efforts at reorder. "Step lively before it gets away!"

"Before what does?" Reinhart screamed into the wind. He was now outdoors; Humbold, already in his eight-cylinder Gigantic, started the engine. The vehicle began to move as Reinhart caught the door handle, and he had to run alongside for half a block before a red light halted it and he could enter.

The boss played the pushbuttons of the radio as if it were an organ, producing a mishmash of sound. At last he settled for a rancorous raving about a deodorant: *Your're a dirty pig unless you use Dream Mist.*

He thrust his face down into his coat and alternately sniffed at both armpits. "Why," he then answered, "whajuh think? Life!"

By the end of Reinhart's first work day there were two new developments, both encouraging. One, Maw was up and around again, showing no damage from whatever her trouble had been, but obstructively trying to talk of some amidst Reinhart's account of his triumph. Two, there was Reinhart's triumph, a feature of which was that suddenly after all these years he ceased to think of Humbold as an enemy.

Humbold was generous—irrespective of the sixty-five per

week, which was not exactly a salary but an estimate of what Reinhart could earn by making sales, fair enough. He had driven first to Gents' Walk, the local clothiers, and got Reinhart reoutfitted from sole to scalp (or, as Humbold put it, "from corns to dandruff"), charging it to his own account, the squaring up to come from his employe's future earnings.

Humbold was egalitarian: he vigorously pressed Reinhart to dress after his, Humbold's, fashion; and while the apprentice politely rejected the pinstripes, the aurora borealis neckties, and any kind of hat, he did appreciate his boss's selfless concern—your typical employer would rather have striven to maintain the distinctions. (Gents' wasn't where Reinhart would have gone on his own; yet he managed to find a harmless brown sports jacket, gray flannels, cordovan-dyed oxfords which might or might not run in the rain, and a single-breasted gabardine raincoat which might or might not shed it, he gave his old clothes to the halitosic clerk to burn. "I'll package them and send them to MISSIONARY, in care of your local postmaster," said the clerk. "An appeal in which your neighborhood clothiers are cooperating, to cover the nakedness of certain tribes in New South Wales.")

Humbold had authority: he operated his great car as if it were a chariot fitted with hub-scythes and the pedestrians were Roman infantry. Walking, Reinhart had always condemned such driving; he saw now how the grass could be green in one's own yard. He felt, if not power, at least his adjacency to it. Their next call was to a gas station, where Humbold flashed a credit card and a herd of lackeys swarmed over the vehicle and filled it and cajoled it and laved it with a variety of their fluids, and stood in platoon formation, saluting, as the Gigantic at length blasted off, just missing a fox terrier with his nose at the tail of another upon the edge of the blacktop.

Humbold had esprit: they roared towards a couple of "live ones," which was to say, clients, people in the market for a house, and the boss already had the scent of prey in his big nostrils; he increased the volume of the radio and whistled through his teeth in accompaniment of the musical commercials; he sideswept his hat brim like an Anzac; he ground two sticks of gum between his molars and winced as if in some excruciatingly sweet pain.

"Keep your eye on me, bud," he said. "It's worth a college course."

Since the boss was going to this trouble over him, Rinehart believed it was only fair to advise: "Which reminds me, sir—"

Humbold buried him in an avalanche of derision. *"Sir!* That

89

went out with Tom Thumb golf and near-beer, bud. You never made a dollar calling 'sir' like a Limey butler. To a client, I repeat, *you* got to be boss. And as to me"—on a shaded avenue, going fifty, he suddenly squashed the brakes, which hurled Reinhart against the dashboard and permitted a woman to wheel a baby carriage across the street in the middle of the block; or rather, she was forced to cross by Humbold's sweeping arm; it was doubtful whether she had really wanted to—"as to me," Humbold repeated, then parenthetically told Reinhart to snap out of it, the dashboard would break sooner than his head, and accelerated forward, waving his hat at the woman. "As to me, everybody calls me Claude, but nobody forgets who pays the bills."

He shot past a stop sign onto an arterial highway, greeting with one raised finger, as if in the schoolroom signal of Number One, the motorcycle cop hiding behind the billboard there, among the early poison ivy. Reinhart cracked his neck to turn and read what wind and weather, or a cunning vandal, had made more eloquent:

CHOICE PROPERTIES SEE HUMBOLD REAL

He decided there was little point in hastily telling the boss he could work only until school started, since at this moment culture seemed irrelevant even to himself. Uncomfortable in his new clothes, he drew a cigarette and punched the dashboard lighter, which instantly glowed like a witch's eye.

"No boy no!" cried Humbold, at the same time gunning off the highway onto a washboard dirt road, the Gigantic much bumpier than the ads, with their photos taken by stroboscopic light at the Gigantic Torture Test Track, Dearborn, Mich., admitted. "Stamp out the King Brothers!"

By the time Reinhart had puzzled this through—he was really very pleased to have been able to: Smo King and Drin King—they had drawn up on the village green, only it was mud, of a cannibal village, only instead of shrunken heads, diapers were everywhere hanging out to dry on sagging lines between the huts, which were made of corrugated iron rather than palm fronds, and the children who burst ululating upon him and the boss were white beneath the dirt.

Humbold broke a passage by flinging a handful of nickels in another direction, saying to Reinhart: "When I was a boy, you could buy off a kid with a penny. I made it by bidniss to be completely nauseating and soon I had more cents than anybody." He asked nothing for his wit, however, and didn't smile himself, but rather studied his shoe-tips in annoyance, which were gathering a film of dust as they padded towards the nearest Quonset.

A respectful half-step behind, Reinhart asked, trying to be professional: "Is this hot territory?"

But he learned that you either knew the jargon or not, simulation was ill advised. Thus Humbold answered as if he had been questioned on the weather: "Temperate."

"Sorry," Reinhart said, and he lowered his voice, for they were almost at the door of the hut. "I mean, this place looks pretty low-class. Are there many clients here who could afford a house?"

Humbold banged the door, the same rusty metal as the siding, with his foot. Instantly it was opened by a skinny young man in eyeglasses, a T-shirt, and an expression of ancient apology. Humbold seized his hand and under the guise of shaking it performed a neat judo type of throw which lifted the man from his threshold and literally dropped him on Reinhart.

"Meet Bobby Clendellan."

Ah, thought Reinhart while helping Clendellan settle shakily on his own two feet, the strong-arm technique. But this fellow didn't seem effeminate, only confused and guilty, other things entirely.

Humbold retrieved poor Clendellan before Reinhart could do too much for him, and holding him by the scruff of his T-shirt, finally answered Reinhart's earlier question: "Can these jokers afford a house? Bud, this is Vetsville, these boys got all them benefits from a grateful country. Ain't that right, Bobby?"

Clendellan adjusted his glasses back of the ears, while looking cravenly through their lenses at Reinhart. He said: "I was a yeoman in the Navy."

"He killed two regulations and wounded a fountain pen," said Humbold. He propelled Clendellan into the hut, patting his slack behind. "Go get your ball and chain and your deductions, if they haven't been eaten up by the vermin in this dump: I got a nice place to show you."

Clendellan poked his head out the door again, and called to Reinhart: "I had limited service because of bad vision."

"That's quite all right," Reinhart answered grandly. He waved the client to his errand.

While they waited, Humbold pawed the ground like a bull and snorted, to maintain his role, but *sotto voce* he advised his apprentice: "A fairly uncommon case, noncombatants being usually the tough ones, with paratroopers and Marines being soft and easy to work."

"I get it," said Reinhart. "Noncombatant service is more like civil life than combat is, and—"

"Wrong, bud. All wrong. Just the opposite: life, real life, is exactly like the fighting, except in the latter you use guns and therefore don't destroy as many people. But if you already had your combat one place, you don't want it in another . . . . The present client is the black sheep, the foul ball, of the moneybags clan who own among other items the Clendellan Building in the city. He lives here like a goat while his family could buy the state from their petty cash. You figure out why?"

"Because he wants to Make His Own Way," whispered Reinhart.

"Absolutely incorrect," the boss said, beheading his gum ball again and again with chipmunked incisors and restoring it with his tongue. "Because he's a Commonist." He let that soak in for a moment, but it didn't faze Reinhart, who had been in Berlin with the real Russians. "Or a Fachist," Humbold continued. "I don't know which, whatever kind of crank it is who likes to live like a nigger when he ain't one. That's seldom a real nigger, by the way. Say bud, do you have a politics?"

"Not so's you can notice," Reinhart answered, sure at last he had said the right thing.

But Humbold turned away in chagrin and punched the side of the hut. Something fell from the wall within and broke and Clendellan's contrite voice was heard: "Be with you in a minute. We're changing the baby's diapers." Perhaps because they didn't answer, he came to the door and explained to Reinhart: "I was stationed at the Norfolk Naval Base throughout my service, which is how I could raise a family."

Reinhart shrugged cynically.

Humbold removed his big hat and extended it, with the hole upwards, in supplication. "All right, then. Can you at least pretend to be a Red?"

"I'm sorry, Claude. I thought we always went against the grain."

"With the men, bud, the men. Look." He literally buttonholed Reinhart—or tried to, but in fact the lapel slot on the new jacket was still sewn shut; Humbold settled for a grip on the notch. "Your job is the wife."

Reinhart felt himself blush in involuntary, anticipatory lasciviousness; his id, or whatever it was, always made his own translation of remarks that linked him with a woman no matter what the intended relation. Humbold however noticed nothing amiss. He was almost a foot shorter than his assistant, but didn't admit it. This was another reason why Reinhart had begun not to dislike him; Humbold was superior to details unless they had a practical application to an immediate purpose. For example, he would never mention Reinhart's size until he wanted someone beaten up.

"You got it?" asked the boss.

"I think so."

Humbold frowned, looking like a rubber ball being pinched. "That's not the right comeback. Be positive, defiant, overbearing, never welch. When you are asked 'You got it?' answer 'Better than you!'"

"Even to you?"

"Especially to me, bud. Who you think's paying you?" Humbold found a handkerchief beneath his coat and snapping it at his shoes in the way a towel is used to sting someone's bare body, cleared them of dust. "O.K.," he said, "now try it. *Got it?*"

Because the boss held the handkerchief as if he would give him a taste of it for failure to comply, Reinhart counterfeited a heavy, sneering insolence that made his stomach curdle, replying: "Better than you, goddammit!" He felt ill and hoped he musn't have to do this frequently.

"There's one thing I won't stand for," Humbold asseverated. "And that is a foul mouth. Clean it up, bud, or you're out of a good opportunity. No taking of the Lord's name in vain; no friendship towards the King Brothers; no suggestiveness about the fair sex. Just listen to your Dutch Uncle Dudley. Remember you wouldn't be in this world without your dear old mother. Write to her frequently, boy. Worship your God in your own way, and go to the church of your choice this Sunday. I say so even to a Jew, for in the eyes of the Big Boy upstairs we are all even as children. He's the greatest bidnissman of them all, bud, and knows a bad property when he eyes one. Don't forfeit your Big Commission."

When Reinhart, more or less sincerely, said: "You know, Claude, you would have made a great preacher," he saw he had at last pushed the right pedal. Humbold uttered no sound, struck no attitude; rather, his eyes disappeared in true humility, he briefly locked arms with his employe in that old knight's embrace where each fellow clasps the other's biceps, and said: "You'll make a great bidnissman, bud, in time."

And there came upon Reinhart in this barren March afternoon a portent of imminent glory, a kind of Star of Bethlehem in whose radiance he saw himself as Henry Ford Reinhart, emperor of the clangorous assembly lines; or Woolworth Reinhart, seated on a mountain of small coins; and finally, John D. Reinhart, withered, digestion ruined, dining on milk and crackers, tipping dimes, his mouth like an empty purse and his purse like a full mouth, not the worst kind of dotage. And for years he had hated business in general and Humbold in particular; we don't know how the other half lives.

"Bandits approaching at three o'clock," warned Humbold,

using his left fist as an intercom; his right presumably on the rudder, he banked towards the hut, from which Clendellan emerged with an armload of baby and extra swathings. Another child, of about two and a half feet—Reinhart was no good at computing age—a girl, and malicious of expression, walked alongside her papa clutching the seam of his chinos. Behind this group, carrying nothing, shuffled a little man in the garb and make-up of a silent-movie comedian, baggy of pants, saggy of shirt, unbarbered, with a face white as flour and hair black as night.

Of course Reinhart knew all along this little Chaplin was a woman and Clendellan's wife, but it was part of the strategy he was swiftly formulating that he pretend otherwise. He saw in astonishment that the boss had turned on a gross gallantry, bowing with fingers to his gut.

"Humbold," Mrs. Clendellan said, a description rather than a greeting.

Straightening, Humbold imperiously signaled the attendance of Reinhart. "My assistant, to take the kids off your hands."

"They're not on mine. Are you myopic?"

"No mam," said the boss. "I speak with all respect." He appealed mutely to Reinhart and back-pedaled to the side of Clendellan, where the girl fetched him a kick in the shins, which could have done little damage considering her height, but Reinhart saw his pride was wounded and marveled at it.

Reinhart himself was now unnerved at a situation that had thrown his boss, and was desperately planning to speak in the character agreed upon—he tried to think of something favorable to say about the Soviet Union—when Mrs. Clendellan shook his hand with incredible strength for so small a woman and said: "I'm Alice."

"My name is Carlo Reinhart. How do you do, madam."

She smiled and slid her grip to his big forearm. "You can drop the feudal designations, Carlo. I'm Alice, and I've been a worker in my time, too: the five-and-ten housewares section. What kind of wage does this reactionary pay you?"

"Oh, a very decent one." For a moment Reinhart thought he discerned a basically attractive woman disguised somewhere within the little creature kneading his arm, and thought oh what a pity, and there was a catch in his voice.

Mrs. Clendellan interpreted it otherwise.

"Strength!" she said, in both sympathy and triumph, and moved her grasp to his upper arm, which was indeed as high as she could reach and it must have been awkward to walk in that manner, for all this while the party was proceeding towards Humbold's car.

The word, however, had to the apprentice a certain Fascist connotation; perhaps after all Claude had been correct in his strange assessment of the Clendellans. So Reinhart answered it with: "Through Joy!" and opened the rear door of the automobile. Frankly he didn't care what they were.

He struggled briefly with Mrs. C. over who helped whom into the car. At last he won, and she clambered in giving him a view of the back of her slacks, from which no valuable data were gained, for they were too baggy to show the shape of her bottom. When he got in, however, he ascertained that her hip was very firm, for she pressed it against his and otherwise sat close enough to allow for three more passengers, though only one came: the small daughter, with a final kick at Humbold, swarmed like a chimpanzee over the backrest of the front seat and violently embraced Reinhart with all her extremities, sharp little kneecap in his ear, little paws in his nostrils, etc., screaming "I love you, big giant!"

Now if Reinhart was flattered, he was also embarrassed, not towards the titular head of this clan—for Clendellan's weak eyes were watery with approval, looking back over the baby's transparent scalp; it was clear his women were seldom pleased —but towards the boss, whose face he could see through the small fingers passionately clawing at his own.

Money? Ah no, it wasn't money which your true businessman lusted after. Reinhart all at once knew this and became a professional in one fell insight. It was love. Humbold looked ghastly, being deprived of it. On the other hand, Reinhart had never liked him more, and wondered if the boss would eventually see that his assistant's success was also his own.

For the nonce, Claude did not. He backed off the mud flat as listless as a grazing water buffalo and droned slowly along the highway hugging the right shoulder so close Reinhart feared he might sever a progression of Burma-Shave verses: IN THIS VALE—OF TOIL AND SIN—YOUR HEAD GROWS BALD— BUT NOT YOUR CHIN.

Tiny Margaret—for that was her name; she said it again and again as she climbed Reinhart's chest and sat upon his head, with one foot in the breast pocket of his jacket: "I'm Margaret Clendellan and I love the giant, I'm Margaret," etc. —little Margaret swung her weight diagonally forward, taking Reinhart's neck along with it perforce, which brought her to the rear adjacency of Humbold's fat shoulders, from which it was even for her short arm a simple maneuver to play streetcar conductor with the boss's earlobe and order: "Make it go!"

There was no love lost between mother and daughter—at the moment they contested over Reinhart, with Margaret, being spryer, holding the edge; though Mrs. C. had somehow wormed one dirty saddle oxford between his new shoes—but Clendellan's frau now contributed her heckle to the same cause.

"Why do you drive so hearselike, Humbold? Surely you must be an honorary sheriff."

"Yes mam," answered Claude, making feeble efforts to free his ear, helpless as the infant in Clendellan's arms, who as a matter of fact was quite self-reliant and had begun to menace Humbold with a blue-and-white rattle, egged on by a proud, no longer cringing dad. "I'm also a big donor to the Police Retirement Fund."

"An overweight one, anyway," rejoined Alice Clendellan, making no move towards the wallet, with all his courtesy cards dangling like an open concertina, which Humbold had pushed over the backrest while steering with one hand. To save the boss's face, Reinhart thought *he* might take it, but was outmoved by little Margaret, who tore the celluloid insert from the billfold and swiftly destroyed its contents.

For Reinhart it was a further insight into the character of both Humbold and business in general to see that when the damage was discovered the boss brightened—the point was, he at last had got a response he could understand—and he actually gave his Stonewall Jackson hat to Margaret, suggesting she tear it to shreds. Some of the old lilt returned to his voice, and he speeded up to forty.

But as anybody could have told him, sanctioned destruction is not the same thing at all. Margaret not only declined; she replaced the hat upon his head and waged no further agression against him.

Well, so it went all afternoon: the family just couldn't resist Reinhart and just couldn't stand Humbold. Claude continued to wilt until he seemed to have changed roles with Clendellan. By the time they stopped at the third house, the latter had got so far as to punch Humbold in the back and say: "I don't think we'll even bother to get out for this turkey."

The irony was that the houses looked to Reinhart like very good buys. He had assumed Humbold would try to do the Clendellans dirty, but no: the first two had been sound bungalows on Presbyterian streets. This one, a block from the northeastern corner of the town line, was old brick shaded by elms; its back yard after fifty feet became an apple orchard; and instead of your modern type of garage, with its vile bleakness, here stood a little green shed which would conceal a car without looking as if it did. Yet this was what Clendellan termed a turkey and declined to consider.

Reinhart believed everybody present save himself was fight-

96

ing some kind of war which had nought to do with buying or selling a house. He understood the justice of Humbold's preparatory comments. The only trouble was that even so the boss had lost every engagement; and he certainly couldn't be happy about an assistant who had won them to no purpose. Reinhart therefore contrived an excellent, if he did say so himself, intrigue. On the taxi ride with the Maker, he had noticed, in the southern district where the Slav kept his junk, a real abomination: a kind of junior tenement of four stories, absurdly distant from the town center for a multiple dwelling, built purposely as a slum, with garbage cans for a yard and a miniature Gobi as a park, where degenerates molested children, children tortured cats, and the latter ate songbirds, while rodents ran with impunity. The building was occupied by emigrés from Kentucky, who had come north to work in the factories and were, despite their salaries, forever indigent; they were also the very same people Reinhart had seen there ever since he was a boy—apparently they never grew older; he swore the urchin eating dirt from a flowerpot had been his schoolfellow in the third grade.

Anyway, this horror of a residence wore a sign on which, under an overlay of misspelled references to the reproductive and excretory activities of Homo sapiens, one could read FOR SALE (and ignore the legend some depraved wag had penciled in beneath: *my Sister*).

Reinhart's plan was this: disingenuously to offer the tenement to the Clendellans, by so doing to shock them into a reasonable attitude towards Claude and the decent properties he had been showing all afternoon.

The best feature was that not even Claude himself understood the scheme. When Reinhart suggested they drive south, the boss pouted. The baby reached over and ran a finger up his spread nose, and its father chuckled idiotically.

Freeing his air, Claude also liberated some of the spleen which had been building up in him for hours: "That's a dumb idea, you. Dumb, dumb, dumb." He abused the driving controls and started up with a thrust that threw Reinhart, Alice, and Margaret together into one amorphous monster with six limbs. Though this far from displeased the girls, they both struggled loose and made their demands, one in tin-whistle coloratura, the other in malignant contralto: they either went where Reinhart said or home.

Humbold furiously drove right to the tenement, which in addition to its other deficiencies stood upon a dead-end street, where he had the greatest trouble reversing the Gigantic and finally was forced to bull, tanklike, into the curb, crumbling it.

He punched his hat, and said sardonically: "This is a waste of time, unless you want to buy the Tenderloin."

"What's the Tenderloin?" asked Clendellan.

But his wife already knew. She leaned across Reinhart's lap —and he began quickly to think she wasn't so bad a dish— and counted the windows in the facade of the building, all broken, some masked with cardboard.

"Something definitely could be made of it," Alice crooned. A cadaverous woman with Medusa hair stared back at her from the second-floor front. On the eroded entrance steps a small boy plucked at his convex navel, which was bare between pants tops and shirt-end. Leaning from the window, the woman advised him: "Don't run with them boys if they kick the shit out'n you." He seemed grateful for the counsel and having drifted along by the trash cans began to break bottles on the sidewalk.

Now it was no surprise to Reinhart that these people cared for one another, but both the Clendellans were much impressed and pursed their lips, while Claude snorted crudely and revved the engine.

"Off we go," he said. "I got to take a shower."

Little Margaret shoved past her mother and, hanging from the car with her feet in Reinhart's face, called to the boy: "I love you, tiny midget!" He replied with a fantastically vivid obscenity for such a small child, who would as yet have only known it as hearsay, absolutely enchanting Margaret, who leaped out and embraced him. He punched at her nose and missed; in no time at all her half-nelson had him grounded.

"Looks like Maggie's making a hit," Clendellan told the infant in his arms, and each bubbled at the other.

"Humbold, I may as well inform you now," said Mrs. Clendellan, "if we buy this building it will be on the following terms: Mr. Reinhart will get the commission."

Claude laughed hysterically and started to drive off. "Oh no, mam, you wouldn't joke so mean with me."

"Reverse this bison!" she ordered. "Try no Cossack tactic on me!" Clendellan tried to add a word, probably affirmative, but she anyway shouted him down.

"Mam," pleaded Humbold, showing a confusion ever ready to become chagrin. "You're a great little kidder but nobody'd purchase the Tenderloin. The town will condemn it next month and—"

"And hurl this underdeveloped population into the street?"

He nodded sadistically. "The owner would unload it maybe for eighteen five, with the rats thrown in. That proves something, being next door to selling it for the nails. The plumbing rusted out in '43; in every room there's muck knee-high like

98

after a flood; the Hunky in his junkyard burns rubber continually; the roof's like cheesecloth; no tomcat's got nerve to enter the cellar where the vermin are big as Shetland ponies; you can't light a match but what the whole shebang would go up like excelsior soaked in fuel oil. And the neighborhood is type Z zoning; they could build a gas works next door."

But before he had finished, the three remaining Clendellans had swarmed from the car and into the tenement, the baby of course willy-nilly though he displayed the greatest interest, babbling merrily.

"Tell um I refuse to come," whispered Humbold as he frustrated Reinhart's apology and pushed him after them.

Reinhart was determined to apolize to someone, though, feeling responsible for this grotesquerie which had got out of control, but it took him ever so long just to catch up with them, who cut through the buildings as if it were a cantaloupe. When he did, Alice said with the inevitable bodily contact (under the mask of discretion, for a host of natives stood nearby gawking and scratching) : "I think you've made yourself a sale!"

His protest was lost as they dashed upstairs. In passing, the baby scraped some filth from the banister and smeared it on its dad. With an effort Reinhart could see how they might fit in as tenants if not as landlords, and began to tell himself: Why not, old fellow, ride with the current?

Clendellan called to Alice, who climbed faster than he: "What does eighteen five mean?"

"Eighteen thousand, five hundred dollars. You can get it from your family."

"Of course that means we'll have to eat dinner with them."

"All right," said Alice, marching fearlessly into the darkened second-story hallway which smelled of faeces and far worse, "I won't say a word about Labor just this once."

An insolent rat, a street-corner bum of his breed, swaggered out of the abandoned carton that was his poolroom and sneered at her. She clattered a tomato can at him, saying: "Your days are numbered, Chiang Kai-shek." Losing face, he slunk away.

Suddenly, when they had reached the end of the black hall, Reinhart conceived an enormous horniness for Alice Clendellan, comparable to that which she had showed for him all afternoon and which if she did buy the tenement was surely her motive. Let's face it, he may be a walking aphrodisiac to a certain type of woman. The very shapelessness of her clothing now excited him as if he were a Japanese.

"Wonder where this leads?" he hypocritically asked, having

99

found a doorknob and turned it. "Aha!" he went on, facing a gulf of darkness where nothing could be seen and much smelled, all unpleasantly. As he expected, Alice was intrigued and found him with much groping of his person. It was made all the more exciting by the proximity of Clendellan, who with the baby paced about over broken glass nearby and sneezed from the dust.

But when Reinhart tried to return the exploration, she eluded him like a dream, and in a moment could be heard going towards the staircase to the third floor, whither he, panting from ardor and ascent, pursued her. Beyond the turn of the landing, they were again alone, and she turned to him, saying lustily: "I haven't been this excited in years!" He seized her waist, with both hands, muttering similar feelings—it was like going after a naked woman through twisted bedclothes—and shortly was embracing nought but air.

With ebbing zest, Reinhart dutifully followed her up through the house, finding one moment after another most propitious as to privacy—the inhabitants of the upper stories were apparently dead in their rooms and Clendellan was still crashing about two floors down—but though he finally had in mind nothing more than a bit of *frottage*, he got nothing more than a verbal concupiscence in which the building and its underprivileged occupants were her lovers. In short, he realized as they mounted the final stair to the loft, she was to be the Jane Addams of southern Ohio and this her Hull, and not whore, House. It was not until they rejoined Clendellan and not really until they all returned to Humbold's car, where the realtor sat piecing together the remnants of his private documents, that Alice threw herself into Reinhart's arms.

"Happy, dear?" asked her husband, depositing the baby, now foul from the tenement, on Humbold's blond upholstery.

"Aroused!" She pulled Reinhart after her into the back seat and chose this moment to give him the kiss no longer looked for, no longer wanted, it was even a sort of horror.

"Wonderful!" said Clendellan, and to Claude: "We'll take it."

No sooner had Reinhart fetched in Margaret from the walk —applying quick artificial respiration to her little friend— than the boss, who had not wanted to sell the building, had produced papers in triplicate, got his clients' signatures and a deposit for good faith, and barreled back to Vetsville at ninety.

"You planned the whole thing, didn't you?" Reinhart asked admiringly when they were again in Humbold's office.

"But," said the boss, "it was better you didn't catch on till after. You might have blown the deal." He put away his hat and topcoat, which were all over tiny black handprints.

"Claude, you are an artist."

Humbold's right eye vanished in deprecation. "Tell you what I'm me, and I'm going to start right out on the square by giving you a full week's commission for your work this P.M. Figure your sixty-five already earned with four days left to go. Now why don't you take off home and tell your daddy you're doing all right? He worries you'll turn bum."

"Thanks, boss."

"Claude."

"Thanks, Claude."

"Yours sincerely, bud."

Reinhart closed the door and went into the outer office, where the secretary was painting a new mouth.

"So you sold the Tenderloin," she asked, "and think you're pretty big. The next thing I know you'll be getting fresh. Well, hands off: I'm engaged."

"No," said Reinhart, "I just tagged along. But what I still can't understand is how Claude was so sure I would suggest going there."

She opened her purse and pitched the lipstick down its gullet. Her penciled brows climbing, she whispered: "Brother, how dumb can you get? He's been trying to peddle that for five years and always carries the Agreement to Buy with him. ... What are you getting, half the commission?"

"I don't know anything about that," Reinhart said pridefully, meaning everything. "But he's giving me my whole week's salary for whatever it was I did."

"Now that's fair," she cried, though still whispering. "He makes nine and a quarter and gives you sixty-five." Her cute little chicken-rump head danced in scorn. "Who's ever going to marry somebody so weak-minded? Not Genevieve Raven!"

Reinhart was not in the least affected by her peevishness, which he believed to be a standard item in an office girl's kit, so he bade her goodbye till the morrow and left, being careful with the door. Yet, in a moment he popped back, and the wind came with him.

"Who in the devil is Genevieve Raven?"

"*Me!*" she screamed.

Chapter 7

So Reinhart had much to tell his folks when he got home, except that of course he suppressed all mention of Mrs. Clendellan's feeling-him-up because it was conventional in his family not to admit that sex existed—which in this case, and perhaps in many others as well, more than we suspect, agreed with reality. Maw, on her feet again, looked ill as he proceeded towards the triumphant dénouement, and seconds before he announced the sale, she had brought the potatoes to a boil which overran the pot and steamed down onto the burner, extinguishing it.

She threatened him with a potholder, shouting; "Don't peeve me with your jabber, fellow, I warn you. This cancer can snuff me out like that gas, and if I go it will be you who drove me."

"But Maw!" Reinhart protested. "A fellow takes his accomplishments to his Old Lady."

With a long-handled fork she pursued one of the potatoes bobbing like baldheaded swimmers in the pan. "You know I won't listen for one minute to brag. You so much as go to the privy and you're back wanting a medal for it."

Reinhart retreated to visit Dad, who sat in bed reading the afternoon paper, his flannel pajama shirt opened to show whitening chest-hair.

"Sit down and take the load off, Carlo. I'll hand you the funnies."

His father had graduated from plain spectacles to bifocals, Reinhart noticed but forbore from mentioning it lest it introduce the subject of his own eyes.

"What do you think of the Reds this year?" his old man went on, giving him a page of comic strips.

"Well," said Reinhart, seeing Winnie Winkle, a really fabulous piece, in panties and brassiere, as young as she had been before the war—he suddenly remembered his high school practice to which she had been muse, and thought he'd better get some nookie soon for health's sake. "Well, I don't know, Dad, I haven't been following the news. That U.N. stuff is pretty tedious." It had been a lascivious day, and now Dixie Dugan was also in her underwear.

"Make first division?"

"Oh," said Reinhart, during the transition to Popeye, "they have plenty of divisions, but we have the atom bomb. . . ." He came to. "I'm sorry, Dad, I just realized you were talking about the baseball team and I about world affairs."

"Mmm. Well, as far as that goes, Carlo, I suppose you know I'm G.O.P. and expect to die that way—and may have to before we ever get another Republican in the White House. You never would have had to waste the flower of your youth on foreign soil if Roosevelt hadn't recognized Hitler."

"I thought it was Stalin he recognized," said Reinhart, feeling despair settle over him like a horse blanket. "Or John L. Lewis. Or both." He decided to try a trick. "What, I wonder, ever became of Haile Selassie, Tony Galento, Wrong-way Corrigan, Dr. Townsend, and Alf Landon?" While his father considered these names, as he knew he would, Reinhart told the story of his new job.

When he was done, his old man said: "Isn't Claude a great guy!"

"He's very decent, Dad, but what I'm trying to get over to you is the real romance of business."

"Ah, you've got yourself a girl. Fine, fine. Time you settled down." He picked up the comics, which Carlo had put aside.

"No," said Reinhart. "You must know what I mean, having been in insurance all your life. I mean adventure. Getting people to buy things they don't want—you make them love, fear, and loathe you. You have a definite influence on shaping their lives. Now take a house—this one you sell them they might live in until they die, and when the children grow up they will take wives and husbands among the neighbor kids, and on and on. All resulting from the original real-estate sale, which they didn't want until manipulated into it by the salesman. Whole

103

cities can be made this way. It's really a creativity not dreamed of in Renaissance."

Unmoved, Dad was intently reading the funnies; so Reinhart thought that in fairness he would expand his enthusiasm to include insurance.

"Your own business, say: look at what can result from your having sold someone a policy. He is struck dead by lightning, and instead of his wife and children becoming wards of the public, they collect the insurance payment, invest it shrewdly, plough back all dividends except what is needed for a modest living, and one day before they die have amassed a fortune, which the grandchildren inherit never suspecting, as they sit before their pressed duck and champagne, that they owe it to one George Reinhart, ace agent of Ecumenical Indemnity!"

"Who is long dead and buried in a pauper's grave," responded Dad, folding his paper lengthwise like a passenger on a crowded streetcar.

"But Dad," said Reinhart, looking for a place to stride about in the room so clogged with the enormous bed. "I'm *for* you and your profession, which now that it won't offend I can say for years I thought was just about the dreariest way in the world for a man to waste his life. Nothing was worse in my opinion than *commerce, economics, exchange, real property, securities, stocks, bonds, finance, annuities, comptrollers, town planning boards, auditors, accountants, ledgers, etc.*— those are some of the words that just to hear turned my stomach. Now here are a few of the words I liked: *paladin, epic, paramour, gourmet, wastrel, mistress, cognac, intrepid, leather, bronze, crimson, alabaster, lance, battle-ax,* and so on. Do you know something? Those two vocabularies are not entirely incompatible."

He saw from the side window that a neighbor was broadcasting grass seed near a garage, assisted by, frustrated by a swarm of children who would grow up to be auditors and poets and epicures and sowers of lawns: everything. *Reinhart was in love with everything.*

As to Dad, he was asleep under a tent of newsprint. Winnie Winkle, in flagrante delectable, was just above his nostrils, and his breathing caused her to do a bump and grind. Reinhart was finally coming out of half a year's funk—his recent emotional history was far from a laugh—and he suddenly found himself wanting to sing and dance and make money, money, money and get drunk and do it with every girl in the world.

But first he had to eat dinner with Maw: potatoes fried in bacon grease, frankfurters whose color came off on the plate, gaseous sauerkraut, and canned applesauce for dessert. They both ate enormously and in silence, until over his cup of instant coffee Reinhart waxed nostalgic and said:

"Remember those drawings you used to make for me years ago of Peter Rabbit and Reddy Fox? And sometimes on summer afternoons we would pack a shoebox with cervelat sandwiches and cheese & crackers and Nabisco wafers and bananas, and go visit the zoo. Remember when Dad made home brew and drew it off into bottles with china stoppers? You two used to play rummy once a week with Charley and Mabel Welch, and little Gladys and I would play Old Maid at a tiny table alongside. Afterwards there'd be a cold snack, and if anybody'd ask Charley for the butter, he would pick up the whole stick and hand it to them for a laugh. Gladys wouldn't drink anything but Orange Crush because it wasn't carbonated."

"You sure can recall anything about food," said Maw. "Want more applesauce?"

"I'll tell you, Maw, I don't like that canned nearly as well as the kind you used to make with cinnamon on it."

"A person gets old, boy, and gets cancer. . . . Charley'n Mabel retired last year to Florida, for he always had TB and spat blood all winter long. Well, no sooner did they get settled down there in a nice subdivision, every cottage on the water, than along came the hurricane; Charley happened to be out in the car, going down to get a *Collier's*—the change-in-address for the subscription not having gone through yet—when it struck. A great tidal wave carried him right off the coastal road and out to sea. When Mabel heard the news she fell into a coma and lived about a hour more, then passed away. As to 'little' Gladys, well you haven't been away so long that you can't remember she grew to five-eleven in her stocking feet at fifteen years of age and stuck way out to here in front. In 1944, at eighteen, she up and gave birth to a baby without a marriage license being in evidence. Turned out to be real filth, breaking Charley'n Mabel's heart, who had given her everything through the years: accordion lessons, a Pekinese pup, and a playhouse in the back yard. Well sir, last I heard she turned nun."

"I didn't know they were Catholic," said Reinhart.

"They certainly were not!" answered Maw. "That's the tragedy." She drained her cup and went *"Phew!"* which Reinhart assumed was her reaction to the coffee; on that they were one. But she did it again: *"Phew!* You're a free white and twenty-one, but if I ever thought you had truck with Filth, I'd slip you strychnine. Do you know what I'm talking about? Filth!"

"What kind, Maw?"

"Why, Smut. All the dirty, miserable, horrible things that bachelors in boarding houses think about; what goes on among the niggers in back alleys in the dead of night; what makes cats do that terrible evil whining in the wee hours and dogs run in packs with their tongues hanging out so disgusting; what ruined Gladys Welch. People touching one another in secret ways. Men rolling their eyeballs and wettening their lips. Girls sticking way out here, fore and aft, wearing bathing suits no bigger than a necktie. The ads for foundations. The kind of pictures men like. Dirty lacy things you can order through the mail from Hollywood. Fiction. Racial comedians like the Marx Brothers, Mae West, Jean Harlow, Clara Bow, and of course everybody French: Morris Chevalier, Simone Simon, and the rest." She rose from the table and stood glaring at him. "Everything warm, wet, soft, dark, private, crooning, sneering, itchy, sneaky, hairy, jokey, shivering, cynical, atheistic, and modern. That's what. And don't try to defend it or I'll slaughter you at my own table."

"Without sex there'd be no people, Maw," said Reinhart brightly. He seized an oatmeal cookie and ingested it whole. "And no animal life, for that matter—though true enough, animals are always more interested in finding food than in reproducing." The next cookie he dunked in the coffee and got to his mouth just before it disintegrated.

"I suppose you're safe then," Maw riposted, running hot water into the sink. "But I can't see but what that'd be preferable," meaning an earth barren of warm-blooded creatures and perhaps even fish as well—any things that touched one another; she was anti-friction. "Don't flowers have it better, though? With seeds carried by the wind. Beautiful, just beautiful."

"Dunno," said Reinhart, rising. "Some things are one way, some the other, and you and I can't change them. I now stick only to what I can have an effect on."

His mother narrowed her eyes at him: "Sure those Russians in Berlin didn't make a Communist of you?"

Reinhart laughingly said absolutely not.

"But you can't be certain, now, can you? How would you know?" When Maw, who was diabolically intelligent, began to talk like a cretin, it was time to fade away. Which he did, into the living room, his ardor now on ice perhaps forever, Filth having suddenly been revealed as the reason why he liked girls. For Maw in an inverse way talked a kind of sense, not to mention that she had always made Filth inordinately attractive to him. Much of what we do in life, he saw, is mere reaction against someone else. God knows what you would do if you lived as a hermit in the North Woods, with nobody to defy,

106

but even then you would have had originally to be born and that required a mother. At any rate, he was getting rather old to go around thinking of girls as merely one vulva after another.

The telephone rang and added to his chastened mood; he no longer believed it a summons to sensuous indulgence.

Maw set up a great din in the kitchen as proof she wouldn't listen: it made a person feel too important if you were nosey about his affairs.

A man's voice said: "Carlo, the game's afoot," like Sherlock Holmes, and it was nobody but Splendor Mainwaring.

"Carlo," Splendor went on, "are you there? I haven't heard from you in days, and as I know you are the soul of dependability, worried that you might have fallen ill or into incapacity. Oh tell me my fears are unwarranted. . . . Yes? Good. And you have read your Goodykuntz, of course?"

Reinhart cleared his throat, groping for an excuse, and luckily Splendor took it as an affirmative, anxious as he obviously was to get on.

"And naturally are enthusiastic," he said. "I don't mean to discount your independence when I say this is as anticipated. You will then be equally happy to learn that the introductory assembly has been scheduled for two nights hence, namely, Wednesday evening at eight o'clock. Please wear a severely conservative suit; white shirt, with if you will a button-down collar and staid necktie, regimental stripe preferred; other accessories in accord."

"Just a moment, Splendor, I—"

"Sorry, Carlo, I was coming to that. Be assured you will be handsomely reimbursed from the first collection."

Reinhart began to perspire back of the knees. Being a good guy is the worst thing in the world; once, out of politeness he had praised his aunt's awful sponge cake, and then found himself forced to eat two more pieces. To be constantly agreeable was actually against his ethic; yet he was, and to hell with it. Talked out of Filth; talked into some nutty project by a crank, who if that wasn't enough was a Negro to boot, so that he couldn't be refused with impunity, because Reinhart just could not bear to close the door on any unfortunate who opened it and asked for him.

He groaned, and Splendor answered: "Grand. I have rented the empty store at 221 Wyandotte Street for the assembly and circulated notices by means of an exceptionally active individual who penetrates all quarters of this district."

Despite the deepest foreboding, Reinhart smiled at this point and asked: "That wouldn't be The Maker?"

"You too know him! That demonstrates his extensive coverage. Every augury is good. I'll see you Wednesday at eight. Meanwhile, Upward to you and yours."

Reinhart, whose mind could move swiftly when he didn't ask it to, realized in a flash that "Upward" was the *Heil* of Splendor's projected group and would have been familiar to him had he read his Goodykuntz. So to maintain his deception he answered likewise and hung up.

Since in all of his anticipatory fantasies of Splendor's meeting he was the conspicuous white, obviously humiliated figure creeping about front and center, he had to order himself next morning, after a night of them, to cease to think about it upon the count of three—a kind of self-hypnotic device he had invented and which usually worked very well, the mind being as craven as a citizen living in a dictatorship.

Nevertheless, he spent all day Tuesday in a shadow cast by the Mainwarings. Even the initial stimulation of his work had diminished like a suntan in two weeks of rain. He wondered whether the midweek slump at the office was habitual. Genevieve failed to be insulting and wore a blouse with smudged cuffs, a real heresy in a person of her profession. She might be enduring her Period, but what of Claude, who had lost his paternalism as quickly as he had, on the first day, assumed it, and now pretended Reinhart wasn't there, staying in his office with the door shut.

When Reinhart finally applied to Genevieve for a ruling on the matter—she being the sort who always had an answer; he had begun to admire that gift above all others—he managed to evoke from her an expression of impatience almost as comforting to him as the information imparted.

She pointed her pencil at the window, which ran with rain. "At last I've met the person dumb enough not to come in out of it."

"I get it!" said Reinhart, rising from the long table where he had sat for hours browsing in the literature of some international real-estate firm which offered for sale Spanish castles, Scottish moors, and all of Austria. "You can't sell a house in this weather."

"Gawd," moaned Genevieve, "the girl who gets you! I'll bet you also eat like a horse." All this while she efficiently typed away with her fingers, never looking at a text. When he inquired, she stated that, one, the forms were in her head and, two, conversation with him was hardly a distraction.

At five, after Claude had blundered out like a sick bullock, unspeaking, Reinhart left too. Genevieve wrinkled her little nose at him when, from the sidewalk, he glanced back through the window. On an impulse, he kissed the palm of his hand and pushed it towards her with a gesture used by policemen to halt traffic. Her face stretched in mock superciliousness, eyebrows way up there, mouth way down here.

Wednesday morning the weather was worse, and Reinhart suffered some painful ague from the night in his basement chamber. You could have got a drink by running a goblet through the atmosphere there; his old zoology notebook was swelling up and bursting open page on page; and the walls leaked not only water but mud as well, in long rivulets which ever replenished his bedside pond. On such a day his parents were sure to develop hideous symptoms if he were present to see them. Therefore he dried himself on an old shirt, dressed in damp clothing, and left without breakfast by the cellar exit. Got coffee at the Trojan Cafe, where he exchanged hubris with Achilles, the proprietor, while at the same time keeping an eye on a number of swarthy little Myrmidons who circulated behind the counter violating the pastry.

Sucking on the first Tum from a handy pocket roll, feeling a certain sandiness between the duodenum and the jejunum, he reported to the office, where Genevieve, since Claude had telephoned that he was taking the day off, assumed the scepter and bossed him about as one might a serf. He knew then the annoyance of a job whose status wasn't specified, and after straightening the books in Claude's office, dusting the window sills, and fetching lunch as ordered, he balked at a four o'clock command to run out for coffee light, hold the sugar, and said something insubordinate like: "Who do you think *you* are?"

Genevieve glared at him for a moment, then ran weeping into the anteroom lavatory and stayed there for forty-five minutes, during which time—damned if he had anything to apologize for—Reinhart tried Claude's swivel chair on for size. What he needed was a real desk of his own. He began to dislike Claude again, he loathed Genevieve Raven, he dreaded sleeping another night in the cellar. . . . He threw hostility around at various imaginary targets—anything to distract him from anticipating an evening among black fanatics.

"Splendor," Reinhart was pleading, three and a half hours later as he towered over his friend in the Mainwaring hall. "Splendor, here I must absolutely put my foot down. I mustn't wear that turban. No, never." The command to wear a dark suit he had obeyed to the best of his ability. Since he owned none, he borrowed a blue serge jacket of his father's, sufficient in girth but clownishly short in trunk and arms. As trousers he wore a pair of ancient oxford-gray flannels tracked through the ragbag, a Siberia to which clothes were banished from the trunk prior to total liquidation. Their legs had been wadded in close community with a woolen scarf used for camphorated-oil rubs: Reinhart therefore exuded an odor from his shanks, but it warded off chills and small dogs.

The turban, however, was too much. Splendor continued to press it on him soberly—indeed, downright morosely for a man with such a gaudy project, his eyes rather obscured as if he wore contact lenses cut from snapshot negatives. The only reason Reinhart finally accepted it was that Splendor manifestly felt worse than he.

"There is only one size," Splendor said dolefully. "So it should fit. Oh, *I'm* sorry!" he exclaimed as Reinhart stoically put it on. "Did you want one, too?"

"This isn't mine?" asked Mohammed Reinhart, giant monarch of the revolting hill tribes. In the yellowed hall mirror he was properly Mongoloid, as well. Relieved that Splendor was not asking this of their friendship, he jokingly barked: "You call me mad, English dog? Haha, Alexander the Great was mad, Caesar was mad, and Napoleon was the maddest of the lot. Look towards yon plain and see my cavalry, mounted on valiant chargers—"

Splendor, who had no sense of humor, wrinkled his thin eyebrows and took back the white-satin cocoon. He placed it on his head himself, but asked Reinhart to adjust it dead center, with the hen's-egg ruby and the little shaving brush that rose from it in vertical alignment with his nose. "Next time, Carlo, if you wish. The costumer's will be closed by now."

From the kitchen Reinhart heard muffled soprano shrieks; Loretta had either damaged herself or been sent hysterical by his act. In either case she was responding to life with more affirmation than her brother, who looked most ill. His turban suggested a bandage rather than the traditional headdress of the seer; his rented dinner jacket jutted high in the back of his neck; and he teetered on tiptoe, as if a giant policeman were plucking him up for vagrancy.

"Do you know something?" asked Reinhart, slouching in synthetic nonchalance. "Since this is the first meeting, you could just as well hold it tomorrow night or next week, for that matter. Besides, it's started to rain again."

Groaning, Splendor sank to the bottom stair, knees in his face.

Reinhart went on: "Really more sleet than rain, in fact. A cold front is moving down from British Columbia. Yesterday there was five inches of snow in Minneapolis, and a man in Eau Claire, Wisconsin, bent over to tie his shoe and froze in that position. So as I say, since this is the first of your meetings, you don't have any obligation."

110

"Except to the truth," said Splendor, rising manfully. "If it's sleeting here, think what the weather must be in Pocatello, Idaho. Yet you can be sure Dr. Goodykuntz is not letting down for a moment."

Reinhart was embarrassed when they left the house and met a thick fog, indeed a warm, suffocating one; yet it served his purposes of camouflage, and Splendor, a petty man only to his own family, did not chide him but rather walked mumbling some private catechism of which Reinhart could catch only discrete words, the usual ones: Prime Mover, life force, etc. He was practicing his address, poor fellow, and did not realize that being profound was the easiest thing in the world. You could say anything at all, and it would be, or come, true, because life was everything. This seemed very clear to Reinhart, to whom it had in fact just occurred, and he felt a faint pity towards everybody who didn't know it—which put him in an ease unprecedented that day, and he stalked along suddenly regretting the presence of the fog, for he wouldn't have minded letting people look at the combination of serenity, authority, and compassion that must show upon his face.

He had gone some distance in such a mode before he noticed that his companion had disappeared in thick air. His calls got no answer; his searches, radiating like spokes from the hub of which he was certain—as advised in the *Boy's Guide to the Wilderness* which fortuitously he had lately found among the childhood memorabilia—made no human contact. It was likely that he, and not Splendor, was lost. He heard a purr and felt fur at his ankles, for cats, unlike small dogs, invariably took to him. A soft voice wrapped, as it were, around his neck at the same time: "Daddy, you like to circumvent the globe?" "No thanks," answered Reinhart. "I'm just lost." "Ah show you to the promised land," said the girl. Reinhart declined again with a thank-you no, the cat meowed, and high heels clopped away leaving behind a giggle like Loretta's. This was the kind of thing Reinhart was wont to do in emergencies, he reflected in shame: panicking, to suspect his friends of dishonor; they were Negroes and the time was night; he was disgusting. Nevertheless, when he heard male footsteps in the murky vicinity and had reason to suppose they were Splendor's, he involuntarily groped for his little pocketknife, with its half-inch blade.

"Wadduh you say, Pops?" asked a person, not Splendor yet very familiar to him. Reinhart saw a suggestion of white in the black fog. "Man, this weather *is* hard on the real estay, don't tell me never. Water fallin' from the sky made that Humbold keep to his bed and you can't fight it. And that hincty little chick G. Raven, she give you many a bad time, which ain't

111

nothin' to what she do if you get married to one another. Mind me of my second wife, who give me numerous scars. Whyn't you tell me that time I assed you about Bridgwater that you had the gift, man? I coulda made you a better deal than Splendor G. Mainwaring. He what you call a stone, man, and will never sprout."

"Obviously it's the Maker," said Reinhart.

"Well it ain't the *Verderber,* which is Dutch for the opposite," answered the Maker in mock indignation. "As you well know, being Dutch as they come. No wonder you never made my action in Bridgwater. You was in the Pantser division of the Liftwaffle!" He laughed like crazy, and added: "Don't you take no never mind to me, Rudolph, I just been turned on."

"That's all very well," said Reinhart, still disturbed at having mislaid his friend, "but how do you know so much about me?"

There was a long silence, and Reinhart, who realized it was quixotic on the West Side, or perhaps anywhere else, to look for causes and effects in geometric progression, had given up and was about to resume his search for the missing nonchemical physican, when the Maker illuminated a pencil-flashlight, opened his great wallet, and withdrew a folded document. He read from it in much the same voice with which, years ago, Splendor had played the magistrate in *Spreading the News*: a Negro's parody of white authority, constipated, effeminate, and unjust, even when, as in this case, granting a right.

" 'Dee following named purr-son is licensed under dee lows of deez state to prectice as a private detective . . . Nicholas Graves,' which is how yours truly was undersigned at birth."

"I never knew a man who had so many professions," said Reinhart, "but—"

"In spite of which," the Maker interrupted, "'I ain't got a brown bare-ass penny I can call my own. What ain't grabbed by them ex-wives is et up by a houseful of relltives. I mean to take a gun after them any time now. And them hoors. Now you never hear nobody give a good word to a procurator, but I tell you it far from easy. You got to keep after them girls for holdin' back their cash, and then they always comin' down sick and needin' a quick fix and I tell you horse ain't gettin' cheaper. Tellphone alone run into money: you don't call them fwequently, they get sulky. 'Sweet man, mah feet hurt god-awful.' 'Awright, baby, you get yoursel a new hat.' 'Green, with a little bit of lace.' 'Sure, anythin' you want, so long as it don't run past 1.98.' Trouble is, you give in like that and they won't cruise all week."

"I'm sorry," said Reinhart, "but that's your problem. Mine

112

is that I don't like the idea of you spying on me. Who hired you?"

"Hunred dollars a day and expinses is what I generally get," said the Maker, "but I'll tell all I know for a picture of George."

Reinhart gave him a dollar bill, in return for which the detective revealed: "Your daddy. He worries you'll be a bum."

"You haven't told him about me coming over here?" Reinhart could have bitten off his tongue. What an insulting thing to say to the Maker, who had no other bailiwick! But the informer set him at ease without prejudice.

"It's a weakness of mine that I always report good about everybody. I never flipped a lip towards him since you sold that tinement house."

"So," said Reinhart. "Much obliged. You're a good fellow, Nicholas."

"I try," answered the Maker, blinking off his flash in modesty. "But I sometimes wonder if I ain't batty in the bell tower."

"That's occurred to every good fellow since the dawn of man," Reinhart said pontifically.

"And what been decided?"

"No decision. But one may be forthcoming at any moment."

"Man," cried the Maker, "could I only talk like you, I'd be the meanest sonbitch ever drawn breath. Why be good if you can say 'forthcoming.' "

Now he was getting invidious, so Reinhart laid a responsibility on him: Where might the missing Splendor be found, or, failing that, where was the store-front house of worship?

"You standin' in the door," said the detective.

Reinhart felt about him, and it was quite true that he stood in some entranceway, flanked by plate glass or, rather, the cardboard surrogate for the same.

"But it must be almost eight o'clock. Where are the lights? Where is Splendor? Where are the people?"

"Now nobody can say I done a bad job," the Maker protested, too much. "But you ain't gonna get off the ground on a expense account of seven dollars eighty cents. There's twenty-nine dollars alone owing on the lectric power, and my cousin's in stir."

"What's he got to do with it?"

"*She.* That there is Big Ruthie, who had a nice policy trade but the bulls closed her up, which left the store empty, and she not going to pay the Power & Light and not get no use from it in stir. And as to the audience, well how many marks you

113

gonna draw on seven-eighty? Hunred handbills, soon lost. No posters, two-colored or otherwised. No public-dress system to scream your message. No big fat soprano on the back of a truck, accompanied by horn men playin' 'I Look Over Jordan and Whut.' No ads in the *West Side Bugle,* bearing pichers of the Reverend or whatever Splendor G. Mainwaring call his-self. I tell you, man, he no more likely to go aloft than a i-ron paperweight."

"Poor guy," said Reinhart. He struck out in pity and inad-vertently knocked the cardboard from the window and what was left of the glass. "Well, we've got to do something." He heard the Maker prepare to flee, and grabbed him. The pri-vate eye went through several Protean transformations, mon-sters, serpents, the bounding sea, but Reinhart held fast, say-ing: "That's right, you and me. Because we're good fellows. Put on your light and look here. I've got fifty-two dollars in this billfold. What can that do for us by nine o'clock?"

The Maker showed the yellow of his eyes and skillfully plucked through the wad while holding the flash in the other hand. "By nine? I can deliver maybe three-four my girls if the meeting won't last beyond eleven, when business pick up."

"How about your boys that hang around the drugstore?"

"That would be Winthrop and the Prince and Webster Small and Little Clyde. Frenchy got cut up lately and Baby Al got extadited to Dee-troit. Man, why don't we pick another night?"

"Got to be now."

"Got to be," the Maker muttered. "Hmm. I could cruise a few saloons, but I tell you, don't look for much. They be a au-dience all right, but I can't guarantee they be human beans. And you get a cigar box at the door with a sign readin: 'Check weapons here,' and put another one on the wall like the city bus, sayin: 'No spittin', chewin', talkin', cussin', going to the toilet, jazzin', or nothin' else while the vehicle in mo-tion, especially with the driver.' Meanin' your friend Splendor G. Mainwaring. Man, he's nowhere." The Maker opened his clothes at the neck and put the bills inside his undershirt, snorting: "Seven dollars eighty!"

Reinhart said: "That's all he had."

"It ain't up to me to destroy your faith in human nature," said Nicholas Graves. "But I'll get you the audience, I'll get you the lights—"

"God," cried Reinhart, "I'd forgotten about that. It's too late now even if we paid the bill; the Power & Light offices are closed." In the interest of symmetry, he knocked the card-board and glass from the left-hand window.

"You worryin' about the only thing *I* ain't. We just tap into

114

the line of the dry cleaner next door; both got the same cellar. Little Clyde do that in his sleep; he was lectrician in the Navy." Reaching high as he could, the Maker patted Reinhart on the shoulder. "Now don't worry, Daddy, we going to come out all right. I just wish *you* was the preacher. Got to be by nine? I'm in motion."

"One more thing, Nicholas. I wonder where Splendor is."

"Take my flash," said the Maker, "and go in the back of the store behind the partition. If you don't find him there passed out cold on Big Ruthie's davenport, then the angels done carried him off to the Isles of Bliss."

Reinhart followed the suggestion and found the man of many callings was right, as he had begun to suspect he always was.

Chapter 8

"Ladies and gentlemen," Reinhart began, drunk as a lord, and then brayed in laughter, for their titles might be many, but never those two. He began again to himself, while the persons of the audience stirred respectfully: "Whores, pimps, cut-throats, degenerates, and fiends," an address that better suited his drunken compulsion towards the truth. "Uh," he went on, "you may smoke." Several people instantly lighted brown-paper cigarettes that exuded a sweetish aroma, and two felonious types, propped against the left wall, took the liberty to drain a flat pint of maroon liquid.

Reinhart bowed slightly from the waist, which motion caused the turban to pitch forward and strike the top rim of his sunglasses. He adjusted the headdress, being careful not to brush the fake mustache attached to his upper lip with library paste, which was pulling his mouth into a sneer as it dried—a purely physical phenomenon, for this was the first time he had been the cynosure of a roomful of moral lepers and consequently had never felt less disdainful.

The Maker, priceless man, as good as his word, had given a hundred cents' value for every dollar; not only had he collected an audience and, tapping the cleaner's power cable, brought light; he also found boxes, kegs, stacked newspapers, stools, and even a chair or two, for there had not been a seat in the house. He posted the wall-notices he had earlier characterized as essential, adding one that read: GOD IS WATCHING you. He directed his scouts in a quick policing-up of the store: there were rats to rout, fallen plaster to sweep, and a grocery counter, dating from Big Ruthie days, to find under a Matterhorn of trash. It was behind this counter that Reinhart now supported himself, knee against the lower shelf where stood his half-empty fifth of gin, another provision of the Maker's.

Splendor, who was personally responsible for Reinhart's debut as orator, had proved a complete washout.

"Splendor, Splendor," Reinhart had called down to him on the couch. "Are you sick?"

The nonchemical interne had revolved agate eyes in the light of the torch, moaning "Very." He rolled against the wall, face to it, the way people show defeat in novels. His turban lay in the debris of the floor.

"You don't have stage fright?" asked Reinhart. "Not you. Why, I can recall your Debating Contest speech before the whole high school. I believe you defended war, while that little skinny girl Angelica Slimp took the opposing view."

"I cribbed most of that from Henry Five, by William Shakespeare," Splendor admitted with a faint smile. "'Once more into the breach, dear friends.' Ah, but I feel very grisly at present."

"Hey," Reinhart cried, "you can't sleep now. It's after eight and the people will be coming soon." He took the light off Splendor's face and directed it upon the leprous wall.

"Nobody's coming, Carlo. Nobody cares. You strive, and for what? You find the electricity turned off."

"But we're fixing that, and the Maker's collecting an audience, and you'll be just great. I thought your idea was pretty punk until tonight. Now I'm enthusiastic. Really! Hahaha." Reinhart turned and kicked an old carton through the back window.

With the flashlight on him again, Splendor said irrelevantly: "You don't know what it's like not being respectable. Your mother didn't run off with Henry Bligh."

But in sympathy Reinhart fervently wished she had, and he said, "I'm sorry."

"My parents used to play cards every Friday night. One evening Seneca Bligh and my father sat there three hours waiting for their partners—who actually had long departed to St. Louis by Greyhound bus. Well, you've seen my father."

"I've met Mrs. Bligh as well," Reinhart answered. "But it was fortunate that you are grown up and not a little child on whom such a thing would be crushing—that you have your plans and ideas and can't be fazed."

"True," Splendor said very weakly. Big Ruthie's sofa had very high ends, and he hung between them like a vacant hammock.

"Anyhow," Reinhart went on, "what is respectability? Pretty boring if you ask me and furthermore a false category. What we want is a celebration of life, because we've only got one."

"True. But now Dr. Goodykuntz writes that the tuition fee I already paid doesn't cover the genuine parchment diploma with seal of fourteen-carat gold."

"How much?"

"Twenty-five dollars, and it's unethical to practice without it. Why can't we postpone the meeting until next week?"

"Splendor, Splendor," chided Reinhart. "Are you losing your faith in Dr. Goodykuntz? I must say you're disappointing me, my dear fellow. Remember that the weather's sure to be far worse in Pocatello and if Dr. Goodykuntz has contracted to give an address tonight, he is already at the auditorium, pouring out inspiration and healing multitudes of sufferers."

Splendor sat up and groped on the floor for his turban. "You've shamed me, Carlo. Disregard the foregoing negativism. It's quite true that I am very ill. I may indeed have cancer. No"—he threw a hand towards Reinhart—"no demonstration. I'm not whining. If this burning pain in my solar plexus gets worse, I may have to go to Pocatello for treatment. You see, the pity is that the physician cannot heal himself; the conjunction of two life forces is called for. But first, my work is cut out for me."

He rose to his feet, and at the same moment the lights came on—one ceiling bulb behind the partition and several out front.

"There you are!" cried Reinhart. "The balloon is going up."

Soon they heard noises of the arriving audience. Now that he had called Splendor back to duty, Reinhart again became reluctant to associate himself with the project. His reluctance turned to terror when, spying around the partition, he saw the Maker's confederates bring in seating facilities and the Maker's chattering girls prepare to use them. The truth was, whores disturbed Reinhart; turning down their solicitations always made him feel like a great swine. In London during the war, he had frequently been almost moved to counter sidewalk propositions with an offer of marriage. Instead of desire, he felt guilt; for the likes of him and a handful of silver, such a woman would recline and accept penetration. This was the female principle reduced to absurdity.

118

When he turned back to assure his friend that prospects were bright, he saw only an empty turban rolling across the floor from the open window; the bee had fled its hive.

"So what do we do now?" asked the Maker, when that person appeared a moment later from the front of the store.

Nicholas Graves was uproariously pleased at Splendor's flight. He chortled so strenuously that he choked, and one of his whores called from beyond the partition: "Baby, you dyin'?"

He ordered her not to embarrass him, and said to Reinhart: "I tole you, I tole you! He never been with it, man, like you and me. He simply run back to noplace."

"Then I guess that does it," Reinhart said. "Tell everybody to go home—and you can keep the money, you earned it. Too bad. I think he's got something, though it's clogged. And you hardly ever run across anybody who believes in anything nowadays. So you can't exactly call him yellow, since a coward wouldn't have had the idea in the first place. I suppose he's just normal, poor guy."

"There you are!" the Maker shouted. "Them folks should blow while you shoot me this wisdom in the back room? Man, you got your chance! How often do you find that, nowadays or never?"

Standing before the audience, Reinhart realized that the Maker's adjuration had probably been sinister. He could not really believe that Reinhart was eloquent; therefore he undoubtedly played the sadist, and his furnishing the orator with disguise, bottle of Dutch nerve, and extravagant encouragement was but the instrumentation of his malice. His roomful of thugs and bawds were to be amused by a Caucasian buffoon, One White Crow.

The drying paste had now drawn Reinhart's upper lip into a pronounced snarl. This was the first time he had ever worn a mask other than that issued him by Nature. He stared through the dark-purple sunglasses, on loan from the Maker's aide Winthrop, at an especially menacing criminal, almost as big as himself in the front row of seats. This man wore sideburns which ran down to his mouth, and on the remainder of his face someone had scored a chessboard with a very dull knife. It was doubtful that he had obeyed the doorside sign prohibiting weapons; and impractical to brood about, since he secured his trousers with a garrison belt terminating in a six-inch buckle of solid lead and both sets of his knuckles were ranks of iron rings begemmed with broken glass. He was a terrible, dreadful, evil sight, and returned Reinhart's stare through protuberant eyes like the business ends of blunt instruments.

119

Reinhart ducked beneath the counter and took another quick shot of gin. While he was there he heard a brute comment from the savage he had temporarily permitted to outface him: "Come on, shit or git off the pot!"

"You!" said Reinhart, bobbing up. "You there, that just spoke. Come up here."

If the man had been frightening before, he was now a perfect horror. He licked his lips and spat between his mastodon feet. In a nonchalant movement of his right hand, he plucked up a small brown neighbor and hurled him at the counter.

"Be of good cheer, brother," said Reinhart to the victim, who was apparently carried about by the big man for just such demonstrations of contempt. To the brute he said: "No, I must have you. Denying the power of the Prime Mover is hopeless. That's what Simon Peter did and he was turned into a rock on which was built the Catholic Church. Now I'm going to count to five and say a bit of Latin, which is the tongue of that faith, and if you're not off that box by the time I finish and standing up here like a man—"

"Praise God and not the Devil," shouted one of the Maker's male shills from the other side of the room.

The criminal lowered his eyes and muttered at his shoes: "Ah cut anybody who bruise me with Latin goddammit."

"Listen to him take the Mighty name in vain, brethren and cistern!" said Reinhart. "Poor Simon Peter!"

"Now don't you call me that," warned the thug, fiddling with his leaden buckle. Nevertheless, he was embarrassed, and dug a cigarette from his jacket pocket and broke it into pieces. "Ah dint come here to be called out of my name."

"What is your name, brother?"

"Stony Jack," answered the big man's little victim, who had reseated himself.

"I don't mean you."

"Neither do I," said the small man, who had a bad right eye like a cracked marble. "I mean him."

"*Stony!*" shouted Reinhart. "What did I tell you about Peter becoming a rock? Your name is already petrified, brother."

"All right," grumbled the monster. "I'm comin'. Just don't go laying any Latin on me." Erect, he was larger than that Reinhart, and carried his great shoulders as an ox a yoke.

"Just put your back against the counterfront, brother, and face the audience," Reinhart ordered, smirking drunkenly. "There's nothing to be afraid of. The Latin I promised was *sic transit gloria mundi* and that can work as well for the good as for the bad."

From the bloc of prostitutes in the center of the audience, a girl sprang up and announced her name as Gloria Monday.

Like her sisters-in-law, she was dressed exceedingly drab and had a voice to match; Reinhart saw that streetwalking was a pretty dreary business, not in the least exotic or even sexy.

"Very well, Gloria, you come up here too."

While she was on her way, Stony Jack glowered at Reinhart. "I got to stand here with a hoor? I never been so insulted in mah life." He brought his iron-and-glass knuckles to the countertop and gouged a peevish mark through its veneer of filthy oilcloth.

"Gloria Hallelujah!" It was the Maker himself who shouted, immensely pleased that one of his people was making out.

"Now," said Reinhart. "Here on my left is Stony Jack, about 250-odd pounds of force, and on my right is Gloria Monday, about 120 pounds of desire. In the middle, representing the mind, is me, Dr. Lorenz T. Goodykuntz of Pocatello, Idaho. This meeting was called by the most brilliant of my students, Splendor G. Mainwaring of this city, but at the eleventh hour he was called away to save a life, and fortunately I was on hand to substitute."

Gloria leaned against the counter and watched Reinhart with the open mouth of awe, two front teeth missing. Small wonder that the Maker never had a penny. Very miffed, Stony stared blackly at his little assistant in the front row. Reinhart coughed and got another drink sub rosa, being conscious of his high responsibility, in which Splendor no longer figured.

He was masked and under a false name. He addressed a roomful of pariahs who had been bribed, threatened, or tricked into coming. The very light that shown down from above was neither his nor theirs; the building was condemned, its late proprietor in durance vile, its latest lessee in flight. The whole situation, indeed, was just like life, and at the same time that it didn't matter, it was very serious. Though not sober.

"How many among you wish you hadn't been born?" Reinhart asked. While the audience labored over this, some persons putting up both hands, some one, and one man, way in the back, apparently three, Gloria whispered to Reinhart: "Sir, you want me to say yiss or no?"

"Just tell me the truth, my dear."

"Then I don't know." She stuck a finger in her ear.

Stony Jack complained. "That's the foolest thang I ever heard."

"Ah," said Reinhart, a bit topheavy from the turban. "Now you see why I picked these two astute individuals." He asked Stony: "Why is it a fool question?"

Flattered, the big man scratched his chin with the rings, which were unavailing against his thick hide. Reinhart saw he

121

had made a tactical error in ceasing to provoke Stony, who might begin to fancy himself a thinker—which is death to the intelligence. He hastily gave his own answer.

"Exactly, because nobody can do anything about it. But kindly observe, my friends, the differences of response between the female and male of the species. The man, pugnacious, positive, dominant, strikes out at the fate which dooms him—because nobody lives forever, everybody eventually fails. Yet he will not admit it. No, he says, meaning Yes. But the woman, not an instrument but a receptacle, is unable to answer at all, which is as much to say Yes, meaning 'You're not asking the right question.' If you have observed, women never answer questions. This is because they are capable of producing new life—a capability which men fiercely resent, so sooner or later they throw the woman down and punish her with the weapon Nature has given them for the purpose, and the result of course is that she produces the very new life the resenting of which caused her to be knocked down and jabbed in the first place. Therefore love is a battle with each side winning a Pyrrhic victory."

Gloria Monday never took her loving eyes from his false face. On the other hand, Stony had begun to grouse in Anglo-Saxon expletives. As to the audience, Reinhart had lost even the Maker, who was edging out the street door. Normally inarticulate, Reinhart felt he could talk all night through the mask, just throwing things out and letting them naturally gravitate into order. But when drunk he also had a fine sense of the lines of communication between human beings. Unworried—being neither a Southerner nor a humanitarian, he cherished the differences among races—at this point he reached under the shelf and brought forth his gin bottle, drained it into his throat, and broke it on the counter with a splendid noise and spray of fragments.

"So much for that. I'm not here to bury life but to recognize it. If I learned one thing from the sovereign of Andorra when I served as his medical advisor, it was: Above all, do no harm and always uphold the dignity of human life. That's as easy, and as hard, to do whether you're a king or a criminal. So all of you have a good chance. Listen to me tell you about the kingdom of Andorra. The palace, which sits on a hill above a green plain, is made out of porphyry, a red stone that gets its color from the blood that is shed in battles and soaks into the earth. The particular stones for this palace were mined at Thermopylae, a place in Greece where centuries ago a handful of Spartans fought to the last man against a horde of Persians and thereby saved their dear country from the foul invader. But the towers, which are really minarets and take

122

after the great temples of Islam, are made of alabaster so white that the snow looks yellow by comparison.

"But it seldom snows there except at Christmas time and then the sun comes out hot soon after and dries it up so that there's no slush to get into your boots or sidewalks to be shoveled. The rest of the year it's warm enough to swim all day, and sufficiently cool at night to sleep under one blanket only. The vineyards, heavy with purple and golden grapes, stretch down slopes behind the palace and on to the horizon, and are thronged with winsome young women with amber hair, who wear only a thin kind of short toga to the midpoint of their supple thighs.

"Now, the Andorrans were a brave, warlike people centuries ago, as everybody was at one time or another—for example, take your Assyrians, who are now extinct; or your Swedes, who fought in the Thirty Years' War but haven't done much since except lie in the sun and turn brown—there's a bit of irony for you folks who were born with a tan. . . . The problem always is how to maintain the spirit while indulging the body. The Andorrans have done this by a shrewd device, having discovered that there are two kinds of people, which we may call the hurters and the hurtees. The first get their satisfaction by working their will on somebody else. The second like to be imposed upon. So every Saturday in Andorra, the entire populace comes to the great square before the palace and line up, according to type, on one side or another, and the hurters proceed to kick the piss out of the hurtees. . . . I apologize to the ladies. I was carried away by enthusiasm for the point I was making."

His sunglass lenses were dirty, and several times he caught himself about to clean them, to do which he would have had to reveal his face. Though he was too drunk to worry for his own sake, and too humble to suppose he would be recognized as other than what he claimed to be, he dared not risk exposure for fear of the deleterious effect it would have on the dear audience, who had absolute faith in Dr. Goodykuntz. He saw respect on those brown faces: either that or noncomprehension; anyway, not pain.

"Ah," he shouted, "how grand it is to be a Negro! Wonderful, just wonderful. You people have more fun than anybody. And while they are frequently niggardly to you, there's not a white person alive who doesn't see in you a symbol of romance and adventure. What is the synonym for 'exciting'? *Colorful!*"

Stony Jack, picking his teeth with a switchblade knife, asked: "You being sour-castic?"

"Not necessarily," Reinhart answered. "Gloria Monday, am I right or wrong?"

She thought about it, hunched in her ancient green coat, her hair like a flight of starlings. "Well, I always kept myself clean, not like some of them girls you see who don't take a baf between now and next Christmas. And while I drink some muscatel now and again and have smoked a stick of pot, I never fool with H, and there ain't nobody can say I do, though they may be them who try—"

"Put a sock in it, baby," called the Maker from the doorway. He had doubtless picked up the phrase in England, when he ran his action at Bridgwater. "We come to hear the Reverent Dr. Goodykuntz, not you troubles, which are endless."

For the first time the audience responded as a unit: they coughed. Reinhart's skull, very warm under the turban, was wet with perspiration, and his glasses had fogged. He saw glimmers of the essential truth here and there, but couldn't seem to maintain a firm hold on it. So far he had delivered a series of disconnected notes, all sound enough as far as they went, but what his listeners needed, not to mention himself, was synthesis—the kind of thing Splendor was so good at, and the real Dr. Goodykuntz, neither of whom were present, though the audience and Reinhart were, neither of whom had come voluntarily. This situation in itself was enormously significant.

"We all," Reinhart said, "are in a world we never made, to use a necessary cliché—and what cliché isn't necessary?—but long as we are in it, we might as well make the best of what may be a mistake. I don't mean we *have* to love anything or anybody—I discussed that just after the war with a fellow in Berlin, Germany; in fact, haha, he was a German; and decided that necessity and love don't mix. I just mean that it might be nice if we do . . . if we love something, that is. Otherwise life is inclined to get pretty dreary, the electricity is turned off for nonpayment of the bill, the telephone never rings except when it's people who want to swindle you, drugs fall from the medicine cabinet, friends let you down, and you never satisfy your parents, nor they you, and unkind people circulate lies about Gloria Monday. But furthermore, what I mean is, perhaps we should try loving even that dreariness and then it wouldn't be so bad, or at least we can see that, in its own way, life is interesting. After all, there it *is*."

Stony Jack looked over a dirty Band-Aid on his right cheekbone, then spat upon the floor. "I was wrong afore. This *here* is the foolest thang I ever heard."

"But you have to admit," said Reinhart, "that if it is the foolest, then it is interesting, because it never happened before.

124

And did you ever think of this: that *each new minute is occurring for the first time*. I'm sorry we don't have a wall clock here, to make the principle more obvious, for it's the most extraordinary phenomenon of a life that is filled with them. For example, I am not the same person who began this sentence, but am several seconds older, all the little molecules of my blood are elsewhere in my veins than they were at the outset, my liver is slightly older, heart, lungs, pancreas, etc., have slightly degenerated. The same is also true of you. You are not the same people who earlier entered this building and took your seats; you are, indeed, some minutes nearer to the grave —if we look on the dreary side of the matter. But take heart! So long as time moves, so do possibilities open up. Keep waiting one minute more!"

Reinhart was excited now, believing he had got to fundamentals and then showed a way out—for who wanted to drive life into a corner and leave it there? Better to dissipate it in the space between here and Neptune, like a meteorite bursting into cosmic dust. That is to say, he was all expanse instead of contradiction, but being at the same time an agoraphobe, he was suddenly struck hard by his essential contradictions and fainted, staying out for approximately thirty-two seconds, during which his turbaned head descended to his folded arms on the counter.

He awoke to hear the Maker shouting: "O noble holy man, thou fallest into a trance!" and could not be sure whether his confederate was authentically impressed or merely resourceful. He himself was very drunk, but felt more desperately than ever his obligation.

"Let me tell you more about Andorra," he easily resumed, never having trouble with a place he knew nothing about— whereas he could have said very little about Ohio—"where they have a national lottery whose first prize is half a million dollars. And here's the feature: *everybody is guaranteed to win it once in his life.*"

"I be goddam if I gotta stan' here listen to this," said Stony, and lumbered to his chair, his jacket-back a great wrinkled sky of tweed lighting.

"Kin I stay?" asked Gloria Monday. "Them other girls always pesterin' me."

"Sure," shouted Reinhart. "Anybody can do anything he wants." He punched at the atmosphere, which seemed to disbelieve him, but the Maker's claqueurs, long silent, rallied feebly: some merely with "Yeah"; others demanding: "Tell it to me, O Doc!"

"You're damned right I'll tell it," Reinhart roared back,

125

the encouragement for some reason making him belligerent. "I'll tell it to the Lord."

"The blessed Lord above?" muttered Gloria Monday, looking shyly at Reinhart as if to ascertain whether that was the one he meant.

So as not to be sacrilegious, in case there actually was a standard God of the type in which he did not believe, Reinhart changed his tune slightly, no point in offending. "I'll tell it to Zeus." He really had a modicum of faith in the old Greek gods, who always did something crummy but feasible to human beings and certainly never considered dying for their sake.

This all made a big hit with Reinhart's listeners, a group that used silence, distended eyes, and fish mouths for their important demonstrations. The orator regretted his long-held conviction that Negroes were a noisy bunch. He also noticed that the latter half of the room was now empty, though he had actually seen no departures. That they were a devious crowd was at least confirmed.

As long as there was still some purpose in so doing, he withheld from himself the realization that he had failed, since it surely took a while for his kind of wisdom, expressed with his kind of energy, to claim their kind of attention. Certainly any moment now he could expect the classic Negro response: they would rise as one man, screaming ecstasy, and cavort in the aisles. . . . One of the brush hairs fell off his lip. He was over the hump towards twenty-two, and already conscious of certain losses. Real estate was his game and not evangelism, yet he had told the truth about Andorra, which he had made up on the spot. He wished terribly that everybody would win, that you could look nowhere without being blinded by grandeur. He also wished he had either drunk more or drunk less.

The Maker's white coat and black visage had disappeared from the street doorway. Reinhart got a premonition of doom when he saw the color combination with which they had been replaced: policeman's midnight blue and Slavic-red face, but the paste helped keep his upper lip stiff, and he remarked to Gloria Monday: "How nice! An officer of the law, of all people, has come to join our devotion."

But she had vanished, probably using Splendor's route through the back window. As had Stony Jack and his small lackey—and indeed every other human being in excess of Reinhart and the uniformed newcomer. A nimble people; at the outset there had been thirty or forty souls in the room, and though Reinhart had seen nobody actually taking leave, now there were none. For a host of reasons he did not himself follow suit: pride, torpor, intoxication, his disguise, and, most important, he knew the patrolman as yet another schoolfellow from before the war.

So he stood, or swayed, his ground, and when the officer had reached the counter, said: "Hi, Hasek."

"Hi, Reinhart," answered Hasek, an incurious man. Far be it from him to ask after Reinhart's unprecedented getup and environs.

"God, Hasek, it must be all of three-four years."

"All of it," said Hasek, his cheekbones a foot apart and his hairline beginning at his eyebrows.

"Still on the force?"

"Yes, sure." Hasek blinked little round eyes.

Reinhart made an overamiable mouth and, indicating his headdress, said: "I'm a little drunk, Hasek, but I guess that's not against the law. Hahaha."

Very solemn in his blue hat, Hasek agreed: "That is correct."

"Uh, just what was it you wanted, Hasek? I've been giving a speech."

"Oh." Hasek scratched his ass with the nightstick. His belt was like a big charm bracelet, with pistol, bullets, handcuffs, flashlight, notepad, holster for twin pencils, two kinds of whistle, leather billy, first-aid packet, and a book of green summonses whose white strings were intertwined into a sort of rag-doll head. "I reckonized you right off in your Mason outfit."

"Hell," said Reinhart, "they make you carry a hardware store."

Something was laboring under Hasek's low forehead, and at last produced issue. He suffered a slow spasm of mirth and said: "It's a living."

"It's a living!" Reinhart repeated, as if it were a riot. "That's pretty funny, Hasek." Laughing, he deftly covered his lip with one hand, went underneath it with the other, and plucked off most of his mustache. He removed the turban, cradling it in his elbow like a football, which left only the purple glasses between him and austere naturalism.

"Now what was it you wanted, Hasek?"

"Why." Seen directly, the patrolman was not nearly so rubicund as he had appeared through the sun lenses; not for a moment, that is; then the blood rose in his cheeks and he averted his juju-bean eyes. "Why, we booked this Niggero. Why, and you know who he is? Old Splendor Mainwaring is who. That good old sonbitch who run every touchdown I ever blocked for. I loved that Niggero like a brother, and I onetime busted the mouth of the left guard from Cheeseman High for hollering 'coon' in the scrimmage. So now the dumb shine turns out to be a user. And it is very embarrassing to me on the force when the chief brings him in and cuffs him to the radiator with me on the desk having to book him. All the while he rides me like he used to on the field: 'Keep your butt down. Hit 'em low. Sixty-three, forty-two, *hike!*' "

"Hasek, Hasek! Explain yourself!" shouted Reinhart. "Splendor Mainwaring was right here in this room not two hours ago. How could he have committed a serious crime within such a short period? Besides, he was sick."

"You don't need no time nor anything but your own person to take dope," Hasek explained. "It's a peculiar crime in that respect. The only thing that's more peculiar is suicide, which is a crime, but the punishment for it is unenforceable, if you get my drift."

"That I understand, Hasek," said Reinhart, who felt he was dreaming all this. "But I tell you there must be some mistake. Splendor taking dope! It's ridiculous. He is a nonchemical physician, among other things."

Hasek removed his cap and rubbed his elbow against the isinglass liner, to match which there was a round bald spot in the center of his crown. "I ain't supposed to remark on charges against accused, whose rights include counsel of his own choice, in lieu of which court will appoint same. Due process, habeas corpus on posting of specified bail, prisoner remanded in custody of, etc., etc., a jury of his pears, hear ye, hear ye. Very interesting stuff, Reinhart. How long you been a counselor at law? I remember you was always very bright in reading English, was you not? Miss Beeler used to give us them poems by Woolworth and others. Well, if you want we can go down to the jail to see your client."

"He sent you here for me?"

"Precisely."

"One minute, Hasek," Reinhart demanded belligerently. "Your name's *not* Hasek! It's Capek, Michael Capek."

"Correct."

"Then why did you let me go on saying Hasek?"

"Rules of the force," said Capek. "No harassment of nor rudeness to the taxpayer unless apprehended in an act where a violation of law is evident. If you want to file a complaint against me, my number is Three."

Reinhart found his coat back of the partition; turned out the lights (no use being profligate with the cleaner's current); hung onto the turban and glasses, which should have to go back to their owners; considered closing the windows and doors but decided the hell with it, why did he have to take responsibility for everything in the world?; and started with Patrolman Capek for the stationhouse.

First time Reinhart had even seen a jail except in the movies, although in earlier years he had been once or twice in the front part of the station, accused of juvenile misdemeanors—throwing corn kernels against householders' windows at Halloween, hooting in the park, etc.—charges dismissed, with a warning. Though this should have been obsolete experience he felt like a current lawbreaker when Capek took a bunch of giant keys from a wall hook and led him clanking down the corridor to the cells. The pokey was too small to afford a warder, the suburb being too narrow for much crime. There were two cells and, at the dead end of the passage, a mop standing head up in a bucket, like a skinny old woman soaking her feet. Capek unlocked the first door and a drunk swayed out, shouting obscenely. They got him back in, Capek and Reinhart; and he sat down in the middle of the concrete floor and derided them.

In Cell Two, which Capek tried next, on a bunk which really hung from the wall on chains, lay Splendor Mainwaring, who stared dully at the ceiling of light bulb and gooseflesh plaster. Capek banged with the key, saying above his own racket: "Accused, here's counsel." He opened the door for Reinhart and locked it behind him. "Kindly notify when ready." Then he wedged his face between the bars and whispered: "He's on the downgrade."

Reinhart put the turban on the floor. There was nowhere to sit, the toilet having no lid.

"You've broken Capek's heart," he said to his late friend, who seemed always to be horizontal at their interviews. "Imagine having to arrest an old teammate. Why don't you ever think about the next fellow?"

Splendor moaned academically, his eyes showing no real feeling. He wore an aggressively white T-shirt.

Reinhart squatted on his heels. "*I* gave the address tonight, if you want to know, and it was a total flop. And when I left, didn't close the windows and it looks like rain."

"Oh," murmured Splendor, an absolute blank.

"Capek told me the magistrate set your bail at five hundred dollars. I guess you expect me to raise it? What's the idea of saying I'm your lawyer?" Reinhart was too tired to dramatize his resentment physically; he fell off his haunches onto his hams and reviled the nonchemical interne. "You're a coward, a fourflusher, a welcher, a fink, a shitheel. A complete washout as a man. What have you ever done for me that I should take care of you, you bum? Haven't you got any more sense

129

than to take dope? What's so bad about reality that you want something else?"

Reinhart knew the answers to these questions—because there is a cause for every effect, which circumstance if you think about it (and perhaps Splendor had) will send you to the nearest heroin forthwith—but as usual he was challenging him to fight back. And as usual he learned something about himself: he was always either provoking or placating.

Splendor's hands raised at the wrists and waved feebly, like the antennae of a dying insect; his head lay quiet and stark on the caseless pillow of striped ticking.

Reinhart pulled the tendons in his weak gut as he rose and went to the bunk. Splendor's lips were quivering. Lowering an ear, Reinhart heard in a gray whisper: "I die, Horatio; the potent poison quite o'ercrows my spirit."

"What's that?" roared Reinhart.

Splendor's nostrils contracted and at last he blinked, saying somewhat more loudly, since the man who was not passion's slave had raised the decibel count: "Absent thee from felicity awhile, and in this harsh world draw thy breath in pain to tell my story."

Reinhart had not figured on this. He was about to yell for Capek to come running with a selection of the familiar antidotes listed on iodine bottles, Drano cans, etc.: mustard, chalk, milk of magnesia—when checking Splendor again lest he expire before they had gone to all that trouble, he saw his friend grin like the radiator of a Buick.

"What aer you doing out *there,* Waldo?" said the nonchemist, still focused on the ceiling. Surely not the statement of a dying man. Reinhart decided to pay no mind to his badinage, and rather to establish the chronology of Splendor's disaster, albeit he would get no help from the principal.

"Let's see." He strolled to the barred window and, because it was night, saw only a reflection of himself in jail, a somewhat romantic image. "You left the shop, by means of French leave, at about eight. Distraught, you repaired to your house. By eight forty, the chief of police, acting on an anonymous tip, was already there to find you with a hypodermic needle, a warm spoon, and an aspirin-bottlecapful of a liquid which proved to be a solution of heroin and water. You were arrested and taken before the magistrate, who set your bail at five hundred dollars. I want you to know that I don't have it, incidentally."

Splendor laughed with his tongue, and said in an execrable accent: "Ah's the coon of Kuhn and Loeb."

"That's all very well," answered Reinhart. "Make your corny jokes, but you're in serious trouble. I'm sorry I ever

130

came into the garage that day." He moved from the vicinity of the toilet, which had just gulped like a frog, though the bowl was bright and its water so crystalline that Reinhart had seen another image of himself in it.

Splendor chortled. "Always call a spade a spade."

That did it. Having picked up the turban, Reinhart called for Capek, who came eating a monstrous ham sandwich valanced with white fat, which he explained had been ordered for Accused in accordance with regulations covering sustenance of prisoners, but since Accused had turned it down, the chief gave him, Three, authorization to otherwise dispose of said provisions, which he was doing with little pleasure. He unlocked the cell with a greasy key.

"To hell with you, Dr. Goodykuntz!" Splendor yelled, and slammed his eyelids shut. Whether he meant the real or the fake was not clear.

"I'm not a lawyer," Reinhart told Capek when they were in the corridor. "That guy can rot in jail so far as I care. Being somewhat gutless myself, I can't stand anybody else who's worse." He didn't know why Capek brought out this candor in him.

They stopped at the desk and the patrolman, his belt toys tinkling, leaned over to throw his crusts in the wastebasket, which being full of resilient, crumpled paper, bounced them out again. Capek made a testy noise and crawled into the knee slot of the desk after his fugitive garbage, vanishing for a moment. So Reinhart addressed his concluding remarks to the surly gallery of wanted rogues on the wall above.

"You see," he complained, "I'm interested only in success." As the criminals stared back unfeeling, out of the moment of truth in which the prison camera had trapped them, he realized that they were not.

Chapter 9

Untypically, Reinhart stuck to his resolve; he trafficked no more in Splendor's problems, and even read with satisfaction in the suburban weekly that his friend had drawn four months' imprisonment in the county jail. But he was never mean; he returned the turban to the costumer, and when his last mustering-out check came from the government, he cashed it and mailed an envelope full of greenbacks, registered under a false name, to the Mainwaring home on Mohwak Street. After all, his encouragement had caused Splendor to quit the jog of Laidlaw's Body Shop & Towing and hence lose the family source of income.

Because of this quixotic, act, Reinhart was penniless by April Fools' Day, for neither had he earned another cent from real estate.

"You ninny," was what Genevieve Raven said to him that morning. "It hasn't rained for a week, Claude's gone out every day, leaving you here, and why?"

"Why?" echoed Reinhart, who had begun to react erotically to her needling and had recently dreamed she was flogging him with a silk stocking stuffed with discarded lingerie.

He had just run out and got them coffee. She drank hers with a nervous little flinch that both annoyed and intrigued him, and between sips put the wooden spoon into the paper cups and agitated the liquid counterclockwise.

"Because," she said, "it's as clear as mud." Meaning, rather, as glass, ice, cellophane, spring water, etc.: Genevieve either misunderstood clichés or purposely violated them, he couldn't figure which. Thus she used "funny as a crutch" for something that really *was* comical. "Do you realize you haven't got one cent out of him in a month? Your sixty-five for selling the Tenderloin was held back for the clothes you bought on his account at Gents' Walk, the cost of which was actually fifty-two fifty, because he always gets a ten to fifteen knockdown there, and as I doubt if you know, that's a very cheap price. If you scratch the sole of those shoes with a penknife, you will find they are largely paper. It's crazy to me that a boy your age doesn't take more pride in his apparel."

"How come I don't remember you from high school?" asked Reinhart, who was sitting on the blunt fins of the radiator that ran below the front window.

"Mmm," Genevieve murmured, "so he's rude too. . . . Why, that's simple: I never went to your dopey place full of factory workers. We used to live in the Heights, and I went to Heights H.S. and took academic, and could have gone to college but wouldn't for the world because Daddy refused to consider any of the nearby universities with their disgustingly low standards. Insisted on Smith, Bryn Mawr, *et al.,* but I didn't dare run away from certain responsibilities here."

"Ah," said Reinhart, sympathetically. "You had to stay and help support—"

Genevieve rose from the swivel chair with such fury that the pencil flew from her bob. "How dare you take such liberties? Daddy could buy and sell you and your whole family and never miss the small change it took for the transaction."

"Ex*cuse* me," said Reinhart, who had vacantly got out his knife and scratched his soles, which looked like leather but it was hard to tell for sure. "I was admiring you. You're certainly quick to take offense, but I suppose that's natural in a girl who is so pretty and charming and bright." He watched with scientific interest while her sharp little breasts quivered, her little butt twitched, and her cheeks blushed. She dashed off to the john.

Reinhart had suddenly got the idea that he could seduce her, which made him too grow hot of skin. He threw some water on his face from the gurgling cooler, and dried himself with an olive drab handkerchief.

When Genevieve reappeared—certainly not with a background of flushing water; she used the restroom only for make-up and tears and never acknowledged its coarser conveniences; and with his typical consideration Reinhart managed at least twice a day to leave the office so she could take an unembarrassed pee, but doubted if she did; her modesty indeed aroused him—when Genevieve marched, like a little circus pony, back to her desk. Reinhart asked: "What should I do about Claude, then?" He made haste to conceal lhis GI handkerchief, as to which she had frequently attacked him (but why throw away a perfectly good square of cloth just because it wasn't white?).

"Honestly!" said she. "You're just pitiful without a woman to tell you what to do." She deposited her round bottom, tweed-covered at present, into the buttock-shaped depressions in her revolvable seat. "You go to Claude and demand to be put on a salary, that's what."

"Sure will take a lot of guts, considering I never do any work."

"Oh my golly! You're about as much fun as a barrel of monkeys." Profligate with office supplies, she broke a new pencil before his eyes—he was leaning towards her across the desk—and squinted hers like a child. "Don't you get the point of business, at all? It's obligations . . . anybody ever tell you you had a funny face?"

In delighted horror, he saw her slender fingers reaching for his nose and got a pronounced erection, to conceal which he strode rapidly into Claude's office and shook a fist at the rubber plant.

"Not like that!" Genevieve called. "Use a little sutt-let-ty once, will you? Like: 'Reason will show that . . .'; 'I have determined, Claude'; 'Look here, Claude, fair is fair . . .' Once he guarantees to pay you a salary, then he'll have to give you work, see?"

Reinhart drifted back relaxing. "He might just show me the door, and then what would I have?"

A host of tiny lines advanced from Genevieve's temples to the corners of her bright eyes; when she played mock-sweet she looked middle-aged. She was unattractive in this aspect, and knew it, as women always know everything about themselves—which is seldom, *au fond*, a real gain though tactically advantageous, for what they know is that one day they will lose their looks, while a man's self-knowledge is limited to the harmless certainty that he will die. A vast difference, *vas deferens*, and it made Reinhart ache to introduce himself into Genevieve's quick little body, for her own good.

"Carlo Reinhart!" she said sarcastically. "You *dear* boy! How did you ever escape getting strangled in your cradle? I never knew a person before who didn't have an aim in life, and it's *so* exciting."

For some reason he was suddenly stung, and answered: "Yeah? It so happens that I just like to live, enjoying every moment as it comes along, if possible, and making the best of the bad ones. I don't care about money or politics or religion

134

or science, but just men and women, and then only the ones I know. I'll never lose any sleep over how many Hindus die of scurvy this year. You know why? Because it's not my fault they aren't getting enough oranges. I'm particularly uninterested in the Negro problem."

"Well who is?" asked Genevieve. "You bring up such dumb things a person would think you didn't have any bats in the belfry." She began testily to ring the bell on her typewriter carriage again and again.

"Ha!" said Reinhart. "If you only knew." His psychiatric experience gave him a secret advantage over everybody.

At the moment Claude swept in from the street, bulled Reinhart aside, and without apology plunged into his office, shutting the door.

"Go get him," whispered Genevieve, who wore a vest of fake leopard skin and bared her teeth apropos of it.

Reinhart was astonished at her ferocity over somebody else's concerns. How had he ever come to float between the Scylla of business and the Charybdis of woman? Now for the millionth time he had to go and earn his manhood.

He tiptoed to Claude's door and drummed upon it with the soft balls of his fingers, looked back at Genevieve, saw her tigrish snarl, desperately turned the knob, and strode in across the beige broadloom that felt like walking on meringue.

"Bud," Claude said to him before he reached the long blond desk, "bud, bud, buddy-bud, bud-bud, buddley, budget. Too bad, bud, but the budget beckons. How's that for a slogan? Get what profit you can from it, bud, because I'm canning you, retroactive fourteen days. Check with G. Raven to see if you still owe us anything on them clothes. If not, goodbye and don't forget your hat."

"I don't wear one," Reinhart admitted happily.

"I know," said the boss, tracing his little mustache with an incredibly slender finger, considering it issued from a puffy palm. "I know, bud. You ain't worked out in none of a hundred ways, though I done all I could. . . . Bud! You're dreaming!"

A just charge, for at the moment Reinhart was gazing out the window upon the growing spring, in which he would wander free. A teen-aged maple, all knock-knees and buds, was waving at him from the edge of the gravel lot behind the office.

"Now, bud, I'll tell you what I'd do in your place," Claude went on when Reinhart reluctantly turned back to him. "Kindly listenyvous. Recall that slogan I put to you"—he threw his wrist in his face and consulted an enormous chronometer showing the date, the phases of the moon, the tides

135

from Block Island to Cape Hatteras, and perhaps the time of day as well—"twenty-nine seconds ago. . . . Kindly repeat what I said twenty-nine seconds ago."

"Bud, buddley-bud . . ." Reinhart began.

"No need for the overture!"

" 'Too bad, bud, but the budget beckons,' " said Reinhart.

Claude bounced up and pressed his assistant's hand. "You see how easy it is when you try? Bud, I *know* I could make a man of you if I had time. You got the stuff, but you fight it. You say Yes, but you think No. Straighten out your thinking, bud. One morning lately I caught a fishy look around your gills that may have been the work of the Kings. Live clean, boy, and you'll be a clean liver and have one. Laugh to show you get it, brother! Good, that's more than enough. Stop it, bud! Sounds like you're choking on a fishbone. Now if I was you and canned—though I never was, see, and why? Because I never worked for anybody else! Haha. . . . Bud! Knock off that laughing! . . . I would take that slogan down to Bauer Dairy Products in the city and peddle it to them for a hundred thousand dollars."

Reinhart frowned in puzzlement and repeated the slogan to himself.

Claude read his lips and hooted derision. "Not just the way it was handed to you, bud. Make it your own, like: 'Buy Bauer Butter, Betty, and Bake Better Batter.' 'Bark for Bauer, Bowser!' "

"Billy Bones, Bridge Builder," said Reinhart brightly, "Begs for Bauer Butter."

Claude shook his round head. Today he wore a mocha-brown sports jacket and a polka-dot clip-on bowtie, fastened nonsymmetrically. "That's narrative, bud, and won't do."

"For Houses and Homes, Holler for Humbold!" Reinhart said.

Claude squinted at him suspiciously and began to pace to and fro in spring oxfords of brown calf and tan suede. His soles were Swiss cheese crepe, and the skirt of his jacket had three slits through its waist closed with only one button.

"Golly, you sure like to fool, don't you, bud? I believe you could stand there all day and gas in this vein. Tell me am I right?"

Reinhart nodded. He was genuinely sorry he hadn't worked out in real estate, without for a moment understanding why he had not. He felt as alien in America as he had in Europe, and it was silly to suppose he would make a hit in Asia even if he got a chance to go there: he had heard that the Japanese, for example, fertilized their vegetables with human excrement.

136

Humbold sat down again, plucked up a pen, and ran it under his nose, as if it had a bouquet. Then he pounded his desk blotter with two fists carrying three rings.

"Durn it, bud, you don't feel no real humility before God Almighty. That takes the form of sarcasm and lack of drive. I'd say you were an atheist, didn't I know your daddy and mom had sent you to Sunny School. But why don't we ever see you at the Masons? What are you doing for your fellow man? 'For when the One Great Scorer comes to write against your name, He writes not that you won or lost but how you played the game.' "

In one of his desk drawers Claude found a wallet-sized card on which were printed the same sentiments, and on the other side a blurb for Humbold Realty. "Carry this at all times in your billfold, bud." He skimmed it across the desktop to Reinhart, and sank both arms into the drawer. Shortly a heap of souvenirs rose before him high as his second chin: a 1946 calendar, mechanical pencil, plastic wallet, tin cigar-holder, lighter the size of a lipstick; a vial of Alphonse de Paris cologne, two pocket notebooks, a key chain with toy-Scottie charm, a Chinese back-scratcher, a combination nail file and corkscrew, a flashlight no larger than a cigarette; a cigarette big as a cigar, in a glass tube; a cigar big as a banana, in a kind of coffin of redwood; a miniature cedar barrel marked BOOTLEG ROOT BEER; and a rubber dog who lifted pneumatic ears when his tail was manipulated. Somewhere on each of these was the legend "See Humbold Realty."

Claude shoved the lot at Reinhart. "Take 'em and blow, bud." His eyes suddenly welled with tears, and he honked into a handkerchief that matched his tie. "Durn it, bud, there is a helplessness about you that gets me here." He indicated his sternum. "I just can't shove you out in the street, you'll be run down like a rabbit."

Anticipating his being rehired, Reinhart grew desperate: "No, I won't, Claude. My God, I was all through Europe in the war."

"Yes, but this is serious, bud. That's what you just can't get through your coconut. This is bidniss, not them silly games like plugging Fachists, or Commonists, whatever them Heinies was at the time, not to mention the goofy Japs, who had a good thing going in novelties and should of stuck to it instead of grabbing the Philistine Islands where there ain't been a loose dollar since little David licked them with a peashooter, according to the Good Book. What's your opinion of Paul, bud?"

"Paul who?" Reinhart asked, his visions of liberty fading, his hand groping for the giant cigarette-under-glass.

"Why, Paul the Epistle. Turns out he was a Jew who made tents. You would know that if you was a Mason, along with various other shenanigans. Ever think of improving the old mind? History ain't the bunk, bud. Some of the finest bidniss-men ever lived were named the Phony Sheeans. Sounds micky, don't it? . . . I can't give you no more straight salary than twenty a week, and don't try to bleed me for better. But I'll pay you in green from the petty cash without writing your name on a payroll, so you can also draw another twenty in unemployment insurance and nobody the wiser. Now what happens is Vetsville is full of ex-servicemen who want to do bidniss with one of their own kind."

Claude rose, came to Reinhart, and began to stuff his protégé's pockets with souvenirs. "Take 'em, boy. But don't let me catch you using the smokables." He snatched the great cig-arette from Reinhart's hand. "Now as manager of Veterans' Division, Humbold Realty, you will need wheels. What hap-pens is the Caddy dealer, who owes me a favor, throws away his waiting list to furnish yours truly with a new four-door. Wait'll you see it, bud! Wop Red, white sidewalls, Futuramic, and the radio's got three speakers, one in the trunk so's you can have music while you change a tire. Bud, come here, I want you to try on this desk for size."

He led Reinhart to his own swivel chair and forced him into it.

"How you feel in the catbird seat, boy? Spin it! . . . You know how it is with cars these days. I have to give that dealer enough to send his punk kid through college, and he'd sooner cut his throat than let you off without a trade-in. But I fought him, bud. No sirreee, I held onto my old Gigantic for my pal. No, fellow, don't offer me eight hundred clams! That car goes to Bud!"

"All right, Claude. What will it cost me?" Reinhart asked skeptically.

Claude squeezed Reinhart's shoulder. "Bud, during the gas rationing I never used that heap but to run my sainted mother to the Methodist covered-dish suppers. She used to sit there holding, God bless her, a casserole of cheese fondue, saying (he went into falsetto): 'Claudy, you're goin' fifteen mph! I won't have it!' So I'd back-throttle to ten."

"I just hope," said Reinhart, "that my promotion doesn't mean I'll have to pay *you* a salary." Claude's chair was not that thrilling, considering that it would have to be given back when he agreed to buy the car. Nor was Reinhart exactly elat-ed over his new post. He had begun to suspect that nine-tenths of every job however grand was humdrum. Not even Claude made sales every day; even Churchill exuded more sweat than

138

blood and tears; and Michelangelo, he read in a popular weekly, had lain on his back four years to paint the Sistine ceiling. The problem was to survive that nine-tenths of banal drudgery. This was another color of horse from what he had described to the Negro audience as the dreariness they should love. What he had meant then was misery and what he said platitudinous: nobody need be told that unpleasantness was interesting: hence that audience were criminals and his parents were hypochondriacs.

He emerged from his reflections to hear, rather than feel, Claude's index finger tapping on his crown.

"Oh bud!" the boss was calling. "Come back, bud. Face the music." His initialed belt buckle was at the level of Reinhart's eye: a great *C*, with a little *H* inside, giving priority, American style, to the Christian name, to private enterprise and rugged individualism.

"But if I take this new job will I get stuck?" Reinhart asked, giddy with apprehension. "Can I stay available for better offers? Maybe somebody will call me from New York. I was in the Army, you know, and made certain contacts." He stood up, passing Claude's nonplused face en route. "Oh yes, I did. Always grabbing the initiative as you do—and I'm not criticizing you for it—you assume I am a fool. I never before had so many people who wanted to tell me what to do. You civilians could stand better manners, for one thing. For another, none of you have ever been out of Ohio. What do you know of the purple fog that rises at twilight from the Devonshire moors? That's just one example, but it makes the point."

From astonishment Claude progressed rapidly into a sort of heart attack. He clutched himself pectorally, fell into the just-vacated chair, and from a mouth that threatened to froth, called weakly: "H_2O!"

Reinhart galloped into the outer office, where Genevieve blocked him before he could get to the bathroom and fill a tumbler. She had undoubtedly been listening at the intercom: Claude kept his transmitter open at all times, in what now proved to be a destructive exhibitionism—for the disloyal secretary whispered: "He's faking. Demand thirty a week with the car thrown in. The tired are bald, the heater's on the Fritz, and besides he's getting the new Cad at twenty per cent below list."

Reinhart could hardly make himself heard; he had a rather thin voice for so thick a thorax; besides, from the inner room Claude was trumpeting like a herd of elephants charging Tarzan's tree-house.

"I just realized," he replied, "after a false start, that I'm not cut out for business. I'm going to get out of town and take up something exciting."

Genevieve shook her head. "Uh-uh."

She was an arrogant little person, and had not, for whatever good reason, been to college. Nowadays Reinhart was constantly surrounded by inferiors, in terms of cultivation and experience, though Genevieve did have the prettiest neck, a supple ivory column that never showed a tendon or a crease, suggesting a like condition of thigh. Her leopard vest swelled and trembled like a living pelt. He fought a compulsion to put his hands inside it and still what was jiggling there. She arched her back in further provocation.

"Well, I've got to get Claude a glass of water."

"Uh-uh." Genevieve inexorably stalked him into the corner beyond the washroom door. "You see, I know your secret."

"Oh," said Reinhart, "I was afraid you might find out." He despaired of making her understand, for women were notoriously disloyal to friends and hysterically afraid of Negroes. Nevertheless, he bravely waded in: "The whole thing is relatively easy to explain, preposterous as it would seem."

"Preposterous?" she said. "If I thought you meant that, and weren't just saying it because you're embarrassed, I'd slap your face." She opened her teeth and ran her tongue along the biting surfaces. The inside of her mouth was exquisite, a pink-satin hollow ringed by an ivory picket fence. If Reinhart had to characterize Genevieve with one word, he might have chosen "clean" over "pretty," and there was no doubt that in a skin-to-skin relationship she would be very savory.

"Oh, you don't know about Dr. Goodykuntz." He suspected they were talking at cross purposes, as a man is condemned to do with a woman, for Genevieve here showed mock shock and shaped her mouth as if to breathe on hot soup.

Claude's sudden quiet frightened Reinhart, and he whispered: "Have you no pity? How can we take a chance on whether or not he's faking? What always makes you so certain?"

"That's just the way I am," said Genevieve. "And I never asked you to fall in love with me. If my fiancé finds out, I can't answer for your safety."

There, presumably, was his secret. The girl was mad. He moved as fast as he could towards the washroom, but she beat him out by a shoulder, and went inside and locked the door. Only after all that did he remember the water cooler standing there like a transparent-domed invader from outer space. So can a woman distract a man that he will forget mortal obligations. He filled a paper cone and rushed back, spilling half, to the boss.

"Gloop," Claude swilled the drink. "Twenty-five a week, bud, and the car for five hundred." He looked perfectly all right; indeed, while he clutched his heart with one hand, he had been making memos with the other.

"I haven't got five hundred," said Reinhart. "And really, Claude, I don't see how I can go on working for you if you think I'm so naïve. In the modern world if you have good manners everybody thinks you're stupid. Now to show you I'm not, here's my idea. Assign the Gigantic to Humbold Realty as a company car, thus getting a tax exemption for it. Besides, it'll save wear and tear on the new Cad."

Claude considered that for a moment, then let his features collapse into the old anguish. He fled from chair to closet and stuck a great tongue into the mirror on the back of the door there. "You're killing me, bud. It hurts me when I laugh. You're malignant, but you don't savvy bidniss one little bit or you'd know I can't let the firm be represented by a four-year-old heap."

"Why not? You've used it up till now." Defiantly, Reinhart took the giant cigar from the redwood coffin and lighted it. He was making his stand here and now, and belched a great mushroom of smoke towards the boss.

Surprisingly, Claude made no objection. He explained patiently: "I was skating on thin ice, bud, and I fell through on my tokus. This firm ain't been conspicuous for sales in the last few weeks. If it ain't my old car, then it's you who jinxed me. With my big heart, though, I'm willing to try anything before I turn you out like an old dog. Always keep a positive face towards life, bud. When you're losing money, up your buying. If you get beat up once, start a fight with a bigger fella. That's the way of Jesus Christ, bud, who got out and walked on the water when his boat leaked. Nothing stopped that tough little guy, because his sainted mother was behind him all the way."

"So was the devil," Reinhart noted sarcastically. "Don't you remember, he said: 'Get thee behind—'" He was interrupted by a piercing whistle from the cigar, and a second later it exploded towards the lighted end and there was a manifestation of excess smoke, very white.

Maintaining his composure, Reinhart looked over the boss's shoulder into the mirror and said nonchalantly: "In the movies a victim's face is covered with black and the cigar peels back like a banana."

Humbold was clutching himself again, this time at his domed gut. He staggered across the room as if in a final seizure, emitting the cries of sundry jungle birds, bounced off the far wall, and caromed back to the closet, where the door was

141

still open and Reinhart stood aside, so that Claude spun right into the hanging clothes therein. When he emerged, he was fully dressed for outdoors in a belted raincoat the color of an unborn calf; there were epaulets at his shoulders, cartridge loops on his chest, and chromium rings at intervals along the belt: he could attach law-enforcement gear in imitation of Officer Capek, or canteens of brandy if he wanted to climb Everest. He wore a rain cap to match. He was still laughing.

"Poor bud," he bellowed. "You'll have to get up earlier in the morning to outfox Claude Humbold. You got the raise, sidestepped the car, and thought you had one on me. *But I got the laugh!* Get the point, bud?"

"No," Reinhart answered aggressively, because he in fact did. Somehow Humbold had won.

"I got one *in* you, pal. En garde at all times, bud. I strike without warning." He went to the rear window and raised its sash. "Get this clue: here's why I never installed the casement type, with crank— I'm too wide to go through half." So saying, he climbed nimbly over the sill and dropped four feet to the ground.

"Claude," Reinhart said, leaning from the window, "I guess I should tell you that I'll want to quit in June to go back to school."

"Typical of you, bud," replied Humbold, eying the gravel yard for ambush. "Gassing about faraway doings when I need a recon man at the front door. June! I live day by day, minute by minute. At this hour I'm a hunted man. Three collection agencies are on my tail. If a dark guy, or a pimply guy, or a guy with specks ask for me today, take him down to the basement and punch him in the mouth. Without no witnesses, he'll never bring you to court. By tomorrow I might have the necessary cabbage. By June I might own the state and you won't want to desert me. Plan to take night courses at the "Y," or study how to fly a plane on Sundays. Hover in the blue over town and look for zoning violations. Report them to the village council, bud, and they'll owe us a favor, which we can use when I rip down that fieldstone dump where Mad Anthony Wayne stayed overnight in the year One, and want to build a nice bowling alley."

He gave Reinhart the two fingered bull's-horns, bullshit salute and hugging the stucco with a grating noise, crept towards the alley.

"I'll admit," said Reinhart, having returned contemplatively to Genevieve's desk, "that this experience has shaken my faith in Claude as a businessman."

"No it hasn't, it hasn't at all," she ruled, smiling through a frown, or vice versa; whichever, her cheeks were stretched

142

tight and shiny, and two dimples appeared that he had never seen before. Women are impossible when they think they've got one on you. Killing two birds with one stone, secretly getting back not only at Genevieve but also at Claude, who would have been horrified at the use to which his riposte was now turned, Reinhart said to Genevieve, to himself: Wait till I get one in you. Aloud, he asked: "Do you have any idea what the word 'invidious' means?"

"Sneaky," said Genevieve. She blotted her fresh lipstick on a Kleenex and studied the impression.

"No, 'giving offense.' You frequently manage to be invidious, like many other people I know, particularly women. What do you mean by saying 'No, it hasn't'? I may be wrong in believing that Claude is a bad businessman. Perhaps he is a good one. But I am right when I describe a certain opinion as being mine. You don't know what I think unless I tell it to you."

"Mmm," answered Genevieve, her upper teeth clasping her lower lip. "You got put on salary, didn't you? I told you just what to do and I must say you did it. Now all that's necessary is to fight him once a week on payday, to actually *get* the money."

"That's what I mean. Is a good businessman so crafty over such small things? I can understand a big, glorious swindle, but what does twenty-five dollars a week mean to Claude Humbold?"

"Everything in the world," said Genevieve, "that's all. He hasn't yet paid for a gallon of liquid soap for the washroom dispenser, which was delivered the same day I started work here six months ago. He owes on the stationery bill from last year, and the company ignores our orders. My ribbon is so faint I have to use a first carbon for the original. You'd think it would embarrass him to send out letters that smear at the touch, except he always uses the phone for important messages. Of course the phone company can't be beat out of their money, but he always waits till they dun him twice—which makes it darn tough when I place a long-distance call for him: they switch me to the business office and some old harpy who checks on our last bill."

"Ah," said Reinhart, "then he runs merely on faith in himself."

"Yeah," sneered Genevieve, "or on other people's in him. How he can still get credit is beyond me."

"Maybe it's the same thing," he replied to her first sentence. "Anyway, I hope you get your pay on time."

"Oh, I'm the one person who does. He's afraid of my father, who's a lawyer, that's why. You must meet Daddy. He would be a good model for you, being very manly."

Taking offense as usual, Reinhart said: "See what I mean about your invidiousness? What do you think I'm like now, a girl? I wish I could understand why you dislike me."

He had no taste for the maudlin, and would have loathed himself for his plaint had she not responded to it so graciously. Women drop us low to raise us up, and vice versa: only our fellow man lets us stand upon the plain and looks us in the eye.

"Carl," said Genevieve, ineffably sweet though not able to resist a small castration of his name; but this was the first time she had ever used it in whatever variant. She reached for the hand by which he supported his standing slump besides the desk, pulled back before she touched it, bit an eraser red, and smirked in the same hue. "Are you always so forward?"

"Genevieve," said Reinhart for wont of anything more eloquent, looking for her momentarily to flee as usual; in fact, hoping she would. He suddenly felt terribly old and weary to be playing this game. He was getting to an age where he wanted only something definite, one way or the other: does she or doesn't she? as the hair-dye ads asked. He hadn't "known" a woman for months, indeed not since he returned to the States, perhaps owing to this very policy, which was either infantile or senile. Sometimes he believed he was in a state of torment so long-drawn-out that it resembled peace.

"Carl," confessed Gen, pulling at the two ends of her purple-velvet string tie, with no damage to the permanent knot. "I'm not really engaged to anybody. . . ." Reacting to Reinhart's depreciatory grin—he had never believed she was —she quickly bridled, saying: "But there's this fellow who thinks we are—"

"Genevieve," Reinhart broke in. "I wonder whether we should do something harmless together, like seeing a movie?"

She answered gravely: "I'll have to let you know" and turned back with compressed lips to her work, but as soon as Reinhart had walked into Claude's office in vague pursuit of his obligations as Manager, Veterans' Division, he heard the outer door swish behind the fading heel-taps of her exit.

Reinhart sat down at Claude's desk and with effort conceived an original plan: he would call door to door in Vetsville, asking each tenant whether he could sell him a house. He remembered this was the means used by certain unfortunates during the Depression to peddle shoelaces, twine, and hairpins. Poor fellows; as a child he would ask Maw to give them a sandwich, and would sympathetically peer out the back door at them as they ate it on the steps. Vignettes of sadness invariably came to his mind when it had been exhausted by scheming. He proceeded to endure a fantasy in which he gave a handout to Claude, who had at last overreached himself; in this vision the boss wore the remnants of his grand attire, there were bird-droppings on his hatbrim, and his boutonniere was moulting.

He didn't hear Genevieve's return. She just suddenly shouted from the other room: "It's all right for tonight, if you don't mind a chaperone."

Oh, you're kidding, said Reinhart, half to himself, but of course nobody ever is.

Chapter 10

Nothing, thought Reinhart, better confirms the integrity of body and soul than a warm bath. He lay back in the one he had just drawn, his privates floating, a cool drip from one tap tickling his left foot and a hot one from the other Chinese-torturing his right—just the proper stimulation; even in a bath the world must be remembered. Maw had been kind to let him use her facilities, for he was no longer a resident of the house and while his own had no tub, it did offer a Navy surplus shower in a stainless steel stall, more than adequate for shedding the dirt though of course deficient in the values of the heart.

Strange how hot water would cool you in June. Even stranger to him was the presence of June itself; no sooner had he got his civilian hide covered with spring clothes than he must strip them off and buy summer garb, for by June Ohio was a second Tunisia, just as it had been Baffin Land in the winter. For a third oddity, this problem of attire had given Reinhart far more difficulty than certain other phenomena of the same period, namely: marriage, change of domicile, return to college, and the pregnancy of his wife. Soon to be twenty-two, he was delighted he could still learn from experience: in this case, that life's big things, at least as a civilian, are subservient to the small. Who could ever know before the fact that a shrunken seersucker would claim a man's mind while his seed lay germinating in the belly of his Mrs.?

(Which is what he got some perverse pleasure in calling his mate, aping the local butcher, a common man in extremis and a great fecund bull who had fathered eight children on a wife no bigger than five-one.)

"Boy," sweetly called Maw from the hall outside, "are you enjoying your warshing up?"

"Plenty, Maw," said Reinhart, raising and lowering a sopping washrag to make a liquid noise for her benefit.

"Do, boy, do, and when you're dry come out and I'll fry you a pork chop."

"Better give me a rain check on the chop, Maw. The Mrs. will be expecting me home for lunch."

"I'll just stick it between two slabs of bread as a sammidge," Maw said, and stole away.

Now there was another singularity to add to the list. Maw had taken on this new, beneficent character from the moment Reinhart had revealed to her his having taken a Frau. It upset all the theories about mother versus wife; Maw not only *loved* her daughter-in-law but liked her son for the first time within his memory. He regretted now that he had not let her in on his getting married before it had been a fact accomplished, but immediate relatives were so inconsistent. He supposed his father-in-law's to be the more predictable reaction; the man had first threatened to murder him unless the marriage were annulled, and then when it was made known that a portion of Reinhart's essence was already inextricably deposited within the body of his darling daughter, he determined to commit homicide on the instant, ran to fetch a weapon while Reinhart stood paralyzed and the females wailed, found a souvenir Samurai sword, and charged the usurper, whom he would certainly have run through had not Reinhart's dear wife-of-one-hour thrown herself in front of hubby, offering her own breasts as target. Reinhart would never forget that gesture, and fell in love with her on the moment, as he had never been able to, despite frantic efforts, before. "You're saved, thug," said his dad-in-law, dropping the blade forthwith, the gilded tassels unraveling from its grip. "But I'll never like you."

Knowing his hand would be spurned, Reinhart did not put it out, but stated in amelioration: "What a nice sword! Where did you buy it, sir?"

Reinhart's new relative was a beastly handsome man with wide shoulders, narrow waist, and a copper suntan already in April; he had the barber cut him bald, and his eyes were the lead-gray of a bullet. He said; "That saber is mine. As a U.S. Marine I took if off a monkey Jap after giving him three slugs in the gut. Then I busted out his front teeth, which were gold, had them strung on a chain, and brought them home as a

147

necklace for my baby girl—the one you violated, Mr. Nobody."

"Reinhart," said Nobody. Something impelled him to smile with an open mouth, though he closed it soon enough when he saw Mr. Raven's interest in his oral architecture.

"You're safe on that count," said his enemy. "There's no jewelry in silver fillings." He clenched his own cruel teeth, meaning levity.

"Oh Blaine!" whined Reinhart's mother-in-law, a thin woman pale as putty, who leaned in a phthisic slump against the foyer wall beneath one of those feather-pictures of a multicolored bird. "Promise me there'll be no violence."

"I'll presume, but never promise," said Mr. Raven. He retrieved his sword, sank it into the tin scabbard he had dropped against the baseboard on his charge, and saying "Genevieve, I'll talk to you in my study," gave them his hard back.

Yes, Reinhart had wedded his colleague Genevieve Raven, who now turned, brushing him with her round behind, and said: "You see, Daddy isn't so bad."

Spend eighteen years remarkable for their lack of event, then have everything happen in the next four. As a high-school punk Reinhart had envisioned having a million at twenty-two, a princess as lover, and the Medal of Honor, yet he had never expected to be married: we daydream glories, not obligations. He had also looked forward to fathering illegitimate issue by the basketfuls, replicas of himself whom he would come upon in mythic ways later in life: "I was born in an orphan asylum, sir, but I feel a curious affinity with you." His bastards would all be athletes and ballerinas, and he would gather them around him to sweeten his still-unmarried dotage.

Reinhart lay his head back upon the cold rim of the tub and hissed to represent the piercing of this sophomoric bubble. Obviously, he was less than desolate at the puncture, but was cautious about calling himself happy, fearing hubris as he had been taught to by his father. It so happened that Genevieve had been a virgin at the moment of truth. He was the one man in the world who could claim to know her as Jacob did Rachel. This was anything but sexy, in his old definition of that quality, but then it was possible he had been hideously wrong about sex ever since puberty, seeing it, pre-Genevieve, as naturally illegal. Just as when as a small boy he would not believe people really did anything in that line—they maybe kissed and looked at each other's parts—when a large boy he thought only married people didn't do it, their mutual possession being recorded with the city clerk and in no need of

148

further proof. Wedded intercourse was so obscene that the language, rich in fornications and adulteries, had no word for it; husbands and wives probably kissed and looked at each other's parts. It was too humiliating to think that a little creature could result from the sport pursued in the back seat of parked cars; and you *slept* with a woman only to keep warm.

In a word, Genevieve had made him a man; with her he *made love* for the first time in his life, as opposed to mere screwing, although he didn't actually *love* her until she defended him from her father. The distinctions were very clear to him as he squeezed the suds from the washcloth onto his shoulders, counted one-two-three until they crawled to the center of his vertebral column, and then brought the brush into play. Consonant with his present mood, in which the commonplace was strange and wonderful (rather then merely sinister, as he usually saw it), he was struck by the circumstances that one owns a back from birth to grave, yet never sees it. Likewise with one's face!

"How about a nice glass of Mr. Ochsenaugen's homemade grape wine?" asked Maw, again prowling outside the door. "Betty O. whom you always thought was cute, still unmarried, crushed the grapes with her feet last September."

"Maw!" shouted Reinhart in the basso given him by the tub, "you advocating strong drink?" Which of old had followed sex on her list of prohibitions, no doubt because it was conducive to sex.

"A married man," said Maw, "needs his strength."

That seemed rather dirty to her son, who heard her set the glass against the door and give a warning to look for it on his exit.

"Phew," Maw said. "What a hot day! This weather must be killing that poor little thing." By which she meant Genevieve, who was short but most sturdy and far from feeble, though it was true that as a woman in her second month she took things easy, on doctor's advice and with husband's blessing. Maw, however, believed it was one month, only the Raven family knowing that sin had preceded sanction, so she went on to envy Genevieve's luck in being delivered next January.

"Don't count your Reinharts before they're hatched," Reinhart almost said but checked himself. He had just returned from Psych class at the university and was overconscious of instances of concealed hostility in his speech. Certainly he didn't wish to curse his own barely formed embryo somewhere deep in Gen's linings, signals from which he believed he had received last night with his ear at her still-small belly. He had heard tiny chirps and though it was probably ludicrous to

149

interpret them as "Daddy" peeped by a fledgling, neither did he hold with Gen's own theory of mere digestive adjustments —wives, he learned, can be extraordinarily antiromantic.

Like a hippopotamus, Reinhart settled on the bottom of the tub until, at one end, only his eyes and nose broke water. Twenty minutes later he emerged and lumbered into the closet, trailed by a fluid spoor. Since his accident with the bathroom supplies they had been rearranged and some staple items—*viz.*, the surplus toilet paper—taken to the basement cupboard, so the pleasure of his present encounter with the linen store was unalloyed: he seized a thick towel and polished his buff to euphoria. A full-length mirror on the inside of the closet door suggested stocktaking, and he did not flee from it, but with a curtailment of breath drew much of his fat up under the ribs and, ignoring what remained, pronounced himself "on the way back," for being a conservative, he believed that perfection had existed at some past time and that true success was invariably retrograde. On the other hand, he disapproved of childhood as it was manifested by your standard American kid, and looked forward to bringing up his own offspring with just severity, relieved by arbitrary instances of massive kindness, *de haut en bas*: "You don't deserve it, but I have bought you a pony."

As an example of the change in his own parent, when he left the bathroom and disremembering the glass of Ochsenaugen '46 propped against the door, kicked it across the hall runner, Maw came grinning with a wet sponge and chortled: "Glad it was of the white and not the red, or it would look as if a person died here of hemorrhage."

Later, having pressed the pork-chop sandwich upon him— having kindly removed the rib, though until he was halfway through he chewed with care, and then in the last mouthful grated terribly on a sizable fragment of bone—Maw reminisced over her own cup of coffee.

"You yourself were never what anybody called a cute baby. You were inclined to make the darndest pickle-face when anybody tried to be nice, and would make funny sounds at them when no more than fifteen months. I forgot when it was you began to defy me, but it was soon." She swallowed and hastened to correct a false impression: "Not that I'm criticizing, mind you. Maybe you'll have better luck with yours. Anyway, when I recall you as a tiny kid, with your mop of yellow hair, I always see you sitting on your little throne. I guess you can't remember that cunning little potty-chair with its rack of beads on the front for the child to toy with while he was doing his business, which you'll find out quick enough that while it seems a simple thing to ask, no kid will be good about it. Any-

150

way, you would have sat there all day if I left you, just running those red-and-blue beads back and forth like an idiot." She quacked with laughter and asked: "Were you counting them?"

"I guess so," said Reinhart, whom nothing could harm nowadays. It seemed an eon since he had got home from the Army and wanted something to do; on the other hand, the time had gone by very quickly. Husband, householder, student, and in the afternoons he still worked for Humbold, which is how he had got the Quonset hut in Vetsville for Gen, the germinating seed, and himself. Twenty-five a week from Claude, ninety fish a month from the GI Bill—in the aggregate, not enough for better quarters. Not that he himself required better—he was delighted with the tin domicile, thinking of it as a kind of amateur clubhouse where camping was a lark.

"What will you call it?" asked Maw, at the sink, where with running water and two fingers she swabbed out her cup. "I still got the name-book your aunt gave me when I carried you, if you can use it. As it happened, I never, liking 'Carl.' Haven't you ever wondered how it got the o? Blame it on your Dad, who claimed to have had a great-uncle in Germany who wrote poetry, was an anarchist, and committed the Dutch act at twenty-two. That man was named Karl, and Dad wanted to make a difference between him and you even if you turned out to sound Italian."

"A poet?" asked Reinhart with a great surge of heart, after the quick passing of a shadow from it: in one month he would reach the age at which Uncle checked out.

"Blew out his brains," said Maw. "No doubt over some illicit romance."

"I wish I had known that when I was in Germany looking for relatives."

"Oh, Dad would never tell you that. He's not one to embarrass a fellow. So don't let on you know."

Neither would Reinhart let on to Maw that Genevieve always called him, with her intuitive tact, by the poet's name. Anyway, she and Maw, while each professed frequent concern for the other, seldom met. Gen had come to his parents' home once, got immediately ill on the glass of Ochsenaugen '46 served by his father as cocktail, and spent the rest of the evening in the bathroom. Maw had yet to visit Vetsville.

"Well, this was very nice." Reinhart pushed away his plate of crusts (he had never eaten one since the night he saw Officer Capek reject them; as in the case of the butcher, he nowadays selected normal men to emulate). "And thanks too for the bath, which hits the spot in weather like this."

151

"Any time," said Maw. "You know the old homestead door is always open for the return of the prodigal. And by the way, I asked my roomer to leave."

"Emmet Swain?" asked Reinhart. "But why, now that I'm no longer here?"

"That's just the point—so's you can visit overnight if need be."

He took his seersucker jacket from the back of a kitchen chair. "Maw, I seldom get your logic though I don't question your intentions. But I've got to go now. The Mrs. will have lunch waiting—"

"I'm sure she'll have a nicer one than I could give you."

"—and then I must get to work. By the way, Claude sends his regards."

Maw opened the front door and spread-eagled herself against it. "That man is a genius. I'm sure glad you decided to stay with him even though going back to college, and I'm certain that poor little thing misses *her* job there, which she quit, though I expect she has more than enough to do around the house all day. Does she do a lot of warshing, boy?"

"Lots," said Reinhart over his shoulder, as he descended the porch steps. Which reminded him that he must stop at the laundry and pick up a bundle.

"My God," shouted Maw, "you're already sweat through the back of your coat again. One thing, though, it must take off a lot of lard."

Reinhart admitted as much and got in behind the wheel of the office automobile, Claude's Gigantic, which he used for everything these days just as if it belonged to him, but drove on its own terms, the car having from long service with the boss acquired a soul. Thus it testily slammed its own door now and began to edge away from the curb before Reinhart was quite set; nor did it honor the stop sign at the next corner, but blasted through with a groan of the horn. To the nearby cop Reinhart helplessly showed his imitation of Claude's one-finger salute, which was accepted and returned.

As it happened, Reinhart's home was the very same hut that his first clients, the Clendellans, had vacated in favor of the Onion. They had left behind a box of newspapers, a broken alarm clock, a bottle of sour milk, and a ripped canvas chair. All of which might still be found, by the curious, in the high grass of the back yard, except that the milk bottle had broken when Genevieve pitched it out the window. For she too had altered. So neat, so deft, so competent as a maiden, as a wife Gen verged on the slatternly, there was no denying it—nor did she try to, but smiled lazily at the mess in the kitchen sink, threw the magazines from couch to floor, lay down and regarded expressionlessly the corrugated vault of the roof, sighing now and again in stupefied contentment while Reinhart rolled up his sleeves and got after the dishes, which was no more than fair since he had also prepared the meal that soiled them.

It had been April 1, Reinhart's patron-day, that marked the point of departure for everybody's way of life. As they left Claude's office at five-ten that afternoon, the secretary said: "Look, I'll make it simple and meet you at the Orpheum at seven twenty-nine."

"But why?" asked Reinhart, wincing as a drop of liquid fell from the sky onto his forehead. Looking aloft for the malicious starling, he discovered that it had instead been and was indeed a light rain, which increased while he watched.

Instantly encasing her head in a collapsible cellophane hood which she had drawn from a tiny sort of cartridge case on her charm bracelet, left wrist, Genevieve replied—

But Reinhart hastily explained: "I mean, I'll get my father's car and pick you up at home, like a decent human being."

"Oh no you won't," was what Genevieve had silently mouthed during his speech and now pronounced aloud while reversing her coat, which proved to be waterproof gabardine on the other side. A kind of compact case, from her purse, yielded abbreviated rubber caps for the toes of her shoes.

"Here," said Reinhart, offering his arm for her to hold while she put them on.

"You'll use any excuse for contact, huh?" She supported herself on Claude's front window, leaving a tiny handprint, very clear, for she was exquisitely made. "I *told* you about Daddy. Do you *want* to provoke him?"

"This is to be done on the sneak, is that it?" She couldn't be touched; he couldn't show his face at her house; he anticipated a great evening. "All I propose to do is take you to the movies."

"Oh yeah?" leered Genevieve from her glassine cowl, like a Martian nun. She saw her bus approaching the corner, and squished towards it without another word.

"Are you kidding?" Reinhart asked his reflection in the plate glass.

But at seven fifteen he stood before the the only movie theater in his suburb, on which they had stuck a tiled entranceway, like a great blue urinal, while he was abroad. BEST YEARS OF YOR LIE, said the marquee, which evidently was still being mounted by the same witty or illiterate manager. Reinhart had gone there for years to see Cark Garble, Betty Grabble, and other celluloid celebrities. From a somnolent woman encased

153

in glass he bought two tickets bearing the legend (for he was the kind of fellow who in idle moments read all such): "We reserve the right to change the price of admission without notice." Thus they could outwit a degenerate with only thirty-five cents to his name, or a parsimonious one, but apparently they had stopped using it against Negroes, for Reinhart saw two go in, looking clean and grateful.

He inspected the glossy stills of a coming attraction, which had also got confused. One caption read: "He had the face of a boy, the lusts of a man, and the body of an animal"; yet the photograph above it showed a well-known actress in regal attire.

"Guy," said a nasty voice nearby, which sounded as if it had bad breath. "You Carl?"

A teen-aged boy-man, with the face of an animal and the hair to go with it, stood beside him, tall as he though fearfully thin. Reinhart was restrained from arbitrarily kicking him into the street only by a habit of seldom acting on hateful impulses, as well as a certain pity: the poor boy had a forehead of vile pimples.

Suffering a poignant recall of himself in that state, Reinhart said in a fine equilibrium between benevolence and distaste, "What is it, son?"

The kid jerked a thumb over his left shoulder and slunk nihilistically through the glass door into the lobby. Receptive even to the most unlikely commands, Reinhart trailed him. The remodelers hadn't yet reached the interior: it was still Bagdad in the time of the more sensual caliphs, though the ticket-taker at the harem portal was dressed more like a corporal in the Austrian hussars. Under a false little stucco balcony with closed shutters, from which hung a fringed shawl embroidered in Arabic runes, next which began a series of those Moslem windows with frames like parentheses, except that they were not in this case windows but rather niches holding jugs more than large enough to accommodate Ali Baba and figured like so many paisley neckties—under the balcony, the punk stopped, cleared the lank hair from his eyes with a spastic movement of his entire body, entended a bony paw and said: "Tickets."

When Reinhart gave him only raised eyebrows, the kid directed a high-pressure stream of saliva between his own shoes and read his forehead welts in Braille, to see if he had lost any. Then he faced the shawl and howled directly into it: "Ain't got!" And who should step out from behind the fringe than Genevieve Raven.

To the punk she said: "All clear?" His neck flexible as a hose, he sank his head to the center of his chest and grunted.

154

Genevieve then addressed Reinhart: "What does he mean you haven't got the tickets?"

He mutely showed the two pasteboards.

"Just go back now and get one for yourself." She snatched them from his hand, and followed by the skinny simian, was admitted to the inner mosque by the hussar, who once the tapestried door closed behind them, said accusingly to Reinhart: "Don't you know that kid is banned from this theater for life?"

"I don't even know who he is."

The doorman, really too young for the hussars, revealed that he went to high school during the daylight hours, where Kenworthy Raven, Genevieve's brother, was his classmate. "And a real criminal," he added.

"Well," said Reinhart, "you let him in."

"Jesus," answered the doorman, who was undersized, "I'd rather get fired than try to stop him. He made a pair of lead knuckles in manual training."

Having reticketed himself and gained entry to the auditorium, Reinhart went in search of his charges. He found Genevieve sitting by herself, one place in from his favorite seat on the aisle. The latter she very prettily invited him to take, removing from it a pale-lavender bolero jacket and a pair of white gloves. For a second he saw the sheen of her knee, as she crossed legs and accidentally kicked his calf. By these visual rewards he was compensated for the loss of Kenworthy, whom he had been planning joyfully to encounter now that he had his number. Reinhart detested fresh kids.

Genevieve laid a hand into the bend of his elbow. "I'm sorry but I told you we'd have to have a chaperone. I know you think Kenny is just awful."

"Not in the least," said Reinhart. "I was beginning to get rather fond of him. Where did he go?"

"He saw some of his friends down front and went to join them. They will probably make noise and be put out. Then he'll get home before I do and when I arrive there won't be heck to pay. But I don't mind being reckless in a good cause." Genevieve squeezed Reinhart's elbow, but when he moved to capture the flexing hand, she quickly retracted it, saying, "Down, boy" and making a remonstrating moue.

Now Reinhart had long noticed that he frequently ran into situations that were always one step ahead of him; by the time he met a challenge, it had passed and his response was obsolete for the next. Small wonder he was always weary. On the other hand, when with Negroes, a grave and careful people, he tended towards the headlong. His big problem was not a career or love, but a matter of timing. His quest, of course, remained: freedom. And the way to it was tortuous because as yet he could not define the nature of his captivity, let alone identify the chief warden, though naturally he knew as well as anybody that we are our own jailors.

"So you weren't kidding about your father?" he noted to Genevieve. "What do you suppose is wrong with him?"

"Why, nothing at all. What a horrible thing to infer!"

"I'm sorry," said Reinhart, as an obese woman with a great head of hair chose the seat in front of him. "I didn't necessarily mean he was depraved."

"*Necessarily?*" said Genevieve. "And *I'm* the one who is supposed to be insidious."

"Invidious," said Reinhart. "Forget it."

"Anyway, what should I care about your opinion? He's my father, not yours."

"True." It occurred to him on their first date they were already arguing like man and wife.

"I realize now what I missed before, because I didn't know you well enough at that time." Genevieve tapped his wrist with a sharp nail. "Mister, you hate love."

"Me?" asked Reinhart in some outrage. One of the many conveniences provided for the patrons of this threater was the Expanso-seat, which did what its name implied on application of the sitter's rump, the seatback encroaching on the leg room of the person behind. Reinhart's kneebones were being crushed and his view was blocked by the woman's Watusi hair, and when he said "Me?" she turned and went "Ssh!" To which he agilely rejoined: "Ladies are please requested to move their heads so as not to cause an annoyance to those behind."

Genevieve, the monomaniac, ignored this exchange, saying: "Yes, you. You are cold, selfish, and vile."

"I'll be damned," whispered Reinhart. "I'm always falling in love."

"Oh, Carl!" Presently his forearm was being massaged by her left breast as she clove to him in the maximum degree allowed by the seat, whose expansible feature worked only from front to rear. And the last thing he saw as the house lights were extinguished in favor of a strident newsreel, was the pink flower of her lips, shaping to whisper in return: "I do, too."

He wished to monkey with nobody's affections, but being in a mistaken relation of love was a damned sight preferable to exchanging piques. Soon his arm was around her, fingers playing slow piano on her ribs, and they were temple to temple. Not even the perversity of the main attraction (an item about several unfortunate veterans, e.g., a cuckold, a guy without hands, etc., and their re-encounter with civil life; typically, the cuckold responds to his plight with melancholy irony, but the maimed chap, whom the VA fits out with a pair of hooks, disembowels a barroom fascist who criticizes Russia), not even this curious entertainment soured his pleasure in close-quartering with a girl for the first time in half a year. He realized he should do this more often; funny how you forget.

Funnier that Kenworthy and his gang of louts went unheard from for the duration of the film. If essential things often slipped from Reinhart's memory, it was nevertheless first-rate on incidentals: he never, for example, forgot a burning cigarette left on the dresser edge. Perhaps a scientist was what he had been cut out to be, and not a poet. Anyway, he was enormously stimulated by a handful of woman and led to expect the imminent coincidence of his aspirations and capabilities. As to Genevieve, she ardently surrendered herself to the movie, taking certain emotions from the actors' surplus and making them her own with readjustments in her clinch with the ex-corporal—paradoxically torturing him with an elbow when the adulterers appeared, though the *wife* was the real miscreant; pinching his wrist on account of the disabled vet, with whose nurselike girl friend she seemed to identify; and so on though never uttering a word, which omission would never make Reinhart complain, for if anybody peeved him, it was that individual who talks during a performance.

All too soon were the house lights illuminated in the brutal transition from reel life to real life, showing the latter as very sleazy: the aisles were runways of waste paper, Reinhart's left oxford was secured to the floor by a wad of chewing gum, and Genevieve's mascara had run so that her eyes looked hollow and feverish. At some instance of corn she had wept, unnoticed by him. So he withheld certain corrosive judgments he otherwise would have made on *The Best Years of Your Lie,* and merely said, simultaneously getting after the chewing gum with a wooden ice-cream spoon he had freed from the discarded container in which it was wound—this item from beneath the stout lady's chair—he said: "Now let's go and have a drink."

"Oh, I never," answered Genevieve. "I would never drink unless maybe an Orange Blossom or a champagne cocktail, and I haven't had *that* since after the senior prom. Anyway, we can't go with Kenny to a place where liquor is sold."

"You don't really mean that your brother"—they were ascending the aisle, and Reinhart noticed that a paper napkin was stuck onto his sole; he had not eradicated the gum; and certain blanched faces at seat level were smirking at his flapping foot—"Kenworthy doesn't really have to go along with us?"

"Carl," said Genevieve at the lobby crossroads where they

prepared to separate for their respective washrooms, "we must get this straight. I have certain obligations to my family. Now you might not like them—the obligations, I mean, though it could also extend to the family—and you're not required to. But anyway I wish you would take the whole thing seriously, and I'll do the same for you, and that puts any relationship on a firm footing. Marriages might be made in heaven, but they have their feet on the earth."

Reinhart was proud to be seen with the trim girl who, finishing her statement, gave him the bolreo jacket to hold and went to wash her hands. That much was established; whether or not she was nuts was probably a meaningless issue. He questioned the sanity of too many people. It was more than likely that he went by an obsolete standard. Besides, proximity to her for hours in the dark had left him unconscionably horny; and you cannot seriously study the essence of a person you mean to devour.

Desire was in sole possession of his heart and made him so impatient that he refused to wait out the queue of swarthy men before the urinals. Instead, he wet his fingers at the basin and ran them through his hair in lieu of the comb he never remembered to carry because of the many years he had been crew-cut. The mirror told him that if anything he had gained a pound or two since the last assessment. His collar, a hair's breadth too tight, kept a good deal of red in the parts above his neck. In everything but height he had begun strongly to resemble his father. Shaken by this realization, he felt an instant loss of concupiscence, and wondered in terror what he could do with Genevieve if laying her was overruled.

A temporary expedient was soon at hand: he waited, first for her to come from the Ladies', which took a good twenty minutes; then for a decision on the matter of the missing Kenworthy, which consumed another half hour and required two trips by himself to the area of the theater where the boy had last been seated, namely, five rows from the screen (on which the giants of the feature were again stalking). On the second of these expeditions an usher, taking him for one of those fiends who wander the aisle in search of little girls, or in flight from them, ordered the ex-corporal to void the auditorium.

"We can't just abandon him!" wailed Gen, when Reinhart returned to her central intelligence station in the outer lobby.

"Nor can you and I stand here all night. It's now eleven thirty."

"Good gravy, and I've got to be home by twelve."

Even at this grievous juncture Reinhart almost said "no kidding" again—there were states of soul in which he would have

158

asked it of a headhunter with a knife at his jugular—but he overpowered his own demon, grasped her (or hers) by the arm, and marched them both to the parking lot.

Always be sure you're right, then forge ahead; Reinhart really lived by such maxims, though he couldn't remember which had been told Edison by his mother and which by Steinmetz to his cigar. Resolution for once triumphed: Genevieve went unprotesting, and once in the car she pounced upon the radio dials and forced them to yield some dreamy music. Already had a miracle come to pass; the auto was Reinhart's dad's and the superheterodyne had been out of whack since November 1938.

"What's your idea of a good place?" asked Reinhart in guilty urgency, for at the edge of the lot, beside an ancient heap without fenders, he had spotted the S-shaped figures of a number of the young, among whom was surely the estimable Kenworthy. They were snorting vilely. Indeed, how strange that Gen had not noticed; but he quickly fired up the Chevy's engine and in first gear it roared like a bomber. "There's," he cried, as he also had to shout down the radio, "there's Fischel's and The Bohemian Garden, or that place with the gilded carriage on the roof. But those date from before the war and I've been away a long time."

"I'm hardly an authority on roadhouses," murmured Genevieve, who with her head on the seatback and closed eyes had been making the hum that Reinhart took for subtle static. "But in the way of swanky bars I've heard Daddy say nothing can touch The Roost."

"On top of the Wexler Hotel, in the city? It will take a half hour just to get there." In the rear-vision mirror he saw the punks' car back immoderately from its slot and follow his; though this may have been coincidental. "I thought you had to be home at twelve?"

"As long as we're in Dutch anyway , might as well do it up brown."

Reinhart's financial resources would hardly permit more than beige; he had five dollars, less three thirty-five centses: for practical purposes, a good four clams. Yet he headed reckless for the highway towards the city, being a veteran of World II with service overseas. The fenderless specimen full of teen-agers took the same route, a block behind. But when Reinhart lost to the next red light, the other vehicle drew up squealing to parallel his and a boy with the face of a rotten banana, half skinned, hung out the window, saying: "Wanta race, Fat?"

"There's where Kenworthy went," Reinhart told Gen.

"Oh-oh," she groaned. "Now you're in for it."

On orange, the punks accelerated through the crossing.

"He didn't like you. He took offense," she went on. "Which I was afraid of, frankly. You should have had his ticket ready when you met us. Turn right, here, and we'll go to The Roost next time.

Reinhart dramatically outthrust his chin though his stomach wasn't fooled for a minute. "If you think a bunch of kids are going to have any effect on what I do or don't—Genevieve, a man can't let himself be bullied!"

"Who's the bully?" asked Gen. "When you must weigh two hundred and fifty and he is sixteen."

Just as he feared, when the punks some hundred yards ahead saw there would be no contest, they skidded to a halt astride the centerline and waited for him to catch up. He did so in a whining second gear, gunning into high when he reached the other driver's blind spot. At its moment of stress the Chevy belched stertorously, and crosseyed with rage Reinhart choked it too ardently, inundating the engine with gasoline, on which it drowned. Collateral with the rear right window of the other car, he was threatened by one of Kenworthy's henchmen: "We're going to get you, fella."

Now Reinhart suddenly passed into a state of clam. "Why?" he asked simply, the corners of his mouth dropping like an old hound's.

"Just a minute, fella," warned the kid, a type even more scurvy than Gen's brother, his neck the diameter of Reinhart's wrist, his murky eyes ringed black from onanism. "One minute, Mac, don't get wise with me."

Genevieve was poking Reinhart's arm. "Be tolerant, Carl. They belong to the wartime generation who have lost their roots. Kenny!" she shouted. "You go on home!"

"Up yours," someone cried back.

"Look," said Reinhart, "you still haven't answered my question. Why do you want to bother us?"

The boy imitated Frankenstein's synthetic head. *"Because . . . you . . . are . . . a . . . jerk."*

"He's got you there," Gen whispered giggling.

Reinhart wondered how Claude Humbold would have replied to such provocation: probably *a priori*, like all men of force; he would never have got into the situation. Meanwhile, such traffic as there was had to go into the left-hand lane to pass them; this included an occasional interstate truck, manned by a brawny driver. No sooner had Reinhart become twenty than everybody started to fear teen-agers. Somehow *he* always managed to miss the power as it was transferred from hand to hand; he might as well have been a rickety runt weighing one-twenty, for his only weapon was guile.

They lay off the bow of a roadside hamburger joint, which was built in simulation of a battleship, with porthole windows and dummy cannon. Foul weather flags hung like drying underwear across its superstructure: each sent a riotous message about another type of sandwich, with two left over for french fries and cole slaw.

"Let's pull in here," said Reinhart to his second-closest adversary (counting Gen as the first). He pointed to the asphalt ocean surrounding the ship, managed to start his own motor, and led the way before anybody could say Frig you.

"Listen," he said to Genevieve as the boys pulled in. "I want you to do something for me. Get your brother out of that car for a few minutes, using any pretext. Either that, or you get in with them. And I'm not kidding."

When her little nose began to twitch, he held up a fist, a symbol of some menace that he had not yet worked out, but she fell for it and called to her brother across him: "You come here and get your allowance, Kenny. It slipped Daddy's mind."

Kenworthy emerged from the other car like an unreeling hose. In a slow wink Reinhart was also out of his. They passed each other with sneers. The punks showed their weapons as Reinhart reached the driver: Stillsons, tire irons, etc.; with comparable armament we might have retained Corregidor.

"I ain't gonna hoit youse," said Reinhart, approximately; he also lowered his voice to a hooligan growl; this was the kind of delivery that impressed young people, who are ever seeking models. It would, however, take a while with these; meanwhile, they were derisive with their front teeth. The driver, who at least had a short haircut and a thick neck, seemed the best bet.

Reinhart went to the far side and, leaning in the window, appealed to him check-by-jowl: "I'm surprised at you guys running with Raven. You don't know about him?"

"Clobber the slob, Bob," urged the skinny kid in rear right, with the venom of the undersized.

But as Reinart had anticipated, the whisper of doubt had already damaged Kenworthy's reputation with the stocky driver, who thereby proved he was normal as he looked.

"Whadduh mean, whadduh you mean?" he howled at Reinhart and ordered his friends to pipe down.

"Frankly," said Reinhart, "I thought you were a bunch of fruits—"

"Listen, man—"

"—until I saw how manly you all look, smoking cigarettes."
He glanced at his own car and saw Gen doing a good job of

retaining Kenworthy. "Then I figured you just didn't know."

"Aw, we know he got clapped up," said one of them.

Reinhart concentrated on the driver. "Well, to make a long story short, Raven is what you call a transvestite."

"What's that?" asked one ferret face.

"Morphadike," explained the driver with a self-satisfied grimace. "You're shit, too, man. I happen to know he likes his ass. Morphadike, huh? Got both kinds of plumbing, huh? You're crap, Mac."

"There ain't no such thing" said the smallest punk.

"Naw," Reinhart said. "What I mean is a guy who puts on girl's clothes whenever he gets a chance."

"Aw," sickly laughed the driver, "that was just in the junior play."

Wonderful the way nature anticipated art. Reinhart had chosen this perversion at random.

"Exactly! And after rehearsals he didn't take them off but wore them around the house, so that it became a scandal in the neighborhood. His sister just told me they might have to put him away; all her underwear is missing."

The smallest boy held out longest, saying: "You just want to get into her pants, Fatso!"

"No," said Reinhart with a hollow laugh, "Kenworthy does, if you get what I mean."

"What do you know," the driver muttered, cocking his head. "Much obliged, fellow. We'll get him. We always guard the honor of the gang."

"Yes," Reinhart agreed. "That kind of member lowers the tone. People are pointing your way already."

The driver stared with blank eyes. "I told you we'd get him, fellow..

"O.K.," said Reinhart, "no offense, Chief." Once again he passed Kenworthy, this time with the springy step of a man who has done the worst he could do to another. On the other hand, Kenworthy already seemed to feel better about him, giving Reinhart the shoulder-twitch and slack tongue that signified tolerance in his jargon.

"You owe me five dollars," said Genevieve as he got in beside her.

"But I must say that you apparently handled it well, for there they go." The teen-ager's vehicle roared off the asphalt onto the open highway, with neither backfire nor blue exhaust (they are always ace mechanics).

"Yes, if I do say so myself." Reinhart was careful to turn his smirk after the vanishing car.

"My brother, poor boy, has many pressures on him. Daddy,

so markedly preferring me, is sometimes unfair to Kenny."

"He seems to give a fair allowance. For God's sake, five bucks," said Reinhart, getting back to normal. He started the engine, praying that its wheeze owed to the common cold rather than a lethal malady.

"Oh, that." She giggled conspiratorially, her true allegiance not clear to Reinhart. "*I* usually give him that, and *say* it comes from Daddy. But what I mean is Daddy kids him awfully about playing a girl in the school play, and then in addition he has those pimples."

"Haven't we all, metaphorically speaking?" Reinhart answered, in an effort to ignore his growing feelings of sonbitchery. He pulled out of range of the mock cannon and on the highway turned back in the direction whence they had come. "No night club tonight, Genevieve. I haven't got but four dollars to my name. I'm sorry if you didn't have a good time."

She clutched at his wrist, causing the car to swerve across a stretch of gravel shoulder and a motorist behind to make his horn go *Waa-waa*. Reinhart missed the other driver's dirty look, though, for he was watching Genevieve cry into a balled Kleenex: She wiped her eyes and added: "Don't you think?"

Reinhart stopped his vehicle, for they had been running along the shoulder, scattering gravel. His lust had turned to melancholia. "Here's all I want to say, Gen: did you ever think about time? Isn't it fascinating? Look at the second hand on your watch, the way it races around the dial ticking off one precious moment after the next."

"I should have been home hours ago," she murmured, and smiled hurtfully at the corners of her nose.

"Ah, and then what? Lie in bed and look at the stars so many light years away from us, and think what a small thing is human life and what fools we are to make so much of it. I mean the kind of person who saves something for decades and decades expecting to use it to the best advantage at some future time, but one day dies missing the point."

"Not me," she said, cheering up. "I can never keep a cent".

"Are you religious?" asked Reinhart, being careful not to touch her, and she had let his arm go when he stopped the automobile.

Genevieve gasped, and said: "You're not a Catholic?"

"Not me", Reinhart rejoined.

"Well because I was going to say—"

"I read a quotation by George Bernard Shaw that went like this: Use yourself up, so that when you die there's nothing left but an empty husk to bury."

She leaned against her door and said: "My, aren't we being ghoulish? You know what I thought? That you stopped here to try and kiss me. That would surely be rather bold, with the traffic going by. Most boys would drive up to Cherry Wood and park on that road going to the abandoned quarry, where the cops never come."

Reinhart supposed it was no use; nobody ever listened to him. He returned the car to the highway and tried again, keeping his eyes on the centerline: "Many of the things we attach an enormous importance to really amount to nothing in the long run. The regret in later years is not that you gave yourself, but that you didn't give enough."

"Better slow down if you want to make that right turn," said Genevieve, who had tucked her legs under her bottom on the seat and sat facing him by three-quarters.

Hard after the turn he had to shift into second, to meet a considerable upgrade. He was appalled by the whining of the gears, and tired in his argument to sound another note: "There's no reason in our day and age for a young, intelligent, vigorous person to protect . . ." (he was hindered here by a deficiency of the language, and not wanting objectively to tip his hand, was forced to choose a collective) *"themself* against experience. Isn't it silly to fear what is natural and as old as life itself?" The last was of course rhetorical and he did not look for her reaction, having anyway to watch where they were materially going: up a forested slope void of houses and streetlamps, and his headlights were guttering.

He began to doubt that Genevieve could cope with any degree of subtlety. From the corner of his eye he saw her peering through the windshield at the profound night twelve feet beyond the radiator ornament.

"Could you put on the brights?" she asked.

Silently he tripped the floor switch, and the lights went out absolutely. In a similar movement he brought back what they had, whether brights or dims, and gained the crest. Most of the town, many little glows, was now contained by the rear-vision mirror, and fixed Reinhart's position in space, the sky being starless.

"Guinevere," said Reinhart, and caught himself; whenever he tried to make himself understood, he thought irrelevantly of King Arthur. "Genevieve—"

"I guess it's left here." Her finger pointed at his nose.

He bumped along a homemade lane of mud wallows, and a kind of buffalo trail, saying absently: "Your house is certainly remote." Creeping through the black forest, again in second gear, he became desperate.

"Gen, I don't want you to think I'm just coarse. I know

164

every guy gives a pretty girl a line, and I don't blame you for being careful. But when two people are attracted to each other and do nothing about it, I believe the situation becomes psychopathic." He and a rabbit in the road ahead saw each other and were mutually startled, though the animal leaped higher; "Huh, you live in a real wilderness."

"You better not go much farther," said Genevieve, whispering though he saw no house from which she could be overheard by her old man. "Or you'll run into the quarry."

"The quarry?" He stopped the engine and was buffeted weak by the stillness. "This is Cherry Wood! While I've been talking, you led me right here." He reached enthusiastically towards her and missed contact, for she was half out of the door.

"How dare you suggest such a thing!" she cried. "And how dare you bring me up here for your foul schemes. I may be ripped by briars and brambles and turn my ankle and freeze, but I'm walking home. If you try to follow, I'll go in the nearest house and call the law."

Reinhart left the wheel and dashed after her in some terror; he always felt exactly like what he was accused of being: in this case, a rapist. In addition, he couldn't see his hand before his face.

"Now you've done it," Genevieve said from the darkness on his left. "I've broken my leg."

"Keep calm", Reinhart screamed. "Show a light, if you've got one."

But by the time she said "I don't smoke," he had found her in some hairy bush. "You want to hang on my arm?" he asked. "I won't get fresh."

"I think the most you would do is carry me," by which she apparently meant the least; whichever it was, he contained her in his arms, the little goof all soft and perfumed and light and solid at the some time, and was her only connection with the earth for twenty-five yards back to the automobile.

"Stay calm," he nervously entreated. "I served in the medics. I'll get some sticks and rip up my shirt and make a splint." He wrenched open the right-hand door.

"Well," said Gen, "I may not have actually broken it. You know how one thinks the worst in the dark. What I probably need is to stretch out."

"That's it!" Reinhart answered in an enthusiasm of relief. "With the affected member elevated higher than the head, so that the blood will recede." He pulled his nose from her hair, where it had been tickled, and suppressed a sneeze. "The back seat will do, with your foot out of the window." There was insufficient space for him to get both Gen and his shoulders into the rear, Dad's auto being a far cry from a London taxi-cab; but while he sought to engineer the problem, she left his support and hopped nimbly in.

"Oh good," said he. "Feeling better? Let me get that window open for your foot."

"Ouch," Genevieve yelped, and because the dashboard glow showed him so little of her, explained: "It hurts when I bend it."

"That splint won't take a minute," Reinhart offered, peering in over the lowered front seat. In the forest an owl asked its imbecile question.

"Oo," said Gen in echo, "it is certainly desolate up here."

"We'll be home in ten minutes." He crawled across to the wheel.

"Do you think I should be jolted so soon?"

"I'll drive easy."

"Actually no, it's definitely not broken. You could feel the break if it were, couldn't you?"

Reinhart preferred to believe she was not badly hurt, for a motive of which he was only half aware and therefore scared of: he had not begun to grow until the sophomore year and thus had known a time when his lusts exceeded his physique and many of the women he desired stood higher than he; his only hope of having them, he was told by his fantasies, lay in their being in some way enfeebled—say with a broken leg. This also explained his attraction to girls who wore glasses.

"Couldn't you?" Genevieve repeated, in a much stronger voice.

"Can *you?*" asked Reinhart, keeping his eyes on the speedometer, which at rest still bravely indicated ten miles an hour.

"I don't know. I feel something . . . oh, that's just the clip on my—sorry."

He turned and mumbled shabbily: "Uh, I was in the medics."

She rustled, and then answered as if through a woolen scarf: "Then I guess you'd know."

"Yeah," said Reinhart, almost surreptitiously opening the door as if it were rather his fly. He clambered awkwardly into the back of the car, and lost all sense of his body when he got there, for technically the rear enclosure of that model would not contain an object of his mass.

"Haha," he chuckled in his hysterical bedside manner, "Herr Doktor Reinhart"—he cleared his throat. "Now where's the complaint, little lady?" He inadvertently touched her ankle, and it seemed to burn him. He reminded himself that he was the veteran of a good many campaigns in the Pubic Wars. What unnerved him in the present engagement was the captiousness of the foe. Since he didn't know where he stood,

166

neither was he sure of where he might wilt. Genevieve suddenly stirred and kicked him right in the mouth with her knee. Had he light, he could have looked right up into her secrets.

Rubbing his sore lip, he said: "That's a relief. The ankle feels okay to me. Probably a pulled tendon."

As if her teeth were clenched in pain, Genevieve left interstices between her words: "The . . . other . . . one." And when he gingerly touched another ankle, or perhaps the same, for he hadn't known which he felt the first time, she went on: "Not . . . the . . . ankle."

Somewhere along the route north he must have passed the site in question, where perhaps the damage was negligible. But he heard nothing but two breathings, of which he failed to recognize one as his own, and in truth and with the best intentions, he could not have stopped before the terminus. Having too quickly assessed the driveway, he thought too soon about garaging his vehicle, and proposing to return his hand to the gearshift, he found it trapped. Her two thighs were stronger than his one arm, at least without exhibitionist brutality on the part of the latter. Simultaneously she complained that the bruise was scarcely *there,* though in an excruciatingly amiable tone. It was hinted that he must go and demanded that he stay. And the owl outside continued to doubt everybody's identity.

Something of a pants-fetichist, Reinhart resented her wearing a girdle like a married woman: all boilerplate, except at the only point worth protection; Fort Knox with an impregnable wall and open gate would drive the subtle criminal mad.

"Don't you hate owls?" asked Reinhart, furiously.

She violently started, and his hand had freedom. Yet liberty is cold, lonely, and embarrassing; he immediately sought a more constricting arrangement. Himself temporarily taken care of, he began to worry about Genevieve—as if she were not present. Indeed, in his mind's eye he saw her in her office person, which was the one he wanted, which explained his remark on the owl: that bird had named his confusion.

"Yes," said the unknown girl he was involved with on the back seat, and put some pressure on his relevant hand. He had forgotten what she was supposed to affirm, and went looking with his other set of fingers. Nylon, taut elastic, skin, more armor, zipper, more skin; the passage here was tight, but he forced it and encountered a hammockful of heavy life.

"Why did you burrow up to my shoulder?" said his apparent friend. "I love you."

Aw no! Reinhart pleaded to himself, the dear emotions are not what I wish; I just want to win.

"Hear me?" shouted Genevieve with remarkable volume for

her size and place. His ears rang. "Love you, love you, love you! . . . And do you me?"

"Ummmm," he muttered, and suddenly took heart at the character of her underfurnishings: in the most intimate connection they could remain fully dressed. Perhaps because of this, life had never seemed stranger to him than at that moment when he worked beneath her skirt. He found room for himself on the narrow seat; he felt warm and thought cool; the rest was art. Genevieve seemed either to be indivisible from him or to have vanished completely, he was not sure until that moment came for the reckoning of other matter, and then it had gone beyond that.

"God, I feel awful," he said into the juncture of her neck and shoulder, or rather to that portion of her jacket bunched there. The one grand fact established, their knowledge of each other was still limited.

"Mpf, mpf," said she from beneath him, and when he shifted slight: "I'm almost suffocated! . . . No, stay!"

"No point in doing anything else, now," Reinhart lugubriously observed. "I'm sorry I didn't take precautions, but if worst comes to worst, I will stick by you." He was naïvely afraid of his own fertility.

"You don't mean—you don't mean—" With a kind of instinctive judo, using only her universal joint, Genevieve pitched him right off onto the floor. "You aren't implying we did something?" No tears now; she beat her knuckles on his head.

"Come now!" said Reinhart sardonically. He made a rain hat of his webbed fingers, to catch her blows.

Genevieve pulled down her skirt and looked as good as new, what he could see of her. Her mind, though, was still being ravaged. "Oh, you couldn't have. You couldn't have taken advantage of my ignorance. Tell me it was just petting."

With this, Reinhart's postcoital sadness degenerated into a boredom in which he was conscious of every night sound; the owl, his question now answered, was silent, but the trees talked among themselves in their soughing vocabulary, and an internal-combustion engine climbed a distant hill.

"Sure," he said wearily, "that's all it was."

"Because," said Gen, swinging her spiked heels to the floor and hence, since he covered it, the small of his back, "because we didn't even have our clothes off."

Eventually they both reached the front seat, Reinhart again at the wheel, but Genevieve was still looking for reasons. "Because," she said, "you didn't even kiss me."

Taking this as an accusation, he leaned over and put their mouths together. Hers was very tight, no doubt owing to a

168

conviction that if you guard one orifice, you retroactively protect them all.

Meanwhile, behind his back he turned on the ignition and found the starter with his left foot. There was nothing left to delay getting her home forthwith. Thus when he left her lips the motor was purring nicely—and a brute flashlight came through the window as if to poke out his eyes as well as burn them, and a voice foul as a man's could be ordered: "Leave the car, and keep your hands in sight."

Hideous apprehensions claimed Reinhart's fancy as he obeyed: lovers' lane bandits, etc., and he got ready to risk death before dishonor. But he had to take a minute or two to fetch back his vision, which was momentarily one burning green ball.

"Hi, Reinhart," said his assailant, in quite another voice from the earlier.

"Capek! I recognize your voice but I can't see you."

"Sorry about my light. In approaching a darkened vehicle, carry flashlight in left hand, have weapon accessible to right, take initiative from suspect. I admit I believed it was you, but couldn't take a chance."

"Why did you believe it was me?" asked Reinhart in pique.

Capek, whom he was beginning to make out, drew him some paces from the car. "I don't want to embarrass your lady," he whispered. "We got a tip you and her were up here. It come from her father."

Reinhart scowled. "Are we trespassing here, Capek?"

"The girl ain't twenty-one, Reinhart, though no charge is placed against you. But I better get her back."

"We were just going."

"Sorry, Reinhart, I'm supposed to bring her." Capek pointed to the police car he had left, with headlamps lighted, down the trail.

"I suppose Kenworthy reported on us to your dad," Reinhart told Genevieve a moment later. He explained about her mode of travel home.

"Oh Carl, it's just a mess," she said forlornly, inclining her head towards her right shoulder. "I know it all seems so provincial to a man of your experience and wide travel. Thank you for not taking advantage of me. I think you should know I had a crush on you since the first day you came in the office and swept the papers from my desk. If you can't return that feeling, well, I guess life in the long run is tragic and we must accept it."

All this while Capek was discreetly waiting down the road; he had even dimmed his headlights.

"Now," said Reinhart, "don't talk as if the world has come

to an end. We'll see each other in the office on Monday. And I will most certainly take you out again. I had a great time tonight!"

"No," moaned Genevieve. "After this Daddy will send me away to school."

"But what have we done that's so awful?" Reinhart asked rhetorically and hypocritically, and as if to minimize his falseness, opened the door, took her in his arms, and nuzzled the apple of her right breast through the blouse.

Genevieve ardently squeezed his bull neck. "No, no, no!" He drew away. She pulled him back. "No, I won't go back at all tonight. I'll stay with you, wherever you go! I'll become your concubine if nothing else."

"Ah," murmured Reinhart into the mouthpiece of her unseen nipple, "you're talking wild." He had introduced her to adulthood, the realm of improbabilities and disappointments, and to abandon her there was perhaps to murder a soul—so important did he think he was at this time, so good did he feel about that importance; to believe you can destroy someone by a crime of omission, there is no greater amour propre than that.

"By God," he said in great elation to the swelling fount of life against his cheek. "That's something for me to do. I'll marry this poor girl!" He then told Genevieve as much to her face.

"But there are only three places in the U.S. and possessions where you can get married immediately: Nevada, the Canal Zone, and Guam," she said in a chagrin so poignant that Reinhart pulled away from her bosom and echoed it.

"There is? Damn!" Then he caught himself. "I didn't mean right now."

"But right now is when I have to go home!" she wailed.

"Oh," Reinhart accepted her questionable argument, so as not to cast his nobility into doubt vis-à-vis himself.

Cradling his head again to ensure their maximum unanimity, Genevieve gave a rundown on marriage regulations in their hunk of America: Ohio, girl and boy both twenty-one, blood test required, wait five days for license; Kentucky and West Virginia, same except three days' wait. "But in *Indiana,* the girl can marry at eighteen without parental consent."

"How long a wait there?" asked Reinhart.

"It's hopeless," cried Gen. He felt her shaking her head. "Three days. It's tragic we haven't enough money to fly to Nevada. Though Maryland isn't bad: forty-eight hours and no blood test. But that time would have to be added to how long it would take us to drive there."

"That might be a week in this heap," Reinhart noted.

"We could steal a better car," said Genevieve wildly, pony-prancing her feet.

"As long as we go in for theft, we might as well steal enough money to fly to Guam." His wry wit gave him second thoughts. Besides, his knees were killing him in their impossible position; and then he had reckless hopes that Capek would just get tired of it all and drive away. These proved vain; the officer's headlamps were now lighted and blinking in signal from bright to dim.

"I guess it's not a good idea, Gen. Look, I'll see you at the office on Monday. We'll talk everything over there. Just remember nothing is bad as you think."

She squinted at him. He wished the whole business had taken place in daylight; it was his peculiarity that he liked to see the women he made love to, not to mention those he had almost married. She followed as he backed from the seat, closely retaining his face with the force of that magnetic squint.

When they stood together on the road and he tried to deflect her towards the police car, Genevieve said, "We *did* do something, didn't we? You must think I'm pretty naïve. Well sir, I mean to charge you with sexual assault." She dashed towards the law, and Reinhart would have admired her speed and grace had he not been hysterical. Nevertheless, he caught her at about the three-quarter mark of the track, symbolically presented his saber hilt-first, and they arrived before Capek's guileless gaze almost nonchalantly.

"We decided to tell you, though it has been a secret," said Reinhart to the officer. "We got married earlier today in Indiana. Now, I think that settles everything."

Capek immediately had to shake hands with the happy couple. "You understand," he said, "I had to do my duty. When you make your complaint, you might say if you want to that I never harassed you. If you want to, that is. I got a wife myself and three kids, and I need this job."

"Capek," Reinhart assured him, "you're such a good egg that I wouldn't report you for using a rubber hose."

Capek bared his teeth in horror and roared away in first gear, not shifting till he reached the main road.

As to Reinhart and Genevieve *nee* Raven, they found U.S. Route 52 and took it west, Reinhart alternating between 55 mph—which is what the Chevy could make with, in the jargon of the road, "everything hung out"—and the 20 ordered by the signs in incorporated villages, population specified. Over the border, near a place called Longnecker, Indiana, they stopped at a motel where the conveniences were infamous but the rates moderate. Luckily, Gen had a wad of money; mainly ones, but enough; which led her intended to suspect some forethought on her wacky part. Wacky because she would allow him no further intimacy till after the ceremony, though they registered with the wino motelman as Mr. and Mrs.

Next morning, Saturday, they proceeded to the nearest town showing cannon and balls and in the courthouse thereof, after first having stopped at a rube doctor's shingle and dropped some blood which he found free of spirochetes, entreated the state of Indiana for a license to fornicate unhampered—which is what it amounted to, sourly reflected Reinhart, whom all this trouble was making an anarchist.

"How do we spend our time till Monday?" he asked his espoused, as they stood on the courthouse lawn near the armament that helped win, or lose, the battle of Shiloh—whichever, the birds had since beshat it. "Since you don't want to—"

"Now don't say something awful," Gen broke in, as if he would have: he was marrying a stranger. She was some the worse for their travels, although having supplied herself with toothpaste, etc., from Woolworth's. "We better place certain calls."

They did. She fortunately got Kenworthy instead of her father; he was under the weather from a working over by his friends; he planned to run off to the Navy; but first he would disseminate her news. Then Reinhart called Claude's office number and left a message with an imbecile phone-service operator, spelling out everybody's name and asking two days off for himself and the secretary.

Finally, he called Dad.

"Carlo! Are you at the drugstore? Would you mind picking up a few items?"

"No, Dad. I called to explain about the car. I have it with me in Indiana. . . . I didn't come home last night."

"Go on."

"I'm serious, Dad. I came over here to get married. Spur-of-the-moment."

"Isn't that nice! Have you got yourself a girl?"

"Of course." Reinhart heard him turn away from the phone and say to Maw: *Carlo went over to Indiana and got himself a wife.* He returned to the wire and asked: "Will you be coming home again, or do you want your socks forwarded?"

"Don't be silly, said Reinhart. "I'll be home on Tuesday. Sorry about the car."

"Oh don't worry about that, Carlo. I won't last much longer and then you will get it anyway. Carlo, Maw would like you to buy a couple dozen fresh eggs from one of those roadside stands, and I will reimburst you in dewtime."

Chapter 11

Genevieve had been better than her word: not only did she
withhold for three days, though their county-seat hotel had a
double bed on which Reinhart tested a number of gymnastic
hypotheses, but immediately after the judge pronounced them
man and wife she began to menstruate and kept it up four
more turns of the earth. Which brought them back to Ohio
and denied Reinhart the knowledge of what it was like to do it
in Indiana, though he was experienced as to England, France,
Germany, and even tiny Luxembourg.

Back in town, for three weeks he and she were constrained
to live separately with their respective parents, meeting only at
the office on workdays. Ridiculous state of affairs, but necessary because of the housing shortage on one hand (he couldn't
himself afford to rent or buy any of the listings he peddled to
clients) and her father on the other (Reinhart wasn't afraid of
him, but it made sense to avoid the issue). So in addition to
these failures as businessman and son-in-law, he went loveless
to boot—as of course did Genevieve, who however did not
seem to mind, the utterance of "I will" having quenched her
premarital spark. Try as he would to get at least some of the
old snottiness from her in lieu of sex, he drew a blank. Her
once-bright eyes were filmed; her head hung interminably
over the works of the typewriter, looking for a stray bobbypin that fouled the gears; she mumbled much.

Claude as usual showed his perfect taste—perfect in what it claimed to be: there is no other standard. "Bud and G. Raven, congrats etcetera!" he cried on their first day back. He gave Gen one of his souvenir vials of cologne and Reinhart a mechanical pencil. "Consider them two days' vacation another wedding prezz, you friends. Name the first one after me and I'm good for a silver teething ring any old day. See him or her grow up to respect their God, country, and bidniss." He collared Reinhart and led him to the front window. "See them two-bit stores across the street? Well I don't! No bud no what I got in mind is a big supermarket claiming the whole block, and rising above it in the noonday sun is a gigantic red sign reading: *Bud Reinhart & Sons!*"

Because of pride, Reinhart wouldn't do the obvious; ask Claude to help him find a home; as a husband, he must begin at least to create the illusion of his own efficacy. However, every landlord with a vacancy was also a man with a high price for his favor in this congested time, and Reinhart's being in real estate seemed only to up the ante. The lowest bribe demanded—for the most squalid rattrap of a flat—was two hundred dollars. The government owed Reinhart no more mustering-out money, and though his application had been entered for unemployment compensation, he had to wait a time for the first check—during which period the bureau kept calling him with one bleak opportunity after another, until he settled it once for all by changing his specification from "general clerical type" to "astronomer." (They could only offer you something germane to your registered profession, and like all public offices dared not reject the statement of a clean-shaven Caucasian; for Reinhart, still heavy, had returned to keeping himself neat.) And as to Claude's promised twenty-five per week, he had yet to receive more than a promise slightly fainter at each repetition.

Anyway, he didn't want to get a home by bribe, which was to start right off on the corrupt foot and suggested a search for a whorehouse or bookmaker rather than a nest to contain one's hen and potential chicklings: no more than two weeks after the ceremony and perhaps seventeen days following their lone intimacy, Gen announced to him in her now phlegmatic way that she was pregnant. They were standing at the water cooler. Owing to the announcement, he drank the cup he had filled for her.

"That proves it then," she said, meaning they had really done something on the back seat, and smirked wanly.

"Well," said Reinhart, overlooking, in the guilt he still felt over the alleged violation, that common sense was here being raped unless her Indiana mensis had been spurious, "well, now we *must* get a place all our own." Besides, he was getting pretty hard up.

He saw nowhere to go but Vetsville. In search of clients he had been calling there in the Gigantic every other day and found that, save for a random crank, it was the choice of nobody, that everyone was a customer for an abode in another district so long as the new house required no cash down, very little per month, and in the aggregate come to no more than, say, $3,000—which, moreover, it was assumed the government would cough up. With these specifications the people with properties to sell disagreed fervently and Reinhart could see no clear right in either case, though now his own ox might be gored it is true he leaned towards the have-nots.

Trying to be dispassionate, for tactical as well as ego reasons, on one trip he stopped by the Vetsville administrative hut and said to the manager there, a fellow who had lost his foot to a German mine: "I think it might be wise from a business point of view for me and the wife to move in here."

"Izzat right?" asked the guy, jerking his artificial hoof, through which motion he got rid of the bad feeling that such an office engenders and leaves festering in the nonmutilate. His smile therefore showed no sarcasm. "If you sold a house to every present tenant, and the next couples on the list moved into our Quonsets, there would still be a hundred and fifty ahead of you."

"That's considerably more," said Reinhart, "than the number of guys from this area who went to war, as you can count from the temporary war memorial they have set up down at the high school."

"This dump," responded the manager, "is principally for GI Bill college fellows from anywhere in the county. You'd see the difference if you went elsewhere: the kids in ours are worse-dressed, for example, and the wives are worse-built, but you will usually hear better grammar. . . . If you are going to college, I can put you down as Prospective Number 267. Of course you have three kids."

"None at all, yet," said honest Reinhart.

"Ah," the manager replied, lifting an ex-Army cuff to scratch his good ankle, "then forget it. Come back when you have two and talk to me. It may be I can work you in with two if you also have a dog."

Reinhart felt too negative after this to call on clients. He drove back towards the office. Whenever he was really depressed, he thought about Negroes, he didn't know why: brown faces just appeared in the gloom of his mind and, furthermore, with no particular message; their expressions were impassive, perhaps representing the incontrovertible facts of life.

Whatever, he was impelled to drive through the colored district, where at the drugstore corner he saw a friend.

He pulled to the curb and called through the open window: "Nicholas, it's me!" The Maker reacted adversely to being sought out—*he* looked for *you;* the other way around, he would offer to escape—however, he halted at the attractive sound of his Christian name, signaled with a shoulder-shift to a henchman half-hidden in the doorway to an upstairs barbershop, and sidled to the car.

"Doc Goodykuntz! I ain't seen you since the lecher, man. When you comin' back?"

"Never," said Reinhart. "I'm trying something else now. I got married, and at this moment that looks like a bust too."

The Maker was as hard to see in full daylight as after dark. Between hat and coat, he showed only a dim mouth. Reinhart would never have recognized him in a Turkish bath.

"Whass matter, the little woman cut you up or burn you with the hot i-ron?"

"We get along fine," said Reinhart, "but just can't locate a place to live."

The Maker's lips closed in a self-kiss. "Whachoo looking for, class or on the other hand, convenience? Near to the streetcah, the saloon, and the poolroom? Near to or avoidin the in-laws? Specify, man. I ain't no good on the hidden motive."

"You want to sit in the car?" Reinhart issued the invite most timorously, lest it be too bold for the Maker, who might be too grand.

"Why, is it hot? I hope you done switched the plates." Nevertheless he accepted immediately and climbed in—lighted a cigar, in fact, to do which he rooted through the glove compartment ostensibly in search of matches, ignored those that he found there but managed to inspect everything else, and finally got his fire from the dashboard gadget. "I can get you five C's for it," he said, careful to belch the smoke in the direction away from his host.

"Your information service has slipped up, I see," said Reinhart. He explained about the Gigantic.

"I long know that," the Maker answered with a shrug. "If Claude the Hum don't pay you soon, he going to owe you five C's anyway. I make you square with him." He reached over and honked the horn at a gaudy couple on the sidewalk, then shouted to them: "Doc Goodykuntz has returned!"

"Quiet!" ordered Reinhart. "That's all finished. It was one big flop."

"You talkin' goofed, man." The Maker produced his billfold. "I done sold twenty-three one-way tickets to Andorra at

176

five clams each, though some is paying them off at one dime per week. You share is fifty-seven fifty. Forty . . . forty-one . . ." He was counting off the bills.

Reinhart went wet as he understood. "What a horrible thing to do!" he moaned. "Find them, give it back. I'm not even sure where Andorra is."

The Maker lifted his white hat for a quick, beady glance. "That ain't how you talked at the lecher."

"I know. It was a terrible mistake. So people really listen when I talk!"

"Ha-hee," laughed the Maker, forcing the money into Reinhart's fist. "I ain't so dumb, man. I know there ain't no Andorra. But why tell them suckers and make them feel mean? Five bucks for a place to dream about ain't the worse bargain. They lose it on the numbers or craps, anyway. Matter of fack, that's just how I lost my share of what I got for the tickets." He showed the now empty maw of his wallet. "Next time, pick a place that will fool me also."

"And myself, too," said Reinhart, looking at the dough and waiting for the enlightenment to clear his conscience. He decided the worst crime was to judge events statistically.

"Though that already is the U.S.A., if you ax me," stated the Maker, staring at the frayed end of his cigar. "Man, we got everythin' you want right here. Oh say can you see—"

"No patriotism, please," said Reinhart, wincing in shame.

But the Maker's mouth fell and he answered solemnly: "Now don't lay no Communism on me."

Starting the engine, Reinhart asked: "You don't have any idea where I can find an apartment?"

"Is *that* what is eatin' you?" The Maker almost swallowed his cigar. "Is that it? I thought it was that daddy-in-law. Why, where you want to stay, Vitsville? Now you just run up there again tomorra. The manager done read his list wrong. You and the Mrs. is the first names at the top." He left the car, but put his hat back into the window. "If you'd ever stop worrying for two minutes, you'd be knee-deep in sugar. Man, I might even run you for President."

Within a fortnight Reinhart and Gen moved in to their very own Quonset, and Reinhart congratulated himself on getting on the Maker's good side; imagine such power used to your detriment! . . . But late in the afternoon of moving day, Genevieve the antiromantic, having hung some monk's-cloth curtains, sat down on a cardboard crate full of disassembled ready-to-paint chaise longue with wheels (gift of Dad), sighed, and said: "Humbold isn't so bad. True, you have to fight him for your pay, but he *did* use his pull to get us here."

"He did?" disingenuously said Reinhart, who had been drilling a hole through the metal wall for the purpose of affixing through it a bolt-and-nut device on which to hang his framed discharge certificate—the environment seemed to demand such an exhibit. She would never hear of the Maker through him.

"Oh sure, I thought you knew I asked him. He could have been a lot quicker about it, but since Vetsville is subsidized by public tax money I believe Claude doesn't want his connection advertised."

"Why is that?" asked Reinhart sullenly, junking all his newly instituted superstitions; he might have guessed that connections and not wizardry would always win out in Ohio.

"Why, because there's nothing rotten in the state of Denmark, not much." She had tied a handkerchief over her head and wore blue jeans which showed to good advantage her perfect rump, even to a suggestion of its cleft. Reinhart reached for it from time to time in exploitation of his proprietorship, which she didn't seem to mind, nor indeed to notice.

"Ah," said Reinhart, throwing down his drill, "who cares? We've got our own place now. You know what that means." He went behind her and, bending over, felt her up through the flannel shirt she wore on loan from her brother.

A naked mattress lay where the movers had coarsely hurled it. Genevieve suffered herself to be led in that direction, but resisted his also trying to undress her in transit. At length he saw, by half, her natural person, and marveled at the quality of her endowments. She tried at least to retain her underpants, which were of an almost luminescent white. During this commotion her breasts leaped like sportive animals. He had her off her feet with his wrist in the crossroads and his hand through to the other rise, boasting: "I can lift you right up to the ceiling like this, on one arm."

She suddenly went limp and whispered: "It's only two P.M."

"I'll pull down the curtains if that bothers you," said Reinhart, swaggering the full four steps to the other side of his house. In the window were the faces of several preschool urchins. Reinhart shook his fist at them; luckily he had had no time to divest himself and therefore offered them no basis of comparison with their fathers. He closed the newly installed curtains, which, designed for the standard window, more than sufficed for this spyhole: he and she were captives in a tin prison of love. He pricked his thumb on one of the clips holding the monk's cloth to the rod-rings, and a drop of blood welled sluggishly from the ball. . . . Reinhart never wasted an

178

accident; he told himself now: Either she was not a virgin or I did not have her that night on the back seat.

Behind his back she had rolled herself in the mattress, a wiener in a bun. Like the crank eater who inspects his sandwich for foreign matter, Reinhart suspiciously unfolded her covering.

"Does it have to be now?" she asked, trying to hide three points of vulnerability with but two quivering hands.

Reinhart said in mock annoyance: "Don't act as if you were about to be murdered." As always at such moments, the various parts of his clothing fused into a single garment, easily shucked. Now, at the moment when, savagely bare, he supposed he would be most frightening, she began to shake with laughter from pearly teeth to rosy nipple.

"It looks so funny!" With tardy consideration, she displayed the back of her head and haha'd to the rear of the hut, where the sink was filled with new dishes still wispy with excelsior.

Now one of Reinhart's many peculiarities had been that while his body performed the act of love, his mind invariably went elsewhere; because of this his potency was seldom in question, though no doubt his sanity could be challenged: having achieved his concrete aim, he did not stay to enjoy it but rather fled to abstractions, did sums, examined theorems, etc., though when not inside a woman—which of course was most of the time—he could hardly add up his change and if forced to, escaped into fantasies of screwing. That is, for him the here and now were always somewhere else. But since marriage is pointless unless you can develop a sense of fact, which is more important than love in this context, which perhaps *is* love, Reinhart set out now to become a husband.

Far from troubled by Gen's jeers, he used them rather for stimulation. They were about to enact that drama of crime and punishment which he had explained to his audience when drunk; and naturally the poor girl was frightened. In human relations, there is always an onus that wants bearing.

"Darling," he said to the groove of her flawless but shivering back, "I love you."

That stopped her hysterical laughter, or rather converted it into what was at once less serious and more useful. "How I hate you!" she cried, scrambled up, and ran nude along the narrow alleyways among the cartons and unarranged furniture.

"Aha!" shouted Reinhart, standing where he was. "We *didn't* do it on the back seat!" For this was not the comportment of a person deflowered long since.

"Certainly not!" screamed Genevieve, her breasts between

the breastlike curves of a loveseat-back. She laughed corrosively again. "I wouldn't let a man touch me, least of all you."

Logician Reinhart, in an Aristotelian pose, finger pointed rhetorically downwards, presumably towards reality, asserted: "But I'm the one you married." Genevieve was touched by this argument. She brushed the curls off her white forehead and frowned with an extended underlip. She was of course still bare and wore a lipstick that matched the hue of her nipples.

"You are so beautiful," he said, inching in her direction with no discernible movement of the body above his ankles.

"Then why must you hurt me?"

"I can sue you for fraud," he warned.

She made a sudden dash for a straightbacked chair and gained it; Reinhart saw her pretty parts through the slats. He feinted the beginning of a move, and bluffed her behind the secondhand sofa purchased with his commission from the Maker's swindle. She was now trapped in a diminishing passage which ended in the metal wall. However, he was far too shrewd to follow, but returned to the mattress and lay supine.

"What are you doing that for?" asked Gen, too proud to deprecate the impasse by coming out the way she went in. In a moment she climbed over the sofa-top and into its flowered seat, where she arranged herself as if for a polite visit, knees together, bare feet on floor, hands limp, and head inclined sympathetically.

Fortunately, the year had reached May and the temperature stood at seventy, else Reinhart would also have had cold to contend with. He balled his clothes for a pillow, and began to whistle a little tune through his teeth.

"Don't *you* look silly!" said Genevieve. "That's really all I've got against you, that you act so *silly*. I didn't ever say I wouldn't *ever* do it, but we aren't even moved in. Otherwise, I really love you and I'm not sorry we got married. Now please throw me my clothes?"

Reinhart's lids fell slowly over his eyes, and a kind of divine catalepsy crept through his trunk and limbs. Certain holy men in India lie in this position and support an erection for days, so that childless women might with a touch of the hand absorb its fertility.

"All right, stay mad." Genevieve fell silent for a while; to get her clothing she would have to step across the yogi's magic body; perhaps she already felt its emanations. Rainfall gushed over their tin capsule in one of those sudden showers that increase self-esteem: you alone have been chosen by heaven for a quick cleansing. Reinhart was absolutely one with the natural world, his spirit at peace.

"I guess I wouldn't mind just sitting there with you," said Gen. "If you want me to." Reinhart could hardly reply to this, since he didn't really hear it, occupied as he was by pure will. At last she rose and went haltingly to the mattress.

"You don't have to sulk," she said, falsely bright. "A person who has never been touched by a person of the other sex has a right to be careful." She knelt. "I think it's awful. I think it should be changed. I mean the way it is. There's love, and then there's sex that makes it dirty. How would you like to be a girl? Carl . . ." She touched his hand. "Carl, let's arrange the furniture now for our little house." Her fingers stole up his forearm, around the bicep, and into the armpit; out again to trace the junction of clavicle and shoulder cap, across and up the neck, over the chin of stubble (for he hadn't yet shaved), with fingers parting to sweep around the nose; her hand reclaimed its integrity between his eyebrows, went through the wheatfield of hair, returned, became a fist, and tumbled limply down the precipice of his forehead, bounced through the hair on his chest, and proceeded to the Mason-Dixon groove that remained as a memory of his absent belt.

All this while Reinhart was in the stasis of authentic power. Her fist became a hand, and arched, like a cat stretching, from the belt-line to his navel. She lay on her side now, face soft against his shoulder, a breast apparently just missing contact with the hollow of his elbow.

"I don't know what I'm doing," she murmured. And without warning her fingers clenched into a small but formidable weapon, and she punched him right in the summit of his belly.

So much for the philosophy of the East!, which proved as inefficacious here as in his other experiments: trying to seduce unknown girls with thought waves, etc.

As soon as he caught his breath, Reinhart turned to her in injured hauteur and asked: "Now why did you do that?"

Expecting retaliation, she had rolled herself into a tight ball like a spider, which any amateur entomologist knows is, contrary to legend, a docile little organism afraid of every undue vibration on its web. He could barely hear her muffled voice: "Because I'm scared."

He said: "They call me Gentle, Genial, Jovial Carlo," and strove to earn at least the first adjective. She murmured: "I think I'm falling asleep."

"Yes," whispered Reinhart. "We'll do it some other time.

181

We've got years." He put his big hand lightly over her eyes. "Isn't it nice and restful here in our own house, with the rain on the roof?" Her even breathing tickled his palm, and under his wrist she mumbled in drowsy security.

True love being known for its treacheries, Reinhart chose this moment to enter her fiercely. This time there could be no doubt he had succeeded in making her his own. It was also legal, for the state has first to come between a pair before it will get out of their way, and its sanction meant much to Reinhart, who was rhythmically practicing respectability with no fear of a cop's hostile flashlight. The conviction that for the first time in his life he was doing what everybody everywhere approved, give him the endurance of Galahad, who had the strength of ten because his heart was pure, though Reinhart wondered why Sir G. was always represented as a eunuch. This was his last reflection, nor did he do sums. As darkness fell he was still occupied with his bride, and she—who proved no fink when the chips were down—him. An inspector of love would have had the greatest difficulty in determining where one left off and the other began.

Like everybody but the perverse, who were not worth bothering about except for laughs, Genevieve liked it once she knew what it was. When you were married, loving was a ready pleasure, always at hand, free as the radio. Because of this, the Reinharts seldom left their hut for the outside entertainments, expensive and hollow, that wives traditionally demand from workaday hubbies with tired feet and sore billfolds. Reinhart could only make the classic assumption that the needs of such women were not met in the domestic arena, i.e., in bed, for his own dear companion never groused. Her premarital complaint had been simply that she was without a husband; obtaining one, she fell quiet. Reinhart loved things that worked out so neatly, the world being in general rather messy. And if he at first missed her needle in his ribs—for though provocation made him nervous, thinking back through twenty-two years until his memory dissipated the mist, he realized that without it he might still be wearing a diaper—he had an obligation that more than made good the loss: shortly Gen was truly pregnant.

He demanded that she quit her job, and "My," said Maw, who saw all manner of things to admire in Genevieve that anybody else would take as commonplace, "she sure agreed to that." He himself got serious about his own, and actually looked forward to his biweekly struggle with Claude for the wages, which he had begun to win. To these were added the unemployment payments of 20 per, making 25 times 52 plus 20 times 52, equaling $2340 the year, or $195 per month. This they could feasibly live on, for the Vetsville rent was 42.50 at every new moon and Reinhart became a shrewd shopper, purchasing the economical cuts—beef hearts, pork hocks, and veal kidneys—at which your typical contemporary housewife turned up her nose (and furthermore he learned to cook them nicely: the hocks with sauerkraut; the kidneys in a pie, the crust of which took six minutes to prepare with a modern mix using cold water; and so on).

Reinhart cooked because he believed that carrying a child was enough for a girl of twenty; with the same motive he performed the other chores: garbage-emptying, eradication of tea-stains from the sink, dish-washing, and the lot. Marriage for him was the marvelous opportunity to use the energy he had stored up for years as a large man who did little. He even purchased another set of basic dumbbells from York, Pa., to replace those that Maw had sold as scrap metal, and in the interstices between his duties exercised for the first time since 1941. By means of these and several performances of the act of love every night, he lost seven pounds in a month; he was still 220 but not flabby.

In the middle of June, when the weather had turned warm enough for Gen to eschew her slip and wear only pants and brassiere under the blue housecoat which her husband opened so often that the zipper was fouled and its function taken over by safety pins, Reinhart let the federal government assume from the state the provision of half his livelihood. Under the GI Bill he enrolled in the Municipal University in the City, and began to draw the stipend of $90 a month. For which he was obliged to attend summer-session classes, three each morning starting at eight, ending at eleven. He made the ten-mile trip, to and fro, in the Gigantic, and by talking real estate to his fellow students between bells, justified the gas-and-oil charges he added to Claude's account at the local Flying Red Horse, which the boss never paid anyhow.

The day Maw had fried him the pork chop, his second Monday of school, he next stopped to claim the laundry from a sullen Chinese whose iron had made sinister little burns at the points of the collars of all his shirts, and then drove to the mud slough, with its permanent tire grooves, in the front yard of Quonset No. 10, or as he had had a jeweler etch into the brass doorknocker, gift of his aunt: SANS SOUCI—REINHART.

Some relentless college girl had lately been hired to divert the children on balmy days, in a simulated summer camp on the other side of Vetsville, now that they were on vacation.

Unharassed, Reinhart walked to his screen door and shouted "Hi-ho." The dust cloud raised by his arrival preceded him through the entrance. "Geneveeeeve," he sang, as was his wont, before looking round the one partition, a kind of baffle just inside the door, which kept area snoopers from seeing, in one wink, right through the house and out the rear exit. He stepped beyond it into the one room that was their all: standard sofa in foreground; double bed made up as a parody of another sofa, against the wall in the middle; sink beside the back door, cabinets above, stove nearby, but the midget refrigerator was closer to the bed, for the outlet was there. Scattered in attendance to these main furnishings were lesser conveniences: straight chair or two; one overstuffed, with footstool and extra pillow; magazine rack; bookcase holding Reinhart's old notebooks, zoology text, and a dogeared copy of *King Arthur*, with "Carlo R. age 10" in a childish mess on the flyleaf. Dad's wheeled chaise longue, really a garden item, had been assembled and put outdoors. Gen sometimes lay there of an afternoon, unless the nearby garbage can, murmurous haunt of flies, had not been collected for an inordinant while and sent forth its effluvium. It was marvelous how she had lost every trace of her premarital snobbery.

As he entered, this valuable person was lying on the real sofa, looking towards the fake one, which wore as cover a huge cloth of dim Paisley, woven by ostensibly indigent Hindus, for it was stamped "India" and had been bought locally for one dollar. On the cover lay a paperbound book, on *its* cover the title *Check for a Short Bier*. Gen whiled away the nine months with reading of this kidney, which Reinhart not only approved; he had suggested it. Nothing like vicarious violence to give you the illusion of movement while you lie still.

"Honey!" shouted Reinhart with his customary ebullience, and kissed her mouth, nose, ears, and forehead, and ran his hand into the housecoat. "What's new with the heir?"

Sitting in the sun had brought out a few amber freckles below her eyes. She was the same girl who had worked in the office, only now relaxed in every part, softer but as firm. For once Reinhart had done something to somebody that agreed with them!

"Oh," she answered with a drowsy smile, "I told you it's much too early. Would you mind reaching me over that book?"

Doing so, Reinhart renewed his acquaintance with the title. "What does that refer to, hon? Is a midget the victim?"

184

"He works in a circus," said Gen. "You get all the circus life as setting."

"Gripping?"

"Very," said she, taking the book with limp fingers that lost their purchase before she had conveyed it to her lap. "Oops."

"No, no," cried Reinhart, "don't you bend over. Let me get it." He reclaimed the book from the uncarpeted floor, and saw light through one of the cracks there. "We have natural air conditioning," he noted. "Comes in handy on these hot nights."

She continued to wear the fixed smile produced on his entrance. It was her standard countenance day in and out; he had never seen anyone so perpetually pleased.

"Any mail come? Any calls?"

"Your government check and a thing about a sale at Milady's."

"Look, sweety, why don't I take you down there and get a new dress? We have the money."

"Why?" she said lackadaisically. "In three months I won't be able to wear it. . . . Then there was a call from a Mr. Melville."

"Yes," said Reinhart. "But you mean Mr. Mellon. He's that ex-sailor who lives in Hut 25. Looks like I've made a sale. Isn't that nice! Do you remember from when you worked at the office, the five-room cottage on Chrysanthemum Lane, one-car garage, automatic-stoker furnace, quarter acre of fruit trees, sixteen-five? Wonder where Mellon suddenly got the money."

"I could have got it wrong," said Gen, "but I thought it was Melville."

"Aren't you glad you don't have to work at that typewriter any more!" said Reinhart in a statement rather than a question. "By the way"—he sat on the floor at her legs—"the Mellons have a couple of cute kids. We'll keep up with them and when ours is big enough we can take him over there to play under those apple trees. Nothing like eating green apples when you're a kid. Then you get sick and your mother gives you castor oil in orange juice. Did you ever do that?"

He reached up and pulled her face down to meet his. Gradually rising while still fastened to her lips, he lifted and carried her front-piggyback, losing his trousers en route, to the pseudo couch—real bed. The skirt of her housecoat was already up when he arrived, and today she wore no underwear at all. *Fortiter in re* met *suaviter in modo*, and both in due time reached that moment of absolute integrity, until which

185

time was cyclical. They at last pulled apart to cool, with a suction noise of navels; he placed his finger in the recessed button of hers and said: "When I was small I thought babies came out here, somehow. It took me years to learn about life. . . . I looked at a marriage book in the library the other day: we can still do it for months. . . . But you're perspiring. Better let me put something over you—summer, contrary to popular opinion, is a great time for colds." He drew the Indian thing over her and dressed himself.

"Shouldn't I make you some lunch?" she asked, her cheeks flushed fruit-pink. A damp curl lay asymmetrically on her forehead, and much of her breast was exposed above the cover.

This was one of their family jokes, and Reinhart gave the traditional answer, which was amusing if you were part of it: "Sure, breaded veal cutlet with tomato sauce."

"No," said Gen, "I don't mean the kidding." She waved the petals of her hand. "You work so hard and I lie around all day. Are you sure a pregnant woman can't do anything? Not according to the doctor."

"Ha!" said Reinhart. "The doctor! What does he know? He has to deal with those slobs who, if you'll pardon the expression, keep their wives constantly knocked up and make them scrub floors as well. So naturally he makes the best of it, telling the prospective mothers that a little hard labor won't hurt them. No, absolutely no. I don't want you to do anything but produce a new life. To see you work would offend me. As if creation isn't labor enough! You let me handle everything else. I've got the energy and strength of a dozen of the washed-out people you see these days everywhere you look." He thrust one wrist underneath the overstuffed chair and, keeping his arm almost straight, lifted it a yard off the floor. He replaced it in slow motion, the hard way, and said: "I'm very bright in class, too, and make penetrating comments. It is all the bunk that you can't be strong both in muscle and brain."

In the kitchen corner, while continuing his lecture, he washed his hands and opened a can of tuna. "You see, it's a question of will, not any mystical thing about aptitude or talent. In Psych we are messing with aptitude tests, which is why this comes to mind. Imagine having to take a test to find out what you're interested in. It goes like this: Do you like to sing? Yes. Dance? Yes. Enjoy being the center of attention? Yes. Diagnosis: You are psychologically equipped to be an entertainer."

He mashed the tuna into some mayonnaise. "Of course, you could never figure that out by yourself. Without the help of some bore with his categories, you thought you'd make a good accountant." He used his newest gadget, an ice-cream scoop that expanded and contracted with a touch of the thumb, to deposit a ball of tuna fish onto a lettuce leaf. With sliced tomatoes, his plate was as professional as any handed over a drugstore counter.

"But you see, it's will. Everything's a question of will. You have to *want* to be an entertainer, say. Then the talent will appear. Take me. I never thought I could cook, and never even tried it. But now I want to, so I can. *Violá,* Madame!" Having placed two buttered Rye-Krisps on the plate, he swept it to Genevieve. "Anybody can do anything. Everybody can have his own Renaissance."

. But she had gone to sleep on one cheek, her mouth crumpled like a child's, one hip high. He might just slip his hand under . . . no, the poor girl was weary. He sat on the floor nearby and, resting the plate on the hassock, ate her lunch.

The telephone rang as Reinhart was washing the dishes. Always here or when one is on the toilet, he complained to the dishtowel on which he hastily dried his wet hands so that he would not be electrocuted. But he spoke enthusiastically into the mouthpiece.

"Mr. Reinhart?" asked the caller, from a throat rich as cream. On the repetition, it lisped to boot; "Misthter Carlo Reinhart?"

"Yeth," replied Reinhart in his automatic sympathy and then hid behind a cough.

"I believe your thecretary may have—I called before. My name ith Melville. To get to the point, I am an author."

"How interesting!" said Reinhart. "Yes, sir. Well, sir. I have just what you want. Don't make a move until you see what I've got to show you. How does this sound: a barn, Mr. Melville. Now wait a moment—a barn with electricity and running water. Bohemian but convenient. Asphalt tiles on the floor. Gas space heater. Half acre with trout stream. I know how you authors love barns. I can pick you up in fifteen minutes, and we'll drive out. It is out of town a ways but that's the privacy you fellows like. Where are you staying?"

"Why?" Melville asked suspiciously.

"So I can pick you up."

"Oh. At the moment I am in the City. Downtown. In your county courthouse."

"Ah," said Reinhart, "no doubt doing one of those exposés, eh Mr. Melville? Well, you just hold on there, I'll pick you up at the main entrance in about thirty minutes; O.K.?"

"Yasss," answered Melville, exhibitionistically abandoning

his lisp. He sounded like a pretty weird bird, but Reinhart assumed that was normal for the profession.

"You were right, hon," he said to Genevieve, hanging up. "It *was* Melville, and he's an author, and they've all got money. I know he'll fall for that barn, because authors are also famous for being impractical. Look, we'll keep up with him after the sale and be invited there to those literary parties where they drink Scotch and make little smirking comments —you've seen them in the movies. But I wonder where around here he'll find other writers to come to them? Ah well, enough of that. Will you be O.K. now? Want me to run up some new magazines or a Coke from the drugstore?"

"Oh, are you leaving?" asked Gen, awakening with her hair flat and her eyes wild. "I must have dropped off."

"No, no, no! Don't get up." Reinhart came to her bed and kissed her goodbye. "Just don't worry about a thing. I've got it all taken care of. There's a tuna plate all prepared in the fridge, and a milk bottle of iced tea. I'll be in and out of the office all afternoon; in case you want to get hold of me, leave a message with the phone service. Claude still hasn't hired another secretary, by the way."

Gen became alert at any mention of the office. Reinhart believed she had enjoyed working there, and he looked forward to inviting her down for a visit after the baby came.

"Oh," she said brightly, "he's saving the salary. He's up to something, the big crook. I wish I could get a glance at his files. Who does his typing now?"

"He takes it to some public stenographer, I think. Of course, as yet I haven't had need of any for myself. But I feel it in my bones that a sale can't be far off. And then you know what I'll do to celebrate, Gen? I'll buy you a big—"

"Carl," she broke in, beseechingly. "Carl, would you let me type the Agreement to Buy? Please? I've got my portable here."

Reinhart guessed aloud that that would not hurt her, if she kept the vibrations down by not typing too fast, but to himself he reflected on the caprices of women. He had taken her away from all that; yet, to go back to it was the favor she asked, not gems or furs or costly scents. Sigmund Freud had made a useful confession, quoted just that morning by the Psych instructor: "The question I have never been able to answer in thirty years of research into the feminine soul is, 'What does a woman want?' "

Chapter 12

"I know it was a disgraceful trick, Carlo. Absolutely inexcusable," said Splendor Mainwaring, as Reinhart drove around the courthouse block and passed the entrance to the jail on the back street. "But in my defense let me say I thought you would immediately recognize my voice."

"How could I recognize you with that fake lisp?" Reinhart demanded. Unfortunately the Gigantic had an automatic shift, and he could not relieve his rage by stripping the gears. "You seem to think I devote my life to studying your habits. You mean nothing to me. Nothing. I owe you no obligation whatever, and I'll thank you to stop trying to claim one for me. What did I get out of your last caper?"

"Well," Splendor answered shyly, "you surely did better than I with it."

Reinhart swung impetuously into the curb in the center of a block. A middle-aged pedestrian stared in frightened supposition that they had chosen him on this hot afternoon to swoop down on and rob, this satchel-faced Negro and this enormous lout: at least such was Reinhart's apprehension. The pedestrian developed greater and greater horror until his eyes threatened to fly from his head. At last he exploded in a sneeze. A mere spasm of rose fever. But before this happened Reinhart had issued Splendor an ultimatum.

"Get the hell out!"

"You don't mean it," said Splendor, with an introverted

look as if he had asked it of himself. He made no move to leave.

"I didn't invite you to enter in the first place," Reinhart said haughtily, because Splendor, however outrageous, had very decent manners. "You insolently climbed in when I stopped for the traffic light. You're lucky I didn't mistake you for a prisoner escaping from jail and beat you up. . . . You *aren't* escaping, incidentally?"

"Oh my no," answered Splendor, showing a paper. "Here's my release. I am rehabilitated, and may re-enter society at my own risk."

"All right, Jack," said a harsh voice with a foul overlay of false patience. A motorcycle cop dressed in a science-fiction getup—helmet, goggles, boots—sneered through his masks into the window on the driver's side. "Jack, this is a restricted zone and you can't even stand here. You know better than that because you can read good as anybody."

"I certainly can, Officer," said Reinhart. "And I'm on my way."

"Not without a ticket you ain't, Jack." With malevolent legerdemain, the cop created a summons-book and placed it on the window ledge, aiming for Reinhart's cheek as he flipped open its long metal cover.

"One moment, Officer. I'm on court business. This man has just been remanded in my custody." Reinhart seized the document from Splendor and shoved it at the goggles.

"How was I to know?" With the other part of his bicameral character, the cop grinned obsequiously, put away his book, and made the motorcycle scream.

As they lurched into motion again, Splendor said: "You see, I have my uses." He took his release from the seat, where Reinhart had aloofly dropped it. He was apparently the source of the strong chemical odor abroad for the past five minutes; in the county jail they probably disinfected his clothes and issued him yellow soap for his person. But thinking of such pathetic details merely increased Reinhart's anger.

"Look," he said. "I have never received a satisfactory explanation from you as to why you took dope that night. Until I do, there's no point in our even talking. And before you brag about getting me out of a traffic ticket, reflect that it was your fault I was threatened with one in the first place."

A boiling day. Sweating, Splendor looked like bronze in the rain. He wore the costume of a white-collared down-and-outer—black suit, shirt without a tie. Now he took from his jacket a piece of chewing gum that obviously had been concealed in a pocket lining for moths, through disinfecting and worse; it was battered and melted, yet still in its paper,

190

which he removed like a surgeon and then offered Reinhart half.

The ex-corporal knew these touching particulars for what they were. "Go to hell with your fleabitten gum; you've got a nickel to buy a new pack."

Splendor chewed deliberately, his eyelids synchronized with his lips, all four opening and closing together in elephantine rhythm. "Despair," he said at length, "ineluctable despair, so profound that it is hopeless to try to explain it systematically. At crucial moments God tends to desert me."

"Then you should get a better one," Reinhart stated cynically. "There's no point in having a religion that is worthless at the showdown." Reaching a less congested area, where there were fewer cars in motion and more at the curb, some attended by undershirted people squinting in the heat, the Gigantic picked up speed of its own volition. For the most part, it did its own thinking; only in the extremity did Reinhart, its God, have to send down an edict.

"But I know there is a sense here that we cannot yet perceive," Splendor went on with the old obliviousness. Jail hadn't changed him one iota.

A snotnosed kid ran into the street after a red ball, and Reinhart had to exert his divine power on the car, which enjoyed running down human beings.

"How arrogant you are," he replied. "Like all people who yap about God, you think He spends His time manipulating your fortunes exclusively, like a personal stockbroker."

"No," Splendor answered dolefully. "No, just the other way around. He pays no attention to me at all."

"That's the same thing. I wish I could make you see that," said Reinhart. "Why don't you forget about having someone else take care of you, and straighten out under your own auspices?"

"Because I have great flaws, Carlo."

You would have thought a man in jail for three months might, when he got out, want to look at the scenery. True, the route home was not much for the eye, yet to him at least it should have signified freedom. But no, he sat like a mummy, wrapped in dogged introversion.

"Your faults are not terribly large," sneered Reinhart. "Moreover, they don't seem to me authentic. I believe your real and only trouble is that you are second-rate."

As if in confirmation, Splendor humbly lowered his head and observed silence until they reached the Negro quarter and he had to direct Reinhart to Mohawk Street, now a terra incognita of sunlight alternating with shade from psoriatic sycamores. Actually, it looked rather nice. In the back yard of the Mainwaring home a grape arbor began sturdily near the kitchen door and then went into rapid decline as it proceeded towards the alley; by Indian summer the weight of its purple fruit would bring it down alongside the broken wheelbarrow, which of course was at rest but gave the illusion of being in slow crazy motion, rustily laughing. As it had for going on a third of a year, the burned-out car lay abaft the shed, its only new circumstance a group of kids simulating a trip to Chicago, brown as if they had been singed in the same fire that cooked their vehicle.

The Mainwaring house had yellow siding with green trim, both colors fading graciously like those of an old necktie many times to the cleaner's; here and there the paint had defected from areas the size of, say, a squirrel—oops, no, it was a real squirrel dangling from an ingenious noose the particulars of which could not be made out from the street, except that at its house-end Mr. Mainwaring grinned through the open window and shouted down: "Got the sonbitch!"

Splendor returned his salute from the car and said lifelessly: "How it buoys one up to see his father."

"What does he have to do, poor fellow," asked Reinhart, "trap to eat?"

"Oh good heavens!" said Splendor. In his efforts towards gentility he sometimes, like a European learning English, used a maidenly turn of speech. This propensity, added to his failure ever to speak of a woman, caused Reinhart to wonder again whether Splendor was a queer—which, if he were, would do much to explain the impasse of his life. On the other hand, he never spoke of men, either—excepting Dr. Goodykuntz, who was rather more idea than person. The truth was, he lived in the universe all by himself and therefore could be characterized by none of the standard definitions. As to whether this was an attribute of Negroes in general or of this guy alone, Reinhart could only admit that he had forgotten Splendor was colored until he saw Mr. Mainwaring's indigo face.

"Good heavens, no!" Splendor went on. "I would imagine it's just simple-minded cruelty. Or perhaps he wants to make a dish of squirrel as a delicacy, 'like they done make in Jawgia.'" His parody was inferior. For the third time he said "good heavens," making Reinhart ache to strike him, and explained: "They don't want for funds. My sister does very well."

"Loretta?" asked Reinhart. "Where does she work?"

"I'd hate to say," answered Splendor.

"Well," said Reinhart, revving the engine, "best of luck to you, Splendor, in whatever you try."

"I was wondering, Carlo, whether—"

But here Reinhart cut him off, in fear of some dreadful proposition. "Just a moment, you had better know that I'm married now."

Splendor acknowledged, or disregarded, this news with a tremor of eyelids, and reached into the inside pocket of his suit jacket.

"Also, my wife is pregnant," Reinhart added, and then perhaps needlessly explained what this meant: "I'm going to be a father."

His colored friend had found a sheaf of papers within his clothes. "I wonder whether, Carlo, you might read this and let me know if I've really said *anything.*"

His manuscript was of yellow paper, ruled in blue, legal length, and written in pencil. All Reinhart could judge at that point, as Splendor handed it over, was the handwriting, which appeared to be that precise, bland, anonymous style used on example-charts in grammar school. Reinhart had not known that any living person wrote in that fashion, except perhaps fat girls.

"Yes, Carlo," said Splendor, smiling in self-congratulation. "It's no mistake. I became a writer while in jail, and this represents my maiden effort. Perhaps it is nothing to be proud of, who knows? That is, you will. But I—well, the creative artist can hardly judge his own work, can he? And I suppose you have studied English literature while in college? And American literature as well?" he asked with his hand apprehensively clutching the door-lever as if a certain kind of answer would send him bolting.

"Only English," said Reinhart, and added ironically: "I hope that is enough to qualify me." What would the guy do next? Once again he had something that was more colorful than what Reinhart had, albeit Reinhart was a prospective father. A writer yet! The ex-corporal found a temporary consolation is assuring himself that the story, or essay or whatever, stunk; but he glanced at the first sentences and was frightened by their grace: "I am a rather elderly man. The nature of my avocations, for the last thirty years, has brought me into more than ordinary contact with what would seem an interesting and somewhat singular set of men, of whom, as yet, nothing, that I know of, has ever been written. . . ."

"Is this fiction or nonfiction?" Reinhart asked, for want of a more articulate response.

Splendor at last wiped the perspiration from his welling forehead, and hung the handkerchief out his window to dry.

"Now," he said with condescension. "Imagination, Carlo, my dear fellow. I am hardly an elderly man."

"I have read essays in which a writer pretends to be somebody he isn't really, so as to make a point," said Reinhart, temperamentally jerking his shoulder; "yet it is not fiction, so to speak."

"Have you an example?" Splendor asked politely, though his chin was insolent.

"Naturally," said Reinhart. He lighted a cigarette to gain time and was inconsiderate with the expelled smoke. "Charles Lamb's 'Dissertation on Roast Pig.' "

"Of course!" Splendor bared his teeth. "You're just the man to read my feeble effort. Now, tell me what you think of it. No holds barred. Tear it to pieces. Give it to me but hard. That's what the beginning author needs, and not the politeness of friends." He opened the door and swung himself out. "I'll expect to hear from you at your convenience, Carlo. Remember to be merciless." He suddenly leaned so far in through the window that, though the car was wide, his eyes were almost crossed on Reinhart's nose. "I'm sure it's inconvenient, what with your being married and almost a father, but I have no one else to ask: I wonder whether you might lend me some money? I can gladly pay you back within a week."

Reinhart thrust the manuscript into the glove compartment and took his wallet from his pocket. "How much?"

Splendor confessed: "I could use a quarter."

"For God's sake, don't be tiresome."

"If you resent it, don't do it," said Splendor, who chose preposterous moments to be proud. Still, he did not withdraw his head and trunk from the car. Anyone walking by would think he was held captive in a sort of modern pillory.

"I mean," said Reinhart. "A quarter!"

"All right, make it a dime."

Now Reinhart did an unforgivable thing. He took a ten-dollar bill from his wallet, crushed it into a ball, and threw it onto the seat below Splendor's forequarters rather than hand it to him; and hardly had the Negro picked it up when Reinhart pointed the indicator at "Drive" and . . . almost blasted off with Splendor still retained; threatened to but didn't. It was unforgivable because the ten-spot was all his folding money: his, his wife's, and his unborn child's.

"So long, Splendor," he said not unkindly, stopping his foot a half inch above the accelerator.

"Thanks for everything, Carlo. I can pay back your loan

when my story is purchased by the *Saturday Evening Post.*'

Reinhart answered "Sure," and watched him cross the yard and mount the rickety porch. He always walked as if mounted on springs and the back of his head was a perfect brown egg.

By about one o'clock the next morning, Reinhart had an altered image of Splendor Mainwaring. Whatever the Negro's failings, as an author he was positively great. Quite likely his foibles were a necessary condition of his talent; creative artists were famous for being weaklings in life. But Splendor's weaknesses, God knows, had been established; his magnificent gift awaited recognition.

This remarkable story of his, which Reinhart had begun in a type of melancholic apathy and then was so subtly ensnared by that he stayed up far beyond his bedtime; this story, which curiously had no title, was about a man who worked in Wall Street as a law-copyist. Splendor somewhere had learned the jargon of that trade, or perhaps made it up; anyway, the narrative was set back some distance in the past, so that factual relevance to current conditions was hardly an issue. Obviously, with the invention of the typewriter the copying of legal documents by hand had died. So much for that.

Now, the story was about the copyist, but was told by his lawyer-boss, an individual in whom good will, naïeté, and guilt combined to make your commonplace man of decency. This was the "rather elderly man" of the opening sentence, read by Reinhart in the car. Why Splendor should pick such a narrator was not immediately apparent; Reinhart eventually decided that having for literary purposes decided to pose as a Caucasian, his friend determined to go the whole hog and simulate elderliness as well, anything to get as far as he could from actuality, which was presumably the idea in writing anything fictional.

The remarkable person, however, was the copyist, whom Splendor named, simply, Arthur. When the story opens, he has just been hired by the attorney, who describes him as "pallidly neat, pitiably respectable, incurably forlorn," and gives him a desk by a little window looking onto an airshaft. Arthur at first does excellently, copying every document handed him. But from a certain arbitrary point on, he refuses to do a lick of work. Now this would perhaps be unnoteworthy except for the character of his employer. That is, you first were struck by the singularities of Arthur: Why should a needy man take a job and then refuse to work at it? What motivates his nihilism? But these questions were soon replaced by one far more to the point: Why does the boss tolerate his defiance?

And not only this. One Sunday morning the lawyer, being in the neighborhood, drops by the office and finds Arthur living there. The poor fellow has no home; on the other hand, his using the office as domicile, without permission or even announcement, is clearly outrageous. The attorney benevolently orders him to leave, gives him a sum of money. The moral confusions of the story were marvelous: the employer habitually expresses his grievances against Arthur by rewarding him materially. Arthur, in return, is defiant with a fantastic gentleness; he never says no, but rather "I prefer not to." Astonishing. The most bitter combat is fought under the conventions of a high civilization; and indeed, as to the boss, of Christianity specifically: whenever he feels impelled to take Arthur by the collar and pitch him out of the office, he recalls the "divine injunction: 'a new commandment I give unto you, that ye love one another.'"

Arthur refuses the boss's terminal-leave pay, because he has no intention of leaving. Nor will he do any work. He continues to linger about the office during business hours, while the other employes labor, threatening by his passivity the general structure of reason and right and the amour propre of the lawyer, who can neither endure his presence nor bring direct aggression against him. That is to say, the aim of each, Arthur and the lawyer, is to make the *other* guy the shit. The lawyer, being a lawyer and thus a captive of all kinds of structure—this united with an idea of himself as a Christian—obviously is the loser. To get rid of Arthur he must move his entire office to another location and hope the clerk's obduracy is related specifically to the old chambers and that he will stay there. He does, and is inherited by the new tenant—who shortly comes to the attorney with a plea: I can do nothing with him; *you* left him behind, it is *your* job to dispose of him. The lawyer washes his hands of the whole mess, but when he hears the new tenant has had Arthur carted off to the city prison as a vagrant—

(At this point Genevieve stirred and muttered in sleep-talk gibberish: "Waaaagotta." For she slept in the nearby bed while Reinhart read his school assignments, and now Splendor's tale, in the overstuffed chair on the other side of the hut, the lamp-shine kept from her by a kraft-paper extension clipped to the shade. Reinhart asked: "Are you O.K., darling?" She answered: "Mpff." He went back to the story.)

The lawyer visits Arthur in prison. The latter implies cryptically that it is the former's fault he is there. And whatever justice there is in the accusation, the lawyer swallows it though protesting otherwise to his ex-clerk. Arthur then turns his back and says no more. As usual the attorney tries to fix this with money: he leaves a generous sum with the prison equivalent of a PX, in Arthur's name, so that the poor fellow can at least eat well while incarcerated. But Arthur eats nothing at all, and on another visit the lawyer finds him in the prison yard, curled up on the ground in the corner of the great wall. Dead.

In an afterword the lawyer confesses he knows nothing of Arthur's previous history save an unconfirmed rumor that he was once a clerk in the Dead Letter Office at Washington. "On errands of life, these letters speed to death," writes the lawyer. "Ah, Arthur! Ah, humanity!"

The story moved Reinhart in a way he could not quite understand. Why was he attracted to the account of an absolute No when he himself had at last become, in extremis, a yea-sayer? Why did he admire Arthur rather than the employer? But he had the answer to one question. Why had he changed his attitude towards Splendor? Because the man was a literary genius.

The third of Reinhart's summer courses, meeting from 10:10 to 11:00 each weekday morning in an unexceptionable room of a characterless building of yellow brick named Coote Hall, was Comparative Literature, which he took to make up the sophomore requirement in English, having run out on such a course three years earlier to go to the war. He had now to make it good or the University would disqualify him for a degree. You needed a degree to be somebody, as everybody said, even the degreeless. Another relevant fact was that he had gone to a different college before the war, a so-called country club where the campus was the feature; and the Municipal University, taking a dim view of this rival claim on the mother lode, would accept in tranfer only three-quarters of each credit from the other.

For a B.A. you must have about 120 points; with 1½ years of college, he had something like 13 3/4. But prewar he had been a callow, lazy, naïve, negligent, dreamy, hopeless, silly, sluggish, fatuous slob. For example, he had had a block would open any book except one on the recommended list. against reading the assignments. Ridiculous but true—he would open any book except one on the recommended list. Furthermore, he had been helpless against this destructive quirk; his defiance was not in the least conscious; try as he would to read Chap. 9, "Political and Social Reorganization," in *The Federal Union; A History of the United States to 1865,* by Prof. John D. Hicks, his eyes would clamp shut at the second sentence. On the other hand he could read three corny novels in one night. At that time he had an aversion to any piece of writing that professed to tell the truth.

But that was all behind him now. Reinhart the fireball: after but a couple of weeks of summer session he had established his pre-eminence in Beginning French, General Psychology III, and Comp Lit. Most of the returned veterans were diligent students, but Reinhart far surpassed the norm, doing not only the assignment but Additional Readings to the right and left of it, the type of thing that textbook authors list at the end of each chapter with an obvious lack of conviction. For example, in the class to which he hurried the morning after reading Splendor's short story, they would in eight summer weeks read all the great works of Western literature from Homer to date. Not the entire work in any case, but rather excerpts from each: first book of the *Iliad;* last scene of *Oedipus Rex* (where he gets the Complex, as the professor said); fifty lines from the *Aeneid;* two cantos of Dante; and so on up through the outputs of Rabelais, Cervantes, Balzac, Tolstoy, and the rest, not to mention brief re-encounters with most of the old English poets dimly recalled from high school ("I saw a host of golden daffodils," "wee timorous cowrin' beastie," and so on).

Pretty comprehensive: the first week they had wound up on the Greeks; today, the end of the second, they would bury the Romans. Reinhart had soon decided that for him there was only one decent mode of action: he would read the whole of each book represented by an excerpt in the text. The resolution sounded more formidable than the performance turned out to be, for the best-kept secret of higher education was that this literature managed much of the time to be fairly interesting. Of course, one expected this of the *Iliad,* but Ovid's *Metamorphoses* were first-rate, too. On the other hand, Horace in translation was a bore, and so was Virgil in the *Eclogues,* though pretty good in the *Aeneid,* especially when Aeneas leaves flaming Troy with his dad on his back and leading his son—his wife gets separated from him and is never found again. That moved Reinhart enormously, as of course did the suicide of lovelorn Dido later on. The Romans wrote as well of women as the Greeks of men. He looked forward to fitting Ovid's *Art of Love* into his schedule, which he believed in large part concerned screwing.

After all, it amounted to only about two or three books a week, which was no insuperable task for a real-estate man whose technique was to let a client look over the property for himself while he, the agent, sat outside in the Gigantic, reading *Agamemnon.* Reinhart saw fewer and fewer reasons why you couldn't be a good businessman and a cultured person at the same time—and for that matter, a husband, father, student, veteran, friend, etc., as well. Why limit yourself to a single state of being? It was at this time that he began to keep his lists: Books Read, Money Incoming, Money Outgoing, Foreign Cities Visited, Physical Workouts, Clients—June, and so on; and he acquired a good many secondhand Modern Library books, old-style with leatherette cover, twenty-five cents apiece, and made for his home a rudimentary bookshelf of stacked bricks and planks, which was sturdy unless you touched it.

Being slightly nearsighted and averse to admitting it to himself, in the Comparative Lit class, as in the others, Reinhart sat in the first row. As he fell into his one-armed chair this morning, two minutes early—the instructor stood in the doorway, droning something to a hairy fellow in a T-shirt showing the University's animal mascot, a slavering jackal or whatever; this student was somewhere under forty, a Phys. Ed. major, and already flunking though summer session had met only ten days and though he was not in the least stupid, as Reinhart discovered upon meeting him over coffee in the Campus Hideaway; it was rather irony that controlled him: "Whoever heard of a coach who was well read?" he asked, with an intelligent smirk—as Reinhart settled in his chair, putting his extra books under it, the pretty, malicious, blond girl on his left said: "Virgil *again today?*"

"I'm afraid so." He smiled, really rather bitterly. As soon as you were married, all the good-looking broads took the initiative. He no longer had the slightest interest in other women, and it was retroactively that he now burned at how she would have sniffed at Reinhart the bachelor. He wore no ring, but they could tell.

She took more liberties. "Damn," she said, maneuvering her shallow blue eyes. "Goddamn," she went on, "there's a dull old bastard."

He frowned and asked: "Mr. Pardy or Virgil?"

"Both." She suddenly crossed her legs in a most awkward fashion for a girl so finely articulated, and he realized that the instructor had come to the lectern directly before them and dropped his briefcase.

"Now, Publius Wirgilius Maro as he was called on his native heath," began Mr. Pardy a few moments later; he was a tall, gaunt man, who had he not gone into teaching could have been a cowboy, "as we mentioned yesterday . . ." He turned several pages in his sheaf of notes and began to read very rapidly: "Been said *Aeneid* is made up of six books *Iliad* and six *Odyssey.* Sixth book obviously modeled on eleventh book *Odyssey;* description of Aeneas' shield much like that by Homer in *Iliad,* but in spite of similarities, differences between Virgil and Homer. Virgil, e.g., worked on epic ten years. Still dissatisfied with it when died and requested it be burned after death. Whereas little is known of Homer the man." Pardy looked at the class and said: "Or Homer the committee," and his students dutifully laughed, it still being early in the hour.

The girl next to Reinhart, whose name was Helen Tarmigan, raised her hand and asked when recognized: "What are some other differences among Homer and Virgil?"

"Of course they are both profound but in a different way," answered Mr. Pardy. "And then it goes without saying"—he sniffed in amusement—"one wrote in Greek, the other in Latin." The class laughed very meagerly at this, and he hastened to add: "I don't mean that altogether with levity. *Mutatis mutandis*, the Roman tongue is another species of—" he coughed. "Perhaps you recall from your high-school Caesar the rubric under which the legions marched: S.P.Q.R. Small profit, quick returns." He consulted the pocket watch he had placed upon the lectern at the outset. The room by now was beastly warm and no one laughed.

Pardy found a piece of chalk in his seersucker jacket and wrote upon the blackboard:

SUNT LACRIMAE RERUM

VARIUM ET MUTABILE SEMPER FEMINA

And explained: "These are two quotations you might wish to remember from Virgil before we pass on. The first is useful at exam time; the second when you get married. The first means 'the tears of things,' or loosely, *'There are tears* in things.' The second, 'Oh, various and changeable is always the woman.'" Miss Tarmigan snickered "But, then," Mr. Pardy said deprecatingly, "I guess you all read Virgil in Latin in high school, and it is a very hot day." He tended to sour when his jokes weren't widely picked up. He now added: *"Troia fuit,* which is the ancient Roman equivalent of *Alles kaputt.* Don't you know Alice Kaputt? She sits in the back row."

He saturninely swung back to the lectern, and crumpled against it. "Well now, if there is no further objection, we move on to Dante, but ah"—he seized his watch and squinted histrionically close to its face—"we have only forty-five minutes left, and that's hardly time to introduce a giant figure such as Dante. May I suggest that we adjourn, then, to meet again tomorrow same time and place. Be sure to read the condensed version of the *Divine Comedy* in your text. What the editor has done is cut out the lard, as it were. You'll find you have read far worse things that were written only yesterday. There are slow moments, true, but there will be other rewarding pas-

200

sages. In the story of Paolo and Francesca you will even find a bit of sex! So bear with it. Good morning."

He clapped his notes together and dashed for the exit, but came nowhere near making it as a number of zealous students swarmed into the aisle and set upon him like mad dogs. The rest of the class melted softly away. Reinhart waited out the zealots, which meant following Pardy and party down several corridors to the teacher's office door and listening to much irrelevant dialogue as the sycophants sought to impress Pardy without doing any actual work and he to get rid of them without their realizing rejection: it should have been a fine exchange but was in fact gross. Miss Tarmigan, last in line before Reinhart, wanted to know how Virgil's opinion of women contrasted with that of the man who wrote a book called *Generation of Vipers* attacking the American female.

"Interesting," mumbled Pardy, smiling wanly at her bosom, and sidled into his office. Miss Tarmigan clopped away on her high heels, waggling her head in a smug manner at whatever had been proved.

"Excuse me, Dr. Pardy," said Reinhart as the office door came towards his nose. No reponse, so he pushed in after. He had checked on Pardy in the catalogue and found him to be sans Ph.D., but used the superior title anyway since he was asking a favor. "Sir, I know how busy you must be, and I wouldn't ask did I not feel it's really an outstanding piece of work." He fished out Splendor's MS from between his books.

"What's that?" said Pardy, still with his back towards Reinhart. "Part of your novel?" He hurled his notes into an open drawer and lighted a cigarette in the desperate, amateurish fashion of professors just out of class.

"Oh no, sir," Reinhart began. "I'm not—" But he suddenly understood the imposition of asking him to evaluate an outsider's work and let the erroneous identification stand. "That is, it's not a novel but a kind of story."

"What kind of story?" Pardy asked pettishly. "You fellows with your 'kind of's.' Why not just call it a story?"

Not wishing to jeopardize Splendor's chances, Reinhart ignored this piece of rudeness and said humbly: "I wondered if you would have time to read it—"

In lanky movement towards the window, under which stood, like an indoor plant that had died, a leather bag of golf clubs, Pardy corrected; "'I should like to have you read it...'"

"Well, will you?" blurted Reinhart, anyway laying the manuscript on the desk.

"There's no career in fiction," said Pardy with acidulous

glee, then snapped the elastic on the suede glove that covered the head of his brassie. "Not for somebody out here. You have to be in New York, you see, and go to their parties. We're all hicks, you see." He snarled at Reinhart, though the venom was directed at somebody not present.

'Pardon?" asked Reinhart.

"Well, go on, then," said Pardy, opening his long lower jaw like a steamshovel. "Find out for yourself what happens when you send a book to a New York publisher."

It didn't take Reinhart long to see the light. "You're a writer yourself, aren't you, sir?"

Pardy made some ironical disclaimer, but he jerked his mouth in pleasure and seized the manuscript in rough good will, dog-earing the early pages. Seeing Splendor's last name and first initial in the upper left-hand corner, he said: "O.K., Mainwaring, I'll look at your stuff, but you mustn't expect to be a Louis Bromfield or a P. P. Marquand first time out."

"I certainly don't," said Reinhart, and escaped.

Two days later they had finished Dante & His Times, and since Reinhart in that period had managed to read the entire *Divine Comedy,* in addition to the assignments in his other courses, plus the performance of his various duties as householder, husband, and realtor, he assumed that Pardy, a professional reader as it were, had had ample time to assess Splendor's talent.

So he had. "Sorry, Mainwaring," he told Reinhart in his office after class, "I'm afraid you don't quite make it. I'm afraid you just don't get off the ground. One, it is not credible when a young fellow writes in the character of an elderly man. Two, where did you get this crazy job of law-copyist? Don't tell me lawyers have not discovered the typewriter. Hahah." He laughed sadly and gestured towards Splendor's surrogate. "One plus two, and the story falls on that."

"But you see, Dr. Pardy, it is historical, which explains your Number Two, and as to your One, what if you read it without knowing the author's age?" Reinhart smiled plaintively. "Dante was never in Paradise, after all."

"Hell."

"Excuse me?"

"You mean, 'Dante was never in Hell.' "

"Or there, either."

Pardy frowned in derision, his nostrils flared. "Not 'either.' Just there, in Hell. That's what the *Divine Comedy* is about. I thought I made that clear this morning. But, my God, if the students can't even get that straight."

"Yes," said Reinhart. "I know that the excerpts in our text are from only the *Inferno*. But on my own I read the other two books, where he goes to Purgatory and to Paradise, though I preferred the *Hell*."

Pardy stared at him keenly. "Where did you get those books, may I ask?"

"The University library."

"Purgatory and Paradise, eh? I suppose it never occurred to you that they might be spurious?" Pardy took Splendor's manuscript from the desktop and thrust it angrily at Reinhart. "Look here, Mainwaring. If you want to be a writer, you had better *write* some instead of reading so abundantly and without authentication. You might also try to cultivate *feeling* rather than pseudo-intellectualism. Get real people in real situations. What do you *know* about Wall Street? Write about college. That's all you *know* at present. Don't make a fool of yourself by pretending to a wider experience than you can *know* and *feel*."

Curiously enough, Reinhart himself had begun to believe it was his own story, and on the spot developed the writer's syndrome: he pressed the button which abolished everybody but admirers of his work, though in this case "everybody" was only poor Pardy, who, himself an unsuccessful writer, had abolished "Mainwaring" before he read him.

In several months with Claude, Reinhart had learned something about business, yet was still a novice before its fundamental mysteries. From one incident, however, and (as usual) under a counterfeit identity, he had learned the only essential secret of literature as a career: spite.

He certainly couldn't pass Pardy's reaction on to Splendor. As usual, he was sorry he had ever got into the situation. He was also sick of being sorry; obviously there was some element in his unconscious that urged him to simulate generosity—if he read his Psych assignments rightly, he was probably, behind the mask, a sadist. Be that as it may, he had now discharged his obligation. But where to, now? If being an author's agent was an unpleasant job, how much more rotten to be an author! What at the outset seemed Splendor's new health had taken very little time to prove his new sickness. Of course Pardy was a buffoon who must have got his job during the war years when 1-A instructors were in uniform—yet his criticism had made a mark on Reinhart. *Was* Splendor's story any good? What *did* an Ohio Negro know about Wall Street?

He went to the periodical room of the University library and pawed through the magazines on the tables there, lousing up their shinglelike arrangement. He had never before appreciated the abundance of scribbling that came monthly from the world's pens, not to mention the daily newspapers that were in another room and the yearly books in subterranean stacks, and this library was small potatoes as such institutions went. Did all these words serve any purpose? Was all this shit worth shoveling? Reinhart savagely, rhetorically asked, for it was getting on towards noon and he was hungry and had not yet found the right magazine. He now doubted whether the story was good, but no one could question its honesty—which immediately disqualified it from any of the periodicals he had yet examined.

Having worked his way through the weeklies and monthlies, he waded into the quarterlies: squat, drab things, their covers lined with unbelievable names opposite nonsensical titles: "John Brabson Slink: 'Alloy in the *Golden Bowl*' . . . Murray Marcus: 'Ain't Gonna Give Ya None of My Jelly-Roll: A Roundup of Recent Verse' . . . Croon Jameson and James C. Wallaby: An Exchange of Correspondence" . . . and so on, but the paper was book quality and they ran no adds.

Reinhart selected *The Midland Review* (edited by John Brabson Slink, except that he was now on a sabbatical and Philip Downing Urn and Irving Washington were alternating as guest editors until he came back), gave Splendor's story a quick, serviceable title ("Arthur"), wrote in the upper left-hand corner "S. Mainwaring, c/o Reinhart" and below it the Vetsville address, and mailed it off in a stamped envelope purchased from the campus P.O.

For two weeks he pounced on the mails so avidly that Gen was at last stirred to ask why, and before he knew what he was doing Reinhart had told her about "Arthur" as if it were his own.

"Oh!" cried Genevieve. She even rose from the couch to come embrace him. "Carl, I never knew you would be a writer, *too*." She hugged him and, bending back, studied the underside of his chin. It was surely nice to be so admired by your little woman and feel her swelling breasts against your upper abdomen.

"Well," said Reinhart in deprecation, "I clown around with it." When *The Midland Review* sent its acceptance, he would direct them to replace the pen name "Mainwaring" with his real one—he actually went so far in his mind at that point.

Two days later, before his inner judge he pleaded that here too he had been clowning. But that was after the manuscript came back with the following note:

DEAR MR. MAINWARING:

This has been a masterpiece ever since the 1850's, when Herman Melville published it under the title of "Bartleby the Scrivener." Your changing the name of the central character is not, in our opinion, a sufficient revision to warrant its republication at this time.

You owe us 18¢ in return postage.

The note was unsigned, and whether it had been written by Philip Downing Urn or Irving Washington, Reinhart would never know.

Chapter 13

Luckily the manuscript had come back on Saturday morning when he was home to seize and hide it and describe the mail for Gen's benefit as a handful of throwaways.

"Gee," she said in commiseration, throwing down her book and rising as she had begun to do at any mention of his art. This reverence was what hurt. "You're waiting to hear about your story, aren't you?"

"Of coure they may not take it," Reinhart muttered, slinking towards the corner where they kept the carpet sweeper. Time for Saturday housecleaning, ten o'clock, Gen not long up. He had been alive since eight, reading his assignments in the back doorway, where it was cool.

"So much the worse for you," said Gen, meaning "them," but being unwittingly right. "That's unthinkable."

To elude his shame he became cross with her for the first time since they took their vows. "How can you say that? You haven't even read it."

"Ah," she said, blinking, "I know it is good if you did it." She winked again; there was a lash in her eye. "Besides, you told me the plot."

"Yes," he admitted, and made the carpet sweeper whirr, "but you know the way it's done may be awful. *I* can't say. . . . We need a vacuum cleaner; this damn thing won't pick up the lint. Maybe the paper will list a used one."

"The check for your story will cover that amply," said Genevieve pretentiously. "But I hope we can find a more exciting way to spend it."

He began to suspect her of malice based on an intuition of the true state of affairs. After all, she had lots of time, did nothing but lie around the house the livelong day. . . . The busy little sweeper wheels suddenly became intractable. He found a bobby pin enmeshed among them—evidence that his wife was everywhere to brake him. Yet when, as long as he was at it, he took the sweeper outside and emptied its dust chamber into the trashcan, among the dirt that matted into long, feltlike strips he discerned other clues to her existence—more hairpins, half-a-Kleenex red with lipstick, the stamen of a paper flower—and instantly throbbed with affection.

He returned to the hut almost chortling, for it was marvelous to admit a wrong to someone you loved. But no wife did he see throughout the length and breadth of his home: she had run away from his bad manners. Ah, there she came from around the front partition. "Darling," she said. "I don't want to bother you, but—well, would you mind looking at—" She held something with both hands behind her and grinned foolishly, putting her right toe forward.

"Speak freely, dear," encouraged Reinhart with a great smile of loving approbation.

"Well . . ."

"Come on."

"It really concerns Daddy."

Reinhart caught his chin as it fell. He had thought they observed a gentleman's agreement to forget about that man. "Have you been in touch with him?" he asked, trying to be nonchalant, but his teeth must have grated.

For Gen answered sharply: "Of course, he's my father."

"What's that got to do with it? He's a swine," Reinhart naturally did *not* say. The sound that came out was a noncommittal mumble. Then he asked: "When?"

Genevieve smiled hypocrisy. "Oh sometimes he comes over during the day."

"When I'm at work."

"Or school," she amplified. "He's sorry he hasn't been able to stay till you get home, but he usually has to run.

"Too bad," murmured Reinhart. "Now what was it you had to show me?" He turned and started back for the sweeper.

"If you aren't interested . . ."

"Didn't I just say I was?" The bad thing about this exchange, which was probably routine in other marriages, was that for the first time since establishing a domicile, they had different aims. Or perhaps it was just that they were revealing

207

them. However, it was only fair that he find out the precise nature of hers.

His grin was probably too obviously disarming—it seemed to annoy her. He said: "Give it here."

She stayed where she stood, and he had eventually to walk to that point. Once there, though, he was instantly reimbursed. Gen kissed him.

"Wouldn't it be kind," she said, "if you would read this and give it your professional criticism." Her mouth was barely off his and the words tickled. He felt a sheaf of paper insinuate itself between his hand and her waist.

He drew back and looked, and my God it was another manuscript: a very thin one, but bearing a thick title in compensation: *The Confessions of a Gentleman,* by Blaine Raven.

"Where's the rest?" he asked lamely.

"That's all I could get him to write so far," said Gen. "But maybe the two of us together, you and I—"

"Are you kidding? He detests me."

"Don't jump for conclusions." Gen wrinkled her nose and sniffed. "My ambition is still to bring you two together." Wasn't it strange that all the while she had stuck stubbornly to her premarital ideas! And never said a word. For the first time he understood that she was deep and, it went without saying, devious.

"Everybody has a story in them," she announced, suddenly defiant, and he daydreamed a ghastly vision of literally that: a great host of human beings vomiting manuscripts. His modest lie had exposed him to a horror hitherto unsuspected.

Up went his hands, and he laughed uneasily. "Next thing, you'll be wanting to show me your poetry, hahaha."

Genevieve colored and turned her shoulder to him.

"I'm sorry," said Reinhart. "I didn't realize you really *had* poetry." He dug her in the ribs. "I'll bet it's great. Isn't it? Isn't it great? Come on now."

She opened her eyes wide as they would go and said: "I don't know whether you understand it, but you're being horrible."

"Then what do you want?" he shouted. "I thought you were conserving your energy to have a baby, when all the time you're writing poetry, seeing people on the sly, and God knows what else. I'm just glad we have an electric refrigerator, that's all." Trundling the sweeper out the back door, he hurled his Parthian shot: "That's why you aren't friends with the ice man!"

Outside, he remembered he had already emptied the dust chamber and in so doing had put down a milder pique. Today

208

Gen was insupportable vis-á-vis, but endearing again when he turned his back on her. What a dog I am, he told himself as he went back inside. . . . Genevieve stood at the sink with a butcher knife near her wrist.

"Stop, stop!" he cried. "I didn't know what I was saying!"

She corrugated her lips and asked: "What's wrong with you? This won't hurt your damn knife." She was cutting the pages of a handsome little notebook jacketed in green morocco.

At the strangest moments Reinhart would develop a passion for *things*: the little book was devilishly cunning, and he could not resist articles made of leather.

He stuck out his hand. "May I see it?"

"No," she said indignantly. "And laugh at my work?"

"Your poems are in it?"

"I'm cutting room to write more," she stated snippishly, threw down the blade, went to the card table where he did his written homework, and began to scribble rapidly with a little pencil that issued from the book's binding on a thin golden chain.

"Darling." He swooped down without warning and gathered her in his arms. His grasp prohibited her from struggling, but she glared as a cat would under similar circumstances and was actually ready to spit in fury. You never saw anything so cute. He slid his hand onto her breast, which was about the size of a green pepper and the consistency of—well, what would you say in poetry—*of flesh,* nothing could compare to its feel.

"Damn you!" she screamed. "Just because you've got that thing, you believe you're God."

"What thing?" he asked incredulously, for naturally he had thrust the carpet sweeper away before embracing her.

"You know what I mean. You act like you've got the only one in the universe!" Her little face was all screwed up, very near his. As if she were rabid, he could neither continue to retain her nor let her go. The pencil was dangling from the book on its chain; the pages had closed of their own willfulness, so he could not read the verse. However, he did finally get the reference and was shocked by it into two kinds of reply: wounded and wounding.

"I never heard you object before. . . . Well, it's the only one in this house, and don't you forget it."

Of course these were both literally false. He had had virtually to rape her the first time; and as to the uniqueness of his position as the only man in her life, or hut, her visiting father nullified that. He let her go and again plunged out the rear door, stumbling on the cinder-block step, into his back yard. What a rotten day! Neither had the grass seed, sown three weeks before, taken hold: the only life in the lawn was the impudent hollow stalks of wild onion, like so many green straws to a subterranean soda. If you pulled them, your hand smelled acrid. There was also a dandelion or two with flowers gone to seed in those tiny powder puffs—he seized one blew it bald, forgetting to make a wish.

Yes, he knew many of Nature's secrets but made little use of them, being habitually enmired in human problems. They didn't see enough other people, he and Gen, especially she. Poets were always turned inward: "If I should die, think only this of me, that there's some corner of a foreign field that is forever England"—the comment of who else but a poet? "When the stars threw down their spears and watered heaven with their tears"—absolutely inexplicable except as the expression of a poet. He realized at long last that *he* very likely was not one, in spite of the distant German relative so poetic as to blow out his brains. In *Anna Karenina,* which he was reading for Comparative Literature (where after two days of *Paradise Lost* they had concluded their study of the Epic and turned to the Novel), the heroine is represented as thinking always of the same thing: her happiness and her unhappiness. That was a woman for you. Reinhart, on the other hand, a man, was at any given moment trying to define himself.

But he could never accept the passing of time. Half a year earlier he had been a soldier on European duty. As a boy he had never really believed he would grow up, though all the while waiting only to do so, for he never placed much value in juvenility. But how did one grow up? And where did the time go? It was already nine minutes, by his wrist watch, since Gen's revelation; already the new situation was more feasible.

But when he returned indoors to admit as much to her, his wife was gone. Really gone this time, for he looked behind the partition. And the car had gone from out front as well, though he never knew she could drive. Either that, or both she and the Gigantic had been kidnaped. He must wait for either the divorce papers or a ransom note. Meanwhile, he went to the makeshift bookcase, at last put down *The Confessions of a Gentleman,* found the old zoology notebook wherein he kept his contemporary lists (without having excised the prewar material, in the early pages, on the euglena, a queer organism half plant, half animal, and armed with a built-in whip, which is how it get its food: flogs its environment, so to speak). He turned past "Books Read," impatient to enter *Anna Karenina,* but he was still only halfway through that novel; reached

"Clients—June" and saw the names of all his Vetsville neighbors though no sales. He had flopped at real estate, as well as marriage.

In a supreme effort to find himself, he started a new list of "Women Had," and counting his age as substantially twenty-two though that birthday was several weeks in the future, his computation came to one for every two years of his life, counting only the complete, standard act and not near misses, virtual victories, and substitute excursions, etc. Also not counting Gen; it seemed pornographic to list a wife.

For example, here was simply: "Anonymous English Girl Met in Pub in Weston Super Mare." He had never learned her name, yet could still recall that of the pub: The Cock and Bull; the condition of her underwear: woolly, the time being February; her cigarettes: Goldflake; but of her person, nothing beyond a vague sense that like all such, she had been cheery.

Now here was another, one Veronica Leary, an Army nurse he had last been with some two-thirds of a year before; he could hardly forget that she was almost six feet tall, but he had lost all memory of her face! Then there was somebody's wife, for whom it had been revenge against her permanent partner, and therefore while giving herself she had held her soul aloof: except at the groin, she and Reinhart remained very distant (thus in a way her husband, whoever he may be, had not been cuckolded). All sorts of options were represented in the names, or pseudonyms, of eleven girls; yet the list was far from comprehensive as to the relationships possible between man and woman.

For example, he had twice been desperately in love without ever "making love" to his sweethearts; while on the other hand he had at best neutral, at worst downright repugnant, feelings towards several of the persons on his list. Suddenly he recalled a shameful twelfth entry, an almost middle-aged cook, weary and coarse, from his prewar college-dormitory kitchen—for him the face-saving upshot of some jest.

Then there had been important experiences with girls he could have taken but never did, and time had taught him that some of these were among the most precious of his gains. A consummated love is grand, but one that misses connections is sometimes glorious, giving you an imaginative lien on the woman forever.

Thirteen: with the utmost reluctance he remembered that he had not always managed to avoid the kind you paid for; though, true, this had never happened while he was sober. The baker's dozen was completed by a tart he had encountered when full of cider and wandering through the blackout in, of

211

all places, an English town named Reading, where he had by inebriate error left the London train. He had been not in the least horny when accosted. Like everyone who has ever frequented a streetwalker, he assented to her offer because, ideologically speaking, it was witty and grotesque, being on the order of: "'ere you go, Yank!" In this case the whole experiment was conducted in the shadows of the railway station. If there were some faces he could not recall, this face he had never even seen!

It is remarkable what you will do because of that which for simplicity's sake might be called the possession of an external sexual organ—for it was not his belief that women, concave, would do nearly as much. He used to get involuntary erections on public conveyances, because of the motion, no doubt, but also owing to the presence of unknown women, whom however he had no wish to enter, being satified to know that he was equipped to do so if need be. There was no reason to believe that a woman could even understand this type of idealism; and for their literalness, as much as anything else, Reinhart pitied them.

"Believe me, knowing only your wife, whom you love, you will know women much better than if you had thousands of them," says a character in *Anna Karenina*. Did Reinhart love Genevieve? He would have put his hand into the fire for her, but did he find her *interesting?* Guiltily he considered whether he should have asked her opinion of whatever the United Nations were doing. He used to jeer at the course in marriage relations offered at his prewar college, but should he have taken it? Perhaps she would like to have her own checkbook. She might be encouraged occasionally to borrow the car, give a bridge party, and gossip over the metaphorical back fence. They would read books together and discuss them, share radio programs, plan an education for the child to come. Going out to dinner would mean little to Gen since Reinhart did the cooking; however, a change of scene might prove salutary.

Home decorating was something women went in for; unless he read his psychology wrong, they considered the house an extension of themselves, rather than, as it was with men, a place to hang the hat. Except it was he, and not she, who kept the place neat. He might have interpreted this, with some self-damage, as effeminacy on his part were not his sexual appetites only too obvious. Speaking of sex, there had been an unfavorable implication in her gibe; he had perhaps gone at it too hot and heavy—he had thought that's what marriage is for; maybe he was wrong.

All in all, they had both of them made mistakes. In future he must be more elastic, and she less secretive. That, he believed, took care of it, but as he nodded confidently towards the front door, he was already half mad with loneliness. He needed only one person at any given time to conspire against the world with, but he *did* need that one. Once you were married, not even a friend could fill the role: it had to be a wife, or perhaps a mistress; something to do with sex, though not in the narrow terms of a lay. A pity that when he was on the verge of important discoveries in this area, his wife had to leave him. Feeling stale, he made the fourth trip of the morning into the back yard. There was no place else to go, especially now that he hadn't the car. Brooding had robbed him of time: the noon whistle groaned from town. Before Monday he had to finish *Anna Karenina,* two chapters in Psych, and a story in French about the inevitable M. et Mme Morel et leurs enfants, but he lost his drive in those disciplines.

"Hi fella," shouted someone across the baked-mud sea between Reinhart's hut and the next. Without raising his head Reinhart knew the call issued from a neighbor so amicable that he had been avoiding him since moving in. Ordinarily he couldn't endure people who were that friendly, feeling awful impulses to punch them suddenly in the mouth and see how they would take *that*: did affection without cause ruin them for reasonable resentment? But now it was as if heaven had sent succor.

"Hi, Fedder." Reinhart waved to him in the fashion of De Gaulle re-entering Paris. That is, whatever his troubles, he still wished to keep a certain interval between them.

Olympian or not, the greeting more than sufficed for Fedder, who took it as license to troop over in a pair of tennis shoes that were gauchely white and too large, slapping the ground like the flippers of a seal. He also wore Army suntan trousers and a T-shirt stenciled USS TICONDEROGA, followed by the last name of a person not himself: his entire wardrobe was war-surplus.

"Hi fella," Fedder repeated when he arrived at close quarters. *"Buon giorno!* How's the lit major?"

Reinhart cupped a hand at his ear and opened his mouth, not putting his incomprehension into words because of a reluctance to encourage Feeder's breeziness.

"English lit, no?" asked his neighbor. "Aren't you in the Comp Lit that meets tennish at one-two-oh Coote? I see you every morning on my way to Econ. I'm pre-law."

"But I don't major in it," Reinhart explained. "I guess you might say I'm pre-psychiatric."

"Working your way up to the insane asylum?" boldly joked Fedder; yet his face was shy and he looked at Reinhart's toes; he wanted so much to be friends that his judgment was warped as how to go about it. Why is acceptance more attractive to him than self-sufficency? Reinhart wondered, continuing in his analytic mood.

"Listen, Carl," Fedder blurted, nudging Reinhart's elbow with his own, his forearm very moist—indeed, Fedder's whole person ran with sweat, and he whipped out an olive-drab handkerchief and mopped his neck—"Carl, I put you up for membership in the Vetsville branch of Citizens for World Government, and we won't take no for an answer."

"I'm afraid you'll have to," Reinhart answered bluntly. He hated to be called by his first name as overture to some plea.

"You're joking," said Fedder. "You writers are always interested in the good of mankind."

For a moment, Reinhart answered internally: That's right, we are, and warmed himself at the candle Fedder had lighted for his exalted profession. For shame. He pinched himself and asked a question that skirted the issue.

"How do you know so much about me?"

"That's all right how I know," Fedder said cutely, simpering and with his head held on the bias. "Never you mind about that." Fedder's hair was clotted with damp and plastered to his scalp like that of the ad-buffoon who uses the greasy tonic rather than the product that attracts the broads. What lies were circulated in the interests of commerce! Fedder had the face of a Boston Terrier, dressed like a vagrant, sweated like a glass of beer on a muggy day, and yet was intimate with Genevieve—how else would he have known about Reinhart?

Why, why, why? What have I left undone? Reinhart asked himself tragically. I was trustworthy, loyal, helpful, cheerful, thrifty, clean, reverent—he recited the Boy Scout Law in unprecedented self-attack (he had never been a Scout), and detected with the greatest alarm his growing taste for the wry and even the sour.

"That's all right," Fedder continued naïvely. "I know *all* about you. Now what about World Guv? And once we nail you for that, next comes the Vetsville Civic Committee. And have you though about the AVC—you certainly wouldn't be the American Legion type. The good people are in the majority here. We've a few Yahoos, but a lot fewer than most communities: 90 per cent of our male inhabitants go to college. What a chance of rational community planning, huh? If only we can incorporate on our own. That's all that's holding us back at present, but once we break loose on our own—well, we'll have grad students in government for our town councilors, a philosophy major for our mayor and each and every

214

one of us will have a direct voice in public affairs, through a sort of Swiss canton arrangement. How about that: Why should we let politicians be contemptible? 'For the triumph of evil it is necessary only that good men do nothing.' " He reapplied the Army handkerchief to his sopping forehead.

What shall I do with my wife's lover? thought Reinhart. Beat him, kill him, or exchange civilities in the European style? He sees me safely into the Comparative Literature class, then races here to my home. The insolent swine, to confront me like this! However, he is far from nonchalant; look at him sweat.

"How did you know I wrote?" Reinhart asked obsessively, for purposes of espionage disguising it as a light, simply vain enquiry. "Have you read my stuff?"

But Fedder, sucking on an empty pipe, had long left that subject. He shifted his feet, blankly said: "Pardon?" and returned to his own interests. "Have you and Jenny talked over the sewer?"

Now it was remarkable that Reinhart maintained his calm demeanor, but he did. Outwardly, he said only: "Mmm," and squinted judiciously, in which he was assisted by the blinding sun, Fedder having maneuvered him around till it was directly in his eyes.

"In case she hasn't fully checked you out," said Fedder, hooking his thumbs through his Army-surplus web belt, talking through his pipe as it were, "when this was a CCC camp years ago, it was in remote country—five miles from town. Wow, that was roughing it! And those fellows had slit trenches and chemical toilets. Came W.W. Two—well, they didn't need another reception center with Fort Budge so close, but if you remember your armed forces, you know the way they ran through supplies. Idea! said the bigwigs. Flashing lightbulbs, etc., as in the funny papers. A Q.M. depot! And so it was, manned by only a battalion, but they got their indoor toilets and branch to the main sewer, which by this time, the town having expanded to within two miles, went so to speak right by the door on its way to empty into the Mohawk River."

Fedder went on talking while breathing in, which of course he did through his empty pipe, as if he were under water and that his sole communication with the air. "Now a sewer that is sufficient, say, for four or five hundred men—however large a quartermasters battalion is—"

Reinhart interrupted Fedder at that point. "Just what branch of the service were *you* in?" There were perhaps countless better questions, but this was in no sense a substitute for them, or evidence that Reinhart was nonplussed: at that moment he had a serious interest in the man's service record, with an idea that were Fedder a combat veteran he might have some small excuse for his outrages: being cuckolded by a hero was surely better than by a 4-F.

But Fedder's voice rose triumphantly over Reinhart's inquiry: he was an absolutely invincible fanatic when it came to sewers, and Reinhart's only comfort lay in supposing that if this was the sort of thing "Jenny" found fascinating, so much the worse for her.

"—insufficient for a community of the size of Vetsville. The problem is simply this: we have outgrown our pipes!" Fedder positively shouted for joy, as if it were an accomplishment to produce more sewage than the next guy. He himself produced more perspiration than most; he was gushing water like a statue in a public fountain. "Now this is the procedure: we petition the town council to—"

A howl of engine and a squeal of tires announced the return of the Gigantic, out front, and no doubt the return of Genevieve logically followed—at the moment, though, Reinhart was not as much impressed by that event as by Fedder's reaction to it: the neighbor broke off the rant about his precious sewer and bent forward, turning his eager muzzle in the direction of the car-noise.

"Is that—" Fedder began, but before he could say "Jenny" again, Reinhart's shoes caught him hard in the buttocks, launching him on a brief flight. He met the earth like a cat, paw-breaking his descent rather gracefully.

What Fedder did post-fall, Reinhart couldn't have said, for the counterfeit writer had turned away from his adversary and gone to meet his wife. He no sooner rounded the corner of the Quonset than she saw him through the windshield.

"Come here and take these packages!" she ordered shrilly. She had changed to a pair of striped shorts that verged on the brazen: a close observer could almost have seen her discreets. This was a mother-elect. Nevertheless, Reinhart did as told and gathered an armload of bundles from the front seat, his strategy being to continue for a while to pay out rope to her. The packages felt like food.

"You haven't been getting enough to eat?" he asked with a faint sneer. "I'm not a good provider—is that what you're saying?"

"Don't be ridiculous," answered Genevieve, twitching her hip. "I'm just going to do something on my own for a change." She piled more parcels on top of those he already held, obstructing his view, then led him into the hut like a blind man. He craftily bided his time, doing an excellent job of transport, unloaded carefully on the drainboard of the

216

kitchen sink and began to unwrap item by item in search of perishables that should be refrigerated without delay.

"You can let that go," Gen said authoritatively.

"But I always—" Reinhart began in wonder.

"I *said*," said Gen, "I'm going to do something on my own for a change. Didn't you understand?" Suddenly she produced a pack of cigarettes, popped one out, lighted it, smoked it furiously once, coughed terribly, put it out under a drizzle of water from one of the taps—which for some reason affected Reinhart like the scraping of metal on concrete—and dropped the butt soggily into the sink, abandoning it there.

Ugh," was the sound Reinhart made, staring at the butt. He was helplessly aware that he became more and more plaintive. For example, he found it impossible at this time to charge her with frequenting Fedder: she might have some ruinously good justification. After all, under the regime of Carlo I, it was true, her functions tended to be perhaps too severely circumscribed. Probably he could delegate certain powers to her without damaging her character, though of course he relied on her understanding that such errors as he had committed could be laid at the door of too much, rather than too little, love. And what about the baby? He wished he could talk to Maw about what she did while pregnant with him, but that subject conjoined with that individual resulted in his always feeling at once curiously weak and preposterously misinformed.

He said subtly: "Oh, I almost forgot to mention. The guy from next door was over. He seems to be a friend of yours."

Gen pushed him aside and began herself to unwrap the packages. From one of them she extricated a great crown roast of beef, its standing ribs wearing little paper pantaloons; from another, an armload of asparagus. There were other goodies in the same vein, scarcely less expensive, and several bottles of the highest type of booze: wine from France and his old friend Courvoisier. Putting the fruit into the refrigerator, she withdrew from it the box of Camembert that Reinhart had just placed there.

"No, no, no," she said. "Must let it ripen. . . . Oh yeah, the man from next door was over yesterday and left a petition for you to sign. I stuck it in the bookcase."

Is that all? murmured Reinhart to himself. It was probably what she would have said had there been more—but could a wife be disloyal who planned such lordly meals for her spouse?

"He's quite a jerk, isn't he?" Reinhart asked happily, trying to fit a long, thin loaf of bread into their short, squat bread-box. Nothing would serve but cutting it in two.

"Noooo," screamed Genevieve, causing him to drop the knife. "Are you out of your mind?" But it was a rather a defense of the loaf than of Fedder; she demanded in the name of freshness that it be kept whole.

"I trust you'll shave sometime this afternoon," she said after the disposition of the food. The last item, for which she let water into a vase, was a bouquet of yellow and white flowers, which, centered on the card table, changed the character of their home; from a machine for living it had become a house of love and light.

"Gen, if you can do it, so can I. I apologize," said Reinhart. Yet he still did not feel up to telling the truth about Melville's-Splendor's-his short story. "You know," he said facetiously, with a sweep of the arm to symbolize the marvelous dinner they would have before nightfall, the first ever prepared by his wife, "quarreling is not so bad when it ends with this kind of reconciliation." Then, as a man will when one thing goes well, he looked for supporting pleasures, and thought of how he had kicked Fedder's ass for what turned out to be no greater crime than promoting a sewer.

He was laughing out loud at the blindness of justice when Gen said: "What are you babbling about? I've invited my family to dinner."

Chapter 14

"Call me Blaine," said Genevieve's father over his brandy, coffee, and panatella. He alternated sips of one or the other with puffs at the third, at which moments his eyes were smugly slitted. If already in April he had had a tan, he now was dark as Splendor Mainwaring—indeed it was difficult for Reinhart to see more of him across the table than eyes and teeth, in the candlelight Gen had provided.

Now, it was once true that you could be accepted into Reinhart's trust by no more than calling for the use of Christian names, but not since he discovered it was an obligation rather than a privilege. Besides, his father-in-law had so far called him nothing at all, while eating great quantities of the food that Gen may have chosen but Reinhart had to pay for.

Gen's mother was present, too—somewhere in the shadows on the right side of the card table: a person of her type was all but eradicated by candlelight. Of the family, only the estimable Kenworthy was missing; he had indeed run off to the Navy. Otherwise, the clan was strategically placed for an explosion of the water heater: *bang,* virtually no more Ravens, whereas the Reinharts would have lost only Carlo.

"The name," Raven went on, "has been in my family generations but it is always given only to firstborn males. It is an exclusive privilege, there having been only six of us since the seventeenth century. However, the tendency of our women is

219

to be spirited and willful, and the line I think has not suffered but—"

"Really!" said Reinhart, doing his best to get along. "You mean that there have been only six men in the family since—"

"Silennnnnce," ordered his father-in-law, and the two women gasped, Genevieve actually kicking Reinhart's ankle. But Raven smiled with his perfect range of teeth and explained: "In our house we get everything right first time out. *Firstborn males* is what was said. And if our Gen hasn't put you straight by this time, you might want to know we sunk our roots on this continent in 1659, when the first American Blaine Raven, ex-lieutenant of Oliver Cromwell, left his native shore after the death of the great Lord Protector and sailed westward on the brigantine *Sobriety,* touching Plymouth harbor some three and a half months later."

A candle almost went out in the gale of his expelled cigar smoke. Perhaps because the brandy was in a water goblet, he mistook it for iced tea; anyway, he threw it down in one swallow and dabbed at his bronze lip with a paper serviette, crumpling it when he finished and hurling it over his shoulder, as Charles Laughton did bones in the movie about Henry VIII. There was no doubt he had style. Genevieve hastily filled his goblet from the flask of Courvoisier, with its big belly that reminded Reinhart of her condition.

Reinhart, incidentally, was radiant with euphoria; he hated being on bad terms with people, and now that he got along with his father-in-law and that the little misunderstanding with Gen was cleared up, he had only to return the MS to Splendor with a blunt note, give Fedder some simple explanation for the rump-kick ("I have a nervous ailment"), and all his problems were solved. He buoyantly tossed off his own brandy. In crossing her legs, Gen kicked his shin again.

"That first Blaine," the latest one continued, "had been a Sussex landowner in England, very handsomely well-to-do. It is all wrong, you know, to think that all the best folk were with the Royalists and the slobs with Cromwell. Far from it. The only real issue there was religious. The Ravens have always despised Catholics, be they even kings!" He smote the card table with the flat of his hand, with the other one protecting the brandy bottle from the vibration.

Reinhart's mother-in-law spoke in her mousy voice, startling everyone and infuriating Raven. "I think it depends on the individual."

"Watch yourself." Raven warned, and flicked a great bread crumb in her direction.

"Help yourself to the Courvoisier, Daddy," said Gen.

"We Ravens never drink anything else but," he noted, rolling his shoulders from front to rear. He wore a knitted sport shirt, lemon yellow, so tight that it might have been sprayed on him in liquid form. His blazer he had earlier removed. "May I compliment you on your choice of dinner wine." He sucked his tongue, frowned, and looking at the corrugated ceiling, "Château Margaux . . . and the year is . . ."

"One moment," said Reinhart, playing Helpful Harry, "I'll go look at the bottle in the trashcan."

Again the women gasped, and again he saw his father-in-law's cruel smile.

"That's all right, all right," Raven said after a moment, threw down another drink, dried his lips with another napkin and pitched it over his back. "The year is . . . Nineteen forty-three," he finished rapidly.

"Right-o, Daddy," crooned Genevieve. "You never miss."

Good old Reinhart, getting a bit high, assumed this was a joke, because before the arrival of the elder Ravens, Gen told him Daddy had order her to serve Château Margaux '43 when he came to dinner. "That was the great one," she had said in explication, "and Daddy refuses anything but the best."

"He never will miss," said Reinhart now, winking at his father-in-law. "He knows the script."

"No, that's all right," Raven said to Gen, interrupting her remonstrance. He put his hand on her wrist. "I don't mind him. He hasn't penetrated the skin—yet." He turned slanted eyes and white fangs towards his son-in-law. "But when you do, mister, I promise to let you know."

Reinhart was still not sure how much of this was in fun; but if the Ravens were as vintage a lot as they made out, their wit was certain to be high and fine, just as his tended to be coarse. He chewed the end of his cigar, and as soon as Gen's glare was off him, seized the brandy bottle and refilled his glass, which was none too big, having lately held chipped beef.

"Where was I?" asked Raven, his sneer shading off into a solipsist grimace of the type people sometimes wear on public buses: they are aware only that they exist and life is mean.

"The first American Blaine Raven," said Reinhart.

"What do you know about him?" shouted his father-in-law. "What did you do in the war? Were you in the Corps?" He picked up one of the crackers accompanying the dessert cheese and hurled it at his wife, who ducked neatly.

For a moment Reinhart was paralyzed because of the sudden breakdown of convention. Then he snatched up a missile

221

of his own—the leftover cork from the wine—and was preparing to fire it at the brute when Gen burst into a sob and ran from the table. Going after her, Reinhart fell over a piece of furniture, for it was quite dark, the Ravens having come two hours late. What an outrage in Reinhart's own house! He picked himself off the floor and caught Genevieve at the screen door.

"Shh!" he warned, indicating Fedder's hut next door.

"Who cares?" Gen asked, her face all tearfully pinched. "Everything's gone wrong. Thank you for ruining my evening."

It didn't take Reinhart long to decide that her condition took precedence over his sense of fair play. "I'll be good," he promised, but while saying it, looking over Gen's shoulder at the candlelit table, he saw his father-in-law throw a whole handful of crackers into his mother-in-law's face.

"Gen, Gen," he whispered, drawing her outside onto the little duckboard-platform that posed as a porch. "Gen, now keep calm, but your father's in there right now mistreating your mother. Don't you think we'd better take the booze away from him?"

Her face caught some light from Fedder's windows. "They've been kidding around like that for years."

"Isn't it strange?"

"Well, *I don't think so*," Gen replied. "You know, if I wanted to, I could say something about hypochondriacs, but I won't."

Reinhart's frustration inflated his head. "Look, I don't want to argue about our families. This is an emergency." Thinking of her pregnancy, he hastily added: "But I don't want you to worry."

"I'm not worrying," she answered loftily. "You just don't seem to understand anyone with spirit. Only a clod is even-tempered at all times."

"You mean me," Reinhart said in aggrieved stoicism.

"Let's put it this way, Carl," Genevieve said softly, "in everybody there's room for improvement. Everybody. We all should become more than what we started as."

"Listen here!" he shouted, and then lowered his voice for the rest, for although his emotion continued to rise, his caution did too. That he was never really unilateral, he felt, saved him from unconditional disasters. "Listen here," he whispered, "the only kind of aristocracy I believe in is the natural one."

"That's just what I'm saying," Gen whispered back. "Not everyone can be born into a family like Daddy's, but there are

222

other compensations. One can develop grace and style and ex-*quis*ite manners."

"Hahaha," jeered Reinhart. "You mispronounced the word." But he felt no real glee.

"That's a good example. Among the better class of people, you don't correct someone's English. Do you know why? Because if *they* say it it, it's automatically right."

"They have to be pretty good people," said Reinhart through clenched teeth. He was seething: to be instructed by a slip of a girl who had never been to college! An educated man knew that to any genuine *haut monde,* American "aristocracy" was a vulgar joke; the original John Jacob Astor, for example, was a Kraut from Heidelberg, Germany, who came to this country and swapped beads for fur with the Indians, no doubt speaking in a clownish accent.

Nevertheless, Reinhart was determined to make every effort to do his part. From where he stood the worst thing you could be called was unfair. So he said: "You mean like Roosevelt, who pronounced "decadent" *deck-a-dunt* and everybody else has followed suit though it doesn't make sense when you think that the word has the same derivation as "decay."

Genevieve brushed that aside with: "Be that as in May—"

"What?"

"Now don't correct me. I know what I'm saying."

"Yes, but I don't," said Reinhart.

"I'm sorry, Carl. Goodness knows I have tried, but your sarcasm is really too much. Added to your lack of breeding, your lack of sensitivity—well, you may be brillant, but that is not enough. There must be heart as well as head. But besides that, how does so much education help you in the art of living?"

Reinhart lowered his head and said tragically: "You never told me any of this before. I am absolutely astonished, Genevieve; it was you who wanted to get married. For your sake I gave up my freedom at twenty-one years of age, and this is how you repay me."

"I gave you enough rope," said Genevieve, drawing back as if from a bad odor, "and here is what I found." She began to enumerate the particularities of his failure, placing her thumb on her little finger, in rather masculine, decidedly common style, the fashion in which a garage mechanic tells you four things that must be done to your Dodge before winter or he won't be responsible. Similarly, so she implied, Genevieve was nothing but a detached and expert observer of their marriage, hired as it were to gauge his performance.

The lights went off in the next-door Quonset: Fedder, ass

that he may be, was realistic enough to keep on good terms with his frau, and bedded with her at a reasonable hour. Elsewhere in Vetsville there were instances of modest revelry: an old college song on the night air, controlled laughter, the clunk of an empty beer can striking the bottom of a trash barrel. This was a harmless population.

"First," Genevieve was saying, resting the small of her back against the little porch rail of one-inch waterpipe, "you try to hide with a great deal of nervous energy the fact that you have no real ambition. You do twice the required amount of college homework, but could do half and get farther if you had a direction—which you don't. Who cares if you read all the *Iliad* or whatever old book? Why don't you study accounting or something useful?"

Her thumb moved to the ball of the next finger. "Second: You will have to face the reality of your job with Claude. You haven't made a sale since the Onion, and that was March. I know you go out every day with clients, but you might as well sit home if you don't sell anything!"

Gen was hitting the target. He could only whine: "I get a salary from him."

"Yes," said she, "and there's something fishy about that. Why should Claude Humbold the world's most famous deadbeat pay you twenty-five dollars a week for contributing nothing to his business? Frankly I don't believe it."

He wanted to ask a question, but she waved her hand in his face, with the thumb on its middle finger. "Third: I wouldn't ask a dog to live in this hobble." She threw her elbow towards the hovel, which just sat there rustily insolent but Reinhart was desperately wounded and caught at himself in the midsection, lurching against the pipe, which made a bleak noise as the flange attaching it to the rusty wall came loose screw by screw. But he had a moment to recover his balance as well as to support Genevieve, before the railing gave way.

Gen never batted an eye. Leaning against his forearm as she had leaned on the pipe, she closed thumb and index finger and said: "Four: Tactlessness, sneering, sarcastic comments, inconsiderate behavior, rudeness—these are some of the things that constitute your flaws. For example, you don't know how to react to graciousness on the part of the next person. I ask about your short story and you tend to veer away, sort of hanged dog—"

Reinhart belched out a confession, and felt great relief. "I'm a liar, too, Gen. I didn't write that story, a friend did—well, actually—"

Genevieve shrugged. "So O.K., that's all there is to it. You're not going to offend anybody by an occasional lie. See, you always worry about the wrong thing. Lack of judgment; not able to size up a situation properly; knowledge of books but not of human nature." She squeezed his hand and said disarmingly: "Excuse me, Carl, but I'm getting a lot out of my system. I certainly don't mean to offend you."

An automobile rolled into the compound, whitewashing them for a moment in its headlights. Their hut was so placed as to check in every arriving vehicle by such a signal; even inside, at night, with the blinds drawn, there was a second of false daylight against the window. It wasn't much of a place; Reinhart had just conned himself for a while into thinking that home is where the heart is, and that Genevieve agreed. Actually, he had taken his fresh bride to a dump. Small wonder she had stayed in bed. Completely unrealistic; he always had been and apparently always would be. One possible interpretation of an incident in Germany was that his foolishness had killed a man. Had he here murdered love? He was scared to ask, now that Gen had got so formal. What a mess he had made of the postwar era, and it not a year under way.

"I think I can summon it all up very simply" Genevieve declared, tapping his sternum. *"You haven't any aim.* It's just about all included in that." She nodded her small head, frowning wisely. "You have charm, brains, good looks—everything required, but they go for nil."

"Really?" asked Reinhart. "Good looks?" He was flattered.

"Don't be smug," said Gen. "That makes it all the worse. Now you are always kidding about my baby, but I wonder if you are prepared to become a father say six and a half months henceforth? It is a grave responsibility. Carl, and not a thing to constantly talk about in a silly fashion."

Reinhart checked the interior through the screen door, at the same time slapping a mosquito a split second before it would have stabbed him in the neck. The patriarch of the Raven clan had seemingly passed out, head and arms on the table. Mrs. Raven had withdrawn to the easy chair under the bridge lamp, where she read a magazine impassively. Reinhart suddenly had an idea that she was strongest of the lot—once again he was thinking along the lines of his toad: true freedom is found only by being consistent with oneself.

"Do you know what it is to bring a new human being into the world?" Gen continued relentlessly. "The poor little thing!"

He thought she had said *"You* poor little thing" in arch satire, and he discovered, by doing it, what "bridling" was: a movement of moral infirmity, like everything connected with

225

a horse, one of the few animals to submit unconditionally to humanity.

"A child needs a Daddy to be proud of," Gen went on.

Now here Reinhart struck back as hard as he could. "Like that drunken bum in there," he snarled, jerking his thumb at Raven. For a second, he didn't care whether that remark destroyed everything between them.

But Gen would decide on her own what was disastrously offensive and what was not. "At least," she answered soberly, "he had something to degenerate from."

Please go back to defending him, Reinhart wanted to tell her. He was not tough enough to accept the winning of an argument involving a betrayal of loyalty. But that was before he understood that Genevieve would make any sacrifice to prove her point; she would even sell out Daddy. Few women are lawyers, because few defendants can afford a counsel whose best efforts will always go towards self-justification: "I know my client is guilty, but I took his case anyway," etc.

"Aw," said Reinhart. "He's not so bad."

"Don't try to conceal your own failures behind another man's."

"All right," he droned. "But where is the point of this long sermon?" He made a surly smile, and scratched the hairless inner surface of his forearm. It was strange how she became repugnant to him when they differed in opinion: her sweet mouth became a great trapdoor that opened to emit vile nonsense; her shortness seemed troglodytic; her scent was as oppressive as that of flowers at a laying-out.

"I'm trying to make it easier for you to take," she explained. "When my parents leave here tonight, I am going home with them for an indefinite period of time. Perhaps we will come together again at a now unsuspected future date. Marriage is not a simple proposition, Carl. You can't just bull your way into it and expect it to take. That was your error. Now that I carry a new life, well I just can't risk it. Meanwhile, I want to say there are things about you I will miss. There's no getting away from the fact that you are oftentimes sweet."

Reinhart's eyes were smarting so fiercely he could hardly keep them open, the side-effect of that filthy cigar, the soggy, turdlike butt of which he still held. He felt three or four mosquitoes attack him en bloc, and didn't care.

At last he said: "Nobody speaks to me like that. Why don't you go to hell, you little Philistine?" He made it a cool question and did not raise his voice. However, he was far from striking a pose; his mind was sketching out a bitter, lonely future with a tragic upshot, such as killing a stranger in a quarrel, twenty years hence, and only later discovering: Ah! It was my own son. The other way around, with young Sohrab slaying Rustum, was scarcely to be preferred. Or something unthinkable in the case of a daughter. This is what happened when you fell in love with a person beneath you in culture.

Genevieve could not be touched, though, if she had first decided on herself as the aggressor and you the victim. She looked at Reinhart in romantic pathos and touched him on the arm as if to say Buck up, poor chap, then swinging the screen aside, went indoors and packed a suitcase while her mother read on. Her father did not move. After watching for a moment, Reinhart descended to the ground and staggered through the tire ruts, distraught. He roamed for a time between the Quonsets until something drew him stealthily to approach Fedder's open window. As he slunk beneath it through the darkness, treading down a petunia bed, he heard very clearly the noise of bedsprings in the rhythm of love. Fedder and his wife Doing It. Extraordinary. Why, why? At present Reinhart felt no such desire and could not understand anyone else's feeling it. He was sexy when afraid but not when angry. He wanted to stick his face in the window and shout: Cut it out, Fedder! No more of that!

It struck him that he had never noticed Fedder's wife; he could not have picked her from a group of three. Fantastic, the data you picked up about people. Seeing them in the sunlight next day, he would know they had made love the night before; yet he would recognize the woman only by her proximity to Fedder. That is, Fedder could be walking with his sister, or female cousin, or mistress, and Reinhart would assume it was his wife and then go on to relate to her this somewhat shameful, though legal, datum: a midnight squeaking of bedsprings. But why should it be shameful? The old Greek Stoics wouldn't have agreed; according to certain authorities they copulated in public, as part of their campaign to reduce everything to the humdrum: What are you doing there, Diogenes? Answer: I'm planting a man. . . . Now Reinhart began to doubt he had ever loved Genevieve. She really was a kind of tramp to have let him take such liberties on their first date.

The scandalous nature of his espionage became known to him at that point, and the blood throbbed noisily through his inner ears. Suppose a car came by and with its headlights caught him among the petunias. He withdrew across the stubbly plain to the shadow of his own abode in quick, short dashes interspersed with frozen moments of surveillance, like a certain type of animal; like a rodent, in fact, who has no defense against his enemies but agility. Yet Reinhart far exceeded the median size of man, and he had just heard from Gen that he was clever, charming, and handsome. Why then was she leaving him? For she was: through his own window, this time, he saw her stuffing underwear into a valise, those white rayon pants he had been wont to pull down whenever the mood came over him. Nothing like this has ever happened to me before, he kept muttering; for as if it wasn't bad enough already, it would make history to boot. Let's see, he would say in time to come, in placing an event, let's see, that happened shortly after my wife walked out. His child would be born half an orphan though its father still lived.

Oh, it was absurd. Yet he saw Gen start to pack her brassieres, of which it appeared she owned an inordinate number. He had never known that before. Remarkable, there must have been fifteen; some were massive molds armatured with wire; others mere ribbons. You could say this for her: she had always been so clean and fresh and firm all over.

He drifted along the side of the building and filtered in through the back door. His mother-in-law looked up from her magazine.

"Can I get you something, Mother?" Reinhart asked, keeping his manners even under stress.

She graciously smiled No; they understood each other, he and she.

"Carl!" shouted Genevieve, as if he were still outdoors. She was feeling her oats.

"Come now," Reinhart said quietly.

She shouted again.

"Why are you yelling? I'm right behind you."

"Would you mind," she asked with some attempt at moderation, "telling Daddy it's time to go?"

"Not all," Reinhart answered frigidly. He stepped to the card table. With his wide figure between Raven and the ladies, so that they could not see his method, he slapped the crown of Daddy's cropped head, arching the palm and gathering in the fingers just after the blow in order that there be no loud report. This had a curious effect on Raven. He raised his head and made a great, groggy, cross-eyed grimace, sneered "Yaaaaa," and fell again onto his folded arms.

"Come on," said Reinhart. He caught him under the shoulders. Annoying work, for Raven was limp as a sandbag and miserably heavy, and though declining the responsibilities of full consciousness, he made a humming, sputtering noise to prove that he was neither dead nor asleep. But the only fact about him that Reinhart found insupportable—for like all sons he was ready to enjoy the weaknesses of all fathers—

228

what Reinhart could not forgive was that Raven really did measure up as a superior person in the basic features that were difficult if not impossible to learn. For example, he was most marvelously constructed: not just in breadth of shoulder and slenderness of waist, which anyone might approximate with effort and self-denial, but in the shape of his ear, in the junction between his neck and head, and the angle of his jawbone. It was hard to get a bad perspective on him, speaking optically. By his mere presence, Raven derided Reinhart's recent struggles to get back into shape; the best he could have got back to was inferior to Raven's worst; and while Reinhart might lose a few more pounds from his body, short of the most elaborate plastic surgery he would never have the face of a noble Roman.

Not to speak of manners. Reinhart was very courteous, but he had but meager acquaintance with the manners of a gentleman, even though he had known some Europeans in their native habitat. It was easy to say that simple decency was enough, that the spirit overruled the forms, but, just as you loathed the relative who though radiant with love celebrated Xmas with cheap gifts, so did you despise the man who with all the good will in the world pulled the soup spoon towards himself when it was genteel to push it away. Yet Raven could have eaten peas with a knife or sucked coffee from a saucer, and it might have started a trend.

As a working hypothesis (for he was interested in all forms of freedom), Reinhart thought this was true because Raven did not care. But the same could be said of the uncouth. Next Reinhart laid it to grace, and while this seemed closer to the mark, it failed to account for such a phenomenon as Reinhart's own father, a very graceful man at table but one who would never inspire emulation as he skillfully dunked a doughnut and got it to his mouth before the coffee-soaked portion fell off.

No, Raven derived his authority from a conviction that he was *always right*. Thus he truly was an aristocrat, whether or not he stemmed from a good family. Reinhart would rather have felt this about himself than have owned a uranium mine; and he immediately forgot Gen's particular criticisms, in the assumption that her fundamental complaint against him was that he came out so ill when measured against her father.

Reinhart was thinking all this, bitterly, as he manhandled Raven through the front door. Taking advantage of the broken rail on the porchlet, he dropped his father-in-law over the side, then came round and dragged him to the car and into its back seat, where the cushions were worn through and vomited naked springs and hairy stuffing. This was Raven's automobile, an old Lincoln Continental in disreputable condition and therefore the *dernier cri* in taste. The Gigantic sat gaudily next to it like a fat boy entwined in tinsel.

"Oh no," said Genevieve, coming up with her suitcase and mother, "Daddy drives."

"Now I realize you are out of your mind," answered Reinhart. "He's unconscious."

Pushing Reinhart aside, Gen went to the back window of the Continental and called in: "Daddy, time to drive us home!"

Reinhart drew Mrs. Raven aside and asked: "What's wrong with her?"

His mother-in-law smiled in simple-minded pride. "She's always been spirited. That's a Raven trait."

"Oh stop it!" said Reinhart. "Not you, too."

"Oh Daddy," Genevieve cried impatiently. "Don't be so weak!"

A muffled sound of aspiration came from the back seat. Suddenly the door was flung open and Raven crawled out, knees half buckled. He shook himself vehemently, then straightened out and exhibitionistically put all his muscles in tension, making a fine show in the knitted shirt.

Raven thrust his jaw at his son-in-law and then his hand. "I take a better view of you, uh—fella. Maybe we Ravens are too New England for our own good. This is essentially the Century of the Slob, and we have to go along with it, willy-nilly. You stole my girl like a brigand and brought her to this pigsty, but I'll say this for you: you lay a good table and you aren't showy. What's your school?" However, luckily for Reinhart, Raven jerked haughtily away before he could have answered, climbed behind the wheel, and started the engine. revving it brutally. Mrs. Raven slipped into the rear.

His bluff called, Reinhart said dolefully to his wife: "Don't you love me any more?"

"What a silly thing to say!" She changed hands on the suitcase. "Why do you think I'm going to all this trouble?"

"But I don't know what you want," said Reinhart.

She put down the valise—as it happened, on his toe; however, it was very light, being filled chiefly with underwear.

"In one word Carl, your idea of life is—well, it's"—she seized his neck and pulled his head down close. "You think that, huh-huh . . ." She laughed nervously into his earhole.

"Go on," he begged, twisting his neck from the tickle.

"*I can't!*" For a moment she was very kittenish, and he believed their troubles were over.

But the next thing he knew, Gen had reclaimed his ear and said into it: "You think that, uh, *doing* it" (she giggled, then

230

turned severe) "takes care of everything." She grabbed her suitcase, leaped into the front seat, and father drove away—not at all fast; no doubt the old Continental could do no more; but Reinhart took it as another outrage that the Ravens whined along the road leading to the main highway at a speed no faster than a cripple could limp, so that he had to stand there watching them for an unbearable length of time. Of course, no one forced him with a gun to stand there, but he knew that that was what you did when your wife—or indeed, anyone else—deserted you, unless you had got the initiative, in which case they had to stand and watch *you*. There were precedents for everything. The old human race was not so dumb as it looked, and had worked out many devices.

In his moment of desolation, that is, he was not altogether bereft of hope. And from any angle, his situation looked better than his next-door neighbor's: a man, not Fedder, suddenly left Fedder's hut and drove away in an automobile; Fedder himself arrived on foot a quarter-hour later, probably from a meeting of sewer enthusiasts elsewhere on the compound. Putting these data together with the information he had recorded earlier, Reinhart could not but conclude, from his observation post behind the curtains, that Fedder was a cuckold.

Chapter 15

That his neighbor wore antlers was not, however, amusing to Reinhart, who reflected again on how his own attitudes had changed since marriage: he was now quite the prude and proud of it. He might even have helped stone the woman taken in adultery. He rejected the theory that desire must lead to disorder, never since his nuptial vows having undergone so much as a dream concerning another woman than his wife. What was the point when you had all you wanted at home?, was the coarse but sensible maxim into which his point of view might be condensed. Its only weakness lay in its narrowness of application. What if you weren't married? Well, have the strength to wait; deprivation *is* good for the soul.

Bluenose Reinhart, contrary to his usual custom, slept very late next morning, which was Sunday, in his chaste bed. Ironies abounded. When he had Gen to snuggle with, he had always risen early, eaten a big breakfast, and got to schoolwork; Sunday afternoons were of course assigned to real-estate clients. Now, however, he had appetite for nothing but coffee, and was torpidly looking forward to a scandalous waste of the whole day, which already stood at the meridian.

A neighbor dog had conveniently destroyed the news section of the Sunday paper, which Reinhart never read anyway: some of the fragments still blew among the nearby hut-tops, like the leaves on which the Cumaean Sibyl wrote her futile data. Safe from news of the world at large, he read the funnies and *This Week*, and the rotogravure section showing, in sepia, local personalities at bay: philanthropist breaking ground for new hospital; coeds repainting interior of Chi Omega house, and so on—it was Sunday, this is what normal human beings did, read the paper and drank coffee while still in their pajamas. He rebuttoned the fly of his, which as always had come open during the night, and had another cup of instant G. Washington, made with condensed syrup from a little tube bearing the signature of the statesman in question. He scratched himself on the right shoulder blade. The weather was sullenly hot, and the iron shell of his residence exaggerated it further. However he bore up admirably under the disaster, and thought of buying a dog or parakeet so as to have someone around the house.

That is, Reinhart's morning-after feeling was one of defiant independence: he would survive even though he might perish. It may have been contradictory nonsense, but a style was established, and when of all people Fedder yelled through the screen door and then entered without permission, Reinhart stayed tough. Where at another juncture he might have been persuaded by the fellow's cuckoldry to be sympathetic, he was now indignant. Where he might have, as an acknowledgment of having yesterday kicked Fedder's ass unjustly, showed a certain restraint in addressing him, he was now rather brassy.

"Fedder! How's your hammer hanging?" was what he said, and thrust his head back into the funny paper.

"Hi neighbor!" Fedder had the same old shameless ebullience. Today he wore only a pair of khaki shorts and lowcut Keds without socks; for a shirt he sported his own hairy breasts and soft stomach; his shoulders were narrow and slanting, his legs skinny as straws. Aesthetically speaking, he was a criminal. "Hi!" he repeated, flopping onto the couch above Reinhart, who was lying on a scatter rug. "If you have reached the comics, that means you've already read about the predicted tax rise. What's your position on that?"

"Frankly," said Reinhart, "I don't think I make enough beyond the GI Bill money to pay an income tax." He petulantly hurled the paper away from him, and it fell like a wind-torn tent near the door to the toilet.

Fedder's stomach rolled over his belt. His canvas shoes were near enough to Reinhart's prone body to have dealt it a return for yesterday's assault, but no doubt it was characteristic of Fedder never even to have such a thought; he had already forgotten that kick by the time he hit the ground. Had Reinhart wished to apologize, he would first have had to explain what for. Never had he encountered such a nonaggres-

233

sive person. Suddenly he felt a great warmth for Fedder and wished to give him a trust.

"I mean" said Fedder, earnestly baring his lower teeth, "the village tax, which of course applies only to property owners—so you say Why? Well sure, but if we get home rule for Vetsville, we'll all *be* property owners!" Guilelessly he passed a hand over his weak features and dried it on his shorts.

Reinhart rose from the floor. Before he spoke to Fedder, he couldn't resist—looking at the mess his neighbor was from the physical point of view—tensing his upper musculature in the manner of Blaine Raven. However, it did no harm: if you can't damage a man by kicking his ass, you can hardly do it by inflating your chest—or can you? Reinhart had lost faith in his judgment of people, and entertained the idea that far from being his forte, as he had always assumed, it might well be his tragic flaw. For Fedder did seem, all at once, to be a bit leery of him; at once got up from the sofa as Reinhart approached it, and dived into a chair that had its back against the wall.

"Fedder," said Reinhart, parking his own behind on the edge of the divan, "Fedder, I wonder whether it would embarrass you if I got serious for a minute."

Fedder's anxiety collapsed into relief. He had been hugging his naked trunk as if in a chill; now he went back to perspiring freely. Reinhart saw that his neighbor had been entertaining the idea that he might be attacked again; yet he had come here of his own volition. This indicated a certain strength, or a certain weakness in the man; only time would tell which. Meanwhile he was the only person available; and of course being privy to Mrs. Fedder's infidelity did not hurt, either, as an aid to confidence. He felt sorry for Fedder and expected him to return the compliment. Yet Reinhart, by knowing everything, would keep the upper hand over Fedder, whose knowledge must always be partial. With everything thus worked out, Reinhart revealed his desolation.

"My wife left last night."

"Oh," Fedder asked gaily, misunderstanding. "Separate vacations?"

Reinhart squelched instantaneous anger. "No, she walked out on me, Fedder."

The neighbor scratched the instep of his foot, sinking a forefinger deep into a tennis shoe, and laughed briefly like Woody Woodpecker, a pyschotic character from a popular animated cartoon. This, however, drew no inimical response from Reinhart, who saw it as sheer delicacy; indeed, to relieve his friend he joined him in synthetic amusement.

Fedder stopped abruptly and asked Reinhart to call him Niles.

Reinhart asked: "Tell me, Niles, you have children, haven't you?"

"Several," admitted Fedder, who was one of those people that have trouble sitting still; he kept moving his legs fitfully; "I have a year or two on you. Bee and I were married in '40. And now we have three daughters: Sewell, Frazer, and Trowbridge." He named them again chronologically, in diminutives. "Trow is five; Sewy, three; ;and Fray, two. Bee had a flat in San Diego, in case you wonder how we managed it in wartime."

"No, I don't wonder," Reinhart said wistfully.

"Of course, Fray did look just like the grocer's delivery boy!" Fedder laughed wildly again, and again he stopped short. "Don't worry," he said, "it'll happen. You are both young and healthy. I'll ask Bee to send Jenny to her obstetrician. He'll make her a personalized schedule of the days on which the ovum is fertile."

At last he had showed his vanity. Reinhart was relieved to have drawn Fedder into the open, and he was happy for him in what was perhaps only a fantasy of potency—there might be a corresponding delivery boy to each daughter—but he saw no good reason to suppress his own data.

He shrugged. "Genevieve's been pregnant for months, so it's not that."

Fedder frowned in a way that warped his upper lip and exposed one tooth. "Why didn't you say so!" he blurted after a moment of thought. "They're all like that."

"Like what?"

"When they're pregnant the first time. Quick to take offense. She'll be back on the next train. Above all, don't blame yourself." Fedder threw his head back and looked at the ceiling.

Reinhart kept alternating in his judgment of Fedder; on the surface the man was 100 per cent fool and nothing he said ever went contrary to that appearance; but notwithstanding that his wife was a harlot, she stayed with him and they had three children besides. That is to say, as a home they were successful—this was something different from romance, sex, screwing, or even foolishness. It was, to be pompous, the continuation of the race. So had marriage, even one that failed, changed Reinhart in his idea of the good life.

"Is it so hard?" he asked.

Fedder took the question warily, bringing his head down between his shoulders; he still didn't trust Reinhart completely.

"I mean," Reinhart explained, "maintaining a home. Frankly, Niles, I haven't done a very good job. I think I probably

235

should blame myself. I don't believe I ever understood Genevieve or even tried. You see, I found it difficult to readjust to civilian life, because contrary to everybody else I rather liked the Army. Does that shock you?"

"Not at all, Carl!" Fedder was quick to asseverate. "I think I can show you your error there, but please don't take it as a *moral* criticism. No—"

"Above all, I got *used* to it," Reinhart went on, here and there pulling his shirt away from his damp chest with an adhesive-tape sound. "There's something to be said for that, isn't it true?"

Bright with his own copious sweat, Fedder leaned forward and sought to interpose—

"Something you can *rely* on," said Reinhart. "The messhall three times daily, rather than this goddam business of the grocery bills! Now there's a strange effect for you: I always feel degraded when I have to pay for food—it seems like something you should have coming to you. But I didn't mind at all giving money to Genevieve for a new dress. Though here's what I don't understand; she never wanted to take it." He decided to let Fedder speak on that subject.

"At such times it was your idea, no?" Fedder asked. "Ah, there you have it, there it is. And if I am right, though it may be difficult for you to admit, you offered it with the conscious idea that you were doing her a favor."

"I might have," Reinhart cautiously admitted. "How should I have acted—as if it were really hostility?"

"Of course it was. Does Procter give Gamble money for a suit? You and Jenny are in this thing together—incorporated, as it were. Remember, that's also legally true. That money you gave her was hers to begin with." Fedder threw himself back into the chair, his chest vibrating flabbily.

"And the thought behind it?" asked Reinhart in his wounded way.

Fedder said bluntly: "That is worthless."

"You mean to tell me one can't give his wife a present?"

Fedder sat up and laid his right index finger into the palm of his left hand. "Why sure. But an authentic one and not a fake. And certainly never in the spirit of an Oriental potentate distributing largesse to his lackeys."

The example showed that for all his common sense, Fedder had a romantic streak: Reinhart as Genghis Khan was pretty far-fetched.

"Can I get you a cup of coffee, Niles?"

Fedder said yes, he might have one if the pot was already made, and trailed his host to the kitchen area. Not a whisper of air came through the little window over the sink, and the

236

view from there was particularly disheartening: a field of tawny, chest-high weeds that marked the southeastern boundary of Vetsville; above, a pitiless sky, so hot its blue had faded.

"Oh," said Reinhart. "No worry about that. This is instant. Isn't it warm today!" His motive is belaboring the obvious was to distract Fedder for a moment from the analytic mood. No doubt Fedder was right, but it did hurt Reinhart's pride to be lectured on marriage by a fellow whose own wife slept with other men.

"Instant," said Fedder, smiling in the guilty, self-derisive manner that some men affect on approaching an area where food is prepared. "You can sure see you are alone."

"No," Reinhart elucidated, running water into the kettle. "I always used this when Gen was here." His ready use of the past tense made him feel awful.

"*You* used it?" Fedder asked with terrible urgency. "You ... didn't ... do ... the ... cooking?"

Reinhart quailed a bit. "I'm afraid so."

"Oh gosh. Well. I see." Fedder snickered nervously.

Swelling back again, Reinhart said: "Now look, Niles, you know I'm not effeminate. It's just—hell, I don't like to be a housewife but how can you ask a girl to work when she's going to have a baby?"

"Uh-huh," Fedder answered, thinking. He tore a paper towel from the dispenser alongside the sink and patted his wet neck.

"I felt rather guilty, I suppose," Reinhart went on. "Women are so little! And what a hell of a big job having a baby is. On the other hand, come to think of it, I seemed more worried than she." He fitted the whistle-gadget to the spout and placed the kettle upon the back burner. "You want a doughnut, Niles?" He grasped the bag that lay on top of the breadbox (not within, where baked goods sweat and grow soggy in warm weather; outside, they merely grow stale). Having opened the bag and withdrawn a sinker and found it hard, however, he suggested toast.

It appeared that Fedder, like so many flabby people, was not interested in food. He neither accepted nor declined, but when the coffee had been poured and they sat at the card table, he ate three of the four pieces of bread that Reinhart had toasted, heaped them with butter and jam, and yet could not be said to have paid them any real attention. But he was profoundly concerned with the love-problems of his neighbor, who on the other hand now regretted having made the disclosure and was chewing his own toast with the greatest care.

"You see, Carl," said Fedder. "Doesn't it occur to you: there may not have been enough *sharing* in your marriage.

From what you say about guilt, and from this thing about your doing the cooking"—he stopped to wipe his bejellied hands upon a paper napkin, then balled the napkin and left it sitting redly, stickily before him—"I just wonder what you left to Jenny. What was her role? You see, washing the dishes is all right for a husband to do, some drudgery like that to relieve the wife of. But cooking is creative. Deprive a woman of this function and— Well, in my opinion the unhappy marriage occurs when everything interesting is done by only one of the team."

Reinhart went to make more toast, as much from curiosity as to how many pieces Fedder would absent-mindedly stow away, as from hospitality. "Genevieve doesn't care at all for the kitchen," he said en route. "If it was up to her, she would live on soda crackers and rattrap cheese. And that's just fine with me. Who wants a wife to have an enormous appetite? I don't think I could get sexually interested in the most beautiful girl who gorged."

"Ah yes," cried Fedder, "but make her cook for you, boy. Don't you see it gives her the upper hand to control your sustenance?"

Reinhart noticed an island of green mold in the center of the bread slice he took from the wrapper. He tore the paper and thumbed through the rest of the load; the mold was a vein running through to the heel—which meant that Fedder's three pieces and his own one, now in their respective stomachs, had probably also been contaminated, and that Fedder might be poisoned unless the toasting had counteracted the properties of the fungus that were unfriendly to man. For himself he had no worries; he currently doubted his powers only in the matter of a wife.

He cut the center from each slice before dropping it into the toaster, and said to Fedder: "When all is said and done, wouldn't you call intercourse an act of aggression?"

Fedder looked uneasy and drank what would have been the grounds, had it been real coffee, from his cup. "I see it as a mutual endeavor, Carl. I don't understand this strain of bad feeling that is so important for you."

"You don't think there is any underlying strife?"

"I can't see it." Fedder had his index finger on the blade of the butter knife.

"Don't we resent those we love?" asked Reinhart.

Fedder smiled and asked why.

"I don't know, I'm just trying to get to general principles." He returned to the table with the new toast, which Fedder soon seized. "Because everything I did with Gen, I did sincerely. I never contrived anything. I felt she needed to be

238

taken care of, though it is true that before we were married I thought of her as efficiency personified. But she is so young. You know there are some girls whom the physical side of marriage frightens. Have you ever read any of those articles in the women's magazines? At one time, in the Victorian era, it was far worse. Certain young ladies, having led protected lives up to then, were driven insane on their wedding night when their husband dropped his pants."

"Go on," said Fedder, waving a crust at him, "you exaggerate."

"And this tie with their fathers. What about that?"

"Bee," Fedder said, "happened to be raised as an orphan, so I can't speak from personal experience. . . . I don't want to sound smug, Carl, but she and I just haven't had any troubles at all in six years. And as it happens, she isn't a college girl." Reinhart started to speak but waited while Fedder said: "Six and a half, really."

That was surely one way, then, to preserve the home: share your wife with other men. Reinhart kept reminding himself of the shameful data he had on Fedder, yet he got great comfort from talking to him and still respected his counsel.

"But tell me," Fedder went on, masticating the crust he had been waving, "tell me about this coming child."

It struck Reinhart as a foolish comment coming from a three-time father. "What is there to tell? Gen has been pregnant since May."

"Ah, then," said Fedder, wiping his mouth with the whisk-broom of his fingers, "she'll be getting big soon." He pushed his chair away from the card table, and lifted one hairy haunch across the other.

"So soon?" asked Reinhart, with a pinched feeling in his bowels. How humiliating. Gen enlarging in her parents' house, he shriveling up in Vetsville.

"Did you never hear the old verse? 'Three months and all is well, three months more she begins to swell—' "

"Sure," Reinhart interrupted. As he remembered, its ending lines were indecent, and he was puzzled at Fedder's loose attitude towards maternity.

"Don't you feel different?" Fedder asked impatiently. "Just a fellow one day, next a father?"

He was some sort of schizophrenic, Reinhart decided, now in one mood, now another.

"You seem to take it lightly enough," he said.

"Me? You see, for you it's the first. That's the difference. Me? When I was in your shoes I suffered torments for every day of the nine months, and when the time for Bee's confinement approached, I went to sick bay, at the base, with total nervous collapse. That's how I feel things." He resented the attribution of nonchalance.

They were out of refreshments again, but Reinhart was damned if he'd toast more bread. In fact he felt very logy and got up from his chair, plunged to the floor and began to do pushups, an exercise he disliked because the obstacle there is your own weight: lifting a barbell, you could contrive extra strength by hating cold iron and thrusting it from you in repugnance; to do so with your own body was somehow self-defeating.

Therefore when he finished he was rather dejected, as well as out of breath. He rolled supine, leaned back on his arms, and looked up at Fedder.

"You know the idea I've had for quite some time?" he asked. "That I should go back and start everything over. That is, everything that's happened since leaving the Army. I should go back to the separation center, turn, and walk into civilian life again, this time through the gate of horn."

"Pardon?" asked Fedder.

"I read the *Aeneid* not long ago," Reinhart explained, and then because Fedder still looked blank, he said: "You know, the two gates of Hades, one of ivory, one of horn. Through the ivory gate 'the powers send false dreams to the world above,' but the horn gate provides 'a ready exit for the true spirits.' Oh well, it's not important."

"Carl," said Fedder, who from Reinhart's perspective seemed to have grotesquely large knees. "Carl," he repeated, looking down at his host with three parts seriousness and one of amusement, "I know you won't be offended if I ask: On thinking it over, don't you find your attitude towards marriage is a bit, well, somewhat on the sophomoric side?"

Reinhart got heavily to his feet. "That seems to be Gen's position on the issue, and it's pretty wild when you realize that all I've done for the past three months is work, whereas all I ever did before getting married was loaf. That reminds me of the favorite principle of psychiatry: that the truth is always the reverse of appearance; the kind man is really a sadist, and so on. I believe it, but the trouble is that once knowing about it, you are corrupted. Wanting to do your friend a favor, you must punch him in the face to make sure he knows you don't hate him secretly."

Fedder by now was smiling broadly, and Reinhart realized that his neighbor had applied these remarks to explain the kick he had received the day before.

"Listen, Carl," Fedder said, leaving his chair. "Let Dr. Niles prescribe. Forget your troubles for an afternoon, hey old boy? You're going on a picnic with the Fedder Family. Now

240

we won't take your No. We've got more than enough food for all and sundry. We insist."

His use of the first person plural disturbed Reinhart, who said: "Hadn't you better check first with your wife?"

"That won't be necessary," Fedder boasted, sticking out his belly and hitching up his shorts. "When you've been married for six and a half years, you know the other partner. Most of these uncertainties are the product of the early months, old fellow. You'll see. It's only a matter of time. Meanwhile, enjoy an afternoon with your neighbors. And don't worry about wives. Yours will come back, and mine will love you."

It was an odd thing to hear, but Reinhart managed to combine the relief of his own embarrassment with the suppression of any element that might give his neighbor pain, by uttering a laconic: "No doubt." Furthermore, upon the instant he resolved upon his honor that never would he succumb to Mrs. Fedder's attractions. This oath was necessitated by his having seen, at Fedder's first mention of "picnic," a terrible image of himself and Bee making mad love amid the crushed fruit in a wild-blackberry bramble, while Fedder fed peanut-butter sandwiches to his children just over the next rise. Some people, like Maw, suffered vision of bloodletting, illness, and death. With Reinhart it had always been sex, and nowadays the fantasy was horrible which in his bachelorhood had been a real joy of life. And he detested picnics.

Some hours later, as a member of a little group of bucolics that ringed an outdoor oven in the county park, Reinhart had nothing to reproach himself for but egomania. The happy truth was that Beatrice Fedder had no discernible interest in Reinhart. Indeed, she seemed to find him barely tolerable, and when by chance they stood briefly side by side, was first to move away, her thin nostrils finely drawn in what, he told himself delightedly, could not be other than dislike.

"How do you want your hamburger, Carl?" asked Niles, squatting before the oven, poking into its fire with a long green stick.

His middle daughter (whose name Reinhart had naturally forgotten), swinging from foot to foot, struck up a silly chant: "Hamburgers, hotdogs, hamburgers, hotdogs . . ."

"Ah," said Reinhart, remembering Fedder's attitude in his kitchen, "so you do the cooking?"

Fedder turned up a soot-stained face. "Only outdoors." He curled his lips in good humor and said to his wife, who stood behind the chimney, which cut off much of her slender body from Reinhart's gaze, which seemed to be her point: "Golly,

241

Bee, I can't get a fire going when I'm watched. Why don't you take Carl for a walk?"

Both principals recoiled from the suggestion so vehemently that even Fedder would have noticed had his head been up, but it wasn't, and he was also distracted by his little daughters, who were continually delivering their minuscule idea of fuel: ice-cream sticks, discarded soda straws, half-burnt matches, and dry grass: It was plain they loved him dearly.

"Go ahead," said Fedder, peering into the grate. "Carl doesn't know this park, Bee."

"Why," cried Reinhart, who was a native to these parts, to which the Fedders had moved only since the war, "I've been coming here since I was as old as—" he pointed at one of the little girls but was halted by the nonrecall of her name, which he knew was hardly the kind of failure to demonstrate before her parents, and was mumbling certain guesses—"Bainbridge," "Crowley," etc. (what ever had become of "Jane" and "Ruth" and "Betty"?)—when a cloud of yellow smoke drove them all from the oven.

"Wood too green," Fedder shouted merrily, and flapped a large, dirty handkerchief to open a channel through the cloud. How gay he was, surrounded by his little girls chirping like wrens, and his stately wife—for so she was, with somewhat elongated features, clean jaw, prominent cheekbones, and suntan. Taller than Fedder, she wore yellow shorts above exceptionally long thighs. Her shirt was the puffy kind that needed the help of the wind to reveal vital upper data, but they were not likely to be voluptuous. Here and there—neck, forearm, etc.—Reinhart saw bones and tendons. She faintly favored the male members of the House of Windsor, except as to eyes; and also an underweight motion-picture actress who always played newspaperwomen.

"Be friends," Fedder, adjured his wife and his neighbor, and dropping his handkerchief, harassed them in the style of a dog herding farm animals.

"Niles!" his wife remonstrated in a whiny alto that showed her dignity in another light. Now that was one for the book: she was scared of good old Reinhart!—who at last decided that the evidence of the previous night would never stand in court: he must have heard wrong. It had of course been she and Fedder, who then popped out for a midnight stroll, returning from which he had been detected by Reinhart. No other explanation was possible, now that Reinhart had seen her. Why, she was so shy that, as Fedder pushed them together like a procurer, her eyes closed in shame and were it not for the tan she would have turned crimson.

"Niles," she whined again, and while Reinhart had begun to find her modesty winning, her voice irritated him.

"Go on," said Fedder, patting both her and Reinhart on their respective behinds. "Run along, and remember what I told you."

"What?" asked Reinhart.

"No, I mean Bee. Bee?"

"All right," she murmured.

"A good half hour before I'll get a decent bed of embers," her husband stated significantly. He gathered to him all three children and returned to the oven.

Reinhart sensed that he was supposed to hear Beatrice Fedder's advice on how to regain and keep his wife; and he regretted more than ever having told his troubles to Niles, who had turned out to be that most terrifying of men: the fellow who is really interested.

"I guess we have to take a walk," he said to her, wryly throwing up his hands. But her head stayed down, and it was difficult for Reinhart to make a point when he couldn't catch an auditor's eye.

"Look!" he cried. "There goes a bluejay."

She lifted her head in the wrong direction. In this attitude, however, her slender throat and narrow eye were seen to great advantage. Men, it occurred to Reinhart, pick wives who have what they themselves lack, so that if it is done well, the married pair is a single human unit in which all possibilities are represented. Thus Bee Fedder, in distinction to her husband, looked as though she never perspired. And Reinhart himself was the last person from whom to expect the decisiveness and efficiency that were, or had been, prime qualities of Genevieve nee Raven. Yet the use of those remarkable faculties were just what he denied her. Was he man enough to call Gen tomorrow and admit his mistakes?

"I guess," he said to Bee, "that you're supposed to be my marriage counselor. Well, tell me this: Is there a formula for keeping the right proportion? A man must be authoritative, or else a woman will have no respect for him. On the other hand, he must not be domineering. He must be attentive, for nothing kills the spirit sooner than indifference, but it is true that everyone, no matter how ardent, needs a rest from unvarying, uh—" he realized he was being a bit bold for their short acquaintance, but said it anyway—"passion."

They had entered a trail leading from the clearing to a field where a host of men played softball with many hoots and catcalls, everybody short of wind and being mocked for it: some office picnic or Methodist outing. With her head down, Beatrice would have walked somnambulistically into center field, but Reinhart caught her bony elbow and steered back into the woods.

"I'm sorry if I embarrassed you," he stated, "but I gathered from Niles's attitude that—"

"That's all right!" she cried, overloud. The sound flushed a blue-colored bird from the greenery above them: as it happened, another jay: scolding raucously, the little crank.

"I knew a flier once," Beatrice suddenly asserted, turning a willowy ankle but gracefully gliding out of the warp. She was no longer shy but rather defiant. "Do you remember Colin Kelly, who in the early days of the war sank a Japanese warship by diving down the smokestack? My friend did the same thing without the publicity."

Reinhart said: "Magnificent!"

Bee looked directly at him for the first time, paling a little in approval. They had come to a fork in the trail marked by rustic signposts with burned-in legends: LADIES to the left, MEN to the right. Again Reinhart steered to the rear.

"You do understand, don't you?" she asked.

He smiled and lied: "Oh sure." Geographically, they were getting nowhere; it was a typical public park, where all roads led to playfields or toilets.

"Ah to be a man!" said Mrs. Fedder, still looking aloft. "And soar through the wild blue yonder. Were you in the Air Corps?"

"No," Reinhart answered vaguely, wondering whether Fedder would mind if they came back so soon; there just wasn't any place to stroll unless they left the trail, and that, according to the little signs affixed to every other tree, would violate the law.

She asked desperately: "You *were* in the service?"

"Oh yes, I was . . . I was . . ." From the corner of his eye he saw certain indications that permitted no leeway: either he produced some claim to adventure or he was a humdrum clod whom she would scorn. The strange thing was why he should care, having no designs on her.

"I don't know whether it's too soon to tell. They warned us—" It was as easy as that, and he didn't really have to prevaricate.

"Intelligence," said Beatrice Fedder. "You were an operative." She clapped her hands, sending more birds out of their treetop hiding places. When she spoke in approbation, her voice was not at all nasal.

"But you know," Reinhart declared manfully, seeing her husband's grimy back at the oven across the clearing, to the edge of which they had returned, "everybody did something adventurous. Some veterans just talk more than others. Anyway, just surviving the problems of normal life is romantic, if you want to see it that way."

"Especially washing and cooking," she answered in a voice so abrasive that it almost took the skin off his neck. "And living in a tin can. And having one kid after another. And talking about sewers. And sitting around the playground with the other hens, who all went to college."

There burst Reinhart's bubble of happy domesticity. But Gen hadn't had to do most of those things, and yet she was also dissatisfied. What did women want? To be men. But that was just impossible, and until they realized it was, he would be out of sympathy with them. They were just like Negroes, who refused to settle for less than being white. And Indians wanted to be Englishmen; Latins, gringos; midgets, giants; and dogs, persons. By this scheme of values Reinhart stood at the very apex of creation. Yet at any given time he was miserable. Put that in your pipe and smoke it, Gen, Bee, Splendor, Pandit Nehru, and Rin Tin Tin!

"I'm sorry," he told Mrs. Fedder, "but there's nothing I can do about it." He regretted having expressed so much resentment in his tone; after all, he was in a way her guest. But when she replied, that kind of regret seemed a joke.

"You could," she said, "if you wanted to." Her head fell again, and by the time they reached her husband, her manner was as if they had never gone.

"Oh," said Fedder, staring from kindly, smoked-reddened eyes, "back already? That didn't take long." His daughters rushed to him as soon as they saw Reinhart, who caught the largest in transit and offered to lift her way up into the sky, but she hid her face and shrank from him.

A breeze of displeasure wafted across Fedder's honest face. "Trow gets dizzy easily," he said, and with a protuberant belly forced Reinhart to fall back.

"Here," said Reinhart, after the meal, "let me earn my keep. I'll police up." He reached first for Fedder's cardboard plate, purposely ignoring Bee, who had finished long before. But she silently made herself his partner, gathering together the children's trash and, though she climbed out of the picnic table more quickly than he, who always had trouble with those joined-bench things, waiting for him so that they could walk to the fire together.

"O.K.!" bellowed Fedder, the jolly pimp. "You make an attractive couple."

Reinhart craftily changed his mind, announcing: "On the other hand, I'll take the kids off your hands, Niles. I saw an Eskimo Pie man down by the ball field." He had not yet got himself free of the stocks, having straddled a cross-member so as to sit far away from Beatrice, whom her husband had placed on his side.

"After all that watermelon?" Fedder asked incredulously, showing the white rind of his. Sensibly enough: those tiny children had eaten like wolves.

And Trowbridge, age 5, who had chattered constantly during the meal but incomprehensibly to everyone except her Daddy, now asserted with great clarity of phrase that she hated ice cream. The three-year-old said little, the smallest nothing at all, but they had managed throughout the meal to get across their dislike of Reinhart, as well as—could it be true?—a conspicuous lack of affection for their mother, who returned it, if her earlier comment was to be believed. And Fedder urged his wife on another man in that perverse way. How terrible! thought Reinhart, who had started on this outing with a desperate need to see a happy family in action. Instead he had got into a snakes' nest. Perhaps fate had saved him from similar straits: if the baby was a boy, Gen would conspire with it against him; if a girl, he had an ally against his wife. Either way, it was all bitter conflict, and where was love?

He and Bee stuffed the oven chimney full of trash, counting on the combustibles to incinerate the melon rinds and bunends, and he tossed a lighted match through the grill at the base. The fire caught on well in the bottom paper, but became clogged somewhere along the middle of the column: dense smoke gushed from the chimney mouth, smelling fearfully of hot garbage. This was an event that failed to touch the Fedders, but Reinhart felt it reflected unfavorably on his outdoorsmanship and began strenuously to poke a stick down the congested shaft in hopes he might clear it before the ice cream man reached them—for that guy, who had pedaled his bicycle-cart up the trail from the ball field, approached them from across the clearing, his bell jingling; and furthermore, his skin was black wherever it emerged from his white uniform, a color combination Reinhart had honestly not noticed when he had seen him at a great distance.

The stickwork made the smoke worse, and Reinhart obviously couldn't piss on the fire as he would have done as a boy, or even now in privacy, so he took a leftover Coke and poured it down the stack.

"Eskimo Pie, sir, madam? Cups? Raspberry, lemon sherbet. Ice-cream samwich?" announced the vendor, who for reasons of his own had chosen to apply first to Reinhart and Bee rather than the obvious choice of Fedder & kids still at table.

"Don't give me a bad time," said Reinhart, throwing down

his empty pop bottle. "Mrs. Fedder, this is my friend Splendor Mainwaring. Splendor, Mrs. Fedder."

Splendor took off his white cap and nodded, staying on the bike seat.

Bee Fedder did a gracious thing: gave her slender hand to the Negro and said: "I'm glad to know you" without a trace of condescension.

He hardly touched it, but wryly called attention to their difficulty with the garbage. "Don't let the park police see that. You're supposed to use those litter baskets."

"My friend is a writer," Reinhart told Bee. "By the way," he said to Splendor, "I still have a manuscript of yours."

"Oh," said Bee in that harsh, almost derisive tone a woman sometimes assumes to indicate she is intelligent. "Oh, is that true. I'd like to read it."

Reinhart smiled evilly at his friend. "You must get the author's permission."

Fedder came up at that moment and shamelessly confessed to Reinhart that now his daughters did want ice cream, now that the man was actually here.

He ordered three chocolate sandwiches from Splendor.

"Right away, boss," cried Splendor and leaned around in his seat to open the cabooselike refrigerator. "Here you go. That will be twenty-eight cents."

Reinhart wished them all in hell.

"Twenty-*eight?*" Fedder complained, showing a new side of his character.

"Seven cents each." Splendor shrugged. "I just work here."

The children hung like dogs underneath Fedder's elbow, looking up at the sandwiches he held; one had begun to melt in a long trickle of brown milk down his pale forearm.

"Oh," he grumbled, and with his free hand paid him.

Splendor took quick, insolent stock of Mrs. Fedder's perfect knees and rang his bell. "Eskimo Pies!" he suddenly bawled at the empty clearing.

"So long Splendor," Reinhart said with no punctuation, as if it were the title of a musical comedy. "Keep up your writing!"

"Oh I will," Splendor answered. He began slowly to pedal away.

"Huh?" asked Fedder, with a quizzical grin. "You know each other?"

Reinhart felt a strange pawing at his left leg. Looking down, he saw Fedder's two-year-old wiping chocolate ice cream on his khaki trousers.

247

"What's this about writing?" asked Fedder, sticking his wet muzzle in Reinhart's line of vision.

"I must borrow it from you," said Beatrice.

Splendor kept going, his jacket-back stained with perspiration, but at twenty yards, he looked back and shouted: "You better get the garbage out of that oven!"

"No, no, honey," Reinhart was busy telling the tiniest Fedder. But he should have heeded his friend's warning, for no sooner had Splendor vanished down the trail to the ball field than a surly park policeman came towards them on the same path. Having reached and inspected the clogged oven, he issued to Reinhart—to whom he went without hesitation—a summons which ordered its recipient to pay two dollars' fine or defend himself in court against a charge of littering public property.

Chapter 16

"I say it was a stinking trick to pull on a friend," Reinhart shouted into the telephone, his voice echoing through the iron house. "Or do you have the nerve to deny it?"

"Hold on, Carlo," said Splendor at the other end of the line. "The juke box is so loud here I can't make out a word. Let me close the door of the booth. Ah. Now what were you asking?"

He it was who had the brass to call Reinhart, rather than the other way around, for when Reinhart was really angry with a person he didn't want to have anything to do with him; then too, he had never sought out Splendor. Third, the Mainwarings did not have a telephone.

But when he was pushed into it, Reinhart could talk turkey in respect to his indignation. He ignored Splendor's diversionary tactics now and said: "I'm not the fool I look. No matter what you say, I accuse you of informing on us to the park police."

"Oh really," answered the Negro. "Of course it's O.K. when the shoe is on the other foot."

"Meaning what?"

"Look, Carlo, I know all about your scheme to resettle the population of the West Side in Andorra."

Reinhart sighed in despair over the impossibility of getting things straight on the telephone. He could not explain about Andorra unless he had Splendor's eye. Anyhow, it was pretty far-fetched to describe it that way, and while it was true that Reinhart still felt guilty about having shared the proceeds of the Maker's sale of fake steamship tickets, they consisted of no more than the amount he had paid out, the night of the lecture, for the benefit of—Splendor Mainwaring, dope fiend, plagiarist, police spy, and false friend.

"I don't know what you're talking about," he said into the mouthpiece. "But I'll tell you this: betraying a friend is one of the baser crimes, and if I recall the *Divine Comedy* correctly Dante agrees with me." He slammed the phone into its cradle, then went to the sink and held his hot face under running water. It was the evening of picnic day, and his present anger had aggravated the aftereffects of the sun. He walked around the house, dripping dry; the night was stifling and he was alone.

He ended up standing before the window that looked towards Fedder's. No sooner had he exonerated Beatrice from suspicion of infidelity than she gave him reason to suspect her all over again. Yet she stayed with Fedder, and in so doing observed the minimum obligation of a wife.

The telephone rang! He rushed to lift it and say: "Darling, how I've missed you."

Splendor's voice replied: "Frankly, Carlo, I think your humor is badly misplaced. . . . And if I wanted to speak of other ways in which you don't measure up to your exalted idea of yourself—well, we all have peculiarities, but I for one am willing to overlook them and fasten my attention on a man's merits rather than his foibles. That is, I try to cultivate a little tolerance. But for that, would I be calling you again?"

"For that matter," asked Reinhart, "why are you? I distinctly gave you to understand that we are no longer on speaking terms."

"I'll tell you why," said Splendor, and no doubt characteristically stretching his neck, swallowed. "We're even again." Reinhart had nothing to remark to this, not understanding it, so he waited for the Negro to continue: "You had it nicely planned! Get me out of the way and use my movement for your Andorra scheme."

Hackles erected, Reinhart answered: "Of course that's why I spent an hour talking up your courage; why I spent my own money to get you an audience; why I made you slip out the back window and run away—you see how childish you are?"

"You did it subtly," said Splendor. "You know how to destroy a man's faith in himself without his realizing what is transpiring. Suddenly, *pssst*, he collapses."

"I refuse to reply."

"Then," Splendor went on, "why would I take heroin? I never saw any before that night, contrary to your stereotyped image of the Neg—"

"Watch yourself," warned Reinhart.

"—wouldn't have known how to use it, even; but a man suddenly darted from an alley, pressed the items into my hand, and vanished quickly as he had appeared. Distraught, ill, I did the natural thing." It was really unfortunate that Splendor couldn't find a use for his gifts—a better use, that is, than harassing Reinhart—for among other things he was an excellent narrator, and Reinhart was now sucked into asking: "Yes, yes, then what happened?"

"You informed the police."

"You absolutely cannot believe that," cried Reinhart. "You simply cannot. . . . But I'll say this: I wish I had."

The operator broke in at that point to announce the exhaustion of the time purchased by Splendor's nickel; and Reinhart, whose reflexes were always amiable irrespective of what he was up to consciously, said quickly; "Give me your number. I'll call you back."

"I have only one nickel—is that what you're saying?" asked Splendor. "Now I should take your petty charity!" He violently hung up, giving his white friend a taste of what Reinhart had handed him earlier. It is not amusing to be on the other end of a slammed telephone.

Reinhart was so angry he thought he might break out in a rash, and when the bell rang again he lifted the instrument and poured through it a gutterful of abuse.

However, the caller this time was Genevieve, who waited patiently for the end of his tirade and, getting it, said with compassion; "Poor boy, you're not off your rocker."

"Gen!" Reinhart shouted lovingly from one part of his character, but his rage had been too recent for any kind of integrity, and the next moment he corrected her: "You always get things wrong. If you mean I'm nuts, then I *am off* my rocker."

"I already excused you for that reason, but if you're going to brag about it!"

"Ah, Gen, Gen," Reinhart wailed pathetically. "What's wrong with me?"

"Have you thought about your breath?" she responded in a nasty parody of a radio mouthwash commercial. "Carl, I just called to say I forgot my nail-polish remover. It's the giant size, and it would be too bad to let it go to waste and buy another. Can you mail it? Put adhesive tape around the

251

top so it won't leak, then wrap the bottle in corrugated paper, then heavy brown. Address it Mrs. Genevieve Reinhart, care of Raven, 25 Hibiscus Terrace, for I haven't yet made up my mind on you and me. But I must say you're no help. By the way, we must work out a monetary arrangement: it's half your child that I am taking calcium pills and drinking extra milk for. . . ." She seemed to shield her mouthpiece, for Reinhart heard a faint "I *am* being tough, Daddy" after her last loud words.

He answered in angry nobility: "You can have everything I've got."

"Because," Gen went on in a deliberate, unreflective fashion as if she were repeating what someone was whispering in her ear, "I'd . . . hate . . . to take you to . . . court."

"That," said Reinhart, "is the coldest, cruelest, most heartless statement I have ever heard. Excuse me"—he wiped the wet earpiece with his handkerchief—"and what it discloses is that you don't love me and never did. And insofar as the polish remover goes, you forgot to replace the cap on the bottle and it has all evaporated."

"Carl!" he heard her cry as he put the phone gently into the cradle—he could never slam it down on his estranged wife. Therefore he had nothing to reproach himself for; and despite his fortune's being at the low-water mark, he had felt worse. All he asked was morally to have one up on the next person— well, it wasn't really all he asked, but having become a victim, he might as well make the most of it.

Now to get to the homework without further nonsense. He picked up *Anna Karenina* in fake peppiness and hurled himself onto the couch. At nine o'clock the day was finally dying outside, and the lamp on the end table behind and above him already drew bugs, not mosquitoes yet but rather a sluggish, fat brand of gnat, which was inclined to fall on the book pages and expire of apathy, making little brown stains. No matter how pointless life seems, look at such a creature and feel purposeful.

Anna, in the chapter he had reached, was suffering from puerperal fever. It looked like curtains for her, and Vronsky and Karenin, lover and husband, had reached an understanding through their mutual grief, as people always do in books —Reinhart jotted a note to that effect, in case he was asked for a comment in class, and added: *Compare Achilles and Priam at end of Illiad.*

Karenin comes off best, being a man of principle. Reinhart was moved by his noble statement to Vronsky, and copied it down: "This is my position: you can trample me in the mud, make me the laughing stock of the world, I will not abandon her, and I will never utter a word of reproach to you." If the truth were known, Reinhart identified with Karenin at this point, as he had earlier, at the time of Anna's seduction, associated himself with her lover; but now Vronsky was at a loss, impressed by the "luminous, serene look" in Karenin's eyes, and "did not understand Karenin's feeling, but he felt that it was something higher and even unattainable for him with his view of life." Reinhart also wrote this in his looseleaf notebook, in his own shorthand: "V. no underst. K's feel'g but f. it higher and unattain' for own life view." Turning to it in preparation for an exam, he would find it incomprehensible.

Yet the great thing about literature, as opposed to science, was that if asked about a book you could make up something quite as appropriate as—perhaps even better than—the particulars you had forgotten. And a narrative got better and better as one's memory of it receded, your distant *Tom Swift and His Big Dirigible* being as good as any here-and-now *Hamlet*.

Reinhart lay there on his spine, the book face down on his chest, insects circling the lamp, the metal vault of his cathedral rising on the left, making its apogee overhead, descending on the right. Could *he* have made Anna Karenina? This was truly the first salacious thought concerning a woman other than his wife that he had had since his marriage. He had never known a Russian broad, but no doubt women everywhere were the same in that they none of them understood history. Precedent was all: a known libertine, having laid everyone, could lay anyone. Women were afraid to oppose a trend. How magnificent, the first man to climb Everest would say, I am all alone up here! Whereas a woman in a like position would cry: How awful that nobody has ever done it but me!

He fell asleep from time to time, from which he kept sweatily waking up and shifting the weight of the book on his chest (Tolstoy wrote them heavy)—but he was startled when the lamp suddenly lost its balance on the edge of the table, to which he had pulled it at the outset, and fell upon his head. For a moment he believed he had been trapped in dreamland and had shot himself before he could get back.

However, he was soon distracted by footsteps upon the little porch and a worry that the visitor might fall off, break his neck, and sue the occupant, for the broken rail had not yet been mended.

"Hold on there!" he shouted for the purpose of establishing legal immunity. One moment he was a mad Russian and the next, his own father, who had an exaggerated concern for the responsibilities of a householder. He clambered off the couch and groped toward the door, a little blind, for the lamp that

253

fell on him had been the only illumination and he had looked right into it.

"Come in," he said to the blur standing beyond the screen door. As she passed him, he recognized her scent. It was Fedder's wife, her bouquet unmistakable: one of those exotic perfumes that erect the hairs of the nose—"Insane," "Fiendish," or "Disaster"—smelling rather like oregano in a base of suntan oil.

"Let me put on some lights," Reinhart said, swallowing with difficulty.

"Oh, not for me," she answered. "I hate glare: it is so scientific." She still wore her picnic shorts, and was all brown leg.

Reinhart coughed viciously, to relieve the tension.

Her voice, which was normally regretful, became expectantly buoyant: "Are you sick?"

"No." said Reinhart. He blurted out the truth. "No, I'm just ill at ease. What will Niles think when he looks over here and sees the place dark?"

She returned to melancholy. "He won't mind."

"Really," said Reinhart. What made him even more uncomfortable was that he had the woman's lines of dialogue and she the man's. It seemed unfair that honor should make you effeminate.

"Won't you sit down." In his confusion he pointed to a straight-backed chair all the way back in the kitchen.

She pouted.

"I'm sorry." He indicated the couch. She took it. "Just what did you want?" he asked, still standing.

"Couldn't we just talk?" She threw her head at a beseeching angle. "Just talk. Tell me about spying." She had sat down right on top of *Anna Karenina*, he hated that kind of insensitivity.

"What was Niles in the Navy?"

"Machinist's mate, second class." She found the book under her bottom and pulled it out, asking: "Is this good?" She riffled through the pages, too fast to read anything but slow enough to lose the fragment of torn newspaper Reinhart had inserted to mark his place: it fluttered behind the couch like a moth.

"I was wondering," asked Reinhart, "whether I might offer you a drink of brandy—of Courvoisier, in fact. It's just about the best. I can say that because it wasn't my choice, though I paid for it. You see—"

"Yes," said Beatrice Fedder, fixing him with her inquiet eyes, indeed staring him down. She was still wearing the puffy blouse and he suspected she might be flat-chested. Her legs, though, were exquisite and probably even better in high heels; she still was barefoot—in fact, her feet were rather dirty, one big-toenail ragged as a saw tooth.

Reinhart had broader tolerances for women than some men he had known, who were quick to see fat where bone was called for, and vice versa. Skinny girls generally had good legs; fat ones, nice breasts; every one had something—of course, that was always his credo. On the other hand, you sometimes saw a pretty face over thick ankles. There are all sorts of compensations, not all of them obviously to the good. Suddenly he realized that Gen when older might become dumpy and walk like a little squab. Such a woman lived in the next block up from his parents, who sometimes derisively watched her go by from behind the drapes.

Blaine Raven's assaults on the Courvoisier had left hardly enough to wet one whistle, let alone two. Working in the dusk of the kitchen area, Reinhart watered the stock, counting on the strength of an expensive booze to retain some pretense of warmth. Wrong. On the test-taste the mixture proved insipid. A touch of sugar made it too sweet. A drop of Worcestershire no doubt helped the color, which however, he couldn't see in the dark, and did something odd to the bouquet. No point in testing more, for he had exhausted the possibilities of reinforcement.

"Mmm," said Beatrice, when he had come back into the light and handed her a glassful over ice. Up went her thin eyebrows as she took a draft. "Mmm, good. You can always tell the best."

"Isn't it true," said Reinhart, more in pity than irony, and tried his. You know, it wasn't brandy but it wasn't bad. He fetched the bottle.

"Careful, Bee," said Beatrice Fedder to herself, mouth at her second glassful. "You're starry-eyed enough as it is."   .

There was something about her, he couldn't put his finger on it, that Reinhart found awfully grating.

"Ah, Bee," said Bee, and then to Reinhart: "Mustn't mind if I talk to myself; she's my only confidante."

"Uh-huh," Reinhart answered. He stood at the little table from which the lamp had earlier fallen on him, and refilled his own glass. He had not yet chosen a seat, though that portion of the couch not occupied by slender Bee yawned at him like a hungry mouth.

"It's a holder from when I was a kid and had an imaginary playmate," Bee continued. "I used to sit by myself and talk for hours. They thought I was warped." She smiled dreamily.

From where he stood Reinhart could see Fedder's house through the window. He supposed that Beatrice did not appreciate what a fine husband she had. He understood, suddenly, how splendid was Fedder's faith in her, to suffer her to go alone on a hot night, wearing shorts, to the home of an attractive man. Reinhart never respected Fedder more than at that moment, because it was then that he decided to seduce his wife.

What had happened was this: The more he reminded himself of how awful it would be in terms of morality, the hornier he became. The more he admired Fedder, the more he wanted to be obligated to him. The more Bee bored him, the more he desired her. It was also true that, accustomed to his regular piece, he feared that another sexless night might drive him to rape a stranger.

Having decided on this monstrous aim, however, he had no better opening device for its instrumentation than to drop heavily on the couch as far as possible from Bee, like a schoolboy. Real booze might have helped, though it appeared his partner, at least, had been hoaxed by the ersatz. She smiled at him through narrowed lids.

"I came originally from upstate," she asserted.

"Yes," said Reinhart. "I remember Niles told me you're an orphan."

"Raised in a Home, sleeping in my narrow iron bed, never knew my parents." She found a squashed package of cigarettes, wrapped in a handkerchief, in her blouse-pocket and lighted one, mopping its end with dark lipstick. Reinhart worried about the irritation to his eyes. And, sure enough, here came a great cloud of smoke directly at them.

"At eighteen, I went out on my own. Bee girl, I said, what do we want to do?"

"You wanted to be loved," said Reinhart, wincing a watery smile.

"I didn't care about that. Love is all you ever heard around the Home, which was full of social-worker types always grinning sadly at you and fondling your behind."

The drink had coarsened her, Reinhart noticed and was not sure whether that made his job easier or more difficult. In his current mood he was tempted to return to an adolescent conviction that girls who talked dirty put out. On the other hand, it meant that the image of her that had aroused him—the dissatisfied, respectable wife—must be altered to the grosser.

He rose, emptied the rest of the bottle into her glass, and sat down an inch closer.

"So," she went on, evacuating a lungful of cigarette, an unattractive thing in a woman, "I got a job in a beauty parlor in

256

Bucyrus. Christ, have you ever smelled the hair of some old biddy under the dryer? Then the guy that owned this place, called himself Monsieur René—he kept waylaying me in the booths, the oily little crumb. At the Home they always told us you've got to be agreeable when out in the world, don't be bitter. But he had a wife, and one night after hours she came in and caught us and went for me with a scissors. Me, not him. Luckily what she grabbed was the thinning shears—you know, without points?" Her cigarette was already down to the nub. She put it out and said: "Honey, you wouldn't have any more?" Holding out the empty glass.

"If we're lucky," said Reinhart with an invisible shudder, "there may be a can of beer in the icebox."

Back in the darkened kitchen, he peered out at Bee in the light. She had crossed her legs in masculine style and fired up a new smoke. Luck was against him: six cans of beer lay on their sides in the bottom of the fridge. Gen had bought them for the ill-fated dinner party, in case Daddy went dry. Of course, he could have told Bee there was none—had he not been afraid of her.

"Don't bother with a glass," she called. "I can take it right from the can and save on washing up."

Grotesque. This type of woman Reinhart had always thought of as being big and burly and found somewhere like teamsters' picnics.

She took a belt from the can he had fetched, and wiping the end of her fine nose, which had got wet from a bit of foam clinging to the far side of the rim, said: "I guess I'm talking your arm off. Don't worry about your wife, honey. There are plenty more fish in the sea, and a lot of them would prefer your kind, believe me."

Reinhart wanted to get her off the subject of his broken marriage. It was offensive to hear the condolences of a lush; moreover, she seemed to take the line that he, and not Gen, was a very special type outside the standard. In love even a genius yearns to be commonplace.

"What happened after the beauty parlor?" he asked.

"After that," said Bee, "I married your friend and mine, Niles Fedder. I haven't ever done anything interesting, unless you count following him to San Diego when he went into the Navy. Did you ever see California? It's not what you would expect. I went up to L.A. once. Did you know that Hollywood isn't anywhere? I mean, you look for something gathered together—you know how they say in the papers 'the movie colony'? Well, it isn't really. It isn't any place you can put your finger on." She handed him the empty beer can, and he fetched her a full.

She widened her eyes over the container at her mouth, and drank *glug-glug-glug*. At the first beer Reinhart had lost all carnal desire, and if that were not enough, he felt sorry for her, and sat down with a long face.

Bee finished the can, and looked at him in prolonged pathos. "Honey," she said, "don't you worry about your wife. She'll be back when she realizes that there isn't a man alive who doesn't have potency problems."

Now, for a moment Reinhart just continued to nod. Then he asked quietly, lugubriously: "Where did you ever get such a vicious idea about me?"

"Why," said Bee, her forearms guarding her bosom—the size of which he had been trying to estimate for a half hour, while she on her part had been sizing him up as a eunuch; it was unthinkable; he might burst—"Why, didn't Niles tell me she left because of that?"

Reinhart shouted: "That sweaty little skunk!"

"There's no need to be nasty," said Bee, lowering her guard when it became apparent his violence was not to be directed towards her. "It has nothing to do with the kind of person you are at heart."

"I ask you," said Reinhart, strangely calm again, "I ask you . . ." Addressing heaven, he said no more aloud. He was saved, by an involvement in the drama of the situation, from embarrassment; it was rather like being drunk. But to get a gain here, you must pay with a loss there. He got nerve, but he lost judgment.

Putting his left hand at her sacroiliac, he thrust the other into the neck of the blouse and found her nearer breast, which as he expected was very small but well-formed. She wore no brassiere. Along her upper lip ran a hairline of beer foam; her visage in general was attenuated, patrician, noninvolved.

"This excites me," he said. "Believe me, it does, Bee. There's nothing I like better." His left hand went into the back waistband of her shorts. Down as far as the coccyx he encountered no underpants. In the depths of summer the temperature of her skin was January. He had lied to her; at this point there was nothing in the world he wanted less than tail, and his groin agreed with his mind. But he panted with simulated passion and labored relentlessly as a mercenary worker on piece rate, two hands going, breathing raucously in her ear. For a long time he spared her lips, supposing them a barometer of sincerity that might show him for what he was, but at last nothing would do but to press his mouth to hers, having lifted her half upon himself by means of the natural handholds though she stayed stiff as a board.

His fears had gone for nought; in kissing Bee he committed

258

himself to nothing; it would have been like eating Jell-O except that his lips tingled from the residue of nicotine on hers and close up she smelled like an ashtray in the office of a brewery.

Very likely the whole business was a foolish idea, yet the history of the West might very well be considered as the product of round-about potency-proving, with say, Napoleon's conquest of Europe as a sort of getting-one-up on a large scale. So Reinhart trudged on, regretting only that Bee was still ostensibly paralyzed with fright.

Or was she? Turning away in false catching of breath, he saw her reach for the live cigarette she had dropped on top of the beer can at the onset of his attack and take a long, insouciant drag. That stung him into more purposeful techniques. He probably should have ripped her clothes off, like the protagonist of a historical novel, but Fedder might find out and, having to pay for new ones, interpret it as the pettiest of bourgeois revenges. So Reinhart was careful with the top button of her side-fly; the rest was zipper, and her shirttail was caught in it, reminiscent of Genevieve.

Gen, Gen, see what you are responsible for!

He freed it and shortly had her bare. She wore pants and brassiere of white skin, between the tan places. He could grant objectively that this was attractive; a noneunch might have been stimulated . . . but not he, to whom the horrors gained access in the most banal of modes: from bull to ox at the flutter of an accusation. He now dared not loosen his belt. Nor could he even perspire: he kept wiping his forehead to check.

"You see, honey?" asked Bee, who understood too well, though he still wore his trousers. "Why keep on? That only makes it worse." She slipped her hands around his neck, which brought a little breast against his cheek like a paraffin lemon.

It is impossible to tell another woman you have made love to your own wife on the average of three times a day since moving into your present domicile—Reinhart formulated this as a law, like Gresham's. Bee stroked his head. She made no move to get back into her clothes, and suggested the modern mother who while bare-ass acts nonchalant so as not to give phobias to the children.

Reinhart turned a corrosive irony on himself, threatening to fabricate substitute equipment of broomstick-end and two walnuts, but in truth there was nothing to do but wage the good fight regardless of deficient armament. At Thermopylae, retreat had been taboo. She was very heavy for a skinny girl— he had to lift her to get himself out from under so as to strip for action. But now she struggled, apparently with an intent to retain him for comforting.

"Let go!" Reinhart whined.

"Don't you fret, honey," said Bee, sympathetically holding him fast. She was more artful than strong; it was as if he were caught in a large hairnet. All this was going on with Fedder in the next hut no more than fifty feet away. Nothing impeded his breaking in at any moment, and Reinhart found himself wishing he would and get served right—but the ill luck seemed invariably to go in one direction: against Reinhart.

"Ah, what's the use, Bee?" he finally asked stoically, and slapped her bare bottom. "Go get dressed."

Putting on her blouse, she said ladylike: "I hope your evening hasn't been ruined."

"Not in the least," answered Reinhart. "It's always worth while hearing other points of view."

She had yet to put on her shorts, and looked very lithe in shirttail and hip-length nudity.

"It's really all relative," she said.

"Isn't it, isn't it? Reinhart responded. "Bee contrary to what Niles told you, and the performance you just witnessed, the situation with my wife was just the other way around. She has been pregnant for weeks." He, too, took his time in dressing.

Bee raised her eyebrows.

"All right," he said, "go check with the gynecologist."

"No, I believe you," she hastily assured him. Whether she did he would never know, but he realized at that point that she had all along been trying to be kind. "But speaking for myself, I always heard it was so great to have kids, but I can tell you it's overrated." At last she slipped into her shorts, and Reinhart felt released from a suspense that he hadn't appreciated till it was gone. "But what's so great about doing something *anybody* can do?"

"Just that," said Reinhart. "Isn't it splendid to be normal?"

She fastened the hook-and-eye at her waistband; he was happy he hadn't ripped it. "That's a man's idea. It's always a man who says a woman's aim in life is to have kids. No woman is so sentimental."

"I'm not sure I understand your use of the word."

She sat at the edge of the couch. "I would say sentimental's when you pretend so hard to yourself you have a feeling you really don't have but believe you should, that you end up feeling sorry for yourself."

"Well," said Reinhart, "you end up with a real emotion, anyway."

Bee grinned. "There you are, the typical man: any old feeling is good as the next. But a woman is very particular about such things."

"That would explain something, then," said Reinhart. "You know, never in my life have I understood my mother."

Bee shrugged.

"Never," he repeated, "and you might say that if I can't grasp the principles of a woman I have known for twenty-two years, how can I expect to with one I've known less than four months?"

Bee shook her fine head; never, in whatever state, had she lost what Reinhart liked to think of as her equanimity. "You and your principles! Stop thinking of women in general. Stop thinking of women at all. If you want to get your wife back and keep her, you'll have to catch her attention." She rose and put her hand out.

"May I ask," said Reinhart, taking it, "what Niles does in that line?"

"He sent me over here, didn't he?"

"Of course." Reinhart only hoped that in gaining Gen's eye he wouldn't have to go as far.

"What I like about tonight is that I have profited by it," he told her. "You never know, do you, when you get up each morning, what the day will bring."

Bee said shyly: "So long, Carl." She was really a fine person.

In saying he had profited, Reinhart meant that he had examined adultery without committing it and gained data on women without actually compromising himself. He was getting to be a real exemplar of the American Way.

Chapter 17

Because his experience with Bee had turned out without prejudice to anybody, Reinhart maintained his admiration for Fedder. He wouldn't have changed him one iota. The world would be a much better place if it were populated with more Niles Fedders. Fedders who keep the old earth spinning. Long Live Fedder!

Reinhart had seen him twice since the day he had got to know both him and his at close quarters, and greeted him both times with an enthusiasm that caused his neighbor to recoil, for Fedder balked at tasting his own medicine. "Niles!" shouted Reinhart on the first occasion, Monday evening when they emerged simultaneously, each from his own hut, to fetch the garbage cans that had been lifted that morning by the Vetsville sanitary squad and hurled back empty. "Niles, where would that sewer main run? Down by Unit H?"

On Wednesday he encountered Fedder on the University campus. Niles and a group of friends, dressed to a man in T-shirts and chino pants, emerged from the Student Union humorlessly sucking at ice-cream cones, some vanilla, one chocolate, one mottled. "Fed!" cried Reinhart. "Wouldn't there have to be an auxiliary pumping station for the sewage somewhere between Vetsville and town?"

Fedder introduced his companions, who all seemed to be named Jack, and amiably chided him: "*Now* you get interested in the sewer, now that your boss has been awarded the contract."

"My boss?" Reinhart asked stupidly and gaped at one of the Jacks.

"Humbold's his name," said Fedder. "Don't you read the papers?" He waxed bitter. "If you ask me, there's something suspicious about the deal. I thought he was a real-estate man, not a sewer contractor. And his was the only bid submitted. Doesn't that sound strange? That's typical small-town politics for you."

"I'll tell you, Niles, I haven's seen Claude for some time. But then, we have never been what you might call close. Businessmen are like that. . . ." From the way they held their heads, Reinhart inferred that neither Fedder nor his companions were ready to confirm this statement, and he went on with some defiance: "For all I know that's the way you *have* to be to make good in business. I suppose it's as good, or as bad, as anything else."

"Not normally?" butted in one of the Jacks, then crunched at his cone.

"Oh, I guess not," Reinhart answered impatiently. He didn't want to get hung up with these guys. What had become of the good old College Joe with his idiot fraternities and junior proms? "And as to the town," he told Fedder, a little chary about meeting his eye even though he hadn't cuckolded him—or perhaps *because* he hadn't—"you've been there only since the beginning of summer and already know more about it than I do in twenty-two years."

Fedder, shrugging, had to step aside for a girl who came down the Union steps and chose to enter the sidewalk at the corner which they were blocking. She had the high, hard behind of the very young.

"No wonder, then," said Fedder, "that the Yahoos have such an easy time of it. I understand the same mayor has been in office since 1928, and the chief of police is his brother." He explained to his friends, who apparently lived in other suburbs. "The Vetsville Civic Committee petitioned for this new sewer, but little did we know that the town would jump at the chance to build it, and thereby develop a damned good argument for gobbling us up. Whereas we're seeking incorporation as an independent community."

The Jacks gasped.

"I mean," said Fedder, "we didn't think of that when we started making noise about the sewer. After all, we are only amateur politicos up against this local Tammany. What can you expect? I wouldn't sneer if I were you, Carl. Most of the rest of us come from somewhere else. Your advice could be invaluable. In addition, you work for Humbold." Fedder fell on the ice cream that the sun was rapidly causing to dwindle, and made short work of it. Reinhart wanted to drive home and get the rest of the data from the horse's mouth, i.e., Claude himself, but felt he owed it to Fedder to tarry here with him.

Wiping his face, Fedder said without warning: "Know who likes you? Bee." Then with a glint in his eye, he asked: "Anything new on the domestic front?"

Reinhart called his bluff by explaining to the Jacks: "My wife left me, is what he means." He had succeeded in his aim: they were all rendered uncomfortable, including Fedder. So much of life consists of embarrassments that sometimes the best you can do is beat the other fellow to them.

Without further ado, he bade them goodbye and repaired to the parking lot; he was actually amused at the thought that Fedder might calumniate him in absentia. It gave him status.

As Reinhart had told Fedder, he and Claude Humbold had not crossed paths for a length of time that could be called unconscionable, if you were looking for an excuse to use that word. It occurred to Reinhart because he had on his conscience a statement by Genevieve that Claude's paying him a salary for doing nothing seemed pretty fishy to her. Having made allowances for her overwrought state, Reinhart still was left with a conviction that it also smelled funny to him. The boss had been eluding him for weeks, though oddly enough paying his salary on schedule, through the mail. The more you thought about it, the most pathological it seemed for Claude to put out money without being beaten into it.

Reinhart had a secret: for some time he had not taken out a single client. It really was impossible to read the complete *Iliad*, etc., not to mention the assignments in Psych and French, and work too. Every afternoon he drove to one of the listings at the edge of town, a vacant cottage in a yard full of weeds, concealed the Gigantic behind a decaying toolshed, crept into the house and lying upon an old blanket that smelled of dog, read till five. Not only did he misrepresent these workdays to Genevieve; he lied about them to himself: the ebullience of ego he had enjoyed until Gen left, owed to his belief that in himself, alone in the Middle West, were both spirit and matter united in Renaissance proportions—the cultivated realtor, the practical intellectual, Carlo de' Medici.

To take money from Claude under such conditions was thievery. Reinhart supposed he could literally be sent to prison for so doing, but that aspect did not interest him at present, no more than did the adjustments that should be made in his self-picture. What he found intriguing was that Claude, who would not without coercion pay you for an actual service honestly performed, here seemed to be naïvely conspiring in a fraud against himself. . . . Which was unlikely. He was cooking up something.

Gen had suspected, with her woman's nose for smelling out shenanigans. Women are very wise. This makes up for the fact that they are seldom well educated. Gen certainly wasn't; she didn't know Dante from Adam. There was something grisly about a woman who did.

He drove straight to the office, intending first to do some reconnoitering in and around the boss's desk, though one of the telling features of the situation was that Claude seemed to have stopped going there. The most difficult phase of the campaign might be in finding him at all. Reinhart planned to start with something modest, like examining his files. But when he rounded the corner by Maybelle's Beauty Salon, he saw the big white Cad parked in the middle of the next block. The Gigantic saw it too and, as always lost face and began to miss in the valves. "You cowardly son of a bitch," Reinhart said to the dashboard, though he knew a mechanism's agony is no small matter. To be decent, he ran on a way and parked it near a shabby Nash.

The glass door of the office, the one that had in a sense brought Reinhart and Genevieve together, was locked. Yet he knew from the Cad that Claude lurked within the inner sanctum; and from certain drifts of blue smoke, that at least one other individual, no enemy of the Kings, was with him.

He stole around the back of the building and, taking care not to trouble the gravel, sidled under the open window.

Claude was speaking: ". . . no, boy, no! Absolutely not, Bobby, never! Bob pal, would you mind pointing that stogie towards the neighbors? I never indulge, old son, and your smoke makes the peepers burn. No offense, Bob. Robert, say you don't hate me for it! Now just let me flush out the old windpipe with a shot of 100-proof H_2O, gents, and I'm your man."

Hardly valuable eavesdropping as yet, but then you could not expect that it would be all pertinent stuff, which only happens in films. Wearing of bending, Reinhart sat on his heels and waited for Claude to return from the water cooler.

He was still there when the torrent descended upon him. Momentarily, all he could see was water; then he discerned, back of the upended bottle, the grim, dedicated visage of Claude Humbold. Imagine, all by himself Claude had lifted the big jug from the cooler, carried it to the window, and tipped it out. But Reinhart could spare no more time for awe. He was being soaked by the fall, which was spasmodic, as air and water struggled for the bottle's narrow mouth with *gloop-gloop* noises. He scrambled away.

"No you don't!" shouted Humbold. "Halt, fugitive! Call out the dogs! Stop or I'll hurl this hand grenade and blow you to flinders."

Squeezing the water from his shirt—luckily he wore no more than that and wash trousers—Reinhart sheepishly smiled and said: "Sorry, Claude, I was looking for a lucky piece I dropped in the gravel."

"Silence, spy!" ordered Humbold, letting the rest of the jug's contents gurgle out to no purpose. "You are covered by an unseen automatic. Just give your age, name, and employer, or you're a dead chicken."

"Claude! Don't you recognize me?"

The boss peered over the bottle, making his eyes mean. "Walk two paces forward, Prisoner. . . . Why are you disguised as Bud? You'd never fool a soul, you poor devil. . . . Bud, that ain't you? Why in the world are you standing there all wet?"

"I had no intention of spying, Claude," said Reinhart. "There is a hole in my pocket and as I was passing the window, all my change fell out."

The bottle at last empty, Claude pulled it inside. He reappeared grinning wide.

"Do you a world of good. Never turn off the old radar, bud. Never show your throat to a wolf, lest he rip it asunder. I believe you'll find that in the Good Book; but if you don't, don't call me heathen. Bud, whyn't you come in, or was you waiting for it to rain?" Gargling a laugh, he fell back indoors.

Owing to one thing or another, Reinhart had not stopped at Maw's for a bath in some time. Consequently, this soaking had done him no harm. Then too, it was a hot day, particularly back there on the gravel. Indeed, by the time he had got around front, he was almost dry.

In Claude's office sat two other men whom Reinhart recognized instantly though he had not seen them in the flesh since before the war, and the photoengravings of their images used by the local newspaper, made in the Twenties, had been run through the presses so often that they nowadays tended to overink and print Negroes.

"Bud," said Claude. "I want to give you a thrill. I want to innerduce you to two of the great statesmen of our era, two of the gents who enrich this country, one nation under God invisible."

"Claude," said Reinhart. "I wanted to explain what I was doing under that window. I had lost my pen, see—"

"Bud," said Claude, "silencio, if you please! And kindly meet the Messers Gibbon, the Honorable Bob J., our esteemed mayor, and Mr. C. Roy, police chief."

Reinhart said how-do and shook their hands. Bob J. resembled his toad in most features, even to a complexion mottled with liver spots, and little forearms that he held in close to a squat trunk. C. Roy, in a blue uniform, was as thick through as his brother but tall as Reinhart and with a larger head, on which his hair grew iron-gray and rather in the shape of a Trojan helmet. He gave Reinhart a hard shake indeed, with a judo twist that sent pains far as the elbow. The mayor shook limp, cold, and oily; it felt like sorting anchovies.

The Gibbon boys had held office continuously since 1928, except for a two-year term won during the middle Thirties by a Reform ticket which promised to remove the slot machines from the confectionery across from the grammar school. Before the war, Reinhart had been wont to jeer at the Gibbons. But now that he was some years older and wiser, and in his new character—young businessman, veteran, husband—his vision was less murky. Actually, there was something reassuring about them. If you had to have politicians, may as well settle for the machine kind; they are steady. Moreover, they will never persecute a man for his own good.

"Well sir, bud," said Claude. "I see you are almost dry. Therefore go get a chair from the outer office and park your carcass on it while I check you out on that opportunity I promised I would open up for you if you did good by me, and you have."

Reinhart fetched a seat and put it down near the window, where he noticed for the first time a rear-vision mirror of the motorcar type, angled to reflect what would otherwise have been the blind spot along the outside wall: thus had Claude discovered him. Nor did the boss fail to characterize the event.

"Bud, I never blame a man for trying to make it no matter how. I don't give a hoot if you tried to sell me out so long as you ain't got no stronger idea than to sneak outside the winda." Claude smirked at Bob J., who sat chin on chest, ruminating on a wad of tongue.

Reinhart decided not to protest further, realizing that it was to everybody's benefit that he be judged as sinister as possible. He was learning all the time. One day Gen would be proud of him.

"Now I don't care what the other side gave you for the goods on me," Claude went on. He wore a green bowtie today, and the points of his sports-shirt collar fell almost to his waist, which admittedly was drawn high. "When you hear my proposition you'll tell them to go buy a cesspool and jump in." This elicited a beastly guffaw from C. Roy, who also smacked his corded fists together.

"Well sir, bud," said Claude. "You are in a pretty position up at Vetsville where I got you a nice hut to live in with your lovely Mrs., the former G. Raven who used to be secketary to Your Uncle Dudley—name one after me, bud, and he'll get a silver cup. Well sir, I guess the kind of monkey you are—in all fairness I believe your best friend would say you was a bit dopey, bud—I guess it ain't likely you heard of a sanitary improvement that we're gonna run through."

Reinhart was pleased to say: "Yes, I have, Claude. I—"

Claude metaphorically impaled him on a finger. "Never mock sewers, bud. If you read your history you'll know that before they had them, the gutters was knee-high with filth—doo-doo floating in plain sight and suchlike."

C. Roy belched a laugh. On the epaulets of his uniform were six gold stars, one better than MacArthur; and his cap, which lay on Humbold's desk, was white on top and blue towards the bottom, with a big oval badge, reading CHIEF, in between.

"I'm not mocking, Claude. I—"

"Fine, fine, fine, bud! Show what you learned from me." The boss told the Gibbons: "You won't find one cleaner-cut. This boy takes a shower as often as you'n I wash our hands, and his brainpower speaks for itself."

"Son," at last said the mayor, his rheumy eyes rising from their toadlike bags, "ambulate into my vicinity in order that I can discern you." He revved the corroded motor of his throat, and spat in excruciating slow motion into Humbold's blond wastebasket. Claude, a fastidious man, averted his eyes.

Like a sissy schoolboy, Reinhart rose and went to stand where he was told. He had an impulse to announce himself in falsetto: "Carlo Reinhart, age 10." However, he knew that satire would be out of order.

"Yasss," said the mayor, a bead of spit winking at the brim of his lower lip. "Son, did you ever entertain this concept? Cooperation with a venture which would not only benefit your fellow men bearing their grievous yoke of life down the pathway to eternity which we all must in our own good time traverse, but result in the accrual of lucre for yourself as a person as well."

"No sir," said Reinhart. "If I have followed you correctly."

C. Roy rubbed his own nose with a hairy fist and said: "You say no to His Honor once more and I'll put a shoe through your belly."

"Easy, Chief," cried Claude. "This is Georgie Reinhart's boy. You know Georgie never taught him no sarcasm. He meant No, he never entertained the concept, etcetera, not No to the cooperation with a venture."

"I say they gotta learn respect," growled the chief. "*All* of them: kids, punks, and wiseguys."

"Chiefy, who's fighting ya?" asked Claude. He nodded at Bob J. "Bud would like you to kindly proceed, Your Honor."

"Bub—is that your appellation?" asked the mayor, his eyes appearing once again. "Bub, arriving at the conclusion that your probity, integrity, and personal honor are above reproach, like the partner in holy matrimony of the late great Julius Caesar, the committee here assembled, directors of Cosmopolitan Sewers, Limited, hereinafter referred to as the Firm, quorum present, do hereby elect you as president of said firm and immediately dissolve themselves as a body. Those in favor say Aye; opposed, No; and so order."

"Ink in the old John Hancock, bud," said Claude, handing Reinhart a pen. He pointed to the spread of documents on his desk.

Had Reinhart not recognized the Gibbon boys—who had been in office since 1928!—he would have taken it for an impractical joke.

"Gentlemen," he protested. "I am of course honored by your expression of . . . uh . . . but you see, I don't know the first thing about sewers. Therefore, in all respect, I must—"

"Listen here, you little snot," shouted the police chief, threatening to rise. "When your superiors tell you to do a thing, you do it, or by Jesus H. Christ, I'll rip your tongue right out of your mouth and throw it to the pigs."

"Boys," said Claude, his round face shining like a new ball, "boys, boys, boys. Let's take a raincheck on the old clowning, fellas, huh, till we do this nice piece of bidniss." He pressed the pen on Reinhart.

It seemed terrible to the ex-corporal that C. Roy's foul mouth should be protected by a badge, and that anybody would talk that way to a veteran.

"I wanted to ask, bud," stated Claude, "if I could keep the pen that signed this historic agreement, like them flunkeys around the White House when the Prez signs a law." He was trying too hard.

"I'm sorry," said Reinhart. "I'll have to think it over."

"You know what I'm thinking over," said C. Roy, "is cutting out your liver."

"Gents, gents!" cried Claude. "Let's have a moratorium on the jokes for maybe five secs. Bud, you sure make a big thing of signing on the dotted. I never knowed you to be so bullix."

Reinhart went back to his chair, sat, and endeavored to comport himself as a company president would, though he had not changed his attitude. But there was no point in insulting them in their choice by appearing as less than what they had taken him for.

"It's only fair," he said, "to express my doubts. Frankly, gentlemen, I think you are pulling my leg. I happened to come to the office today just by accident. You couldn't have expected me. Thus how could you have the papers ready for me to sign? And furthermore, what's a mayor and police chief doing with a construction company that is to build a public project in the very town where they hold office?"

"Are you, sir, *barrrrroooommm*"—Bob J. cleared his throat —"are you, good sir, making charges of malfeasance?" A cigar ash fell onto the plateau of his vast belly. He used the end of his tie to whisk it off. "Abuze of public trust? Betrayal of civic confidence?" He sought to light his cigar-end, but it was too soggy.

"Certainly not, Your Honor," answered Reinhart, discreetly lowering his eyelids. "I'm just saying that as evidence you are kidding me."

Claude plunged in. "Bud, if you washed your ears today, you just heard Hizzoner dissolve himself, his honorable brother, and yours sincerely from the *organization* committee. Get that important term, bud! *Organization*. Where would we be without it? If our public men don't channel our efforts in the right directions, buddy boy, we'd be no better than them poor benighted coons in darkest Africa, with only a little rag around their tail. Recall *Trader Horn,* bud, or uz that before your time? *Yeaou, roaaaaaarrr, screeeeeech*"—he simulated the cries of certain wild animals—"life in the raw, bud: it ain't no laugh. The Holy Word is that the lion will lay down with the lamb, but who knows the schedule, bud, that's the question. Nobody but the Big Boy Upstairs. Remember that and you'll never get too big for your britches."

"Claude," said Reinhart. "In all respect, what's that got to do with the subject at hand?"

"You little snot," snarled C. Roy. "Let him have that paperweight right in the mouth, Claude."

"Bud, to put it in a walnutshell, if the smart boys like you and me don't take a hand now and again to keep the boobs on the rails, I don't know what this country will come to. God bless America, bud. I'll defend it with every drop of my blood and I know I speak for you when I state that no Hitler nor any other dirty Wop is going to march in here and tell *us* what to do!" He was shouting now, with awful fangs. "Millions for defense, but not one cent for tribute! Fifty-four forty or fight, bud! Wait till you see the whites of their eyes! My only regret is that I have but one life to give for my country! Send us more Japs! Bud, you must have ice water in your veins if you ain't thrilled by the music of John Philip Sousa!"

"Claude,' said Reinhart, "that patriotic stuff is swell, but seriously, what does it have to do with being president of a sewer company?"

Humbold's face cleared, as if it were a stage after the curtain calls, with the players scurrying off.

He asked without prejudice: "All right, bud. What's your price?"

Reinhart smiled and said: "Just as I suspected, Claude. You'd rather even pay out money than answer a question."

The boss's bowtie jumped with his dirty little chuckle. "Can't say, bud, I don't recall ever doing either one."

The mayor gargled and spat, then said: "Bub—have I gotten your appellation correct? Bub, to put it succulently, the duly constituted legislative body of this municipality in Janooary of Nineteen hundred and forty-six voted in the affirmative to bring before the people a special bond issue, which was, pursuant to that decision of the counsel in deliberative session assembled, in the month of Febooary, same year—we are still in that year, incidentally"—he stopped, put a new cigar between his lips, puffed, removed it, and struck a kitchen match on the edge of Claude's desk, leaving behind a long superficial wound. When its job was done, the match dropped from his limp fingers to the floor. Claude stabbed out desperately with a black-and-white oxford and killed the flame before it did more than scorch the hardwood in approximately the diameter of a nickel.

The mayor's head suddenly fell upon his chest. Somewhere inside him stayed the smoke from his second drag.

C. Roy laid a big clamshell of a hand on his brother's arm.

"Bob, I didn't think you was through."

It took more than that to stir the mayor, whose cigar was burning a hole in his vest. But at last he was shaken awake and, beating out the embers with the paddle-end of his necktie, he resumed: "In the due course of events, said special bond issue was brought to the polls in Murch of Nineteen hundred and forty-six, aforesaid year, carried to the citizens of this great town, who exercising their franchise, approved it to a degree characterized by the Fourth Estate as, I believe, overwhelming."

"There's your data, bud," said Claude, getting ready to thrust the papers at Reinhart again.

"I guess that was about the time I got out of the Army," Reinhart noted.

"Ah," exclaimed the mayor, and the cigar fell from his teeth into his lap. "You are a veteran of the late unpleasantness! Claude Humbold, you never told us that. We got a medal down at the town hall for you then, Bub, and will arrange for a public investiture. Never say our 'umble community balks before recognition of the vast and massive debt—excuse me. C. Roy, was I not smoking?"

"You was," answered the chief. "And your stogie is at present laying on your lap, underneath your belly."

"Hear, hear!" shouted Claude. Every time Reinhart looked his way, he shoved the papers and pen at him.

"It has been decided," Bob J. went on, "most expeditious and advantageous to run the main adjacent to the veterans' community, thereby servicing the needs of those heroes and their families as the obeisance of this municipality to the late example they set for all Americans by trouncing the Heinie and stemming the Yellow Tide. It is the least we can do to flush away their wastes."

C. Roy sniggered: "Shee-at."

"But what about this company that won the contract?" naïvely asked Reinhart.

The mayor pointed the cigar at him. "No individooal can level the finger of calumny at that award. Cosmopolitan Sewers, Inc.—"

"Limited!" shouted Claude.

"—had the low bid, my friend, I refer you to the record."

"But Your Honor," said Reinhart, "and please don't take offense, I just want to understand. You and your brother are on the board of Cosmopolitan Sewers."

"I tole you I would ream out your guts, and I sure will," said C. Roy, extending his bristling jaw.

But the mayor nodded benevolently. "A fair question, Bub, the fairest of queries. Precisely as you have remarked. But we are resigning. I refer you to the documents which your employer is striving to hand you. We made a mistake, and are big enough to amend same. Bub, what more can we do?"

"Why," asked Claude, "are you—" And the chief joined

him in objection, but Bob J. overruled them with his three chins.

"No, gentlemen and colleagues, let us admit our misendeavors. We have nothing to conceal." He solemnly chewed his tongue, having once again mislaid the cigar.

"Nevertheless, bud," said Claude, "only a dirty skunk would reveal a confidence, and you was made this offer mainly because of your integrity." He succeeded in forcing the papers on Reinhart.

"I don't see my name here anywhere," Reinhart said after a once-over. "You seem to be resigning in favor of Blank Blank. And why are *you* quitting, Claude? You aren't a civic official."

"Buddy" said Claude, and hooted in exasperation. "You married my typist, for one—I ain't got nobody to sock the L. C. Smith. Just you go and write yourself in. For the other, I got two reasons: *Uno*, you know I ain't got time for nothing additional. *Zwei*, I'm trying to keep my promise to your daddy to make a man of you, and this is the thanks I get. You wanna be an expense to him for the rest of your life?"

"Just what does that mean?" Reinhart felt a chill mince between his shoulder blades.

"Why," said the boss, leering on a circuit of the Gibbons, "who you think's been putting out that salary per week, for which you laid around the Mason place and read books instead of pushing real estate? *Me?* Bud, you got solid cast iron from ear to ear if you think you can bamboozle your Uncle Dudley."

Reinhart couldn't meet his overbearing eye. He watched his own feet and said miserably: "My dad has been paying my salary." Without the help of his father and the government, he wouldn't have had one stinking dollar.

Claude kept his grin. "This can't be news to you, bud. You knew it all the while. No? Go on. Go on. . . . Anyway, that's over now. In your new position you get fifty fish a week and I'm moving you and the former G. Raven to one of my empty houses in a classy neighborhood, rent-free. How about that, how abou-ou-ou-that?"

Reinhart again protested, feebly, that he knew nothing about sewers, and in return heard that no officer of such a company ever did: the technical doings were the job of the subcontractor, whom Claude had already signed up. Nor was Reinhart conversant with finance, tax moneys, and the like— nor must he be, according to Claude, who would arrange for all that.

"Then what's the point of having me at all?" asked the ex-corporal.

"Bud, the first thing you yourself suspected when you heard of this project was a stink in Denmark, and you ain't no different from John Q. Public in that wise. Everybody thinks his tax dollar goes into a crooked pocket when it leaves his own—and I for one won't fight him on that. But say you get the point here, buddy, O tell me you savvy this: go look in that mirror on the back of the toilet door and then let me know if you ever saw a honester phiz."

But what Reinhart saw instead was a weak bastard deserted by his wife and supported by his father, and he came back into the room and signed on as president of Cosmopolitan Sewers, Ltd.

"By the way," said Claude, waving the signatures dry, "don't sweat about *this* salary, bud. I ain't paying it, so you're safe. This is feed from the public trough. Now as to that auto of mine which you been driving. Tell your daddy he don't owe me any more rent on it. The Sanitation Commission of this town has purchased that there vehicle and earmarked it for the use of the president of Cosmopolitan Sewers." He awakened the mayor and handed him the documents, then told Reinhart: "You made yourself a nice deal, bud. You're on your way up, and when you get there, don't forget who gave ya your first boost.

"Cosmo has also rented this office, by the way," Claude said. "Dint I say you would be sitting behind this here desk? A fella will come tomorrow and change the signs, bud. Take a piece of paper and write the way you want your name to show. I'll be in bidniss from my home from now on, but I'd appreciate it if you would forget the address when certain parties call."

C. Roy put on his police cap, and Reinhart noticed that the badge actually read CHEIF—though it is true his vision was still blurred by shame.

"Now what else was it—right, right!" asked and answered Claude, squinting towards the ceiling. "Bud, who ever heard of a firm with only a prez? Who's gonna take the reins if you come down with the virus? Didjever think of that? I'm taking suggestions."

"Pardon?" asked Reinhart.

"Name one more director, bud. Individual of integrity, etcetera, like Hizzoner says you are conspicuous for. Young leader of the community. Specimen of the nation's manhood. Veteran who stemmed the Yellow Tide."

Reinhart immediately thought of Fedder and his colleagues on the Vetsville Betterment Committee. The irony attracted

274

him; for the same reason no doubt, some king actually gave Plato, a know-it-all on the subject of government, the chance to implement his theories, which of course flopped and that was that.

But before he could speak, Claude said: "Bud, just how close are you to the niggers?"

Reinhart blushed dark as one, and the boss hastened to add: "No criticism, fella. I admire you for it. The Almighty made some of us black—and some black and blue." He winked at the chief, who looked very solemn when he himself was not making the sadistic allusions. "I personally give them up some time ago on account of I never understood their lingo. And you never find a spade who can resist the King Brothers—but that's personal with me, man—ain't that what they say, 'man'?—but we all got our peculiarities, bud, don't you forget it, and Old Glory waves over us all."

The mayor suddenly awakened and gave him a nice hand.

Having nodded graciously to both sides of his audience, Claude went on: "Now here's what comes off the top of the noodle: Why don't you get a nice shine boy with you on this board?"

C. Roy lip-farted and took his cap off, saying: "I still don't like it."

"O.K.," said Reinhart, who had reached the end of his rope. "I suppose you mean Splendor Mainwaring, since he's the only Negro I know. But, look, Claude, if you have that much, you know he also just got out of jail. What kind of impression is it going to make when they find that out?"

"Who's 'they'?" asked the boss, amiably gritting his teeth.

"Your enemies. The ones you referred to a while ago when you wetted me down. Whoever you've got that mirror mounted up there to catch."

Claude leered so violently that his upper lip curled right up over his little mustache.

"It always takes you a while, don't it, bud? Bud, you should know better'n anybody that them natives is restless. . . . The *niggers*, bud, get it? Our black brothers are the enemy at present. Last night an individual representing them tried to gain access at the movie house and took the name of the Lord in vain when turned away. He also threatened to go get his black gang. He denounced the legally constituted authorities of this municipality, bud. He left when threatened with the law, but I doubt has changed his mind. This individual was described by a source as none other than—"

"Yes," said Reinhart. "Splendor Mainwaring. I figured he would get around to that sooner or later."

"I shoulda pegged out his skin on the jailhouse wall," said the chief, "while we had him."

"Well sir," Claude said, getting cheery again. "If one dark fella gets uppity, there'll be more to follow. Tear gas, machine guns, National Guard. See ourselves in the newsreels, bud! Might get a nice piece of bidniss out of it, selling them little wood pickaninnies sitting in a outdoor crapper with "Souvenir of Race Riot" burned in the door with a electric pencil—"

"I don't get it," Reinhart interrupted. "Negroes are admitted to the movie; I've seen them there myself."

"Never when under the influence, bud. Never while stinking."

"Then it was because he was drunk, not because he was colored."

"Buddy, he was a *drunk nigger.*"

"Look," said Reinhart. "Have they ever turned away a drunken white man?"

"Look yourself, fella," said Claude. "You know I take a dim view of elbow-lifting, white or black. I tell the ticket girl to give a bad time to anybody she smells liquor on."

"I'm trying not to get lost here," Reinhart admitted. "*You* tell the ticket girl? You own the theater?"

"It ain't illegal, pal. I leave it up to Hizzoner."

The mayor mumbled affirmation without opening his eyes.

"I don't mean it is," said Reinhart. "I just mean . . . well, why not say a drunk is never allowed in the theater and let it go at that?"

"You're getting bullheaded again, bud. Kindly tune in on the following message: *He was a drunk nigger.*" Claude slapped the desk edge with the tips of his fingers. "I never weasel on moral values, pal. And I never looked for you to do it, either, the way you was raised. But that's between you and your Maker, bud. Now to go on with what I was saying when I was so rudely. You can't build a sewer if you're going to fight a jig war—and that's what we are going to do, bud, *build that sewer,* for the convenience of black, white, purple, or polka dot—that's democracy, bud, and that's the way of that terrific little guy who was born in a manger. You prove to me Jesus Christ ever took a drink, and I'll say call me a Red. And I don't wanna hear no crossback argument that was muscatel they drank at the Last Supper: pure grape juice, bud, and noncarbonated—only one who boozed was Judas. . . . What we're up against, to put it in a peanutshell, is your chocolate-colored friend threatens to sue the movie house, which comes down in the end to yours truly, for turning him away because he was a nigger. I never knew that was against the

Constitution, did you? I figure it's all hot air, but why take a chance? You won't hear no more about it when he's vice-president of Cosmo."

Reinhart shook his head in recognition. If he had had any sense, he would long since have brought Claude and Splendor together.

"A nigger's exactly like anybody else," the boss added. "He just wants to be noticed."

"Bub," said the mayor, not only awakening but rising from his chair with remarkable agility—but then the toad, while fat, is certainly nimble—"Bub, I don't anticipate you will have cause to regret affixing your assent on this historical compact in any wise. We will be in communication *ex officio*." He laid his hand in Reinhart's, soft and damp as a half-chewed sandwich, took it back, and waddled out.

What Reinhart waited for was C. Roy. He caught him as the chief was just coming up from the chair, and got his fist over C. Roy's fingers between the second and third knuckles. Reinhart was very strong in the hands; even so, he probably outdid himself in this demonstration, which was all the more interesting for the chief's reluctance to complain. Indeed, he grinned in a beastly way as if he were giving rather than getting what-for, but tears at the corner of his eyes betrayed him: it hurt awfully.

Reinhart suddenly let go, at approximately the point beyond which C. Roy would have been permanently maimed. Enough is as good as a feast. Furthermore, Reinhart had used as much trickery as muscle; it was not clear that, though thirty years younger, he could have out-gripped the chief in a fair contest. Anyway, he had got across his message; that he was not the kind of fellow you could threaten all afternoon with impunity.

Chapter 18

"Dad, I don't mind telling you I had made a mess of just about everything, but finally my luck changed at long last. At long last," Reinhart repeated, because it was a turn of phrase that he liked.

Dad ducked out of sight behind the fender of his Chevy, which they were washing with a dribbly hose minus its nozzle. Reinhart pioneered into the dirty surfaces while his pop followed along with the chamois.

"I don't know if you realize just how low I was," the ex-corporal went on. "I had too much pride to let on. But look: Gen walked out on me; I fell behind in schoolwork; I wasn't on good terms with the neighbors; I was at odds with this colored fellow—and I don't have to tell you about the job; I'm still humiliated that you had to pay what amounted to an allowance, and I want you to know that you'll get every penny back just as soon—"

"Carlo," Dad interrupted, speaking through the grille, as it were, so that his voice had a rather metallic tinge, "would you please run that hose down along here?"

"Here?"

"Yeah," said Dad. "Oops, you got me a little there. Sure don't want to catch cold. Think I should go in and change?"

"Naw," Reinhart scoffed. "It's unusually warm for October. Besides, you were just splashed, not soaked, and are dressed snug." Dad wore serge pants; a shirt of cotton flannel faded from red to a sort of bruise-blue; a brown sweater; and at his neck you could see the edge of what would be, if Reinhart recalled the schedule, the medium weight, three-quarter-length, 30 per cent wool, 70 per cent cotton underwear that his father donned circa September 21st every year if the woodchuck had seen its shadow on the Labor Day previous. Dad also wore a black hat—as it happened, the same under which Reinhart had discovered him that bleak night in the railway station half a year before.

"Got a new chapeau, Dad?"

"Yeah that's why I'm wearing this one out here. The one I used to wear out here I'll give to some nigger, I think, if I see one going by." He looked down the driveway into the street, but none passed at that moment, and disappointedly he stuck his nose again into the grille, asking: "Carlo, did you ever notice how dead leaves get stuck in all the little places here around the radiator? I wonder why."

Reinhart laid the hose down to gurgle alongside the driveway, squatted alongside Dad, and said: "Well, they get sucked up off the road by the air that is taken in there, and then they get stuck."

Dad chewed on the elucidation while trying to get his thick fingers between the close-set grille fins so as to dry the beads of water off their chromium.

"Then let me ass you this, Carlo," he said. "Is it your opinion these leaves do harm? Because I defy anybody to fish them out without arms the length of a baboon, and skinny enough to get in through these here what-do-you-call-ums. You'd think somebody would do something about that problem."

"They probably will, Dad," Reinhart said, putting his hand on Dad's old wool shoulder, over the moth holes. "And I do not believe they do—harm, that is. . . . Anyway, there I was. I don't mind telling you, right down on rock-bottom, even farther down than I myself realized at the time. Funny how you don't know how bad it was till later. You know, if we didn't have either memory or imagination, I guess we would never be in trouble."

Dad sat back on his haunches and stared wistfully at the hose.

"Then," said Reinhart, giving his father a shoulder-whack, "it all changed. And it was by means of Claude Humbold that it did. And I want to acknowledge how your advice was right from the beginning. I was too dumb to see that last spring when you were trying to get me associated with him. I thought I was too sophisticated for this hick town. I didn't get the point of normal life."

"Carlo, if you could just reach me the hose, I'd do the rest. There's some mud on this bumper still."

"Here you go," said Reinhart, handing it over as he squatted, dousing his father partially. "Well sir, you were absolutely right, Dad, no question about it."

"Carlo, if you don't mind, I'll need the sponge too."

"Oh, I'm sorry. Here, give us back the hose. I'm supposed to do that. Sorry, Dad."

Dad repeated a protest he had made at the outset: "How does it look for an executive to be helping a fat old man clean a dirty old Chevy?"

The condescension was of course just the feature that attracted Reinhart. He had lately taken to admitting to himself his worst motives for every option—to beat fate to it, as it were, for he was still on uneasy terms with success and feared that the disasters he nowadays missed were piling up somewhere in preparation for a massive sneak attack. Just as when in bad times he asked why he should have all the ill luck, he now wondered why he deserved so much good—this in spite of the fact that he had no religion. There was still much about life that would bear discussion; hence this attempt with Dad, whom he had, naturally, avoided during the time of trouble: no one wants to be humiliated in front of his father. Moreover, Dad was embarrassed by the difficulties of others, perhaps because he overrated everybody. If X then failed, it was an adverse reflection on Dad; maybe it was even worse to be Dad than X, at least so Dad would have you believe. Indeed he was strange, and not just as a father. With friends like Claude Humbold and the Gibbons, with whom he had grown up, he stayed an insurance man.

And speaking of embarrassments, Reinhart felt very awkward nowadays just to be in the vicinity of an old, economy-priced automobile. Talk all you want about the vulgarity of large, gaudy cars, but Reinhart lived in the United States of America and not, say, in the Orient, where it might be good manners to run a shabby rickshaw, for all he knew; here, there was no getting away from the fact that it lowered your tone to drive a seedy heap, notwithstanding your spiritual worth.

"Aw," said Reinhart, "don't talk like that, Dad. You're not . . ." But he really *was* old and fat and the car *was* dirty and outmoded; and it made sense to take another approach: "Why don't you let me see what kind of deal I can get you on that convertible you told me about the night I got home from the Army?" He squeezed a dirty torrent from the sponge— queer marine creature whose skeleton ended up in this role— and smeared the mud off the bumper.

"Convertible?" asked Dad in an awe-filled whimper, as if he might be run down by one.

"Well, maybe that is a bit wild," Reinhart hastily admitted, making an accompanying motion with the hand that held the hose: again Dad got it, though again only the periphery of the main gush.

"Carlo," said Dad, shaking droplets off his arms, "in your opinion, wouldn't it be advisable to finish off with a bucket? I believe we waste a lot of water this way, and not to mention the expense, there is this drought you read about in the papers."

"O.K.," Reinhart said brightly. "I can just shut it off here by putting my thumb over the end, until we are ready to go around to the spiggot. No wasted motion, eh Dad? That's something you learn in my job." After a moment, he learned something here, too: that if you plug even a weak dribble, it is no great time before the pressure has got very strong indeed. Yet he had a muscular thumb, and hung on.

"Carlo," said Dad, "I wanted to ask you how the sewer is coming." A dead leaf suddenly tumbled down through the air and settled in the groove of his hat, stem down, resembling a feather; he suggested a retired Indian scout. "It must be nice, associating with the Honorable Bob J. Gibbon, who is a fine statesman, and that nice coon boy, who is a credit to his race, as I always say—you know how they always mention that on the radio about Joe Louis. No doubt he has the makings of a second George Washington Carter, who rose from slave to . . . well, I don't recall exactly what it was he rose to, but you can look it up in the *Reader's Digest*."

"Car-*ver*, I believe it is, Dad." Reinhart said this through clenched teeth, so hard was it to retain the hose; his thumb felt big as an orange.

"Oh," said Dad, "you know of him. Then you get my point. Honest as the day is long. One time it rained on a book he borrowed from the library. Wasn't his fault, he stuck it up among the rafters in the attic of the log cabin where he lived as a boy with his old mammy. Well, the shingles were rotted there and let in the rain. Well, he felt it was his responsibility to pay for that book, and he did, by doing manual labor for months."

"Wasn't that Abe Lincoln?" asked Reinhart. Suddenly there was no more force against his hold; apparently the water had at last learned who was boss and retreated back into the pipes. Or Maw had turned it off. Anyway, a great red ring was incised in the ball of his thumb.

"I never enjoyed your educational advantages," Dad admitted, half sitting on a fender, "but I think those stories are

281

swell. Somebody to look up to—that's what the big fellows provide for us little guys. Imagine that, walking four miles through the snow in leaky shoes—or was that another story? Anyhow, that illustrates why Granpa was glad he came here and stopped being a German."

Not a drop coming through the hose now, so Reinhart let it fall. "I don't believe," he offered, "I ever told you of my curious experiences in Germany." Dad looked at sea, so he clarified: "The war."

"Ah," said Dad sympathetically, "that's O.K., Carlo. I'll never ask, you can rely on it."

"Anyway, Dad," Reinhart said, "the point is, I haven't done as badly as I might have, in the prewar era." By standing near the windows of the automobile he could make an image therein that was not unflattering: blue-serge suit that he had not deigned to remove for the present chore, white collar, striped tie, clean handkerchief in breast pocket. He had jazzier costumes, but not for a Sunday visit to his folks. He honored the memory of his late penury and lifelong parsimoniousness by continuing to wear Army-issue underwear; otherwise he was all new as to clothes, and all items were charged to his account at Gents' Walk, where the chief executive of Cosmopolitan Sewers, Ltd., had unlimited credit.

"You know there's a one and only thing that will take your tar off a hubcap," Dad stated, sitting on his heels and fingering a bit of the former on the right front latter. "And that is carbon tetrachloride. Yes sir, you can't sell me a substitute."

"Do you mind my saying something?" asked Reinhart, a certain agony in his smile, which Dad however would not see. "Half a year ago, all you could talk of was Claude Humbold. Now when I want to, you won't." He took a cigarette holder from his pocket and put a Pall Mall into it. Nowadays he smoked a good deal; he was also working again towards the portly—it being impossible for an executive to maintain a Calvinist face towards food and tobacco; yes, and drink as well, which may have contributed to his color: several times he had been asked whence a sunburn in autumn. He strolled to and fro upon the oily grass within the parallel concrete strips of the driveway, hands linked across the sacroiliac, cutting a figure for the benefit of the neighbors, who, according to Maw's old testimony, always had offspring who did better.

When he looked up from his shoes, off which the grass was whipping the shine, Dad had vanished. But moving swiftly, Reinhart cornered him in the garage, near where the garden hose was looped for the winter.

He repeated the statement. Dad feinted left and went right, through the side door into the back yard, where he tipped the

282

dirty water from the birdbath, saying: "A early freeze would of split it wide open."

"Dad, do you mind?" asked Reinhart. "As a matter of fact, I have *always* wondered why it's so hard to talk to you."

"Looky there." Dad pointed to the bottom of the garden, where his lawnmower stood against the only tree—matter of fact, a maple to which Reinhart was in the relation of parent to child; he had brought it home from school years ago one Arbor Day, as no more than a twig with roots like hair. It grew now in a vigorous sort of young-manhood; though at the moment, as a step towards going bald for the winter, its leaves had turned yellow, in some cases tinged with a red of the same hue as the dominant tone in Reinhart's new complexion.

"The tree?" asked Reinhart. "Yeah, hasn't it grown well!"

"No, my lawnmower," said Dad. "The darn Whipple boy didn't put it away the last time he cut the grass. And that was last . . ." He was gone again. Ah, there he went, down the stairway to the outside basement door. Though breathless, Reinhart plunged after him.

"Time for storm windas again, Carlo. Got to replace the old putty, paint the sash, and clean the panes with Windex and Scott towels; you'll get streaks with anything else. Izzat what you use? Say, you know I'm still wet from that hosing down you let me have, and will get pneumonia if I don't change." He hung his hat on a rafter-nail and would have taken the steps to the first floor had not his son denied him access to them.

"Jig's up, Dad. Afraid I must insist."

"On what?" asked Dad. "What jig? The one you work with?" Behind his pale eyes lay no discernible guile. He could have used a hair-trim over his ear on each side. On his upper lip was a small razor cut, very minor, but he was conscious of it and did not smile as wide as usual, when he smiled. Right now he was neither amused nor grave, just blank, and nobody could be as blank as Dad.

"Humbold, Dad. The sewer project, Dad. There's something you don't like about it."

"Oh." Dad first satisfied himself that all escape routes were blocked, then looked straight ahead, which for him was on the level of his son's necktie-knot. "Well," he said at last, "isn't it crooked?"

"I'll straighten it when I get to a mirror," said Reinhart. "Wait a minute—you mean the project?" As always, it made him uneasy to loom so high above his father, and he slumped against a metal pillar that had a built-in jack to raise a sag in the floor above. "Why, sure," he lightly admitted, "aren't they always? . . . What?"

Dad had mumbled something. Now he repeated it audibly: "You aren't even building a sewer."

"They're *your* friends who are in back of it," Reinhart said. "That's the way *your* town has always been run. *I* am a citizen of the world." Then he responded to what Dad had said: "Sure we're building a sewer. Haven't you seen the crew with the steam shovel and concrete mixer down by West Creek? The crooked part is that the Gibbons engineered the contract award so it would go to our company, which they and Claude secretly own. Splendor and I are just front men. They think I don't understand this—Claude and the Gibbons, that is, and had us sign some phony papers as corporation officers. . . . I don't know if I ever told you, Dad, but there are a lot of people who think I'm dumb. This is because of my light complexion, I believe. If you have blond hair and blue eyes, and in addition are big—well, you'll find a number of people who will doubt you have much upstairs.

"But I have found out how to use this, see: let 'em think what they want, while all the while quietly going your own way." He brought his eyes out of the slits he had affected to dramatize the point. The coldness of the metal pillar had worked through his jacket tail and trousers seat and chilled one ham. "So in regard to this sewer business. It has given a job to Splendor who, having had certain misfortunes, needed it. You should see what it's done for him: he's stopped thinking of himself as a Negro every minute of the day." He lowered his voice so that it might not be heard through the floor above. "And it brought me back my wife, and I'm going to be a Dad myself in December."

"But," Dad said stubbornly, looking at Reinhart's Adam's apple, "no sewer is getting built."

"Why do you keep saying that? Go down to West Creek and look at the concrete mixer."

"I have," said his old man, "and got a stick and lifted the cover of that manhole they poured cement for last week, and there isn't any sewer underneath it, just earth."

"There isn't?" asked Reinhart, shifting against the pillar. "Odd. . . . Well, there must be an explanation. I can't imagine a whole crew of men whose profession it is to dig sewers, not digging one; it doesn't make sense. For such men it would be harder, I think, not to dig than to dig. And *why* wouldn't they dig, since that's what they are being paid to do?" He stamped his feet, the basement being cold as a tomb. "From what you have indicated, I should say that the men in question are concrete-pourers, exclusively. They proceed along the line where the sewer is to go, setting in a manhole every so many feet. Then, later, along come the sewer people underneath, boring out the main and running up the manhole connections at the appropriate place. That would be somewhat similar to the way sandhogs build things like the Lincoln Tunnel in New York—one crew starts boring from the New Jersey side, and one from the Manhattan Island side, and they meet in midstream. Incidentally, seldom are they more than a few inches off, owing to the modern systems of measurement, etcetera. You can look that up in the *Reader's Digest,* or maybe it was *Life.*"

Dad looked remarkably sympathetic throughout the explanation, and now nodded enthusiastically. "Sure, I've seen that in the newsreels. Big, sweaty fellows wearing dirty undershirts and tin helmets. They always shake hands with the other side when they break through, and grin at the camera."

From this reaction Reinhart took courage to accept his own theory, which had been rather desperately formulated: he could not bear to have his father believe that he was out of control, or that he was crooked, for that matter. He understood for the first time that when he had become a man, the exterior representative of his conscience had changed from Maw to Dad, and he breathed easier. Foolishly, for however successful the sandhog example, it was soon exhausted, and Dad obstinately returned to the issue.

"The only thing is," said he, still squeezing his sweater in the damp places—he hadn't forgotten that, either—"I been along the whole route of the sewer and haven't found one place where they started to dig."

Reinhart impatiently expelled his breath. "What are you snooping around for, anyway, Dad? I thought your business was insurance."

"Why," his father answered, taking no offense, "I'm a tax-payer."

A sacred word, and Reinhart pulled in his horns. A taxpayer had even more rights than a veteran, standing in relation to the latter as the Lord to Jesus, and of course properly there should be no clash between the two: the fellow who paid for it and he who defended it. The Gibbons regularly invited the public to attend council meetings and inspect the jailhouse; the sewer could hardly be exempt if the citizenry footed the bill.

So Reinhart smiled tremulously at his progenitor and said: "They do that later, as I pointed out; they first situate all the manholes, then the diggers come along. All very simple, Dad, *when you're in a position of responsibility.*" He relied on Dad to take the hint when it was put with so much regard for his feelings, and Dad did, throwing his head back to sneeze and then lowering it to follow his son upstairs.

285

Genevieve, so to speak twice as big as life, sat upon the living-room sofa listening to Maw. She had returned to Reinhart three months before, and was now in her high time with a great swell beneath her maternity smock that would have impeded her running away again. Nevertheless he always felt some anxiety when out of her presence; and when in it, kept close company so as not only to block any flight by force if necessary, but also to anticipate and dispose of the circumstances in reaction to which she might wish to flee. He had become far more subtle a husband than he once had been. For example, he delegated to her many of the duties he used to perform himself—some of them, such as taking out the garbage, even demeaning. He knew pain as he watched her bend with difficulty to extract the paper bag from the kitchen step-on can and carry it to the back porch, worry the lid off the big galvanized container, and drop in the parcel before the liquid from the wastes had caused it to disintegrate. Sometimes she didn't quite make it, and orange rinds, eggshells, and veal-cutlet leavings were scattered wide. Nor would this stir her husband to report with the mop; he had sworn never again to usurp her functions, notwithstanding the gritting of his teeth, which sometimes worked independently of his resolutions; when you truly loved someone, you had the strength to let them clean up their own messes.

Not, certainly, that Gen found her chores pleasing, but like all women she had an instinct for reality, and he at last had come to understand it, which in turn gained him her respect. These interlocking arrangements were what marriage consisted of, being but translations into other areas of existence of the basic connection of the genitalia which your amateur supposes is all.

Anyway, there sat Gen, as it were a giant Easter egg in her lap and noncomment on her face, while Maw talked from across the room—from as far across as possible, as it happened, from a chair in the corner beyond the cabinet radio. They had never been close, these two, and perhaps never would be. But they seldom met, so it was no issue.

"Oh hi," said Maw to Reinhart as he entered the room. "Whajuh do with your father, bury him in the basement?"

Reinhart looked around. "Dunno. He was just behind me."

"Aha," Maw said. "It's all right, I hear him in the toilet. I believe he's coming down with something. You didn't put that hose on him?"

"Only by accident, Maw." Reinhart went to his wife and, taking her two hands, prepared to help her leave the sofa. He

286

winked at Genevieve, who must have had a bleak forty-five minutes, and informed Maw that they must go.

"Go?" cried his mother. "Then who's gonna eat my roast?" This hapened to be a polite lie; he had gone earlier to the fridge for a drink of ice water and seen no meat but wieners, and the oven, which had a Pyrex door, was empty. Maw maintained the illusion of hospitality, and he respected her for it.

But when he sought to support her cordial fraud—"Sorry to have caused any inconvenience"—she viciously bit the hand that fed her.

"You're darn right you should be sorry, brother. That piece of meat cost your father a pretty penny, and for him it don't grow on trees." Maw had returned to her old condemnatory tone just at the time he joined the sewer project, and he couldn't help thinking there was some connection. "He's never been a big businessman," she went on. "Just being an ordinary slob is good enough for him."

Genevieve had let his hands fall during this conversation and made no move to leave the couch. "Hadn't we better go, honey?" he asked. It struck him when she answered, how much softer her voice was than his mother's, indeed, softer than her own at home, virtually a whisper.

"Your mother will want to finish her story," Gen said, with a sanctimonious inclination of the head.

"Oh do you, Maw?"

"How's that?" cried Maw. "Gee, I must need an ear trumpet, I didn't hear a word. Couldn't be anything wrong with your voices, so it must be me." She smote her temple with an open palm.

"Did you have a story that needed finishing, Maw?" asked Reinhart, wishing that his wife were in this instance less polite and more opportunist, while at the same time appreciating her tact.

"Well sir, isn't that something! I finally got me somebody who likes to hear what *I* say." But in reality she glared at both of them: Maw worked best with her back to the wall, and the whole concept of gracious gain was alien to her. "Well sure, I was telling her about Margie Platt, who was in your class but after graduating instead of going to college like yourself and of course not off to the Army, married a boy from Indiana and moved to Fort Wayne. That started it: one miscarriage after another. To date, poor girl has had five, I believe, or maybe six. Every time but the first she got as far as her"— Maw jabbed a forefinger towards Genevieve, whose name she had apparently never learned—"when boom! there you go.

287

It's mean, just downright mean, and I could of sat down and balled when I heard of it."

"Well, that's about the size of it," said Reinhart to Gen, feeling for her knee so as to distract her; he had been taken unawares, never suspecting that Maw would wield the knife against Genevieve so blatantly. Gen's smile was a trifle sick, but no more so than when they had arrived.

"Poor thing," wailed Maw. "Sometimes I wonder if it's worth all the pain and agony to bring forth a human being, just to have them walk right out of your house without so much as a thank-you and run off for the Army or wherever. Maybe it's better to have your miscarriages and suffer severely only for a short time than to carry it out over a life long. Maybe—"

"Yes indeed," said Reinhart, trying to hide Maw's voice under his own. "Indeed, yes. Must get our girl home, and feed the cat and the dog, though not to each other, haha! Lots of chores, yessiree." He ignored Gen's wry look as he pulled her up, and informed Maw: "That big house keeps us busy. We may have to get a maid."

"Does it?" asked Maw. "I wouldn't know, this bungalow being more than good enough for me, and I sure never got a helping hand with my housework. Recall when I was carrying you, your aunt offered to come in to run the sweeper, but I would druther have laid down and died than not been able all by myself to keep a nice place for your Dad to come home and hang up his hat and eat his hot grub."

"Oh, it isn't Gen's idea for the maid," said Reinhart. "It's mine. Actually she dotes on housework and got very sore at me once because I wasn't letting her do enough."

Long before he finished his speech, though, Maw began to shout down the hall for Dad, and when that individual had sent back a muffled reply that he was on his way, she swung on her heel and stalked off through the dining room.

Reinhart opened the front door, but Gen made him push it shut again.

"You want to stay?" he asked incredulously.

"She will have something for you," Gen told him severely. "Take it and don't be rude."

It was only a matter of moments before his little wife was proved to have second sight. Maw appeared carrying something wrapped in wax paper. She had never done this before. Of the household chores she disliked cooking most, and therefore would not have made a gift of food. Her strength was in the laundry department, but he could not recall having left any dirty clothes behind last time.

"Take this, boy," said Maw, shoving it at him.

"Should I open it now?"

"If you're hungry," his mother said, assuming a bluff stance before him, but there was vulnerability in her eye. "It's a meat loaf. Probably isn't any good. If you don't like it, throw it to the dog."

Pregnant Genevieve shouldered her husband aside; for some reason he had been standing between his women, so that one could not see the other.

"I'm sure it's delicious," said she. "Just delicious, and we will make supper of it tonight."

"Dinner," Reinhart said instinctively, and saw the girls co-operate against him, Maw and Gen: he brought them together at the cost of himself. His wife made a negative sound, and Maw said: "I see Mr. Know-It-All gives you the same trouble he gave me." She told Reinhart, "For your info, sap, supper is *in the evening,* dinner elsewhere."

"The latter is the main meal, Maw. See Webster."

"Why, you dirty—" she began as of yore, but had to call a quick halt before the suddenly asserted authority of Genevieve, five feet two.

"Thank you *so* much, Mrs. Reinhart. It was *so* nice." She indicated by a pressure on his arm that now Reinhart should open the door. Which he did with one hand, the meat loaf in the other like a football though rather more heavy. Dad lumbered up the hallway at that moment and made a melancholy congé. He held an atomizer and sounded as though he had already developed quite a nice cold.

"Look, Genevieve," Reinhart had said into the telephone that day after leaving Claude and the Gibbons, "look, Genevieve—now don't interrupt me until I've had my say. Fair is fair—huh?"

"I just mean I'm not Genevieve. Dear me."

"Then who the hell are you?" He realized it was preposterous to be rude to a wrong number for which his own finger was responsible, and softened the pitch: "Aren't you POmegranate 4321?"

"I'm your mother-in-law. How are you today?"

"Sorry, Mrs. Raven. I don't think I have ever spoken to you on the phone before, and didn't recognize—"

"I seldom use it, I feel uneasy when I can't see a face. Pardon?"

"I didn't say anything, Mrs. Raven. We have a bad connection."

"But then the advantage is you don't have to meet an eye and all that sort of difficulty. I suppose I really prefer to use

289

the telephone. Isn't this nice! Have we ever talked so much together?"

"Never," said Reinhart.

"I rarely talk to anyone, at least on this plane." Her voice became very bright: "You might say, what's the point when our days are so limited and we'll probably be with a completely different crowd on the other side."

"May I ask," said Reinhart in some apprehension, "whether I am connected to the Raven residence?"

Gen at once came angrily onto the wire: "How dare you talk to my mother behind my back?"

"Now, I can't control who will answer when I call POmegranate 4321, can I?" asked Reinhart. "Just *think* for a minute."

"Do you know what always strikes me, Carl? How you never face anything directly, but make a little wry question of it. I can just see your little sarcastic grin lurking at the corners of your mouth. You are an enormous person physically but you have the psychology of a weak and small someone. You're always *explaining* things in a kind of crafty, sneaky way, as if the human you're talking to is a dupe."

"I'll ignore your abuse," said Reinhart gravely. "If you were as ready to think carefully about a subject as you are to attack, *toujours* attack, why—I don't want to quarrel, Genevieve, and I certainly have no intention to be wry or sarcastic. . . . How are you, by the way?"

"I'm—oh, you're just horrible. Of all the mean tricks I ever heard of, getting that awful woman to call up with a pack of lies."

"What lies?" he asked, rather than "what woman?" though he couldn't identify either.

"Do you think she dared to reveal herself?" cried Gen.

"Now *you're* putting everything as a question. Calm down and give me a clear statement of the facts. This comes as a complete surprise to me, Genevieve—I might add, like everything you do."

"You are just a goof, sir. Because now I have grounds. I bet you never considered that feature. No sooner do I turn my back than you bring in the chippies. I will see that you are ejected from Vetsville on a morals charge."

Somehow she had found out about Bee Fedder without getting the whole story, which unfortunately he could never tell. As regards Bee, what kind of nut was she to have telephoned Genevieve?

"You don't even offer a defense, is that it?" asked Gen. "All right for you then. The die is passed. I hope you are satisfied that you have ruined my life." But she didn't hang up as he expected, rather stayed on, breathing indignantly through her mouth. Finally she said scornfully: "Did you think I would swallow that story?"

"For the last time, my dear Genevieve," Reinhart stated, "I don't know what you're talking about. I did not get any woman to call you up, and if one did, it was to perpetrate a vicious hoax in the interest of my enemies. A man in the public eye attracts all sorts of cranks, willy-nilly."

"Thank you, kind sir, for confirming my own theory. She insisted you were grief-stricken over my departure, couldn't eat, study, and were on the point of being asked to leave Vetsville—made you out the most miserable wretch this side of a kennel, and all for love. Well I'll say this: not for one minute was I taken in, but I don't believe in cruelty to dump animals and because of this natural weakness in me was seriously considering returning to you on a trial basis, or at least until you would get up off your alleged bed of pain and begin to resemble an adult man. But now I am relieved to know this was girlish foolishness on my part, and that you are getting on famously, better than when you were tied down with me—what do you mean a man in the public eye?"

Bee, he understood now, had tried to do him a kind turn. Wasn't she nice! He had had little experience with girls in the relation of mere friendship—getting between their legs eventually and on whatever pretext was always in the back of his mind: but in the case of Bee, he was exonerated of that criminal intention before the court of experience, proving he couldn't have her if he tried, which he had. Perhaps that's the kind he should have married instead of this one the thought of whose round behind enchanted him even when listening over the telephone to her obloquy and threats. Love was sometimes crippling.

"That's why I'm calling," he said. "If you'd be a little more patient, Genevieve. If I had to name one quality above all others that should be cultivated by human beings, it's tolerance. There's always a reason why the other guy acts as he does, Gen. He may still be wrong, of course—"

"I'm warning you," she said, "that I will disconnect in about ten seconds if you don't cut fish or bait. You are hardly the person I would choose as my moral authority."

"All right, all right." He symbolically threw up his hands. "I've just become the success you wanted me to be." Speaking fast and ruthlessly, he told her about the sewer project.

Only silence from her end. "Are we cut off?" he asked.

A small voice, near tears, answered: "It was the fact that I wasn't there. You consider me a detriment. Well maybe I am.

291

I didn't go to college. But I'm human! I suppose in the years to come you'll forget that I predicted great things for you if you would just go out and get them. At the time I didn't know it was I who you felt held you back. With me out of the picture you soon enough began to make progress by heaps and mounds. Well good luck to you, Carl, and if we meet someday—"

"Gen now don't be asinine. I'm going to give you another piece of news, after which I want you to go and pack up your pants and brassieres again, and I will be there shortly to bring you back here to your rightful abode. It is true that this good fortune came while you were absent, but it was as a result of your galvanizing me into action *by* going away. You must understand that!"

Genevieve constricted her lips and said: "Carl, if this is a type of gag. . . ." She swallowed, loud in his ear; she really was moved. "If you could tender some evidence of good faith. . . ."

"Talk to Claude if you don't believe me," said Reinhart. "But these crass material matters are not important enough to fake. 'Come live with me and be my love and we will all the pleasures pruv.'" He burlesqued it a little in acknowledgment of her antisentimentality, but like all clowns was basically sad.

"In that awful hut again?"

"Certainly not!" Reinhart promised wildly, feeling unconditionally powerful at the thought that his love life was to be resumed, as if all the world could be cowed by an erection. "Just for a day or two until we regroup our forces. . . ."

"Carl don't think I won't hold you to it. I'll tell Daddy and it sounds fine, but I'm sure there's more than needs the eye." But then her voice softened. "Meanwhile, I'll be waiting for you."

Suddenly Reinhart's pride demanded a more ardent expression than that. He after all had or would become a new person in accordance with her recommendations (and had already long forgotten that his change in fortune owed everything to chance and nought to his own initiative—he was frequently out of spirits but never morbid).

"Is that all?"

She protested: "*Cah*-rll, Othermay's right in the extnay oomray!"

"Well aren't we married?"

"*Just what should I say?*" she whispered indignantly. "*Something dirty?*"

"I don't know, Genevieve, you are a married woman since April and a prospective mother since May, and yet sometimes I believe you haven't changed one iota from the virgin you were in March."

"May I remind you, dear sir, that smutty talk on the phone is a criminal offense?" She spoke so officiously that for a moment Reinhart took her for the operator and hovered on the brink of a fantastic imposture designed to hoodwink the authorities.

But he disciplined himself and went on to make his point: "What I mean of course is you still can't see that intimacy is perfectly normal." *Hummmmmmm,* said the dial tone that had replaced a living girl.

Ten minutes later he went to fetch Gen home, just before dinner time on a summer afternoon. He was sweating like a horse, but made an occasion of it and wore his tan tropical worsted with bow tie. Fortunately, her father turned up missing. Reinhart chose this time to wonder whether his habit of getting on well with women and badly with men meant his masculinity was above average or below: practically any mode of action could be proved queer in the long run. But even when he had difficulties with a woman, as in the case of Gen, it was interesting; trouble is, men are bores.

Having said goodbye to his mother-in-law, an intriguing person in her own way, which she had hinted at in the short conversation on the phone; one day when he found time he must interview her—Reinhart brought his wife to the car, her valise on his other arm. It was novel to have her back again after three days, a combination of alien and familiar. For one, she seemed to stand lower. When he asked why, her answer was New Look.

"The skirt is longer, silly. Therefore the legs look shorter."

He felt himself blush at the mention of limbs. Face to face, she took the reunion with less wear-and-tear than he. She had a real fiber that he had always lacked. He might do worse than study the girl he had married.

Having fired up the engine, Reinhart asked: "Shall we eat first?"

But she was not amused by the old joke, just looked hurt and said: "I regard that as bad taste."

Within a fortnight they had moved into a large house two in from the intersection of Buena Vista Lane with Krausmeyer Street, still in the town, approximately two miles from Reinhart's parents in distance and even more in tone, the neighborhood being principally German brick occupied by retired grocers; whereas that of his folks was chiefly one-story shingled, populated by depressed clerks.

The first, or Vetsville phase, was now history, like the Continental Congress or the Beer Hall Putsch. Luckily, Fedder spent moving day at College—not that they transferred anything but a few books and the door knocker; the new place was furnished; the old stuff they simply abandoned—Fedder was not around to take leave of, and Reinhart didn't dare communicate with Bee until, after arriving at the new residence and faking the loss of his fountain pen, he returned to the compound without Genevieve. He really had to thank his friend.

He knocked her up, in the British sense, i.e., pounded on her door and she answered.

"I just have a minute," he said. "As maybe you didn't realize because we didn't hire a truck, we moved this morning. The point is, my wife came back to me. It's now been about two weeks, and I've never got the chance to thank you for calling her."

Bee smiled shyly. "Oh that's O.K. Would you like to come in for a cup of coffee?"

"It wouldn't look good," said Reinhart, "so I'd better not. But listen, what in addition to the obvious I liked about it was —well I am always interested in schemes. It's a personal weakness. How clever of you! I should have thought of that, but didn't have the talent."

His compliments pleased Bee. She pulled at the leg of her shorts and said: "But I bet you would have been plenty sore if it hadn't worked—me telling her you had a different girl every night!" She looked so wickedly merry at this that Reinhart ceased to believe she had been interested solely in his welfare.

"Is that what you told Genevieve?"

"I know women."

"I'm beginning to, myself," said Reinhart. "Oddly enough. I know you really hate one another."

"Now you be tough on her," Bee said, with her hip against the door frame. "You *aren't* mad?"

Reinhart shook her hand. "Not me," he answered. "It worked, didn't it? Oh, and would you please tell Niles: I'm going to get him his sewer. True, not exactly for Vetsville, but I think that just the thought of a new sewer anywhere will be welcome to him. Now I must close your screen door before any more flies get in." Deciding it was discreet, because on a Monday the other Vetsville wives were all in their back yards with wet wash, he kissed her hand and took off.

Chapter 19

Reinhart had one of those electric-eye gadgets that opened his garage door automatically when the Gigantic passed a certain point towards the end of the driveway. He was always a little anxious during this operation: Halloween approached, and it was not unlikely that a juvenile attempt might be made to jam the beam. He planned to let his dog course freely about the yard day and night for the next week, for all the good a dachshund would do.

He walked around front, so as to gloat over the fa ade. ule and with no hands. Genevieve he had already let out of the car at that section of the drive nearest the house, it being negligent to have her walk the enormous distance back from the garage. So extensive was his domain. Such a far cry from Vetsville, so grotesque a change, that there had been nothing for it but to adjust immediately. From the moment Reinhart crossed the threshold of his new abode, he accepted it as his due, and indeed, a moment later glancing through a front window, seeing a poodle micturate against one of his evergreens, he dashed outdoors and stoned that impudent animal (which lived two houses down, and afterwards would have denied to him the sidewalk in front of its own place had he ever offered to walk there, which he didn't; nowadays he walked nowhere except from house to Gigantic and vice versa).

As Reinhart left the garage, the electric eye registered the passing of his burly figure and pulled the doors down. Everything was in perfect working order, for that's the way Claude kept his possessions, and if they went bad he was inclined to get a new replacement rather than have it fixed. Claude Humbold continued to own this house; Reinhart only rented it from him; but the greatest feature was that Cosmopolitan Sewers, Ltd., paid the rent with no charge to the tenant except for the telephone, mere peanuts.

He walked around front, so as to gloat over the façade. Quite a lawn he had on all sides, separated from his neighbors' by the driveway on the left, a mesh fence on the right, and from the street by a hedge the corner elements of which were clipped in the shape of big hand grenades. The design of the house was basically Stratford-upon-Avon, with leaded windows, roof high in the middle and descending at the eaves to four feet from the ground, timbered-and-stuccoed second story; but certain other reminiscences had been thrown in: side porch with New Orleans ironwork between Parthenon columns, and an orange terrazzo floor; atop the ridgepole, a tiny cupola à la mode de Mount Vernon; and two lamps from a Venetian canal, their poles aslant, flanked a front doorway more medieval than Elizabethan, being low, vaulted, and monkish—Reinhart, a Friar Tuck of a man, forgetting to duck, sometimes butted his forehead on the keystone and emitted a lusty oath.

Inside, which is where he now repaired after surveying the world from his stoop and answering a hail from the middle-aged neighbors across the street, who were about to enter their new Shoat V-8 for a Sunday drive—inside, he walked directly into the living room, there being no prefatory hallway of any description. He had remembered to duck for the doorway but not, once in, to look for the cat, which inscrutably had chosen to lie just beyond the threshold. If anything will throw the shivers into you, it is the scream of a cat when you tread upon its tail. The vile sound served to remind Reinhart of Dad's grave charges, another discord.

"Honey," asked Genevieve, emerging from the first-floor lavatory off the solarium to the left of the living room, "did I hear the telephone ring?"

"No," he answered curtly, exchanging stares with the moose's head above the fireplace.

"Sorry. Uh, you want to think now or talk?"

"The former, if you don't mind."

Gen said O.K. and tiptoed through the dining room towards the kitchen. She was always like this at home, sustaining Reinhart's role as lord of the manor. Indeed, he could have been a good deal more magisterial to her taste, but he felt silly when it got too thick. He had discovered that more authority and more possessions paradoxically diminish true responsibility, for a man tends to worry about these rather than himself; thus they stay sleek and he gets flabby.

He dropped into a great green leather chair before the fireplace, so right for the kind of cogitation he must now do that it was almost stultifying. Below the moose's dewlaps hung crossed krises. Claude had had the house decorated with an eye to his own eventual tenancy—he no more shot the moose than he wrested the weapons from a Malay, but rather bought them all from a catalogue of some Monkey Ward of the exotic.

So the sewer project was *that* crooked. He hadn't dreamed. The contractual shenanigans had been normal enough, the point of small-town government being that relatives and friends get the favors, not gangsters as in the big cities or storm troopers as in foreign countries. Insofar as Reinhart had a political faith, it was more strengthened than violated by the neighborhood fraud, which he saw as a guise of love. But this one looked unfair: they really should build some kind of sewer. When Dad objected, who would put up with anything, decent men should listen.

However, he regretted exposing the whole thing to Gen at dinner, for women are notorious for having no principles. They ate in the breakfast nook, the dining room being so large that only two people felt stranded, like survivors around an ice floe; whereas in the nook their knees touched cozily. That was naturally *all* he got nowadays. There were theories that you could continue to make love almost up to the birthday, but he couldn't see it after Gen had begun to swell. Anyway, as he had always maintained, marriage had other compensations—for example, just looking at the childish white mustache left from her last drink of milk.

"You see the spot we're in, hon," he said after giving her Dad's information.

"I told you Claude is never on the level." She drank more milk, this time without wetting her upper lip; he realized the first time had been specially arranged for him: wives are capable of such niceties. "Well, it's not likely you can do anything, so I would forget it." She took a miniscule forkful of Maw's meat loaf, which was inedibly dry; whether that owed to its original composition or Gen's sabotage—she had heated it overlong—Reinhart couldn't and surely didn't want to say. He himself was off his feed, eating four or five slices merely to fill the void.

"That's pretty cynical," he stated with a frown. "You see, I don't mind a swindle—for instance, like the Army, since we

297

won the war. But in this case a lot of sewage is going to—oh, excuse me, you're still eating."

She dropped her fork. "I'm quite finished, though it was very good."

"It was awful," said ruthless Reinhart. "My mother couldn't fry a decent egg. Why lie when you don't have to."

Genevieve lowered her eyes and munched on a sweet pickle. "Because there's the human element."

"All right, and that's what I mean about the sewer. The scheme has now assumed an inhuman air, if you ask me. You know I was with the medics in the Army and we were taught something about sanitation. I believe I am safe in saying that pestilence owing to improper sanitary facilities has mowed down more people than all your wars. You know, these local things aren't all just corny ways to waste your time as long as you can't get to New York or Paris."

"Whoever said they were, Carl?" Genevieve reached up to arrange a string of ivy drooping from a small wall-pot. She had lost interest in the subject, now that it appeared he would talk his qualms away and they would continue to live in the big house and enjoy the other advantages of corrupt prosperity. Like most women, she had no sense of real power; pride meant nothing to her. If the baby was male, Reinhart must assume responsibility for his education lest Gen bring up a sissy, that is, a boy who confuses charm with character.

"I did, for one," Reinhart answered, as she got up to serve his coffee, East Coast style, with the dessert. "You'd be surprised at the big ideas I had when I left the Army. Or rather, not ideas, I suppose, but wants. You understand that during the war I went halfway around the world. I don't mind telling you that even yet I haven't given up all my dreams."

Genevieve ran thick cream over his baked apple. "This is just a suggestion," she said decently, "but wouldn't it help if your hopes were specific? You know, like wanting to be an attorney?"

"I'm sorry," Reinhart responded frostily, "that I'll never measure up to your father."

"Now who meant that?" She shook her head, on which the hair was rather lank nowadays and in front brushed across from one side to the other, secured by one bobbypin. Neither did she wear much make-up: her face was clean and faintly freckled, with that bare, soft cast of feature that you see on someone just wakened from a good night's sleep. Luckily the nook was not the booth type, for with her belly she couldn't have sat in it without Reinhart's expanding her space by diminishing his, which owing to his own girth he could not have done comfortably.

"If I interpret you correctly, then, you are advising me to go back to school?" For he hadn't at the onset of the fall semester, sewage and culture being too incongruous a mixture even for him: the ideals of the Renaissance were impossible of attainment in the middle of the twentieth century.

"Golly." Gen turned away to show her sensitivity. "I don't want to bud into your affairs."

"I'll tell you this much," said Reinhart. "I always want whatever will make you proud of me."

Genevieve had the tip of her left index finger between her teeth, but probably was not genuinely attending to the matter. She was not much good at discussing problems, preferring to reach her beliefs in private and promote them sneakily. She would not have been one to toss the logos around with Socrates, but then neither would any other woman, so much the worse for the Greeks.

"I wonder if it's a boy whether he will hate me."

"Carl, do you feel well?" Gen's eyebrows really showed some distress, which gave him a nice feeling.

"That's just something you learn in the study of psychology. . . . Uh, would you fetch me more coffee." The latter was more command than question. He watched her struggle up and waddle to the stove. With his long arms he could have reached the percolator from where he sat, but that wouldn't be showing her she was needed.

"Love," he went on, raising his replenished cup, "from the point of view of depth psychology, is a very complicated emotion, including many hostile factors. St. Augustine, an early psychologist before the field was known as such, stated that the source of evil, as well as good, was love."

Gen set the coffee pot down upon the table and said: "That clenches it for me. I think you'd make a marvelous psychologist. How long would that take?"

"Genevieve, we are making a point, not discussing my career. Keep the personal element out of it for a moment. . . . It is *common* for a son to *loathe* and *abominate* his father."

She clasped hands across her belly, as if to protect it, and warned: "Oh Carl, please don't talk like that, even if in fun."

"As a matter of fact," Reinhart stated dispassionately, "I am very fond of my old man. But that may be because we are so different. He has no ambition, and that helps. But what if our son turns out just like me? There might be a clash, and that's all I meant."

"In that case I'm sure you'll be understanding," said Genevieve. "As you were with my brother." She employed no irony. "He certainly admires you, and send regards in every letter."

Reinhart had heard this before but never grew accustomed to it, with his shaky conscience towards Kenworthy.

"How is he getting along, by the way?" His coffee was a little acid on the tonsils.

"Wonderfully. He is a pharmacist's mate on the *USS Trout*, at present on patrol in Alaskan waters. The Navy made a man of him, there's no question about it. He's grown a half inch and put on fifteen pounds. Recently the crew gave an original stage show on the base, and he played a girl. Good-looking, too. Did I remember to give you that snapshot?"

"Uh-huh," he grunted. "Swell. . . . On the other hand, if we have a daughter, you may run into a ticklish situation."

"Oh Carl, let's not talk of that silly stuff; it really sounds deformed."

He pushed back his chair and crossed legs. "I was wondering, dear, whether a cigar would nauseate you."

"I'll just switch on the exhaust fan."

But he waved her down and performed this chore himself, being a man who cherished the moral distinctions: the serving up of his sustenance was the woman's role, whereas that which concerned the indulgences—tobacco, drink—was his.

That is how Reinhart and Genevieve got along in the third stage of their relationship (1—premarital; 2—newlyweds; 3—reconciliation and preparation for parenthood). Reinhart was serious, even sober, yet if the occasion seemed to call for it, he might crack a joke. His style was more vivid than hers. He was oftentimes ebullient, and if a song could be heard behind the bathroom door, it was surely the work of the master rather than the mistress. But Gen had a sort of common sense that he had often heard imputed to women but never before seen at close range, it being a thing one never notices in his mother.

His moods were more violent than Genevieve's. Because she was pregnant he tried to spare her the worst of them, crept rather up to his attic study and punched the rafters when upset by a joint of meat all gristle or a neighbor's guest whose car blocked the driveway: so much of everyday life consists of these petty frustrations unknown to the rich and glorious, who shrug them off onto lackeys—Reinhart's conception of the advantages of power frequently took this negative cast, and he asked himself whether he were really cut out for anything big.

Fortunately, they were both elastic, because you ran into

such things as this: a throat-clearing mood sometimes stole over Genevieve, and she would flutter her palate every ten seconds for hours, didn't even know she was doing it, in a kind of substitute for smoking or chewing gum. After the first minute it became unbearable and even retreating to the attic was no good; the insidious tremor seemed to penetrate floors and climb heights, or perhaps it was just that he could imagine her still doing it, below. But when you love a person and live in proximity to her, you understand that there are reasons for every phenomenon, usually of a nervous nature. It has long been said that everybody these days is a bundle of jangling ganglia, but beyond stating this truism your average individual disassociates himself from the problem like Pontius Pilate.

Not Reinhart, whose new home came equipped with a radio-phonograph long as one living-room wall. Of course its original guts had gone flooey, but on top of the cabinet sat the extra turntable which the home technician installs in such cases, having washed his hands of the regular repairman, who is a bandit and charges your eyeteeth for doing a job that won't last a week. The cabinet-top apparatus worked however, though you saw undue wire. On this arrangement, when Gen began to clear her throat, Reinhart would lose no time in placing a record chosen to ease her. Not a word, mind you, or a frown on his part, nor a beefing up of the volume to drown her out: it was to be a true if temporary cure. If he had chosen well—South American tunes, with their jerky rhythms, seemed to be more successful than the typical oleaginous ballad—Gen would stop humphing; the inner uncertainty of which the ticklish throat was but a symptom, soothed, without the possibility of her developing a phobia towards the doctor, who stayed anonymous.

She, too, the situation reversed, was subtle, if not to the same degree (but he was a year older and had far-flung experience): owing no doubt to his present high responsibilities rather than Gen's cuisine, which was above all bland, Reinhart's meals did not digest so readily as they had in the carefree days of yore. He was wont to utter odd sounds after dinner—not outright belches, certainly, but their suppressions, as well as certain faint gurgles, susurruses, and even squeaks.

Genevieve's technique: In the downstairs lavatory, where, following the instructions of the dentifrice commercials, he went after every meal to brush his teeth, he would find the toothpaste hidden behind a Pepto-Bismol bottle. In the living room a roll of Tums lay alongside his favorite ashtray. And if he stepped to the kitchen for a drink of water, there was the cylinder of Alka-Seltzers, a midget monolith erected on the embankment behind the sink. . . .

Naturally there were traits of each that exhausted the other's capacity for adjustment, and sometimes corrective measures were so unobtrusive as to be overlooked entirely. Gen had not really reformed from her old habit of never quite closing things, from jar-tops to closet-doors, and she was one the few people whom a dripping faucet doesn't bother. If she opened a large root beer, say, and couldn't drink it all at once, she would return the uncapped bottle to the fridge, where naturally it went flat in ten seconds —all the while the rubber-cork gadget thoughtfully provided by Reinhart went unused. But then, and perhaps worst of all, Genevieve didn't mind later drinking still root beer; indeed, would not even notice the bubbles had fled.

Reinhart's habit that most annoyed Gen (judging from her reaction) was rubbing his head while he talked. How long he had been wont to do this he could not have said; no one else had ever pointed it out; it was his sniffing that Maw had always objected to, but that tic disappeared when he had outgrown adolescence. Nowadays it seemed he could hardly utter a word without putting a hand to his scalp—at least, so stated Genevieve.

Again it was his head in another of Genevieve's criticisms: he didn't take it to the barber nearly often enough. She was particularly averse to sideburns verging on the feathery, maintaining that feature linked a man to the Kentuckians who emigrated north to work in the factories of Ohio, a race which the aborigines in Reinhart's town put only just above the Negroes. Having for years worn a crewcut and only recently let his thatch grow towards a length that an executive might show without embarrassment, Reinhart could only, as of this time, offer a feeble rebuttal to his wife's argument. Thus, another point of abrasion between them.

But, like the others, ridiculously inconsequential when you thought of all the problems that could arise from the impulse of the sexes to couple. Illegitimate births and VD of course were always on the increase. But to make it legal solved nothing. The divorce rate climbed. Naïve brides were forever made frigid by the terrors of the wedding night. Husbands were castrated by the loss of their independence. More than half the national wealth was controlled by widows, who endowed dog kennels, Hindu seers, and health-food maniacs.

Marriage was a creation of civilization, not nature: no two tigers cohabited for twenty years; and a rabbit will of course sock it into anything that crosses his path and then hop on, contrary to the fairy tales that bring him home each evening to a Mrs. Bunny waiting with easy chair and slippers. On the other hand, certain human fanatics disapproved even of legal coitus: St. Paul, Count Tolstoy, and Mahatma Gandhi. But there were those like Plato who maintained anybody could do it with anybody else as long as the state said when. The Gods assured Aeneas that founding Rome was more important than loving Dido, so off he sailed leaving her to suicide. St. Augustine screwed like a mink and then, going for priest, knocked off the sex absolutely. They made Abelard a bullock for hopping Heloïse, and Tristan and Isolde ended up scarcely better.

You would get no comfort from literature or history: except for the exemplary Brownings, the great lovers always went mad, betrayed each other foully, or lost their taste. Thinking about this, Reinhart grew very impatient with tradition and decided that history was indeed the bunk: either that or you never heard of all the couples who hit it off, on the ground that harmony had no general interest. It was true that the one instance of absolute fidelity that mythology had to offer—Baucis and Philemon, who after a long life together died and were transformed into adjacent trees—was much more dispiriting than an account of how Venus and Mars put the horns on Vulcan. But the gods could handle themselves, whereas the miseries of love were sometimes disastrous to men.

And Reinhart was utterly bored by any kind of wretchedness, suffering, despair, agony, negativism, and failure. There was no reason why you couldn't be successfully married; no reason why the commonplace could not be enormously interesting, it was where most everyone spent their lives. Normality had been sneered at too long, said Reinhart—meaning: by Reinhart, who was intolerant towards the reckless opinions of his youth. So long as he was going to be a father it made no sense to hold out any longer from joining the American Legion, the Masonic Lodge, and the Kiwanis. Let's face it, you couldn't support a family and also run away to New York and live in a penthouse.

. . . Genevieve lay with her bottom pointed his way, pregnancy towards the wall. He used the outside half of the bed, so as to protect her against the world. Goddammit, you can have your chorus girls and riches and power, there isn't anything that sets up a man like his own dear woman with a spark of new life glowing inside her. She stirs her shoulder and mumbles some dream gibberish; "Bur-bla-bloo-mmm-ba." Asleep already, the healthy little savage, and radiating warmth. One of the cleverest acts of his life was marrying

Genevieve Raven, and he derived a perverse satisfaction from remembering it had come about through accident or at any rate the sort of off-the-cuff volitions that depend so much on chance—Reinhart the schemer, ha! Making plans was merely a way to kill time while fate decided on the next move. Owing to his understanding of this state of affairs, he was curiously free of despair—and consequently nowadays suffered insomnia for the first time in his life. The despondent flee to the Land of Nod, but the happy man cannot bear to set aside his attention.

Chapter 20

Reinhart of course used the big blond desk that had been relinquished by Claude Humbold when that entrepreneur turned over his real-estate bureau to Cosmopolitan Sewer, Ltd., but there was now another, only slightly smaller, against the left wall of the inner office; and behind it sat an individual named, unless the sign was in error, *Splendor G. Mainwaring, Vice-Pres.* A conservative man, as one could see from his dress, which was navy-blue pinstripe of suit, white of shirt, and foulard of necktie.

"Carlo," he was saying to his superior across the way, "I hate to say it, but your cynicism is appalling."

Whatever the changes in the man, he still could outrage his friend and colleague. Although Reinhart had slept very little the night before and until this moment had been drowsily apathetic, he was now jerked awake. Splendor had criticized him more than any other non-relative he had ever known and while Reinhart used to tell himself that that sort of thing should be easier to take from a black man than from a white, owing to the history of the Negroes in this country, in actuality it was precisely the reverse, and probably for the same reason.

"I don't recall that I asked for that analysis," Reinhart answered without lifting his head from the documents before him: specifications, as it happened, for that portion of the sewer called the East Link.

"The only reason I am taking the liberty of making it," said Splendor, who as a matter of fact had since taking this position been remarkably correct with the president of the firm, "has more to do with personal relations than with the welfare of the commonweal. Your father tells me there is no—"

"Christ," interrupted Reinhart, leaping up to close the door into the outer office, where foremen of the working crews were wont frequently to track in mud throughout the morning and leave with the secretaries certain papers detached from their dirty clipboards.

Building anything at all meant you used more paper than cement, and every document concerning the sewer-in-progress (or, as Dad would have it, the non-sewer) came to Reinhart. Certainly no one could question that phase of the operation: everywhere you looked there stood filing cabinets, and papers littered the desks like leaves in the vale of Vallombrosa. Some glided to the floor and were there masticated by passing heels. Now and again a girl came in from the outer office to empty the Out box and to fill the In.

The blueprints, to which Reinhart now referred, were to be measured yard by yard, too big for rolling; bound horizontally, along their upper margins, against a sheet of plywood, they made a great sheaf which hung from screw-eyes set into the ceiling near the windows. When not being examined, they had to be got out of the way so as not to obstruct the natural light: by means of a pulley arrangement, with ropes to the inferior corners of the plywood, the ensemble was drawn up against the ceiling. It weighed considerable, and as he now paid out rope, Reinhart was careful to give it leeway; however, it came down without miscarriage.

"Look," he demanded of Splendor, having lifted sheet after sheet until he found the appropriate plan, that for the West Bend, the conversion of which into reality was what Dad asserted had not taken place—though if that hadn't been dug, it was also probable that there was no excavation anywhere else.

"Look," said Reinhart. "The blueprint is very clear on this matter. Here's that manhole that Dad is so interested in, and . . . yes, here it is: the main. *There definitely is a sewer main underneath it on this plan.*"

"With all those blueprints over your head, I can't hear a word you say," said Splendor, which naturally Reinhart couldn't hear, either. This kind of dialogue continued for a while, and was no more futile than their usual, for onward from that first encounter in the garage, these two men had alternated in miscommunicating with each other—or at least so Reinhart understood the situation as he emerged from the book of plans and let the leaves fall shut. He ran it back up against the ceiling, then through the intercom warned the girls they were not to be disturbed until further notice.

"Now, Splendor, my fine-feathered friend," he said, degrading him as a prelude to incrimination, "now don't tell me you didn't know this project is a swindle."

Splendor uttered a laugh, his indication of gravity rather than its reverse, for he was never gay.

He answered: "There's no need to get hysterical." He adjusted his necktie with prissy fingers, in executive appearance outdoing Reinhart ten ways from the word *go*. "There do appear to be serious irregularities on the part of the subcontractors—"

"Balls," cried Reinhart, whose intent was to rub Splendor's nose in it, for once to make this guy acknowledge that reality is here and not somewhere else. "Don't be like the movie starlet who on her knees before the producer pretends she's being knighted." The vice-president winced and as a matter of fact Reinhart colored slightly, for Splendor had always set a sort of moral pace that was here being disordered.

Just then the intercom buzzer sounded, and when Reinhart flipped its lever to the listening position he heard the secretary say; "Mail's in, Mr. R."

"I said don't disturb," Reinhart told her and switched off. He appreciated that Genevieve had been a real gem for Claude; these girls were cretins. They were also still leery of Mr. Splendor Mainwaring and became apprehensive if Reinhart went out of the office leaving him behind. Everybody knows America's crimes against the Negro, but who protests against what it has done to the office girl?

"I just like to preserve whatever good I can find, rather than rejoice over the bad," Splendor stated. "Otherwise, the world would seem hopeless."

Reinhart swept off his revolving chair some of the papers that had fallen there in his brief absence, and sat. It was horribly unfair that another man should line up with one's father. "Well," he asked in high dudgeon, "what the goddam hell do you and Dad want me to do?"

"Let it suffice to say you know the right," said Splendor.

"Oh yeah?" Reinhart sneered, but he knew that there are no heights to which the human being cannot attain when impelled by the expectations of others.

At that moment one of the secretaries, defying orders, entered with an armload of paper. It was as if she had to go to the toilet no matter what: the mail, etc., was piling up in the outer office; he *had* to deal with it. In the face of such desperation, Reinhart accepted the delivery without protest, but lurked behind her on the way out and locked the door.

"Look at this crap," he said to Splendor. "I believe most of it emanates from Claude. Bills, bills. Here's one for a dozen outdoor oil-drum stoves of the type called salamanders. Three of them are in service at our worksites—I assume that's what the diggers are doing when they're supposed to be excavating; warming themselves—that leaves nine that to my knowledge have never been delivered. To boot, why should they be charged to Cosmo when they are used exclusively by the subcontractors? Now I also happen to know that the firm whose name appears at the head of this statement, Paramount Surplus Suppliers, is a dummy company consisting of Claude Humbold and a ream of letterheads. And he bought the oil drums, which used to hold creosote, from Drako Shingle Company for two-bits apiece and charges us twelve fifty."

He shrugged despondently and opened the next envelope. "Here are the eminent-domain papers by which we are empowered to run a trunk sewer through the southeast corner of a marsh allegedly owned by one Walter Hasenbacher, for the 'reasonable compensation' of what figures out to be 1,000 dollars a square foot. Walter Hasenbacher of course is none other than Claude Humbold."

"What's the point you're making here?" asked Splendor, making his ruminative-camel mouth.

"Just that while it is evident to everybody that the building of this sewer is crooked, the skullduggery is so complicated that nobody can understand it. At the same time, it can probably be proved that more people benefit this way than if the project were honest. For example, as you know there is a real Walter Hasenbacher—the brother-in-law of 'Pup' Agnew who hangs out at Joe Laidlaw's garage: he married Pup's sister Margie when she was three months gone, and works in the lumberyard. Naturally, Claude gives Walter something for the use of his name. . . . Then there are all the extra workmen on the payroll: they are all real people and family men besides. Not to mention the union. Why do you think the subcontractor isn't bothered by the International Sewer Excavating Workers though his men aren't organized? Because Claude—"

"—pays them off," Splendor broke in hastily, apparently in fear that the progression would soon reach the Negroes, for not only was there his vice-presidency, but the digging gang showed many dark faces.

"Yeah," Reinhart said flatly, because the payoffs were the lesser reason, the union being not so enlightened as Claude and the Gibbons; it could do without a membership of coloreds. In every human endeavor there is more than meets the eye. Sometimes less: Splendor was No. 2 executive of Cosmo and had been given nothing to do, a very grave error on the part of those responsible, thought Reinhart, and then realized he meant himself. When you came down to it, his own authority could be exerted only in reference to three people—Splendor and the secretaries—and several things all of them inside the office: furniture and the like. Outside, everything was controlled by the subcontractor, unless Reinhart had misunderstood the documents that covered this arrangement.

"Mr. R. Mr. R.!" the other secretary now cried through the locked door. "Mr. Reo says you have to sign a requisition for galvanized siding."

"Awright," said Reinhart, opening up. There stood Reo himself, the subcontractor, a swarthy, criminal-faced man with a little spurt of hair between his eyebrows. He wore hip-boots and a plaid jacket, as well as a hunting cap with those integral earmuffs that when not in use tie across the crown.

Reinhart was a great deal larger than Reo in body, but something less in assurance, though his intention was not to show it. For example, he asked here: "What part does galvanized siding play in the *digging* of a sewer?" He did make that emphasis, watching the subcontractor's reaction. Result: nil.

Reo merely answered, in his beastly manner: "Fuh duh hut."

"What does that mean?" demanded Reinhart. "What hut?"

"Duh liddle houze."

"Since when does a little house have anything to do with a sewer?"

Reo said something like "Wake Jack," and Reinhart had him repeat it several times before being able to translate it as "work shack": a place to safeguard fragile and/or valuable equipment at night without transporting it off the worksite, by day a refuge for malingerers. The latter Reinhart added gratuitously, playing boss to the hilt; just as, had he been a workman, he would have malingered.

"Look," he said to Reo, who was really too unshaven for one to see a reaction anyway, "why does Cosmo have to buy materials that you will use exclusively for your own purposes?"

Reo had no more patience than others of his ilk of semiliterate specialists. He simply shoved the requisition at the president of Cosmo and said; "*I* done know. *I* done know, Mitter Reinhart. Just sign."

There was an old schoolboy retort that you made to the over-officious fellow: Who was your nigger last year? Of course with Splendor behind him Reinhart did not pronounce this, but it expressed his attitude: weak irony of the sort he wished to, and thought he had, got over. You can't afford irony if you are seriously interested in acquiring power. Lucky that Splendor was there. Once again his presence inspired Reinhart to rise above himself—*as it always did*. Reinhart suddenly understood the significance of the Negro in the human condition—but like all great pieces of knowledge this appeared at a moment when it could not immediately be exploited, and by the time it could, Reinhart decided he was guilty of bigotry towards the majority in characterizing as peculiar to a segment of mankind that which should distinguish the entire species from the other animals.

First, though, Reinhart told Reo: "I'll have no insubordination here. Be so good as to remember your place. *I* am the contractor, you are the subcontractor—not to mention that your honesty is seriously in question, while I am a man of integrity."

Reo's mouth fell open at this heresy. "Kid, you know Claude Humbold? He ain't gone like this." Both secretaries looked up from their typing, frightened little geese, and back of him Reinhart heard Splendor say: "Don't go too far." But he would never have started it at all without the hope of being excessive, and brought forth the rest of the cards for his grand slam.

"Furthermore," he announced to Reo, "don't think I am ignorant of those manholes without mains underneath them. By God, we're going to have a real sewer or you're going to the penitentiary."

At that, Reo fled as fast as his hipboots would carry him, the girls threw on their outer clothes and followed him out the door, and when Reinhart, with thrills of pride chasing up and down his spine, turned back into the inner office, he saw Splendor at the closet—

"Mainwaring," he commanded, "put your coat back on that hanger or I'll have you shot. As I recall, you maintain your Army court-martial was unjust. Here's a chance to clean the blot from your shield. Damn the torpedoes till you see the whites of their eyes! Full speed ahead and send us more Japs!"

"I don't know, Carlo," said Splendor, sitting down but leaving one arm in his topcoat, as a fervent Mormon does with his ritual underwear while taking a bath. "You just don't have any sense."

"Well damn me," swore the president and commander in chief. "Wasn't it you, not more than five minutes ago, who goaded me into doing the honorable thing? What the hell do I care whether or not this town has an efficient drainage system? I'm just motivated by a need to be adequate, like everybody else."

"But surely you won't deny a tendency toward quixotism," said Don Quixote Mainwaring, with a typical deficiency of self-knowledge: Dr. Goodykuntz! Herman Melville!

But Reinhart answered him quietly: "I take it you don't think we'll win."

"On the other hand," said Splendor, at last removing his arm from the coat, "what have I got to lose?" One thing, he always had plenty of self-pity.

"Bud," said Claude, "I see right off I won't get nowhere with you by mentioning God, Mother, and the U.S.A. I do believe you turned atheist and traitor behind my back. All I can say is, I truly hope your tortures in Hades are as short as your ingrate's memory, for I never bear a grudge, buddy boy, you know that. Nevertheless I got a bite like a adder, whatever that is. Kindly inform me what a adder is, Mr. Splendor Mainwaring."

He spun around to face the vice-president, who quailed. However, Claude himself was none too potent there in the inner office for the first time since he had vacated it in favor of Reinhart. Thus he now had to take a position on Reinhart's ground, and the fact that he had come to his protégé, rather than vice versa, showed who held the reins. He was surrounded, standing in the center of the room with an executive behind a desk on either side of him. Yet he was far from out.

And Splendor wasted no time in proving himself of dubious value to the good fight. Claude seemed to have the same effect on him as heroin, with the decent difference that he did not assume the coon accent.

"I don't know, sir." He displayed some extra white of eye, and Reinhart, who would rather have punched him, said: "It's a type of organism that crawls upon its belly."

Taking this personally, Claude faced Reinhart again and gestured with his cavalry hat. "Bud, nobody in my long history of human relations ever turned on me the way you have. I never thought I'd have my own crown of thorns and Judas to taunt me for my big flaw: love of people."

"Claude," said Reinhart, "why don't you cut it out? All we are going to do is insist that a real sewer be built to serve the citizens of this town. You can even take pride, since it actually represents your own idea before the crooks took over." He made that excuse available if Claude wished to take it, for he really was sensitive to the charge of ingratitude.

With a wave of his magic hat towards the windows, Claude transformed the gravel waste outside into a cemetery. "Here

311

lies C. Humbold," he read from the nearest tombstone, "Done to Death Most Foul by the Hand of—here's a buck to go buy a cold-chisel, bud, and chip in your John Hancock. I won't say your name: the Lord has paralyzed my tongue in that area."

"You never did."

"Awright then, I will: *Benedick Arnold.*" Claude gave a so-there nod to his head, and strutted some. With renewed self-respect, he turned again on Splendor.

"Just when, may I ask, did you get this idea to defy me, *my dear sir?* I always knew your principles was very high indeed and your record to match, but I never knew they was suicidal, if you grab my meaning."

"Yes sir, Mr. Humbold, I understand," Splendor responded in the quick-syllabled, thick-lipped (though his were thin) mode used by slaves trying to avoid a whipping—Reinhart had seen that in the movies and historical fiction and assumed those also were Splendor's sources because nobody hereabout ever took a hand to a darky.

Reinhart addressed the back of Claude's checkered topcoat: "Think of it this way: as a success of yours, because you trained me."

The ex-boss came slowly around, saying: "Benedick, I hope you know what it means to be all by your lonesome behind six foot of rock and steel. Ben boy, you'll have only the Almighty to talk to where you're going. Think about it, Arnie, and don't come sniffling to me when it's too late and you are already up the river. What is it, ten to twenty for fraud? And then when you get out, Ben, all the good folk spit on the ex-con. Arn boy, you lose your franchise, the sanctified privilege and obli-gation to vote for the man of your choice whatever his creed, code, or color." At the last word he did a sort of bump and grind for the benefit of Splendor behind him. "And don't show up at the Presbyterian Church, they don't want a wor-shiper bearing the smell of the hoosegow."

"You can sit down if you like, Claude."

"Never in the presence of the heathen and dissolute, Ben. You know that. Nor will I bare my head before an atheist." He pulled his hat down so far that his ears were horizontal projections.

To cap his heresy, Reinhart at this point lighted an enor-mous green cigar. He said: "I just wanted you to be comfort-able while I give you a bit of data."

Claude put his features through venomous calisthenics, hissed, and then endeavored to strike like the notorious reptile whose name he had cited—except that the American puffing adder is more properly called the hognose snake and, though

312

it can swell to more than its natural size, altogether harmless.

"Ben you make me merciless," he said. "I got them contracts you signed, and likewise your scribble on all them orders, requisitions, invoices, checks, statements, bills of lading, agreements to buy, eminent domains, *nol prosses, jus primae noctises,* not to mention *sub specie aeternitatis* and *circumspices.* Arnie, your goose is reamed, steamed, and dry cleaned. The things you done with public moneys would grow fur on a fish! Misrepresentation, Benny, fraud, malfeasance, mayhem, etcetera. Sections 1 through 285 of the charter of every decent municipality in Christendom, violated. Anglo-Saxon jurisprudence, Ben. Don't monkey with it!"

"That's what I wanted to point out to you, Claude." Reinhart seized one of the documents from the litter on the desk, turned it over, and wrote upon it: CARLO B. REINHART. "There you have my legal signature, as used on various Army records which can be found in the files of the Adjutant General's Office in Washington."

"One second, Benny boy," said Claude, leaning over to study the hen tracks. There was some dampness in the crown of his sombrero. "I would say that was the work of a five-year-old imbecile, didn't I know any such sympathy was wasted."

"Be that as it may," answered Reinhart, "in point of law I think you will find that signifies me. Now then, here is what I put at the bottom of all those papers you speak about."

He wrote CARL L. REINHART, slanting left, letters tall and thin, whereas the genuine were short and fat, went rightwards, and towards the end of the name grew giddy and eventually fell off the line to the next below.

Claude drew from his pocket the contract Reinhart had signed on accepting the presidency, and compared signatures, lowering his face almost to the paper.

"What got me," said Reinhart, "is how you never noticed the missing *o.*" He looked to Splendor for a little appreciation and saw the vice-president refuse to meet his eye.

"You say there is an *o* there?" asked Claude.

Reinhart grinned. "It really couldn't be clearer, and you know it. And I call your attention to the middle initial."

Great black circles were forming around Claude's eyes, and his lips were cracking in a kind of instant fever. It was astonishing to Reinhart that he was beating the boss so easily. But it went to show that entrepreneurs were not so tough as alleged. All it takes is a little counteraggression, of course supported with a certain intelligence.

"Ben," said Claude in a voice that broke, "I ain't the one to lead the Light Brigade into the Valley of Death when the Russkies hold the overwhelming odds, and I only mind when someone beats me fair and square, whereas I admire you for winning mean and dirty. As a bidnissman, you are rotten to the core, and God bless you." He reached across and patted Reinhart's shoulder with his left hand while reaching for the desk set with his right. The set was the one he had left behind, offering pen, mechanical pencil, and between them a little brass clock, all on a slab of green onyx into which was sunk a silver tablet engraved with his name and the compliments of the Southern Ohio Realtors Assn.

Claude chose the pen, which as a matter of fact Reinhart had used to sign every document at Cosmo, including the original contract.

"The only trouble is," he stated, still lugubrious, "you are so darn dumb, if you will excuse the French." Then, snorting away his crocodile tears, he spread out the contract and made the necessary improvements in Reinhart's signature thereon: adding the *o* to "Carl," and converting the *L* to a *B* by means of two tiny loops.

"I suppose," said Reinhart, keeping his chin up, "that you are hardly serious, performing this forgery in the presence of witnesses."

"Eggs-actly," Claude answered ruthlessly. "It is a joke, like what you wrote in front of Honorable Bob J. and C. Roy." The balloon of his face was again inflated smooth. He replaced the pen in its socket, put the contract inside his suit, and smiled but failed to jeer. "It's swell to work with fellows who will stand up like a man and admit it when they're wrong. But, I wish you a happy Halloween and Mr. Splendor Mainwaring, Your Honor, the same goes to you." He fluttered his fingers at the V.-P., who had begun to grin toothily. "And I am sure glad, bud, that with a baby coming soon you won't have to leave that nice home on Buena Vista."

Reinhart remained in a state of shock for some time after Claude left. To Splendor's credit, the vice-president did what he could in the way of consolation.

"You see, Carlo," he said, "your trick would never have stood up in a court of law, anyway. Whatever name you wrote, it was definitely you who signed it, and not, I believe, under any type of duress. Perhaps if you had arranged for some other evidence that you intentionally used a pseudo-signature so as to gain the confidence of the guilty parties to a swindle—say a registered letter to some individual not involved. . . ."

"Ah," said Reinhart, "what do you know about it?"

Splendor winced. "If I were as rude as you, I could point out that it might have helped if I had been taken into your confidence." Reinhart's failure to alter expression offended him further, and he expanded his charges: "Why did you give me this job If I was not to have a function? It destroys a man to sit here day after day, accepting money for doing nothing. You talk of the big swindle, but ignore the little frauds of which—"

"No," Reinhart at last interrupted, "no, that's not what concerns me this moment. . . . I am just struck by the realization that for the sake of my own pride I almost got my wife and unborn child turned out into the cold. You can talk all you want to about a man's honor, but it is different things to different people, or even the same person in different situations."

Splendor agreed, and added: "If I may be so bold, Carlo, you will make a commonplace discovery into an enterprise of great pitch and moment."

"Well it is, for me," Reinhart admitted. By his failure he had let himself open to a certain amount of impudence from his friend and colleague, and it would have been too shamefully easy to point out Splendor's inadequacies.

The latter had gone into quite a good mood and was rubbing his beige palms together.

"Now," he said, "we can get to work."

"On what?" Reinhart asked in a clipped, sarcastic manner. "No irony, please. I may have to accept the status quo at present, but as soon after the baby is born as is feasible, I'm going to resign. I will not permanently remain in a job where I have lost face."

The vice-president left his desk and took up Claude's late position in the center of the room. Reinhart recognized the old fanatical look he had not seen since the days of Dr. Goodykuntz.

"Isn't this what we've always wanted?" Splendor cried, his lower jaw continuing to tremble between sentences. "Our backs to the wall, no hope of succor, food gone, and ammunition in short supply. What do we do now, boys?" he asked an invisible Lost Battalion, and gave the answer as if from them: *"We attack!"*

"Take it easy, Splendor. Don't you remember? We just did that." Reinhart unobtrusively reached towards the water carafe which was part of his desk equipment, meaning to dash its contents at the Negro if reason would not calm him. He absolutely would not again join in any extravagance.

"I beg to correct you. And don't drench me until you've

315

heard me out," Splendor said more moderately. "What we have seen is an attempt at negotiation, and its inevitable failure. Now for the frontal assault." He hastily waved Reinhart down. "O.K., disregard the military idiom: I use it only because you have always shown an adolescent taste for glory."

"Yes," said Reinhart, "at one time that was certainly true about me; but the very fact that I can listen to you sneer at it now without punching your snoot proves I have matured."

Chapter 21

"You've got me wrong," Splendor said evenly. "You've *always* had me wrong from the first, but I don't mind."

"Well, why don't you mind?" asked Reinhart. "If anybody had always had me wrong, *I* would mind. It's the normal thing to do. Go on, mind."

"Because, simply because I want to get on to more important things." You couldn't say that Splendor struck a pose; he always stood like that if you were seated.

Reinhart said: "Personally, I find your nobility irrelevant, or perhaps just late. What I cannot understand, to put it as decently as possible, is why your high principles are reserved only for me. And not ten minutes ago you backed down disgracefully from Claude Humbold. Is it unfair to mention Dr. Goodykuntz? Whose head wore the turban at the moment of truth? Who had to endure being accused as a plagiarist by the editors of *The Midland Review*? I can tell you right now that two things in all the world that I do not want to be are non-chemical physician and writer. I was deeply humiliated on both occasions, and the latter almost broke up my marriage."

Splendor continued to stand between the desks, untouched, in the neat pinstripe with a white handkerchief above his heart.

"I'll tell you, Carlo, some other time we'll draw up your bill of particulars against me, but at the moment I ask you to put aside my delinquencies, your plans for wreaking revenge, Dr. Goodykuntz, *et al.*, the whole kit and caboodle." Splendor spoke with some passion, and his saliva spray could be seen against the light. "I ask us now to go beyond all these petty specificities, to move out of the strait passages onto the broad plains where are enacted the events of magnitude and scope which give our civilization its peculiar character. Materialism, my dear Carlo, the superstition that we consist in no more than three yards of intestine beginning with an open maw and terminating in a rectum, is our enemy, and not its poor disreputable advocates, the victims of the delusion so coarsely expressed in the maxim you and I both heard while serving with our armed forces in the late conflict: 'If you can't eat it or copulate with it, urinate on it.' "

Splendor wiped his mouth with his breast-pocket handkerchief and replaced it messy. His eyes were preoccupied. He resumed: "You know why we must build this sewer, more than ever now that Mr. Humbold will oppose us with all his might?"

He was the only person in the whole organization, not excluding the secretaries or the guy who came to read the electric meter, who addressed Humbold in the polite style—no doubt for the simple reason that he had never been told "call me Claude." But Reinhart suddenly liked to think that Splendor would have been formal anyway: the last gentleman on earth, with his back against the wall, and nobody else here but us Visigoths.

"Certainly not to benefit the population." Splendor answered himself. "The present sanitary facilities will be adequate until at least 1980, according to the statistical projection made last year by the county engineers. The average town resident unit produced 1,512.7 cubic feet of sewerage annually. The annual percentage of increase for the next 35 years, allowing for a steady rise in the number of automatic washing machines, extra bathrooms, exterior water hydrants, etc., added to existing homes, allowing even for the construction of more additional residences than the town has space for—as you know, because of surrounding communities we cannot grow much—this on the one hand, and on the other, our only real industry, the Amalgamated Pencil Company, providing it expands beyond the wildest dreams of avarice on the part of its management"—Splendor cleared his throat—"could increase its present flow of sewage by 150 per cent without overencumbering the present mains, which after all date only from 1932, with a new treatment plant in '38."

He stopped here, in full cognizance of the effect on Reinhart.

"You know all this for a fact?" asked the latter, in lieu of anything more striking.

"For three months," said Splendor, "I had nothing to do as vice-president but study the field. In all modesty I can describe myself as a sanitary engineer in all but the certificate." He returned to his desk and produced from its drawers sundry volumes, graphs, and charts that Reinhart was willing without argument to accept as the last word on the theme. He had always wondered what Splendor was reading while he, Reinhart, signed requisitions for Johnny Reo.

"You did not get these by mail from Pocatello, Idaho?"

Splendor laughed politely—that is, not in Reinhart's face but towards the windows. "Never fear. Ah, no, the county engineer's office, with its excellent library, is very cooperative on such matters."

"Yes," said Reinhart with no malice, "and that office would be in the courthouse, whose location you would know, having been in jail there last spring." Splendor nodded benignly. Reinhart then chuckled, though feeling as exhausted as if he had run a mile. With approaching fatherhood, he suffered a marked diminution of the old endurance; yet he would not let this make him mean. "Well," he said, "I guess you have showed us."

"Please," Splendor protested, "I'm hardly interested in exhibitionism." His eyebrows came down. "I was hoping you'd ask why then we should build the sewer when it's not needed. And I trust I have proved it isn't—except for the West Side, the one part of town where it will not go. The present facility in my home district is disgraceful. You can fake a new sewer elsewhere, because the old one does an adequate job, but—"

Reinhart at last cleared things with his amour propre and sprang in here: "I get it, I get it!"

"You don't," Splendor said coldly.

"Wait a moment," Reinhart cried. "Hear me out. Our funds may have been reduced by three months of fantastic graft, but we still have surely enough to put a new main through the West Side. That's about half a mile at the outside, and it can link up with the trunk line just north of Mayberry Place."

"No, no, no," shouted Splendor. "I an officer of the company building the Negroes a new sewer? How would that look? Collusion and influence-pedding all over again."

"Christ, you've got to benefit somebody. You mean, out of some highly abstract conception of honor we should make an altogether purposeless excavation in the middle of nowhere? That is what they call—"

"Reductio ad absurdum."

Splendor pronounced it with so much satisfaction that Reinhart was moved to wail: "You read in *Life* magazine about those Existentialists and have become one."

Splendor just loved to be accused of something or other; he protested, but you could see it made him happy just to be charged. However, he really had improved, in his own way, ever since leaving jail: having Reinhart fined for littering the park was a means of striking back. Now he had grown beyond mere negative aggression and wanted to establish himself ethically, like one of Conrad's young captains who yearns for bad weather to steer his ship through so as to prove his worth as mariner and man.

Reinhart got his cigar butt from the ashtray where it had gone cold some time before.

"Look here," he said. "I am the legal president of this company. To put me where I would catch the blame, Claude and the Gibbons had to give me real power. There's a lesson in that. I don't know the Existentialist position on the matter, but a rather varied experience of life has shown me that one necessarily involves the other; power: obligation: honor. Now, since the responsibility is primarily mine in this case, I must make the decision. But I shall need you for the performance, my dear fellow. In fact, I must abandon the project if you refuse your aid.

"We shall build an honest, efficient sewer, not to spite Claude or because we are good citizens and godfearing men or any such hot air, but because we have contracted to do so. We will restore the value of a man's word!

"Second, we shall dig it through the West Side, not because the residents there are more deserving than those elsewhere, or because the vice-president of our firm has personal interests in that district, but rather because that's where it is needed."

Splendor tried to look sinister, to emphasize his warning: "You are prepared to lose your house?"

"Not," said Reinhart, "until I've used the tricks up my sleeve. If they fail, of course Claude will throw us out. But I'd rather see my child born in a cheap hotel room than have it grow up with a gutless father." He gestured at his friend. "By the way, we'd like you to come to dinner, but you understand it is inconvenient for Gen, being pregnant."

"I apologize, Carlo, for accusing you of getting me wrong. Indeed we see eye to eye," Splendor graciously admitted. "You know of course that we shall probably fail. Ranged against us are the mayor, the chief of police, and the biggest businessman in town; and Johnny Reo is essentially a gangster."

"None of that materialist talk," cried Reinhart, using the tiny cigar butt as a saber.

Reinhart felt much less confidence than he professed, but temporarily everybody else had a false sense of security and would not bother him, at least not for the rest of the day, Claude, Genevieve, and Splendor. Of course he must let Dad know without delay, who had really headed him for the new goal, just as he had steered him to the old. Way last March, Dad said, go to Humbold; and now, build a real sewer, and, his son had acquiesced after only token resistance. As a result he no longer felt guilty about the old fellow, but just resented him for telling Why but not How. Very normal situation on both sides; he would get his revenge on his own son; and so the world keeps turning.

Meanwhile, we all must do our jobs. Reinhart swore Splendor in as technical director and sent him off to the county engineer's office, not neglecting to pave his way by phone and written authorization, lest that official be not as cooperative as Splendor had, to make a point, represented him.

Next Reinhart placed a call to the number that the office book listed opposite the name of Johnny Reo. At length this got him a phone booth in the rear of the Star Tavern and Grill.

"Are you sure?"

"Whadduh yuh sure?" asked the bartender. "Don't I know when I walk all the way back here?"

"I wonder," said Reinhart, "how I happened to get this number for Johnny Reo, the sewer subcontractor."

"Maybe because he's usually in the booth alongside only not now gimme your phone he'll call yuh."

Reinhart did so and hung up. He was now about to draw his ace from the hole, and his audacity had not yet reached his throat: if he talked just now, his voice would quaver. At the same time he grew maniacally horny, and believed that if the secretaries had returned (they had not) he might have violated them both in the outer office, in full sight of passers-by. However, it was the compensatory lust of little faith, rather than a symptom of overconfidence—when you are married, you learn such things—and after two quick shots from the bottle he kept in his desk as an antidote for self-doubt, it went away.

He seized the telephone again and dialed Long Distance.

"Listen, Operator, I want to place a person-to-person call to James T. Marsala, Brooklyn, New York. I have his number."

She rang and buzzed and clicked, and eventually someone answered from deep in that terra incognita. Another bar &

321

grill. Party referred them to a numbah rin Bridgeport, Conn. Jimmy apparently then was back from the Army; Reinhart's hopes rose. The Bridgeport phone was in a barbershop. The proprietor said: "He ain't in Bridge-a-port. Gone to New Jerse," gave an address, added: "I don' wan' no troub'," and rang off.

"Shall I try this Whoopee Club in Hamhurst?" asked the operator with her *noli me tangere* diction.

"Naturally," Reinhart answered, taking another shot of booze with his right hand. He had always understood that Jimmy's brother was the hood, and taken even that as a bit of forgivable hyperbole.

"Yeah, he's here, wait a minute," said the male answerer at the Whoopee Club, and in a moment there was the voice of Marsala himself, the great old Army buddy whom Reinhart hadn't seen since his last day in Berlin, September 1945.

"Awright," Reinhart bawled, "your bunk looks like a hoor's nest, you jerk. What do you think this is, a guinea holiday?"

"Aw no," said Marsala, a man of infinite sentiment, and choked up. "You goddam crummy rummy Carlo Reinhart, I know ya voice everywhere. Wadduh yuh doing in Newark? Come on over and we'll eat a steak." But it still took him a while to cope with the miraculous event, and here and there throughout their subsequent conversation he pronounced the ingenious obscenities for which he had been famous in the 1209th General Hospital.

"I'm calling from Ohio, Jimmy, and will give you the whole story in a minute. But first, *Come sta?* When did you get back? What are you doing?"

"Listen, you know you need money, what's mine is yours, you goddam punk. I stick a check in the mail. Ain't I your mother-loving buddy, you Kraut bastid? Hey how about that little Trudy hoor in Berlin! She gave me the clap after you left. Where did she pick it up, you dirty college guy? You goddam lousy stinking Carlo Slob Reinhart." There followed several incestuous epithets. "It's worth a grand to talk to ya, you old schmuk. Hey I wanna bring you up here at my expense. Whatdduh yuh, fly? Or you like the train? Shit, I buy ya a car, a nice ass-wagon all your own. My brother's got a Gigantic dealership. I been back since November '45. Why dint you get in touch befah? I hang around this club for Mr. Esposito, kind of like a collection agent. Hey, you getting much? Them college broads lay for yuh?"

"I'm married now."

Marsala groaned. "Oh Jesus, I'm saw-ry, Carlo. Oh shit, no offense to your lovely wife."

"Let me get a word in edgeways, Jim. I'm doing pretty well

322

myself, so while I sure appreciate your generosity, I don't need a loan. I've also got a Gigantic, as it happens, at least for a while yet. Let me brief you on the situation."

After Reinhart had pretty well sketched it out, Marsala asked: "Lemme get this straight, Carlo. You with or against the law?"

"It's complicated, Jim. I don't know if I can make it clear, but you see the *law* is against the law. The police chief is party to a fraud."

Marsala chuckled. "Then you got nothing to worry about, kid."

"No," said Reinhart. "See, I want to dig this sewer, and they are trying to stop me. Now at that point I thought of you. There is this subcontractor Johnny Reo, who is in with them, but I need him and his work crews to excavate and pour the concrete—what do I know about that sort of thing? I have a fellow on my side who claims to be a technical expert, but I don't trust him." Well, at least he didn't say Splendor was a Negro.

"Jesus, what do I know?" asked Marsala. "But I could let you talk to Patsy Romano when he shows up, whose old man Black John's a contractor in Leonia. Wait a minute." Offstage he shouted: "Hey, *Gazzo! Dov'e Pasquale?* Yeah? *Succhia questo,* somonabitch! . . . Carlo, lemme have him call you."

"That's not quite it, Jim. I could hardly learn the business talking to a guy on the phone for fifteen minutes. I have to get Reo to stay on the job, and thought you might have some idea how it could be done."

"You need Reo himself, I guess," Marsala said regretfully. "Becawss I was gonna say we could have him knocked off and that would settle it."

"Oh never!" gasped Reinhart. "I don't suggest that for a minute." Yet it certainly was thrilling to hear, and very useful for one's fantasies to know he could pull a trigger, so to speak, by remote control. "What I had in mind was just some sort of pressure."

"Sure, kid, sure. Though I say this: you always got to show some muscle, see. That's the point, if you don't wanna have just some comedy, get me? See, there's the talk, like you do so good being college and all, what we call square, no offense. And then there's this Other. Now you got to make up your mind whadduh yuh want. Why don't you let me talk to Mr. Esposito and call you back? He might know this Reo. He's got friends everywhere. A real great guy. You come up here and I'll innerduce you and he'll buy you a steak. So all right kid. Keep your ass on ice for another hour. You'll definitely hear from me soon."

323

"Thanks, Jimmy. You're a friend."

"Ya crummy bastid, I love ya." He broke the connection with a crash.

Reinhart poured himself another drink. He heard the secretaries creep back to work in the outer office. They would flee again when they discovered what he was up to. Nobody defied Humbold except him, Reinhart. He could have people knocked off: not even Claude could say that, whose power consisted in part of money, but mainly in a kind of magic which probably should be called love. Opposition to Claude really was heretical, atheistical, and seditious, as he charged; and no sooner did you plot against him than you found yourself at least considering crimes of violence, in distinction to those of the pieties that he practiced. But Mr. Esposito also represented a solid American tradition, in another line of endeavor. And Reinhart was already beginning to think of himself as a synthesis of these two strains, that is, no longer culture and commerce, but fraud and force, and of course directed towards the achievement of progressive ends like a new sewer for the Negroes.

Reinhart always remembered the exact terms of a promise, and Marsala's had been to get in touch again soon: he did not, during the rest of that day or on the next. Reo insolently ignored the request to call and sent a flunkey to the office with more spurious documents for Reinhart to sign. Splendor frequented the county engineer's office, and telephoned in occasionally with technical details that Reinhart couldn't make head nor tail of but didn't let on so as not to discourage the poor devil.

Wednesday still showed no change, though Reinhart stayed at the office till nine P.M. waiting for the phone to jingle, the bleakest hope of modern man. Trouble was, he had no strategy beyond putting the pressure on Reo. There were probably other contractors extant, but Reo had already been paid, near as could be figured, forty thousand dollars for making ten Potemkin manholes. He owed them something—besides, Reinhart wanted to avoid the complication of trying to get more tax money from Claude, the Gibbons, and their captive town council. The district attorney he didn't seriously consider, being no fink, though he intended to threaten Claude with the idea, to ensure keeping the house till the child was born. Actually he might have finked had he any assurance that it wouldn't backfire on himself, one twenty-two-year-old veteran versus the entire town administration. The D.A. was probably in political cahoots with the Gibbons, for example, and Reinhart's signature, altered or not, appeared on every obligating paper.

He put on the gray homburg he had purchased at the first cool breeze of early October and wore to work though nowhere else lest pretentiousness be implied. It was his first hat since a prewar semi-zoot number, and gave him the look of a national chairman of the Democratic Party. If he pulled off this current effort, he might indeed have a future in politics. National affairs had never before been of interest for the simple reason that he couldn't see a connection between them and himself, except in the case of the late war. He was intrigued by his habit of going on to greater ambitions when lesser ones had flopped. Marsala likely would never call, yet Reinhart was already in the White House.

He left the building, locking the glass door, and took a deep draught of night air at the curb alongside the Gigantic. It smelled of pencil: the wind had changed. Using his lungs to full capacity made his head swim briefly. He was a fine figure of a man but could use some exercise. He sucked in his belly but there wasn't much of a place for it to go.

"Hey mister," said a weak voice behind him.

He had been alone on the sidewalk until that instant. This person must have issued from the passageway between the buildings. Reinhart looked him over in the fair light of the street lamp: a mousy individual, haggard with worry.

"Could you gimme a hand?" asked the man. "We took the short cut through the back lot. I don't know what happened. I can't budge her alone." Being small, he was probably married to one of those buffaloes.

"Sure," Reinhart heartily averred. "Twisted her ankle, I guess." He followed the little fellow behind the building, where the light of a bleary moon was dim but sufficient to show an automobile alone on the plain of gravel.

"There she is," said the man. "Stopped dead. Probly the carburetor."

"I thought you meant your wife." Shrugging, Reinhart went to the hood. He was on the point of asking the man how she opened, through the grille or from inside, when several other human beings leaped out of concealment behind the auto and set upon him in furious attack. And after a moment it developed that they weren't people so much as genuine thugs efficiently practicing their métier. Unfortunately, the judo stuff Reinhart had been taught in the Army required your opponent to stand stock-still while you fitted a hold onto him or simulated kneeing his testicles. These adversaries declined to cooperate: they punished Reinhart without giving him a turn. Something limited Reinhart's anger—he learned something even while being beaten half to death: that receiving aggression makes you a lot less angry than handing it out, the popular conception to the contrary notwithstanding.

By now, his hat was off and he lay on his back, in real trouble. Just as well he was in bad condition: the layer of excess fat was all to the good as padding. Not that he wasn't fighting back. He was, but his enemies had every advantage, including rolls of dimes inside their fists. His great strength was therefore harnessed by a number of straps: surprise, ignorance, respectability, and a bourgeois concern for his topcoat and homburg. He was not even able to count how many men he stood up against, or fell down for. A number of hard feet descended upon him, and he had enough and passed out.

Whenever it was he came to, he felt for his wallet first and looked second to see whether the assailants had gone. Indeed they had, but not with his billfold. With difficulty he sat up and picked gravel from his hair, feeling as a peach must after falling from the branch. If they hadn't wanted cash, then the thugs must have been hired by his enemies to do to him what he had tried to arrange for Johnny Reo. Ha, there was a certain justice in it. When Reinhart was hurt he had a tendency towards moralism.

He found his poor homburg and corrected its crush, but could not deal with the torn brim. Topcoat apparently a total loss: in his position one couldn't go about with patches on the tail. A necktie more or less was of course no great problem. Would he could have said the same for the trousers to his decent gray-herringbone suit!

He staggered around to the street and, having luckily retained the doorkey in the lining of his coat though the pocket was ripped away, re-entered the office. The washroom mirror reflected the image of a wartorn priest: not only had the tie disappeared, but his collar was severed from the neckband and turned half-circle. No marks on his face though it hurt fearfully. He drew a basin of water but could not get his head into it because of the faucets in the way—an inconvenience that fictional detectives never seem to suffer. Neither was a towel in evidence. Those asinine secretaries had concealed the supply, probably to discourage Splendor from washing there. Finally he had to shake himself dry like a dog.

Now what? Futile to call the police, since C. Roy Gibbon had probably arranged for the beating. Anyhow, Reinhart would have been humiliated to ask a cop to defend or avenge him. In the good old days, Americans carried each his own weapon, and there has been a certain debilitation of fiber since that practice was outlawed in favor of a man with blue uniform and nightstick.

Nor did he wish to hear Gen's consolation for his hurts. Your wise husband appears before his wife only as victor, especially one as large as Reinhart: winning was his only justification for eating so much, for expatiating so readily, in short, for being boss.

That left Dad. So Reinhart called the old homestead. Luckily his father answered rather than Maw, who might have made some rough banter utterly inappropriate.

"Hi, Dad. I've just been beaten up in the lot back of the office. My clothes are ruined, and I have a few scratches, but appear to be O.K. in the main."

"Ah," responded Dad. "Sure you have the right number?"

"I said it's Carlo. What's the matter?"

"You must have been hit in the mouth, then, for your voice is changed. Sorry, Carlo. How's your supply of Mercurochrome?"

Reinhart cleared his throat. "Sorry Dad. No, they seem to have missed my mouth and concentrated mainly in the midsection. I can hardly stand up, but outside of that, it's essentially my coat and hat that suffered. I never told you that I was in a bad fight once in Germany and hurt my head though not irreparably. That's also where I received that slight scar on my cheek, in case you noticed."

"I wonder," said Dad, "where you ever got so pugnacious, because I should think such a talker as you wouldn't have to rely on the fists. But I don't want to criticize."

"A funny thing: I swear to you that none of these fights has ever been my idea. They are kind of thrust upon me. Anyway, I didn't do very well in the present one. I soon fell down. I don't have a taste for that sort of thing any more, and don't know whether it is because of what I did to the other guy in Germany or he did to me."

"What was it you wanted to know Carlo?" asked Dad somewhat impatiently. He had probably been called away from a radio program, perhaps *Gangbusters*, and he tended not to take exterior damage as seriously as maladies due to germs.

"Well," said Reinhart, "simply this: I took your cue on the sewer, and told Claude I meant to build a good one. Then he pressured me to renege. However, later, I found a way that he could be defied, and had barely started to plan it when this assault occurred. Now, he didn't know of my latest decision, so why would he have me beaten up? The same applies to Johnny Reo. Uh, excuse me. . . ." he shifted his position in the chair, but when you are bruised all over, nothing much helps. "Now, as regards Reo, the irony is that I arranged to have him—" But he supposed he shouldn't tell that to Dad. "Well, it doesn't matter," he wound up. "Just wanted you to know I'm O.K."

"That's sure swell," Dad droned. "Always cooperate with Claude Humbold and stay out of vacant lots, is my advice. There are fellows hanging out there who just like to pick on people, and if you couldn't see their faces in the dark, they were probably coons."

All this while Reinhart had been astonished at his father's apparent unconcern, but at last he understood. Beset his life long with fantasy-fears, Dad was happily immune to real dangers, seeing them as anti-climatic. All dark alleys to him were filled with assassins: an idealist in the true sense of the word, he was only bored by your sauntering up one and getting murdered anachronistically.

"My best to Maw," Reinhart told his father. "And thanks, Dad. In your own way, you always tell me what I want to know, though never what I ask. The deficiency is all mine."

Hardly had he lowered the instrument than the bell summoned him to lift it again, and the operator announced a person-to-person line from Hamhurst, New Jersey.

"Carlo Reinhart, you goddam old buddy, you," cried Marsala from six hundred miles away. "Your troubles should be over. Some friends of Mr. Esposito was supposed to discuss matters with this Reo a couple of hours ago."

"Thanks for clearing things up," groaned Reinhart. "Your boys just kicked the hell out of *me*."

Marsala for a long while cursed furiously in Italian, and then told Reinhart: "Ya know what? They were probably stoopid Sicilians." He was almost hysterical with shame. "Buddy, I wish you was here so you could hit me right in the mouth. C'mon, I pay ya a plane ticket so you can kick me inna ass."

"Now, now," said Reinhart, who was curiously free of indignation. He hated to see anyone embarrassed. "Obviously it wasn't your mistake. These fellows were incompetent. Thinking I was Reo, they administered the beating but didn't say one word about the sewer. It should have been just the other way around."

"I lost face, pal."

"You've been going to too many movies about the Japs," Reinhart assured him. "Lose face today, regain it tomorrow, Jim."

"That's what happens when you send an order to a crummy hick organization wid a couple of slot machines and nothing else goin' for them but to sit around and jerk off. Whyn't ya move up here someplace and build your sewer, buddy? Jersey,

New Yawk, or Bridgeport, Conn, huh? I could take care ya like a baby."

Reinhart realized that Marsala intended to do nothing further, being one of those persons whose resolution can be summoned for a single effort which will succeed or fail without encore. He thanked him sincerely, mentioned a few reminiscences to cheer him up, and broke the connection. He would rather have taken ten beatings than been made so aware that friendships are at the mercy of current conditions.

Chapter 22

"Ah, Carolo," what was Splendor said when apprised of the failure of Reinhart's strategy, next morning, "whatever could have been in your mind? If we forsake reason, my friend, we have regressed to the level of the brute beast." He had showed up at the office a few minutes earlier, overladen with rolls of blueprints and sketches on transparent paper, and dressed in riding pants and boots such as engineers always wore in the popular conception.

"Not to mention the moral aspect," Splendor went on, suddenly dropping all his rolls to the floor of the office, where they tumbled every which way. He was also wearing a military khaki shirt with shoulder straps and paneled pockets, and a trenchcoat hung over his left forearm.

"Anyway, it didn't work," Reinhart admitted sourly, "and before you get too sanctimonious, reflect on that fact that *I* was the one who took the beating."

Splendor, at his best when given an adjuration of this kind, did consider the point, becoming for a few moments all forehead. Then he said: "I'm sorry. I hope you weren't hurt too badly"; and limberly, without flexing his knees, bent to gather up the blueprints. He placed them carefully along the broad sill of the window, but indifferently threw the coat over his revolving chair and sat upon it. There was a Negro for you: the garment would be ready for the ragbag before the last installment was paid.

"No doubt," said Reinhart, "I should have discussed it with you beforehand. But you'd sing a different tune if it had been a success."

"Though what that would have proved is at least arguable," Splendor answered.

Reinhart ached all over from the beating, and sat upon a cushion so as not to be damaged by vibrations.

"You know, the interesting thing is that not only was my skin not broken, but I haven't been able to find a single wound anywhere on my body. These professional hoods are artists at their work. There's a lesson in that for us, Splendor my boy: Precision. They knew exactly where to strike and how: hurt, but don't mark. So here I am, apparently sound, but I can hardly move. I crawled to work this morning only because my wife's curiosity might have been aroused by the sight of me sitting around home, groaning. That's hardly a good example to set. Remember that if you ever get married: for peace in the home, never show an Achilles' heel."

Splendor raised one eyebrow and, after a moment, did likewise with the other.

"What's wrong?" asked Reinhart. "You don't agree?"

"I beg your pardon." Splendor put a hand to his closed mouth and looked blankly at the window.

"Well, good," said Reinhart. "I was afraid for a moment that you were opposed to precision. Now, let's see where we stand. It's clear that we can expect no cooperation from Reo, and my attempt to force it from him has, as we have seen, miscarried." The word reminded him of Gen and her condition, and he superstitiously hurried on. "Fortunately that whole disaster began and ended with me, with nobody the wiser." He spoke this hoarsely through a cupped fist, as he had when telling Splendor earlier about the beating, lest the secretaries be listening behind the door. "We were right to concern ourselves first with Reo, because of the various individuals involved, he is the one who would dig the sewer—this doesn't interest you?" Splendor had not yet turned back.

He did so now, saying, as if there had been utter silence since Reinhart commented on his quizzical look, "I *am* married."

"Is that right?" said Reinhart. "Isn't that swell." He would have liked to go over and shake hands, but—with reference to his hurts, which stopped throbbing so long as he didn't move —thought he had better postpone that salute until later, combining it perhaps with a trip to the john. Anyway: "Congratulations! A sudden elopement, I take it?"

"More or less," Splendor admitted dolefully.

"Here I thought you were poring over sewer specifications

in the county engineer's office, all the while."

Splendor answered resentfully, pointing to the blueprints on the window sill. "You haven't even perused them, yet stand ready to bring a charge of malingering."

"The longer I know you, the more touchy you get," said Reinhart. "So you had time for both. I admire you. And it goes without saying that I wish you and your new bride every happiness." He started to repeat his earlier promise to have Splendor, and now the Mrs. as well, to dinner when Gen was over her confinement.

"New?" asked the vice-president. "I got married when I was nineteen years old."

Reinhart glared at him for a while. "How the devil was I supposed to know that?"

"Now who's touchy?"

"All right, forget it."

"I'll be glad to," said Splendor. "My wife ran off last year." He gave Reinhart a keen eye. "I recall telling you."

"I could bite off my tongue," Reinhart said. "It was just one of those meaningless things one says from time to time—forget about it."

"I suppose I have the right to talk as much about my private life as you do yours."

"Look, if you're going to take that tone . . . you told me it was your mother who ran off, I don't want to be snide, but I remember it very well."

"Then," said Splendor, "I must have been out of my head, because my dear mother passed away when I was five."

"It's not the kind of thing I would make up," Reinhart pleaded. "But I could have heard wrong—in fact, I'm sure I did." He smiled weirdly.

"Set yourself at ease," said Splendor. "Your memory must be accurate. There are moments when I am capable of uttering absolute fantasy without a basis in temporal existence. Indeed, how ironical that this quirk should be made evident in a discussion about my wife—this very foible could be found at the crux of her objection to me. She was a tasteless woman, but there was some justice in her complaint. She fled with a pianist—one of those putty-colored, spiritually impoverished individuals who affect long sideburns, a thin mustache, and alligator shoes."

Reinhart wagged his head in sympathy regardless of the pain that issued in radial filaments from the base of his neck: his body was now at that post-punishment stage where those parts ache most that were not touched, as if they had jealously sucked the hurt from those that were.

"Yes," said Splendor, apparently taking it as agreement.

"This woman was not notable for her cerebral vitality. She could not find an address by number. One had to say: 'Two beauty shops past the Baptist church till you reach a jewelry store, then cross the street towards the bakery and proceed to the mailbox, turning then in the direction of the motion-picture marquee, at which count six doors along, and if you see a green awning, you are there.'"

"It is well known of women," Reinhart said, "that they tend towards the concrete. Now in thinking that over, I have arrived at the conclusion that is because they must literally carry the child for the first nine months of its life, towards the end of which time it is a burden of some substance. Whereas being a father is rather abstract if you think about it."

"I have six offspring," Splendor stated dispassionately. "Whom I never see because they went along with their mother to Biloxi, Mississippi, and the aforesaid trumpet player."

Reinhart called him on it: "Six kids? You were married at nineteen and you had six kids? You can't be more than a year or so older than I. And I heard you say the man was a piano player."

"That type of individual can perform on any musical device known to man, Carlo. He starts at ten with a piece of paper on a comb or perhaps a stolen tambourine, and will do a little tap dance on the sidewalk. He will go throughout life without one solitary higher impulse, and when he isn't drumming in the compulsive manner of a cretin imbecile, he can be found in the nearest restaurant devouring barbecued ribs."

"I've heard the later ones aren't too tough," said Reinhart, "but how about the first? Was your wife in labor long?" He disbelieved that Splendor was father of six, but neither did he charge him with lying 100 per cent: two or three, was more like it.

But Splendor took no more account of Reinhart's obsession than Reinhart did of his.

"Carlo, these details are not important. One day we will get beyond animal life as it is now known, for was it not incredible just a century ago that a human being could fly? You may jeer, but I think it wholly possible that man may in time be able to take off his body as we can now doff a coat, and pursue an existence of sheer thought."

"Speak for yourself," Reinhart advised him, not being the sort you could rebuff with impunity. "But I think even you will admit that since that time has not yet come, that as of this moment man still must dispose of his wastes, we had better get back to the sewer." So much for trying to communicate with Splendor; the longer he tried, the more difficult it was, like pursuing spaghetti with a tableknife.

Splendor's head fell, and he seemed to be peering into his crotch. Then he said: "Perhaps I was wrong."

Reinhart was instantly sympathetic. "Never blame yourself for things past and done. Just think that she would have run off regardless. If she had been married to the musician, she would have run off with you." He thought he had put it very nicely, but Splendor still sat grimacing.

"I should have apprised you, Carlo, I realize that now. But you did appoint me company engineer, and it was in accordance with my conception of that office that I proceeded as I did."

Reinhart laughed considerately. "I doubt that I could have done much to help. One has to be left pretty much to himself in matters of love. Nor can I see that being company engineer is related to your marital troubles, which, believe me, have also been known by king and potenate."

Splendor got up and went with his springy step to the window sill.

"You see," he said, indicating the blueprints and the rolls of semi-transparent tracing paper, "I have evidence of good faith. Those are copies of the plans for the Chessville sewer, dug in 1939, Chessville being, as you can verify, our suburban neighbor to the west and, again a matter of record, a community of approximately the same size as ours."

"I know where Chessville is," Reinhart said impatiently.

"Well then." Splendor struck one of the rolls, and its open end pointed towards Reinhart became oval for an instant and then recovered round. "There they were in the county engineer's files, ready to hand. Why spend months drawing up new ones? Especially since we determined to start with a mere half-mile branch through the West Side, joining the trunk north of Mayberry Place. I have here," grasping the roll he had just flattened, "precisely such a branch line from the Chessville system, with a few differences from our needs that can be adjusted by simple mathematical computations. For example, the Chessville branch is nearer two miles than a half, services more large institutions than ours would, and so on."

Reinhart shook his head, forgetting, until it did, that it would hurt him. "Splendor, you are a marvel, but for the first time since we have been closely associated, I believe I have some hope of understanding you eventually. For example, am I not right in taking the foregoing commentary on your marriage as a red herring?"

The vice-president pantomined surprise.

"Intended," Reinhart went on, "temporarily anyway, to lose me in the bushes while you pursue some monkey business on the main highway. But this I say to you: you might as well come clean now without further equivocation, because I'll know it in the long run. Anyway, I am too weak at this moment to protest very much—but also, I should add, to play Dr. Goodykuntz again."

"I suppose you'll never let me live that down," said Splendor, in a rare resort to the vernacular. He looked tired, and suddenly rested his narrow behind against the sill. "Contrary to what you may think, I *am* capable of embarrassment. . . . I'll put it to you candidly, Carlo, if that's what you wish. You are a man of good will but little faith, and thus more gifted in the critical area than the creative. You know how to deal with what already exists, but are altogether without the power to bring something new into existence. Not even your remarkable courage can overcome this natural limitation, for it is primarily an instrument of defense. You are like the present-day English, who cannot be defeated and at the same time never win. I admire you enormously, and if I did not, would hardly dare to be so frank."

"Thank you," said Reinhart, fearing the worst, because, as it happened, he agreed with Splendor's assessment of his character.

"Now I of course am the diametrical opposite, a person of poor judgment and fundamentally craven. The worst man in a pinch. I am saved from being an absolute failure only by my fecund imagination and my irrepressible audacity, which I am enabled to exercise by reason of a social situation in which no one expects anything of me."

"It's the sewer, isn't it? said Reinhart. "My scheme was to work on the men. You went directly to the thing." He put this as an accusation because he was thinking with reference to Splendor's otherworldliness.

Splendor shrugged. "I had no choice, Carlo. I realized that when I witnessed your feeble efforts to overcome Mr. Humbold with the false signatures. And now this hiring of thugs—well, really."

"So you got a shovel and pick and started to undermine one of those concrete manholes?"

Splendor shook his head.

"Worse than that?"

"I am afraid so."

Reinhart shut his eyes, the only physical movement he could make without pain, and said: "Where?"

"I think I had better insist at this point, Carlo, that caprice played no part in selecting the place of excavation. Mohawk Street was obvious, being centrally situated in the area to be served and at a lower elevation than the adjacent thoroughfares: indeed, I cannot recall a rain in recent years that hasn't

335

overflowed the existing system and backed up into our cellars."

Keeping his eyes shut, Reinhart mumbled: "Yes, I realize that you live there."

"Along with a great population of rats," Splendor added. "That curious beast who by his mode of life reminds us that man is still filthier. Everywhere we human beings look in Nature, Carlo, we see our moral superiors. It is a crushing burden. Have you ever observed the way an animal voids its wastes? Rather banally, as it were."

"That's quite true," said Reinhart, opening his eyes and shutting his mouth as if he were stuffed with sawdust and seated on Splendor's knee.

"There were efficient sanitary facilities in the palace of Knossos in ancient Crete. On the other hand, as late as the fifteenth century in Paris, the practice was to empty slops out of the window, and on one occasion a student did so on King Louis XI, who was on his way to mass. In Germany at about the same time, the Emperor Frederick was holding a council meeting when the chamber floor suddenly collapsed and half his advisors were drowned in the cesspool underneath. . . . From one aspect, the history of civilization can be seen as the chronicle of how man has disposed of his filth."

"Splendor," said Reinhart, "so far as I am concerned, you need no philosophical or historical justification for whatever it is you have done while I thought you were harmlessly amusing yourself, safely out of harm's way, in the county engineer's office. I'll admit I was wrong. It is true that experience has made me cynical. And though I started with the idea of helping you achieve self-assertion, in retrospect I see that instead I have persistently blocked you. . . . Mohawk Street, eh? How far have you gone?"

"Carlo," said Splendor, crossing his high-laced boots, "I wish to read you certain expert objections to locating sewers in suburban back yards. This is from a recognized authority." He unbuttoned the flap of the military pocket over his heart and brought out a memorandum, from which he read; " 'One: manholes get covered and lost. Two: residents object, sometimes violently, to trespassing by maintenance men. Three: dogs are dangerous. Four: shrubbery, trees, and landscaping may be ruined, and their presence adds to the cost of maintenance. Five: there is greater trouble from roots in the sewers. Six: good public relations are jeopardized.' "

"I won't fight you there," Reinhart assured him.

"The intent," said Splendor, "was to justify taking to the street itself."

"I assume, then, that for convenience's sake you started to dig very near your own curb?"

"Carlo," said Splendor, "I think we may have exploited the subject to the full, insofar as words will take us for the moment. The appropriate move, as I see it, is that we now visit the excavation itself, for good or ill." He stood up, stepped to his chair and invested himself in the trenchcoat. "Look at it this way: you will have to see it sometime."

"True," answered Reinhart, wincing for effect. "But I tell you today it hurts me to breathe. I can't understand how I was even able to drive to work. So you dug a hole in the middle of the street. I'll take your word for it. A sort of moral protest. Fine! Now just wait, can't you?, till I get into better shape. Say two days. Your hole won't go anywhere. Meanwhile, be sure to put oilpots around it at dusk, if you haven't already, and also some sort of barricade during the day, for that matter. My mind hasn't been impaired, and I shall be thinking intently. But even this early, I am inclined to approve of your impulsiveness. After all, ground had to be broken sooner or later."

Splendor ran a finger around the circumference of his left ear, the helix of which took the light like an inlay of rare wood.

"Oh," he said deliberately. "Perhaps I could drive the car. You can lie down on the rear seat, which will be quite as restful as your bed or divan at home. And arranging a system of mirrors so as to permit you, without altering your position, to see through the window, would be the work of a moment."

"I really don't care to go over there today," Reinhart announced firmly but decently. "I really don't feel capable today of evaluating whatever it is you've accomplished beyond the general statement which I have already made: tentatively affirmative, that is, so set your mind at ease. No harm done. After all, a hole is a hole, isn't it?" He chuckled. "We really should tell Claude about it and let him stew for a while. He may make a deal if he thinks we are ready to go around chopping up the streets, which Cosmo is of course empowered to do without special permit, under the terms of our contract with the town. And you are an officer of the firm. So don't let him threaten you with charges of destruction of public property."

Splendor slowly continued to do up the fastenings of his trenchcoat. "How different the arrangements might be," he said, "were comfort and convenience our chief criteria. But we know they are not, Carlo. And if I say I must insist, you will understand that the circumstances are speaking rather than I personally."

"You insist?" asked Reinhart.

"Afraid I must," said Splendor.

"Is it pretty bad?"

"Do you," asked Splendor, "wish me to construct that mirror arrangement?"

"Don't be ridiculous," said Reinhart. "I can stand, walk, drive, etcetera, just as if I were alive." He fetched his own streetwear from the closet—the second-string outfit of covert-cloth topcoat and brown felt hat that he was reduced to now that the chesterfield and homburg were *hors de combat*—and biting on an imaginary bullet, led Splendor through the outer office, where one of the secretaries tried to press some correspondence upon him, but he motioned her aside and got away with it. He meant to fire both of those girls as soon as he could figure a way to get his and Splendor's paychecks without them.

"It might be wise," he said to his companion when they had seated themselves in the Gigantic, "to check me in before we get there." In spite of Splendor's fishy manner, Reinhart intended to stay calm, having been impressed by those check lists run by various popular magazines on what to do in case of emergency: in the great Coconut Grove night-club fire, and other disasters, panic caused more casualties than the flames; on the other hand, reason had prevailed on the *Titanic*, most of whose passengers drowned serenely—though it is true that a man wearing a dress had tried to enter a lifeboat with the women and children.

"Oh, I'll get blamed whichever," said Splendor in the sullen manner that he could slip into at will, but he dropped it for a moment to wince as Reinhart's cowboy getaway burned rubber. "Isn't that childish?"

"Certainly," answered Reinhart, "but tell it to the car." The Gigantic sounded a Bronx cheer very similar to Claude's, as if he were under the hood, in fact; and stepped on its own gas. In his current debility, Reinhart dared to comment no further; every so often one heard that such a machine of its own volition leaped the curb and slaughtered innocent pedestrians simply to embarrass its driver.

When he had recovered his head, which had been whipped back against the top of the seat, Splendor patted the dashboard. "I have a way with engines. The trouble at the excavation occurred when my back was turned. No power shovel would run amok under my direction."

The Gigantic settled down to an even purr. Reinhart wished he could say as much for himself..

"Power shovel," he repeated idiotically. "Run amok."

"Certainly not." Splendor made a stout gesture. "It was the

338

foolish associate of that scandalous individual who calls himself the Maker. My error consists in permitting him to assume the controls, but I was overwhelmed by his childish enthusiasm. 'Let me run that big motherfu—' well, anything to stop his cursing, thought I. You have to consider the populace, Carlo."

Reinhart breathed with the sound of dottle being blown from a pipe. But extremity or no, he was first concerned to establish the rights of property.

"I was wondering, Splendor, where you might have got a power shovel."

"You might say I stole it," Splendor answered as the Gigantic stopped for a traffic light, as it had seldom been wont to do. "Although I suspect that there are clauses in our agreement with the subcontractor that might be interpreted as a sanction: the shovel belongs to Mr. Reo, and is the one which has been ostensibly digging the West Bend but, as we know, was simply parked in the adjacent field. I merely climbed into the cab the other day and drove the monstrous device to my house. The machine that I cannot operate has never been built."

"That must have been an interesting spectacle," said Reinhart. "Did no one see you?" Though he trod the accelerator at the onset of the yellow light, the Gigantic refused to move until the green.

"Good God, yes," answered Splendor with puzzled vehemence. "But what's so odd about a man driving a power shovel?"

"That's true," Reinhart agreed, so relieved over the clearing up of this minor point that for a moment he completely forgot the alleged disaster. What a priceless trick if they could complete the excavation and return the shovel before their enemies were the wiser!

"Would that I had never left the controls!" Splendor suddenly moaned, casting Reinhart back into fear and trembling. "I fear that what was so hopefully begun is ill finished." He retracted his hand from the dashboard and the Gigantic's engine developed a sort of catarrh. "I swear to you, Carlo, that my plans were sound sewer-engineering and my provisions adequate according to standard practice. I had my lumber ready for sheeting and bracing, which are technical terms for the supports one must place in the trench lest its sides collapse. If I mention these, it is to forestall your inevitable accusation that I did not take the proper measures."

Reinhart laughed madly. He had no other mode of release, since a middle-aged woman operating a fat sedan had settled down at ten miles an hour ahead of the Gigantic and would, he knew, stay there forever in cahoots with the automobiles coming the other way on the narrow street; one frequently ran into such a conspiracy, the aim of which was to stifle aspiration.

Oddly enough, Splendor noticed his blockage. "Ah," he said, "no short cut is available. Therefore pull to the curb and wait until the drone is out of sight. Better an outright stop than a deadening crawl; it does not ravage the personality to nearly the same degree."

Reinhart tried it, and taking off again after an outright halt of one clocked minute, found no hindrance to his travel for three good blocks. Moreover, when he again approached the woman's rear bumper, they had both reached the main east-west artery, and he swept round her in a great turn, the Gigantic roaring in exultation.

"I've got to hand it to you, Splendor. You do seem to have worked out a certain style for getting through life," Reinhart was glad to admit for the nonce, reversing, as he was wont to do, his whole attitude. And though startled, Splendor had the good taste to follow suit.

"And then I destroy everything with a massive failure of judgment," he answered. "I realize, Carlo, that your most ferocious criticism of me has been too sympathetic. Any resentment I have shown against you is sheer bravado. You have given me every opportunity to display the—uh—stuff that I am made of and—"

"Oh for Christ's sake," said Reinhart.

Splendor blushed after his fashion, which was necessarily mystical: a shadow moved across his eyes.

"Do you or do you not want to hear about that disaster?" he asked with sudden asperity.

"Then get it over with!" bawled Reinhart, as the Gigantic hurled them around a corner and wallowed for half a block on its soft suspension.

Splendor sneered faintly and gestured with his thumb like a gas-station attendant indicating the direction of the men's toilet. "It would be superfluous now. We are there."

Reinhart saw they had indeed reached the West Side, the recent corner having been that of the drugstore and the next being, so said the signpost, an ingress into Mohawk Street. He took it to the left, then had to brake sharply to avoid precipitating them into a horde of dark-skinned people that filled the roadway.

Splendor leaped out of the vehicle before the crowd could surround it. "Make way here for the duly appointed officials," he pompously proclaimed, becoming grim of aspect, and raised his right arm like a baton.

340

Reinhart left the wheel leering hysterically in every direction at once, still in ignorance but determined to reveal neither that nor the peculiar despair which it caused him to suffer. But he moved slowly and a number of Negro children reached the door of the car before he emerged from it. They stared at him with paralytic curiosity. "Excuse me," he said, for to his mind a child deserved quite as much courtesy as an adult.

"Tell them," said Splendor, beyond the hood, "that— Oh, I shall." He strode back to the children.

"I will personally," he addressed that assemblage of round black eyes, "put in jail for twenty years that boy or girl who *touches* this car; and I know who does it even though my back is turned, because of a secret electric eye which takes a picture of whoever approaches this automobile and sends it to the police." Reinhart would have liked to see him wink, and a kid or two jeer, but all played it so straight that there was no telling who hoaxed whom, and Reinhart had no faith that his hubcaps would still be there when he returned.

"Now, Carlo," said Splendor with no change of tone, "try to keep control of yourself. What is, is. And what will be, will be."

At their approach the crowd broke like water before a boat. Splendor marched on austerely, but Reinhart nodded and smiled at as many individuals as he could pick out. He loathed and feared masses of humanity and always tried to reduce them to their components. Thus he would have plunged into the yawning pit had not his authoritative friend seized him.

Nevertheless he stayed very calm, and asked: "Isn't it rather larger than necessary for a sewer trench?" What he saw was an excavation probably fifty feet deep; the street had disappeared altogether from curb to curb and then some: indeed, taking the sidewalk and several houses with it to the east. As to longitude, the gulf extended to the next corner. But he recognized the neighborhood: up ahead on the left lay the Mainwaring house, with now but half a front yard, and beyond it the alley, now debouching into the crevasse. He sensed some alterations closer to the left hand, but cautiously forbore from examining them more thoroughly until Splendor stated his case.

That person leaned over and looked into the pit, as if he were seeing it for the first time.

"Yes," he said, "that would be putting it conservatively."

"Now the way I understand it," said Reinhart, "is that this friend of the Maker's, operating the machine, grew too zealous and before he could be restrained had scooped out all this earth. . . . By the way, where is all the earth?"

Splendor moved back from the edge of the hole, which was

ever crumbling with little wisps of dust. "There you are," he said. "We no more than pierced crust, when suddenly the whole block sank. It must have been undermined by a subterranean creek."

"Is that water down there?" Reinhart asked. "So muddy it's hard to tell."

"Yes," said Splendor, "and it is apparently rising."

"The power shovel, I suppose, is beyond recover. Did the Maker's friend survive?"

"That type of individual is nimble as a goat, Carlo. He leaped from the cab as it was in the act of falling. As to the machine itself, you can still see the boom there on the right. I believe it is slowly going under."

"Yes, the water has certainly risen just since we've been standing here," Reinhart observed. "I can see it is water now and not simply mud."

"Yes, I believe we inadvertently severed a water main."

Reinhart put the tip of his little finger in his nose, not picking it but rather feeling for a hair that tickled.

"No subterranean creek, then?"

"Well, there *could* be one, in addition," said Splendor, taking up another notch in his trenchcoat buckle, the belt now so tight that he appeared to be cut in half. "But I believe that the immediate source of the flow is the main that burst when we used the dynamite."

"That could easily happen if you're not careful," Reinhart admitted. "Along with the gas mains, too, I should imagine. The latter probably accounts for the strange odor I have smelled since we left the car. You had better warn these people not to light cigarettes near the excavation." He looked back at the crowd, who were keeping their distance, but seemed not in the least apprehensive; in fact, here and there were broad grins, and almost universal was an air of sanguine anticipation.

"Well, morale is good," he observed and, as he did so, noticed for the first time a large signboard mounted between the sidewalk and the right-hand curb, very near the precipice. This board read:

WEST SIDE IMPROVEMENT PROJECT

Hon. Bob J. Gibbon, *Mayor*
Hon. C. Roy Gibbon, *Ch. of Police*
Hon. Claude Humbold, *Sponsor*
Mr. Splendor G. Mainwaring, *Sanitary Engineer*
Col. Carlo Rinehart (Ret.) *President*

Perhaps because of his proximity to so many Negroes, Reinhart had fallen into a strange mood: about the general situation, now that he had a fairly definitive view of it, he had lost all concern. We will also one day die, but who finds it possible seriously to worry about it? On the other hand, he was fascinated by such particularities as his name and grade.

" 'Reinhart' is misspelled," he told Splendor, but never said a word about being listed last. "Also that *o* should be a *p*, in the rank. I was a corporal, not a colonel, but I would be obliged to you if the whole line were repainted, leaving out any reference to my being an ex-serviceman, which is not apropos."

"To emphasize that you were a Veteran was the idea," said Splendor. "You know that publicity value of the term these days. 'Veteran Robs Candy Store,' 'Veteran Bites Dog,' and so on, in the headlines. They used to do the same thing with the designation 'Negro,' although not so much nowadays in reference to the sort of incident that any human being might engage in."

"Well, that's the point here," Reinhart said. "It rather embarrasses me to be labeled that way. . . . You say dynamite? How did that come about?"

"About four feet below the surface we encountered solid rock," Splendor explained. "This person who is a friend of the individual that calls himself the Maker, claimed to have been in demolition work in the Army and undertook to 'loosen up the dig,' as I believe he put it."

"You just had some dynamite lying around?"

Splendor shrugged. "For all I know of those gentry, I wouldn't be surprised if they kept a stock on hand for the detonation of bank vaults. They are very bad men, Carlo, but one must use what he is given, or progress becomes impossible."

Reinhart breathed in slowly, so as not to absorb too much of the illuminating gas that he now could see bubbling candidly up through the murky waters.

"You really have a vision of aspiration and expanse, haven't you?" he asked. "I don't think I ever quite realized that before, Splendor. You really are an opportunist, in love with the possibilities of life—and that necessarily involves the occasional meanness I have observed in you. My friend, you have out-Reinharted Reinhart—you are all I ever wanted to be, and twice as vivid. Whether or not that is because you are a Negro is beside the point."

"Why?" said Splendor, not defiant but authentically curious.

"Why, because that is something nobody can do anything about."

Splendor looked dubious for quite a long time, not seeing

the hand Reinhart extended towards him. When it did come to his attention, he seized it ebulliently as if it were a reward for his ingenuity and daring. But in fact Reinhart was bidding him goodbye.

"There's no doubt in my mind that you'll make it," said the president. "Certainly I can do nothing more for you—or ever have done, for that matter. The debt is all the other way. By demonstrating your freedom from limitations, you have shown me a prisoner of mine." He had begun sincerely enough, for he did admire Splendor, but as he continued to praise him he grew ever more false. There was a reason for this; the other Negroes were coming out of their initial shyness and moving near the two executives, and Reinhart yielded to an impulse to play to the crowd.

Splendor finally understood, and when he did, dropped Reinhart's hand in resentment.

"You're walking out on me? You're showing the white feather?"

"Of course," said Reinhart. "I have been trying to make clear to you that you no longer need me."

Splendor caught his head in his hands. "I have never been more astonished in all my life." He turned and stared dumbly into the pit. "What am I supposed to do about all this water, not to mention the escaping gas?"

Reinhart chuckled. "Splendor, in modern society there are agencies to take care of these incidentals. You simply call the gas company and then call the water company."

The crowd let him limp through to the car, which had stayed sound and in full possession of its accessories.

Chapter 23

So long as he was in Splendor's presence he had kept the faith, but now that the Gigantic caused the West Side rapidly to dwindle in the rear-vision mirror, Reinhart had to admit this latest debacle left him with no stomach for more. Outwitted, beaten up, and now he was liable for what might be the subsidence of the whole Negro district. It seemed always to be true of him that he was unsuccessful and responsible at the same time: unfair combination; Splendor for example invariably failed but could not be held responsible; Claude had responsibilities but succeeded. Civilian life was shit.

In his despair he had, without even thinking about it, strong-armed the Gigantic onto the state highway that left town by the northwest—the same route he and Gen had followed a half year before to go get married. This was another way of reminding himself that for a grown man to fail in business was also to fail in love, which the longer you are married gets farther and farther from the simple idea of lips on lips, or even penis in vagina, while still comprehending those. There are things like authority and who has it, and money likewise, and respect; and moral emasculation, rather more deadly than the physical version. No, he could not face Gen now, and her very condition made it worse: he would now actually be under an obligation to crack up when she was in labor—the world imposed upon the failure a definitive script giving him both dialogue and movements until further notice: bent back,

345

sick eyes, apologetic noises interspersed with a sort of plaintive venom. Into what kind of trauma was born an infant through whose misty first vision moved a hung-over, defeated dad?

That is to say, as Reinhart tooled briskly along the concrete he was seriously considering knocking himself off, doing the so-called Dutch act, though he was well aware that it was no longer popular as a means of reclaiming honor, just as honor itself was no longer conspicuously in vogue, although more of it may be around than one suspects, subterraneously or at least in B movies, or perhaps disguised as something else more fashionable. He had at any rate to rely on Gen's understanding when she got the news: greater love hath no man than to lay his life down for his self-respect. His son would then start off with an enormous advantage: "Poor devil, lost his father before he was born; no wonder he turned out delinquent." Or: "Splendid fellow, made out wonderfully though having no dad to guide him." Similar gains if the child were a girl—which he did not go into now because thinking of the male Samaritans who would aid a daughter might weaken his resolution to do the right thing by her: namely, remove himself.

And as to Genevieve, a dear person who deserved far better than he had ever delivered, she would prosper so marvelously as a widow that he wished awfully he could be around to see it. His Veteran's insurance came to ten thousand simoleons, rather more than he could bring on the hoof. Her twenty-year-old behind draped in black, and ten grand to boot. He believed she loved him as is and would miss him truly, but she was hardly the sort to mourn forever, or to become what you might call unhinged even temporarily. He had always cherished her common sense, for obvious reasons. Yes, he just wished he could be around to see it.

"There you are," said Reinhart to Reinhart, "you no sooner get an idea than you also think of the fake corresponding to it, and the latter is always vastly more attractive to you than the former. What you are planning at this moment is not a genuine suicide, any more than you looked forward to the digging of a genuine sewer, or wanted to be genuine friends with a genuine Negro. You certainly have an enormous distaste for reality." So Reinhart berated himself aloud, even as he made a U-turn and headed south towards the Ohio River.

"Well," he said at last in answer, "I think that while what you say has a superficial justification, it is basically unfair. I have had occasion more than once in the past to sense in myself a certain creative talent. True, I don't draw or sing or write verse, but I do manage to get involved in situations that seem to have artistic form and I do frequently feel an exaltation for which no other explanation would suffice than that I am something of a poet. That is, while suffering the most grievous disappointments I am inclined to rise above them and actually enjoy the spectacle.

"Now, as to your comments about fakery. My position on that is Platonic: Every earthly condition or entity is but the pale shadow of the perfect fake that stands for it in heaven, or America, which are for all practical purposes synonymous. Therefore to be is human; to seem, divine."

His other self made no immediate rejoinder, because he had reached a stretch of highway flanked by used-car lots whose owners in collusion with the police had put a traffic signal every hundred yards to arrest the flight of prospective buyers; and when he stopped at each of these, the other motorists who pulled alongside might have seen him talking to himself, a practice which though widespread on the streets of New York is frowned upon in the Middle West.

Thus inhibited in his dialogue—it was perhaps evidence of advancing age that he could not continue it without moving his lips—Reinhart turned as a person will to practicalities: he needed money on the one hand and on the other he had the car, the title to which had been transferred to Cosmopolitan Sewers, Ltd., of which he was legal president. Morally his case was weaker, for the Gigantic was essentially the property of Claude, and Claude had actually dealt squarely with him on the personal level ever since the organization of Cosmo, paid him generously and on time, given him the use of the house and car, and so on: in civilian life there was always this discrepancy between public and private.

But if he were to commit suicide, he needed a few dollars for necessary expenses, but didn't want to be seen around home or bank. *Ergo,* he whipped the Gigantic off the highway and into one of the lots, driving between parallel lines of prewar chariots until he reached a hut that evidently constituted the office, for it wore a sign: PSYCHO SAM: TAKE ADVANTAGE OF MY LUNACY AND BUY QUICK BEFORE I AM HAULED OFF TO THE HATCH!

The poor old Gigantic, cowed by these exhortations, mumbled to a stop. Reinhart had pretty well licked it anyway by his highhanded driving since leaving the West Side, so naturally he felt guilty about what he was ready to do now. "You weren't the worst car in the world," he said graciously to the heater-grille, which might be taken as its ear, and climbed out. Two men were pawing the gravel several cars down, and several others at the back of the lot, but no one appeared for him. He opened the office door and poked inside.

"Never," said a sweat-shiny, catchup-faced man who con-

347

tinued to wear a felt hat though he sat behind a desk. "I'll put your name on a list, brother, but don't look for it to come up before you're old and bald. So long."

But Reinhart had already steeled himself for the unpleasant encounter that any kind of commerce seemed to turn out to be for him.

"How do you do," he said. "If you are Psycho Sam, I want—"

The man developed an interesting combination of snarl and grin. "No sirree, brother, you don't want *nothing*, not one iota. It's what *I* want all the way. Me, Myself, and I are the only three fellas I pay any attention to nowadays. You know what 'sellers' market' means? It means *I* got the merchandise what *you* want and you're going to have to crawl to get it."

The same kind of situation they had had in real estate, except that not even Claude had exploited it in this fashion. There must be something abominable inherent in the idea of cars, which are also used as lethal weapons on the great national holidays and have made more casualties than all the wars since the dawn of man—or however it is phrased by the newspaper hacks on July 5th.

"All right, then," Reinhart said pleasantly. "Sorry to have bothered you. I'll sell my 1941 Gigantic to Max the Maniac, next door."

The red-faced guy rose from his chair and swept towards Reinhart in one fluid motion, as if he were being swung aboard ship by breeches buoy.

"Friend, whyn't you say so?" He made as if to kiss Reinhart, but dodged at the last moment, pinched the slats in the little door-blind, glanced perfunctorily through the window, and cried: "Beautiful vehicle! You get our top price."

Anticipating some difficulty with the registration, Reinhart started to explain: "You see, it's a company car, and—"

"Uh-huh," said Psycho Sam (if indeed it was he), "never you mind, big fellow, that auto*mo*bile will be in Flaarida before they know it's gone, and in South America next week, where we peddle that class-type car to rich Spiks for an arm and a leg, and they don't complain, getting nothing from Detroit for the whole war and they got the wherewithal, raising coffee and such, nothing a greaser woont do for a Gigantic Flameburst Straight Eight, he would sell his old lady on the street. . . . I can take all you get. Forget about Maniac Max. He will hump you on the price and if you holler, blow the whistle to the cops."

Reinhart got out his driver's license and the registration. "I can prove this isn't a hot car—"

Psycho unlocked a desk drawer, took from it a metal cash-box, unlocked that, and counted off eight 100-dollar bills. Stretching forward to poke them at Reinhart, he let go a long, low, half-muted fart, and said to himself, aloud: "I hear you talkin'."

Reinhart suddenly understood he was getting a good deal only because Psycho believed him to be an auto thief (strange when you considered that Negroes usually figured him for a policeman), so he took the cash and insolently flipped the ignition key onto the desk, the way underworld figures do in the movies.

This however offended Psycho, who gave him a pissy look and rasped: "You could use some etiquette, brother."

"Sorry, Psycho."

"Let me set you straight about that, too: I'm Harry. There ain't no Psycho. Just a name, get it? Kind of a come-on."

'Yeah," answered Reinhart, who with the cash in his pocket found his mood changed: essentially he hated this type of person. "Yeah, a come-on, but when a guy takes you up on it and wants to buy a car, you give him a bad time because it's a seller's market. What's the idea, or are you in this line of work just because you're sadistic?"

Harry pushed back his hat. "Who?" he asked. "I happen to be Lithuanian, but that ain't neither here nor there. No, after all, get it, you want to get a guy in here inna first place, no? If you already give him the works on the signs—'Frig You, Jack, Keep Going'—that's what he'll do. No, first you pull him off the street with his balls in a uproar, *then* tell him go jerk hisself off. Get it? Nobody can hold up under that kinda tension. He'll buy anything and kiss your dilly for it. Course it won't work for the rest of your life now they got rolling in Detroit again. Couple of years and lots of cars, we go back to patting *their* rosy rumps. I don't know what's so hard to grab about that. You just stick to the merchandising, brother, and leave the thinking to us."

The phone rang at that moment and he stuck his face into it. Reinhart left the lot on shank's mare, first time he had walked in ages. He seemed already to have a blister when he passed Maniac Max's, so in front of the next establishment, a wholesale house for tires, he sat on the pile of discarded whitewalls that made a fence around the place and put up his thumb at the traffic—though his billfold held eight hundred dollars and he could well have afforded a cab. But it was rather pansyfied, he thought, to run away in a taxi like an eloping debutante. Also he didn't want so precise a record of his trip as a taxi driver would be likely to make.

His fellow men showed their usual disinclination to be serviceable, passing by with accelerators to the floor and noses towards heaven. And who could blame them? Reinhart himself would not have stopped for Reinhart—you could get held up, beaten to a pulp, and flung into a culvert that way. He tried to look like something smaller than he was, scrooching down against the tire, but then of course his arms seemed longer, apish.

He had put on his reading glasses and was surveying the immediate area for a piece of cardboard on which he could letter MINISTERIAL STUDENT RETURNING TO SEMINARY, when a squeal of brakes lifted his heart.

It was a late, prewar Buick four-door, with one whole fender covered in red lead as a preparation for repainting: the front bumper had been taken off no doubt for the same reason, and the hubcaps as well; newspaper, held by draftsman's tape, masked the back windows. The radio aerial flew an enormous hairy tail, the size a fox might grow if he were big as a pony.

The driver stuck his head out the right-hand window—to do which he did not have to slide as far as another might: his neck seemed unusually long.

"Come on, boy!"—actually he said, " 'mon, bwa!"

He wore sideburns that fell to his jawbone, a mustache thin as a sprinkling of cigarette ashes, and a sort of blue cowboy shirt with white two-headed-arrow piping over the breast pockets.

Reinhart caught the door as it was flung open, got in and—

"Watch yass," warned his host, but too late, and he fell through empty space onto the floorboards: no right-hand seat. "I bought this machine off a nigger," his friend went on, "and you know what he did to it—used it right up, lived, eat, sleeped, shit in it, never got out the door from the time he bought it to when he sold it to me. I'm cleaning it up, boy, and putting in a new rear end. You never seen a machine like I'm going to have. I'm going to cut her down like a racer and run her at Indianapolis. I'm going to rebore her block, and I'm going to drive two hundred miles an ar, and run them p'lice off the road. One of 'em old boys stopped me yesserday, come up and put his hand right here on the winda, and I said: 'You bear pull it back, boy, or I'll break it off rat at the wrist.' You bear believe he pulled it right back too, boy, or I would of done it. You goddam right I would of done it." He clawed some hair out of his eyes and drove a quarter mile in low gear. Neither did the car have a muffler. With his behind on the floor, and the dashboard above his eyes, Reinhart felt as though he were being shot out of a cannon.

"I would of put my knife in him," continued his host, a

350

specimen of what was called locally a "Briarhopper," a person with Kentuckian antecedents. "I saw my daddy do that one-time. Put a double-bit ax right in some old boy's head for get-ting smart with him. FBI ran him to China and we never saw him since. Over there still with them Chinks, probly. I had a Chink girl once. Her gash run crossways, like they say, and that's no lie. I can go eight times a night, and then I get tared and it hangs down like a old sock. Where you from Cummins-ville?"

"No," answered Reinhart from the floor. He had an under-chin view of his benefactor and consequently a perspective on several boils. From the rear-vision mirror dangled a naked kewpie doll in a nimbus of red and blue feathers. The back seat seemed to be filled with old tires and extra auto parts, be-cause Reinhart looked it over, thinking he might retire there, but no.

The Briarhopper had one of those little swivel-knobs on the steering wheel, and drove with a hand on it, freeing the other to finger his crotch, pick his nose, and hail—girls, Reinhart assumed though of course he couldn't see, and what he heard was the frequent repetition of "Got damn! What I need is a piece of cock." Such are the variations in American idiom that certain terms reverse their meaning from one to the next: Reinhart had served in the Army and hence knew this fellow was anything but a queer: on the other hand, it was not im-possible that he might have been waving at chickens.

"No," Reinhart answered. "My name is Lorenz Goody-kuntz of Pocatello, Idaho, and I am just passing through."

The next moment he was hurled into the back of the auto-mobile and saved from serious damage only by the cushion of an old tire. The Briarhopper had suddenly climbed on the brakes. When the skid finally petered out, he pulled off the road, then turned and thrust his wiry hand at Reinhart.

"Doc Goodykuntz, I be a sonbitch! Recall me, Doc? Homer A. Blesserhart of 119 Snell Avenue and before that I uz in the Army: PFC Homer A. Blesserhart, Twenty-Seventh Messkit Repair Battalion, APO 93, care uh Postmaster S. F. My God, I must uf tuck every course you sell, and I got four of your de-grees, though them genuine sheepskin parchments must of got lost in the mail."

Reinhart sighed and crawled forward, dragging with him a wooden carton of wire and such, which he emptied, upended, and sat on. He was now at a higher level than a normal seat and feared that when they got the show on the road again, Homer's cowboy driving might send him through the roof.

"You realize, Blesserhart," he said severely, "that from my thousands of students it is difficult to remember any single one. . . ." He saw Homer's slack mouth begin to tighten in a pout. ". . . Wait a minute—nonchemical medicine, wasn't it?"

"Nuh," said Homer, going sullen again. "Nucklar Science and Industral Mechanics, Radio*tell*agrafy, Psychic Energy, and Advanced Seminar in Martal Relations."

"Oh sure, the marriage course. I remember you very well. How's the wife?"

Homer put his head out the driver's window. They sat on the shoulder of the road, between a wholesale tile house and a gravel pit, and a little farther along was a giant plaster cone from a window in the base of which a red-haired guy in a white overseas cap sold frozen custard, and one of those gas-pipe-rack establishments that offered two-pants suit for 19.95, alterations included. However, Homer had averted his head from embarrassment and not to enjoy the view: a blush ran over his pimples.

"I ain't got no missus," he confessed. "I tuck that course because I figured it to be dirty." He put the car in motion again, running her up close to the ass-end of a big semi that encapsulated them in blue Diesel exhaust. "And my God it was, Doc. You must of got a lot of poongtang in your time if you'll pardon the exprayshun—'swat them gooks call it in the islands." He at last swung around the truck, choosing a place where the highway narrowed to two lanes and went into a tight curve: it was a close game for several seconds with an oncoming coupe, but he finally bluffed it off the road, into the adjacent gully, and through a chicken-wire fence on the rise—Reinhart could see no further, for by then they were negotiating the next turn. One thing, his malaise was lifting.

"Then what about those baby shoes hanging in the rear window?" he asked.

"Belong to muh baby uncle Pearl," said Homer. "He be three years next week. . . . Doc, don't tell me you come up here to deliver my diplomas? Got dam. You recollect I wrote you I uz getting farred from my job? Well I was. I left one of your Martal Relations lessons in the tollet at the garage where I had been reading while taking a dump during my lunch ar, and some woman come in to get gas and slipped in for a quick leak—because we just had one tollet, not like the Sohio with men's and women's—and saw it there and come running out to Joe Sawyer who's the prop. of that station and said you got a sex-fiend hereabout, so Joe come to me and he uz sore as a boil and said you goddam prevert, I don't want no twenny-two-year-old mechanic who still pulls his pood in the tollet, and farred me. I uz going to put my knife in him but he uz holding a big socket wrench at the time and looked like he

352

would cold-cock me as it was. But that was real nasty, Doc, and I tell you I never abused myself after the age of maybe ten, looking in the Sears catalogue at ladies in their undies. These here pimples must have come from something else."

"I'm sure they do, Blesserhart," muttered Reinhart, who was trying to remember, from one of those magazine filler-articles on What to Do When You Expect a Car Accident, the proper sequence of safety measures: cross arms over face, crouch down below windshield, relax, etc. Fate had ironically elbowed him into what promised to be a suicide most authentic. This is where his hubris had led him: you should not even joke about shuffling off the mortal coil.

CROSSROAD, said a sign showing a black $+$ on a yellow field, and from the real one for which this was but a symbol, crawled an old Ford station wagon with sides of diseased wood.

"Hold ya hat," cried Homer, the foxtail outside his window flying horizontal, "we going to sheer off this sonbitch at the tailpipe."

But it was likely that they would hit nowhere near so far aft. Reinhart found that in an emergency he was more inclined to guard his crotch than his eyes—strange, but his hands were paralytically cupped there while he shouted: "Brakes, oh for Christ sake, brakes!"

"Ain't got none at this fast," Homer answered merrily, accelerating further in lieu thereof and still steering with one hand on the swivel-knob.

Homer's estimate was right on the nose: *brannng*, the Buick's left fender severed that portion of the Ford's exhaust pipe that extended beyond the rear bumper, without touching the body. A masterful piece of driving on the part of Blesserhart, who waved his no-grudge at the other driver—an old man with a load of egg crates, Reinhart had time to observe before they barreled over the next rise, who never knew what didn't hit him.

Onward, Homer driving as if in exemplification of Splendor's philosophy, which they had both got from Dr. Goodykuntz, whom Reinhart was impersonating for the second time. Small world. Pocatello might be a feasible hideout after he had taken simulation to the limit and faked a departure from the world. He must consider the particularities.

"Going feeshing down the river, Doc," said Homer, when queried on his destination. "And be proud to have your company." He flashed a mouthful of nothing: his front teeth were gone, top and bottom, at age twenty-two.

Down the river, splendid! Immediately Reinhart had his plans: drowning was the most satisfactory kind of death to counterfeit. A fire wasn't bad, but you had to provide some sort of organic material, say the body of a pig, to be found afterwards in a charred state; still, they would look for teeth that agreed with the chart of your fillings provided by the family dentist. Then too, Reinhart did not like to destroy property, which was also his objection to spuriously polishing off oneself by blast—TNT, dynamite, gas, etc., you name it, they were all hard to harness, the noise was abominable, and once again you would need that pig or whatever, to be found in fragments.

You couldn't beat drowning, with driver's license, social security card, and checkbook left on the riverbank—and of course a note announcing your intentions and pleading your regrets.

"I'd be proud to come along," he answered solemnly, gulping to relieve the ear-pressure as they roared down a slope, and catching the dashboard to hold himself on his box as they began a new ascent. "And," Reinhart continued, "I'm sorry about those missing diplomas, but you must know from reading my literature that I have many enemies. Indeed, banding together, they have at last succeeded in flushing me out of Pocatello, Idaho, altogether. You see me at a very low point, Blesserhart. Frankly, I am on the run. I shall never forget the kindness you have extended to me. I confess I was at the point of doing away with myself when I met you."

Homer was touched and blew both nostrils, alternately, plugging the other with a forefinger, out his window.

"Just let me catch one of them boys trying to pressecute you, Doc, that's all I say. I'll put my knife in him and that's no lie. I'll turn my dog on him. I'll carve him inta a woman. I'll cold-cock him with one blow of my mighty fist, and I can do it, too, I got hands like arn. I'll lay his belly open and grab his hind legs and flip his guts out like you do a rabbit. I'll snatch him bald. I'll bend his ears like a aileron, and he'll take off straight up in a stiff wind. I'll string him on a ramrod and cook him over a slow far. I'll rip out his gizzard and use it for bait." And so on, adding several more stanzas to his never-ending epic. Reinhart was a little embarrassed to the shown up by comparison as prosaic, he who was supposed to be the poet. Trouble was, the most romantic of his doings had usually to be concealed, such as his project at present, and as for talking colorfully, he couldn't without a bellyful of drink.

"Pull in here," he ordered all at once, and Homer was equal to the occasion, swinging with the scream of tortured rubber into the parking lot of the roadhouse they had just been about to pass at seventy miles an hour.

He ripped the hand brake on, and stared at Reinhart in respectful obedience. "If you want to go to the toilet, Doc, you could use them booshes there. Don't look to me like the Kit Kat Klub is open yet."

"Matter of fact, what I wanted was a shot of red-eye," Reinhart robustly announced.

"Whyn't you say so?" Homer brought a flat pint of drugstore port from his back pocket, spun off the cap, and passed his hand, with its glaze of grease, over the muzzle.

Reinhart refused very nicely, confessing an aversion to sweet tastes at this moment, so Homer said O.K. Doc, threw his head back so far you would have thought it would topple off his neck, and drained the last drop of the purple contents, breaking the bottle with a *whaaaap* on the blacktop when they left the car.

Homer was was almost as tall as Reinhart, but thin as a snake standing on end. His shoulders were broad when you faced him, but let him turn in profile and be vanished. His hips were nonexistent. He wore western-style pants with horizontal pockets, in which while walking he carried his hands, thumbs protruding; and his shoes were yellow to match his eyes, with points like stilettos.

They barged into the roadhouse. The interior held no surprise: the chairs were upended on the tables, the air was dark green and smelled like a kennel of wet dogs, and the bartender, who had hairy forearms, came in from somewhere out back, lifted the trap door that admitted him behind the mahogany, and asked with cynical courtesy: "What's yours, gents?"

Reinhart motioned Homer to a stool and ordered grandly: "Give the gentleman whatever he desires and pour me a Courvoisier while I use the phone." He grouped through the gloom towards the telephone booth he could just barely spot at the right rear. Inside it smelled of urine and of course neither the dome light nor the little fan was operative. He dialed home by the flare of his Zippo.

"Gen?"

"Carl, hello."

"Well, what's happening?"

"I gained a pound and a half last week, but the doctor said though it's abnormal, don't worry."

"Swell," said Reinhart. He had forgotten her visit to the obstetrician, if the truth be known; she must have gone in a cab —for which it was characteristic of her that she did not reproach him, swine that he was. Still, he couldn't help being impatient: "And what else?"

"He said for my constipation to eat ordinary licorish candy

rather than take all that milk of magnesia that has begun to turn my stomach. Did you know that ordinary licorish has a cathartic action?"

"I certainly didn't," said Reinhart, "and I think it's wonderful. Any calls for me?"

"Not so's you could notice," gaily answered Gen, who was in a very bright mood for no reason at all, whereas yesterday she had been depressed almost to point of coma: so it goes with gravid women.

"Listen," Reinhart began, opening the booth door slightly to freshen the air, but that of the room was scarcely better and Homer had brought the jukebox obstreperously to life, so he closed it again lest Gen misinterpret. "Listen . . ."

"And I had the usual nosebleed, quickly over. And he said that varicose vein behind my left knee will go away after delivery, as will the heartburn, the insomnia, the rash, the backache, and the leg cramps."

"But you knew that already, darling," said Reinhart, touched by her naïve need to catalogue. How come he leave her at such a time? But Claude and the Gibbons would get him if he returned; and she was in no condition to come along. He had called merely to get the lie of the land, but he now resolved to tell her everything.

"Listen, hon. Things have gone wrong with the sewer—"

"Now don't be angry," she said. "You were out when I called the office to remind you today was my appointment with the doctor, so I had no resource but to call Daddy."

"Genevieve," Reinhart said gravely, "If I've told you once, I've told you a hundred times that while we don't see eye to eye, your father and me, I would be the last person to want to come between you. Besides, something has come up regarding my work that may make it necessary for you to rely on him for a while. I may have to disappear—"

"I think he has begun to accept you, dear. Really. I noticed a definite slackening off of bitterness. You might even think of taking him to lunch one day soon. Which reminds me, it's past one o'clock, and I wonder if you are ever going to get home to have lunch today."

"Not today, Gen, and not tomorrow," Reinhart said portentously.

"Oh good," cried Gen, only too pleased. "Then I can have liver, which you despise."

"Yes," said Reinhart tragically, "you'll be on your own now." He had meant to tell her the truth but couldn't seem to

356

get it out, hence this fishy sort of idiom that revealed very little while making him feel as if he really were about to destroy himself.

"Yes," said Genevieve. "Did you have anything else to say at this moment, dear?"

"Maybe I have, Gen," Reinhart answered reproachfully. "Perhaps I have something of overwhelming importance to tell you. . . ."

"Well do you? Because the doorbell has been ringing constantly for the last two minutes, and I can see through the window that it's the boy from the drugstore with my vitamin capsules."

"No," Reinhart said simply. "Just don't believe everything you read in the papers." He hung up. He might try again if he could work up any conviction that he would get to first base with Genevieve, but it seemed unlikely. The nearer she got to giving birth, the more she resembled her own mother in woolly-mindedness—whereas premaritally there was a certain equivalence between her personality and that of her old man; both had a certain sharpness though his had rusted. Anyway, somewhere along the line Reinhart had got out of touch with Genevieve while growing closer to her—which is something the hacks who write on problems of marriage never understand or least pretend not to. He wondered whether you could become so intimate with a woman as not to know her at all, to pass on the street without recognition: "Now let me see, could that be Isolde, dearer to me than life itself?" Whereas the waitress in a greasy spoon, say, to whom you were altogether indifferent, was an open book. Such a girl, for example, was waiting outside the phone booth: a stingy-haired blonde with vivid make-up, a little droopy as to tit, a trifle wide in the haunch, and—he would bet, for she wore bell-bottomed red slacks in the fashion of the day—a bit thin in the calf.

"I'll bet," he addressed her defiantly, "I'll bet that I can give a pretty good analysis of your character though I have never seen you before."

She made simple-minded googoo-eyes at him, which were of such a pale blue that had they been outdoors he would have sworn he could see the sky through the back of her head.

"Gee kid, you can?"

"How about this," said Reinhart. "You are patient, but you don't know anybody else who is. Considerate of your friends, you suffer from inconsiderateness of others. You are nervous, but most other people think of you as the soul of calm. Everybody tells you his troubles; but when you have difficulties, you suffer them in silence. You are generous to a fault, but this generosity is seldom returned, and never by the people who have profited most by yours. You—"

"Oh golly," squealed the blonde, "you are sure a genius like Homer said. You got me to a T, honey. Go on." She laid her breast against his arm, then giggled. Curious sensation.

"You know Homer?" asked Reinhart, who in truth had momentarily forgotten his friend. "I thought you were waiting for the phone."

Her hands instantly ran all over him, like a team of hamsters. "I'm ol' Homer's lit-tul cousin, and I'm your date, and I am goeen to call you Goody."

Chapter 24

Billie-Jo proved to be this girl's name, complete with hyphen; she wrote it on the bartop with a finger wet with condensation from her glass. Her smile had too much gum in it, her teeth being small though clean, and her cheeks were flaccid unless she smiled; she was not unfair to look upon in the present, but you thought she might be extraordinarily pretty in the future, if, straight-faced, she would smile, or, smiling, she would sober: thus she was always at once both a disappointment and a promise, like life itself.

But Reinhart was annoyed with Blesserhart for having picked up these quiff—for Homer had one too, a brunette with features strong as a Turk's—when he had said he was going fishing down the river. So after considerably ordering the girls' drinks replenished—rum and Coke for Billie-Jo and bourbon and a gingerale for the other, who was called Grace and looked about the age to have that name which had now passed out of fashion, that is, about ten years older than the others—when the bartender with rude deftness had splashed in the Coke with one hand while simultaneously foaming in the gingerale with the other, Reinhart dragged Homer off to the men's room.

It was reasonably clean this early in the day and furnished with a vending machine from which you could purchase a comb for one dime. Over the urinals were those birdcage things holding a disinfectant the emanations from which opened up your sinuses, and in each drain a ten-pound chunk of ice lay melting. Homer stood a considerable distance from his stall, legs spread, as if he were watering the lawn.

"Blessherhart," said Reinhart, "I thought we were going fishing. How did your cousin and her friend get into the act?"

"I sweared I never knowed they was hereabout, Doc," Homer answered, stripping the gears with his zipper. He then bought a new comb, though one already showed in his back pants pocket, ran it twice from eyebrow to nape, and discarded it in the flip-top wastecan. "They got a tent show in the lot neckstore and come in here when they seen ar machine setting outside. I can't say if Billie-Jo knowed it was mine or thought it belonged to a couple a salesmen with hot pants. Anyway, them two come in and Billie-Jo reckonized me right off and said, 'Hi, Homer.' An I said, 'Hi, Billie-Jo.' An she said, 'Homer, I wanna innerduce you ta' "—

"Yeah," Reinhart interrupted, "that goes without saying."

"Sure," Homer agreed. "And I tell you this, Doc, when Billie-Jo fown out who you was an all, why, you could'nt hold her back from going right over to that telephome to wait on ya." Staring at his shoes, he exclaimed: "Well, will you looky there—I peed on my toes!" He slid under a compartment door, for the sit-down toilets were all pay-type, and then climbed out over the top trailing a long string of tissue.

"So I uz thinking, Doc, you're sure right about that feeshing down the river, I uz sure going and am still." He frowned upon seeing that the dye from his shoes had come off on the paper, and accused them of inverse practices. However, he quickly regained his bonhomie and said to Reinhart: "But what I uz wondering about, Doc, is if you'd care to take a minute and drop your load."

"No thanks," Reinhart answered, grimacing. "I don't have to go."

Laughing like the devil, Homer figured out the confusion. "I don't mean take a crap, Doc. I mean take Billie-Jo over behind the tent and put it to her. I guarantee you won't regret it, though it's true I ain't laid a hand on her since she was fourteen an she must be twenny now if she's a day, got damn." He squinted. "If it's all the same to you, Doc, I'd just as soon leave this tollet because that chemical smell is getting to my eyes. Got damn, I druther smell shit than that, woon't you? . . . Anyway, I thought we could take in the tent show, and that don't open till seven. We can just as well go down the river later: I ain't got nothing else to do, as I told you being farred from my job, and you're sure welcome to join me. There ain't nothing beats feeshing at night." He smiled with

360

his vacant mouth and swung out of the men's room. Reinhart stayed behind to reflect that he either played along with Blesserhart or found another means of getting where he wanted to go: Homer had obviously decided to stay and would not be dissuaded even by Dr. Goodykuntz: you find such strong wills in people who otherwise have little recommendation, and their existence must be acknowledged and come to terms with if you are ambitious.

He ran a washbasin of cold water and threw some on his head, for fatigue had set in at the thought of spending several hours with Billie-Jo. Suppose they were seen by someone he knew—it would spoil the pattern altogether: Sewer Official Flees with Carnival Girl. That could never be explained to Genevieve, who would not forgive him even if he then proceeded to commit ostensible suicide. On the other hand he had very little inclination towards going out onto the highway again and thumbing another ride; he was psychologically comfortable with Homer and in the role of Dr. Goodykuntz: you could hardly count on the next guy's being as amiable as the former, or swallowing the latter, at least to the same degree as Homer. . . . No paper towels, but the washroom was equipped with one of those hot-air devices which could be swiveled upwards to dry the face. *Better*, said an enamel plate on its top, *Than Towels: Avoids Chapping!* Or so, anyway, went the theory. In practice Reinhart confirmed what he already knew, and left after ten minutes still dripping.

"Where'd everybody go?" he asked the bartender, who was refilling a nest of stainless-steel compartments with cherries, olives, lemon slices, lemon skin, pearl onions, orange segments, pineapple chunks, and lime rounds, having already checked his extensive stock of potables.

"And yet," the bartender admitted to Reinhart, leaning on his balled towel and speaking from the side of his mouth as if the place were packed to the guards, "before we close tonight some wiseguy will roll in and ast for pinecone cordial with a cumquat in it, like they serve in Manitoba, or somewhere. The Joker is what you get a lot of in this business and is worst than your drunk. Sometimes you can't tell him from the expert, who knows better than you how to mix a thing, leans over and supertends running the glass-edge through powdered sugar for your sours and so forth. Then comes the Sophisticake, who wants for his girl to have you reckonize him and so will call you by the first name. You get all types in a bar. This is where to learn *human nature*." He smugly leaned away.

"Or anywhere else," Reinhart could not forbear from stating; he had little taste for the arrogance of barkeeps, barbers, and taxi drivers and saw no good reason why they should know more about man on the basis of drunks, dirty necks, and addresses of ill repute, than a cost accountant or shipping clerk with his statistics and manifests, or for that matter, than an agoraphobic spinster with her African violets on the window sill. "Where'd you say the others went?"

"Who?" said the bartender, after the fashion of his trade, though Reinhart's party had been the only people in the place. "I got my job to do, sir. I can't keep track of every customer." He backed off, smiling by the book, and took a little sip of the Coke-over-ice-chips that such a fellow always keeps in a recess below the bar.

Reinhart spotted the dim orange glow of a booth-light midway along the gloom of the west wall, and soon found his friends beneath it: the light, not the booth itself, though Homer and Grace, in a clinch, looked as if they might manage the other as well, and were gradually sliding sub rosa. This movement was checked by the entry of Reinhart's long legs. Grace for some reason sat on the outside, and the booth was so narrow that his right knee extended into her crotch, so that she could go nowhere and Homer's hand was pinched. They of course continued to ignore Reinhart.

Would the same had been true of Billie-Jo, who instantly molded herself against his right side like a great piece of soft cheese.

"Kuh-yoo-it?" she said close, referring to the other couple, and he knew his ear was all over lipstick.

Having brought with him his third tot of brandy, he now consumed it neat, and tried to avoid her personal attention with a merry but superficial reaction which missed the point at every interchange. Thus when she again said "cute," this time meaning him, he laughed blatantly and vibrated his arm so as to shake her loose—however, she not only successfully rode out the tremors but improved her position by means of them: his shoulder was now clamped between her breasts and his elbow on her belly.

Meanwhile, across and under the table, Grace was doing something to his captive knee, sort of jazzing it slowly though otherwise occupied with Homer, who was gobbling like a turkey behind her head. "Ah!" cried Reinhart, jerking himself from the booth, Billie-Jo of necessity coming along partway and falling one knee on the floor. "I'll buy another round for all." The girls declined, which should have made him suspicious, but he refilled Homer and himself, and so it went for hours, all afternoon, and—though he switched to beer—in no

362

time at all, not having eaten since breakfast, Reinhart was stinking drunk.

However, it had always been Reinhart's peculiarity that alcohol never put him into oblivion. His coordination suffered, but his senses grew ever sharper. For example he had not while still sober realized, as he did now, that the girls were trying to pick their pockets, Grace succeeding with Homer, if a jackknife, a coil of wire, and a burnt-out sparkplug constituted success. She also found a condom, naturally in his watchpocket; it was loose, i.e., not in the little regulation red-and-white Trojan folder, and therefore may have been secondhand for all anybody knew. Snickering, she dangled it as public property and might even have inflated it had not Reinhart expressed opposition. Homer of course was himself altogether unconscious, his head lolling in whatever direction he was pushed by Grace, who gave him a shot with her elbow from time to time to emphasize his helplessness. His eyes stayed somewhere in the upper region of his skull; you could see only their blank underparts. His mouth wore a fixed smile: the man to whom no damage could be done. He had even left the key in the Buick's ignition and the windows open: Who wanted it? Who wanted him? Who gave a damn? Reinhart, having his cross to bear, envied Homer greatly. For him, Homer had succeeded Splendor as an image of freedom, yet the fact remained that Reinhart, always Reinhart, still represented reason, order, and responsibility, because if he didn't, who would?

That is to say, in this situation he alone had valuable property which could be robbed, and therefore as much as he might have liked, he could not forget himself in the fashion of Homer. This was the story of his life, but he was not without devices. In the present case, on one of his trips to refill the drinks, he had ducked into the john and switched his money from inside coat pocket to right-foot sock, all the way under the instep, where he could feel it wrinkly, tickly, on his way back to the table. So he was safe enough from Billie-Jo's maraudings, unless he passed out, which was unlikely.

But what he could not for some time understand is why, now that Homer was unconscious and would hardly be able to see the show, he, Reinhart, did not tote him to the car and himself drive down the river and proceed to fake the suicide, etc., afterwards hiding out until the stink blew away from the sewer disaster, then reappearing, or if not, having Gen join him in Salt Lake City or wherever, that is of course after the baby was born, and together carving a new life.

Why he did not do this was a mystery to him until he felt

Billie-Jo's hand working like a mouse in his pants pocket. The liquor and the *frottage* had made him horny. And not only Billie-Jo. With Homer out of the running and anyway money-less, Grace shunted him like a wad of old clothes into the corner of the booth and rode Reinhart's knee with new vigor. There was something merciless about her strong nose and stark eyes that both appalled and attracted him; and his feelings were the same, in reverse detail, towards Billie-Jo, who like a wad of cotton candy was both clinging and intangible and inspired in him a desire to wreak some cruelty upon her while at the same time he was being victimized by Grace. In their combination these two girls made up a parody of one exemplary woman.

Which went to show that it was not really lust that detained him, but the possibility of isolating the truth about that condition. He never forgot his mission to bear witness to the principal phenomena.

Billie-Jo lingered for a moment in the misapprehension she had found a roll of bills.

"Ah, but you have!" said theoretical Dr. Goodykuntz, including Grace in his audience. "Money is power, is love, and vice versa. All the good things are one, and this is their homeland. Abe Lincoln rose from log cabin to White House; about his sex life there is a deficiency of data, but it can be safely assumed that he would attract many women with his sad, emaciated face alone. George Washington on the other hand, looking like the portrait of himself, which is to say, in one dimension—no profile or back-of-head, if he turned sideways he would disappear—where was I? Oh—G. Washington is said to have perished from the effects of leaping unclad from a lady's window into a snowbank in Alexandria, Virginia. Which, whorehouse or private domicile? On entry of the police or husband? Who can say. Stories vary. The whole thing may be a canard. But the point remains, why won't you find it in the history books but, instead, told around Army barracks? Four-F's thus never know this terribly important detail—whether true or false—about the Father of Our Country. At least he wasn't a fairy, like Alexander the Great and Julius Caesar."

"Wha you find, B.J.?" crassly asked Grace, who on the precedent of Homer seemed to think Reinhart was drunker than he actually was.

"Only his dummy," answered Billie-Jo, giving Reinhart a push as she came out of his pocket with the other hand. "Hey, Goody," she shouted in his ear as if he were passing out, "wha you give me and Grace to let you do wha you want? C'mon, hoss." She kicked his ankle. "You want a party?"

Now Reinhart, the valve-lifters of whose mind were clattering so loudly he could barely hear her—and besides, Grace's presence stirred something infantile in him—thought she had asked him if he wanted a potty, and he declined: no, thank you.

"Tole you he sounded fruit to me," Grace averred. "All thet talk."

Her evil look pierced Reinhart's oysterish consciousness. "Yeah?" he rejoined. "That's what so negative about your world-outlook, my good woman. You're always opting for dead ends. Ignore the pun and reflect that lust is ever temporary, like the appetite for food. Neither the steak nor the sex you had yesterday have any bearing on that for which you hunger today. That is why eating and screwing—I beg your pardon—coitus, are crafts rather than fine arts like epic poetry and portraiture. Not to mention that gluttony is finally paralyzing: when you satisfy such a taste, all movement stops. And one of the ways a person can turn into a thing is by going into a condition of absolute stasis—a characteristic of an inanimate object being that it cannot move of its own volition. . . . And you are only parading your ignorance if you state your belief in some kind of equation in which silence is a necessary condition of potency in the man. The male Zulu [Reinhart made this up] chatters incessantly during the sexual act, that is to say, gives everything while his mate accepts anything, and I don't have to tell you what a stallion he is."

Reinhart sank his glowering face in the beer glass. He felt the girls signaling above him, but failed to take alarm, for he could handle anything in the fields of sex, pocket-picking, roadhouses, or carnival tarts, and they had better believe it.

He must have muttered the last phrase aloud because Billie-Jo ran a lock of hair over his nose and said: "We don' believe you, Goody. Show us you are a man. Come over inna tent and show us, Goody. I don' think you kin." She edged him out of the booth. "But you better pay the man fore we go, hon. Where's your roll?"

Grace slipped out before they did, hard and mobile as a greased bearing. She wore spikelike bangs, among the black of which there were threads of gray, and the same kind of sailor-slacks as B.J., but hers were stuffed into low cowboy boots with spiked heels. She grinned knowingly at Reinhart as he registered how she was shod.

She said: "Mebbe we can do business with this stiff, B.J."

Meanwhile, deprived of his support, Homer melted all over the booth-bench and dripped onto the floor.

Reinhart shrugged at that, but sounded a deep, testicle-laugh at Billie-Jo's obsession with his wad. "Ignorant people

365

like yourself always assume that they are craftier than the person of culture. Of course, sometimes they are, like the rotten little chippie that made a fool of poor John Keats. But I don't have consumption," he gloated with his chin in the air. "I paid the bartender as we went along."

"O.K.," B.J. answered good-naturedly, and took his right arm as Grace clamped onto his left. "I won't fight you, Goody. I do *anything you want*. Don't be shy to ast me."

They were strong, though of course Reinhart could have overpowered them; the drinking had altered his sense of balance, but hadn't touched his strength. However, he staggered along quietly between, only rarely using the girls' arms for actual support, and swallowing a lot, for a strange sensation, which resembles nothing so much as thirst, follows on an afternoon of beer.

"I'll come back for him," he shouted to the bartender, indicating Homer's putative corpse. "He'll be all right. Don't worry about him."

"I wouldn't think of it," answered that person, who had changed identities since Reinhart last noticed. No, nothing nightmarish: the other's shift had probably ended. Reinhart was not of the persuasion of drunks seen in movies, for whom the world spins around like a pinwheel, and who are always encountering weird, masklike visages, voodoo-looking types— these usually in murder films. No, he was high but reasonable, and took an epiphany of his father-in-law, sitting at the bar, as not the real thing but rather an apparition created by his conscience. He knew that what he should have done, he had not: jettison these trollops, reclaim Homer, and set off down to the river. But he simply couldn't resist seeing what concluded from the premises established; and surely, in Western civilization, curiosity is a good.

Other customers were extant, and as his little party left the establishment he discovered that day had become night. In the lot next door there were indeed a congeries of tents, linked by garlands of illuminated lightbulbs. Ah then, time for the show; no orgy was planned; the girls were simply capturing someone for the audience, which from the looks of things would be spare enough, though the big mouth of a loudspeaker mounted above the ticket booth was blaring bizarre promises to one and all: *Strange and Exotic Rites Hitherto Forbidden, Weird Pleasures of Alien Peoples*, etc. Inside the booth, when they reached it, Reinhart saw a square-jawed man with gray hair and the complexion of a slice of ham. He looked at Reinhart, likewise, and said with the timbre of loose plumbing: *"Come on Joe see the girlies ya can't lose."*

"He's with us, Al," announced Billie-Jo.

"On da house," Al said mechanically and struck a little bell.

Reinhart made some effort to pull himself together as they trudged up the dusty midway towards a large tent at the far end—though hardly far: it was obviously a crappy little show, and between here and there the route was flanked only by several small canvas lean-tos covering plank counters and wheels of chance, each administered by an individual saturnine, nay, downright sullen of mien.

These persons exchanged greetings with Reinhart's guides, who made certain smirks and gestures that they assumed he did not notice, Grace all the while with her nails in his arm. It amused him and still fitted his needs to be thought a patsy: victims made the best investigators, having no positive principles to clash with those of the subject under study; they want only to survive, and with such a negative obsession the vision stays unclouded.

Heroic girlie posters rose before the large tent, three of them side by side, a big triptych to the left of the entrance flap; to the right stood a platform from which a barker would harangue the crowd when one assembled—if that ever happened, which seemed unlikely at this point, Reinhart being, so far as he could see, the only non-employe at large. The posters were worthy of note, representing a trio of long-stemmed American Beauties, limned, as the saying goes, by some unsung master, and on a base of tin, for they had here and there been dented by rock-throwers—and it was interesting to speculate on the identify of the latter: homosexuals, kids below the age of desire, or an enraged citizenry banning the show from their town? Whatever, the one on the left showed a rusty nipple through her bathing suit.

Yes, bathing suit, and a conservative model at that, for when an amusement is really dirty, the illustrations are modest; and vice versa, as everyone knows who has scanned the stills outside a movie house. Reinhart had actually never attended this type of entertainment before, but when in high school he had talked to others who had, and this was the setup: a center curtain divided the interior of the tent into two equal parts and also bisected the stage, which lay in the middle. For the first act, the audience was admitted to that compartment nearer the midway; the girls paraded briefly in G-strings and fringed brassieres, then slipped behind the curtain onto the back stage, and the audience, upon payment of another fee, filed into the rear. Here, the reports had it, promises were fulfilled and compromise was unknown: the girls stripped to the buff and performed in little tableaux that robustly acknowledged the interests of ardent virility. As in burlesque, there were classic routines: e.g., a flowing festoon of femininity, each girl with her hands on the breasts of the next, called the "Milkmaids' Delight." In another, half the performers became human wheelbarrows with outspread legs as handles and hands representing the forward wheel, and were trundled about the stage by the remainder of the company. There was also a simple whorehouse scene, for which one of the male roustabouts was enlisted: the girls formed a naked rank, he selected one, led her to a canvas cot, and the lights went out as he unzipped his fly. For it was a general rule that not even such a show displayed a man in the altogether, this type of diversion being smutty but not perverse.

The tent was empty as Reinhart entered on the arms of his friends, though the lights were lit. Plain dirt lay underfoot, and seating arrangements were never provided. The whole plant could be struck and folded away in an hour, and the troupe on the road towards their next location, which, like this, would be on county ground where jurisdiction was lax, outside some city limits.

"When's show start?" Reinhart mumbled; he hadn't spoken for a time and his lips were thick.

"Ain't going to be none," said Billie-Jo as Grace left them and went through the curtain to the rear. "We can't get no audience. I think all of the fellows in this locality have turned queer."

He shook his head. "It's really terrible if even your kind of woman has the wrong slant. . . . I don't mean to insult you, I mean simply with all your experience in the field. . . . If the men aren't here, they're probably out having direct contact with girls, which if you ask me is a lot better than if they came to this show just to look and then go practice self-abuse."

"Yeah, turned queer, I figure," repeated Billie-Jo, in that half-witted oblivion that takes anything for assent. "That's why we uz so glad to run onto you, Goody. Can tell you're a real bull, and I'm sure glad you prefer me over that Grace, who is thirty years old and got gray hair all the way down." She suddenly undid two buttons at the neck and pulled the blouse over her head, coming into view in her show-bra, a loose, faded hammock of greenish-gray tulle with flaking sequins.

Mind you, they were standing beneath a sagging light bulb, on the dirt floor, before the bare stage, of this empty tent. Reinhart fought against an impulse to reach into his shoe and buy his way out untouched and untouching. He was capable of great sympathy for an entertainer without someone to play to, not to mention a member of the passive sex forced by circumstances to become active. On the other hand, if he had not already lost all desire on the walk along the midway and the entrance into this canvas desolation, the brassiere alone, which was both washed out and dirty, would have been enough to do it.

B.J. had turned her back to him and was smiling garishly over her left shoulder while her hips rolled up one side and down the other: the standard parody of the female tempter.

"Will you listen a minute?" he said. Damn that beer; it seemed to have coagulated in his esophagus. "Stop shaking it for a moment, will you? I don't find your behavior exciting, see. You know what makes a woman attractive?" He knew he was raving, and lowered the volume. "Well, it isn't anything blatant, I can tell you. It is an air of receptivity to change, with at the same time a hint of defiance to it. . . . For Christ's sake, put your slacks back on." For Billie-Jo had, with the always startling rapidity of a woman undressing, divested herself of the garments in question. Her upper thighs, of which he had the posterior view, were already, at twenty years of age, rather lumpy, and the back thread of G-string emerged from the division of a bottom that hung conspicuously low. The ensemble was exceedingly melancholy.

Reinhart backed away as she turned and vibrated towards him.

"C'mon, Goody," stated she, livid tip of tongue showing, "everybody deserves a good time once inna while."

"It's a sort of radical conservatism," said Reinhart, desperately returning to his characterization of the female temperament, for, as someone has said, ideas are weapons. "Or vice versa, but the point is, a tension between contradictories. Armed pacifism!" In retreat, he found his heels at the base of the little stairs rising to the stage, and went up one, B.J. pressing him hard. "Pacific warmongering!" Three steps more, and he strode the boards as if in some old melodrama turned inside out, heroine pursuing villain. "You see, the peculiarity of women is that they are all born wishing to be men, and their big problem all through life is to get over the resentment engendered by that seemingly dirty deal. Therefore they must first be assured that being a girl is good—" he continued moving backwards, B.J. having by now undulated to his level— "and secondly they must be disabused, by force if necessary, of the misconception that one can be a man without having the appropriate organs. I'm not saying it's the best of all worlds, believe me, but you see it's the only one we have." He smiled apologetically, as a man does in righteous expectation of forgiveness for a situation which, though he never made, he profits by; and threw out his hands in that gesture designed to look like supplication but really signifying *it's no skin off my ass*.

A specialist in the spreading of limbs, Billie-Joe made her own interpretation of his open arms, and rushed into them hurling him against the curtain, into it, and finally through it to the back stage, when an old friend struck him with a carriage whip. It was indeed Grace, who aside from a great deal of hair wore nought but her cowboy boots.

Reinhart asked: "Say, what's the big idea?"

"Down, boy!" ordered Grace, lashing him again about the shoulders, and from the audience sounded several snickers, two chuckles, and that one outright guffaw that can always be expected.

Audience? Unfortunately yes, some fifteen or twenty souls stood in the pit, near enough to rest their jaws upon the rim of the stage, explaining why nobody had been seen either on the midway or in the front compartment: the show was on the back. Indeed, it appeared that Reinhart had been precipitated into the whorehouse scene itself, with Grace as madam and three more naked girls representing the stable, which Billie-Jo now joined, dropping bra and G-string enroute.

Now it took Reinhart no time at all to see that what you had here were two groups of humanity each of which believed the other to be a preposterous and degrading spectacle. In the girls this conviction manifested itself in a fixed sneer; in the men, an anxious smirk.

"C'mon, Rover," said Grace, goosing him with her whip handle, "pick your mate for breeding purposes." She snapped her fingers at the girls, and number one stepped out of line and pranced about like a toy poodle, behind high and her hand bunched above it like a pompom tail. Number two was squat and bowlegged as an English bull, and her choice of role was obvious. Three coursed the forestage as a greyhound bitch; and Billie-Jo bayed like a hound.

During these doings Reinhart stood there in felt hat and topcoat, curiously at ease though ostensibly an object of scorn being simultaneously tempted by the whores and punished by the madam. Man of iron? Not really: for example the lash itself was made of soft felt with a little wing of cardboard at its extremity to provide the sound of pain without the effect. Secondly, the fluids he had drunk earlier still supplied the inner reassurances. With a constant snootful he could have been a great actor.

Having waited courteously until the last doggie fell back into rank, he proceeded to address the swarm of white faces some four feet beyond his toes.

"Well, fellows, there you have it. With all respect to these misguided but hardworking girls, I think you'll admit it's not much. Finally you must ask yourselves: 'Why did I ever come in here to see the imitation of a cat house when I could have gone to a real one for a couple dollars more?' Reality, friends. That's all I'm asking you to consider, reality instead of fantasy. Is that so difficult?" *Craaack,* Grace's fake whip snapped past his nose.

"The answer is Yes, of course. Don't think I can't understand that you have come here because here failure is impossible. Even in a brothel, not to mention the ordinary walks of life, you are required at the minimum to *get one up.* Let him sneer who has a perfect record in this respect—if he can be found." He paused a moment to allow the popular expression of cynical mirth, but none came. And before he resumed, Grace gave him a big push in the small of the back and said: "Go home, Jack, your act is over."

Next a tough-looking male individual—probably the barker, whose presence had gone unnoticed—appeared and, grasping Reinhart with tattooed hands, endeavored to hurl him off the stage. Too bad that when attacked by thugs, only the night before, Reinhart had not been caught in a rhetorical mood. Now, showing only the briefest twitch of exasperation, he lifted his big fist like a sandbag and felled the intruder stone cold.

"Jeesus," said the long-necked girl who played the greyhound, "he's one of them athletic preachers from the YMCA. I'm taking off." And she did, running bare-ass through the curtain, followed by three of her colleagues. Billie-Jo, however, remained and started again to croon her ritual invitations, the perfect model of half-witted solipsism; she would have seen a grizzly bear as merely a big stiff in a fur coat, looking for a good time.

But indomitable Grace, now wielding the leather-bound whip handle, struck Reinhart with it in back of the knees, causing him momentarily to buckle.

She said: "Go away, you bastid."

Of course the audience took these events as part of the show, and when Reinhart forcibly disarmed her, which involved certain close-quarter work, they were moved to cry ribald encouragements: "Don't stop now, boy!" "Shove it in." And so on, advertising, so to speak, their disregard of his earlier commentary. He then appreciated the fact that uttering the truth is one thing and getting anyone to believe it, another —which made him one with all the great prophets. John the Baptist had to get his head cut off before anyone would take him seriously, and everybody knows about the lengths to

371

which went Jesus of Nazareth.

Reinhart really was convinced at the moment that, unless he got his message across to this representative sample, the entire male element of the great American nation would degenerate into voyeurs and onanists. He decided he must make the sacrifice, and let go of Grace so as to prepare his martyr-costume. Up to this monent, she had taken each incident more ill than the last—one had to admire her spirit while deploring its object—but as Reinhart dropped one by one his garments to the floor, she shed her ferocity to the same rhythm, and when his hat, topcoat, suit jacket, shirt, necktie, and undershirt were gone, and his belt unnotched, had nothing left but fright.

"Listen, Jack, our permit don't cover pulling the job on stage, for Christ Almighty!" She dashed for her own heap of clothing, down right, incidentally trampling the recumbent barker, who whimpered "Uncle!" in his profound sleep.

But Reinhart, still in his pants, waylaid her from behind, lifted her with boots kicking, and said to the audience: "I hope you're not missing any of this. Your manhood is at stake, friends, and no less. What I ask of you is merely to exercise it; Do, instead of Look. Act, rather than Imagine. Move, in place of Talk. You will thank me in the years to come. And—here's the irony—the women will thank *you*, because can't you see that *they don't want to win!*"

At this point, Reinhart's trousers fell about his ankles and, while still holding Grace, he found it easy to step out of them, which was more than he could do with any kind of equanimity in the privacy of his own bathroom. Billie-Jo, who with her blank self always accepted the prevailing temper, confirmed that the power now was Reinhart's: she had wandered down amongst the crowd and, clutching everywhere, found three takers at once. They bore her to the ground.

"Excellent!" cried Reinhart from the platform above. He was at the first button of his drawers, and had put Grace on her feet while retaining her with his free hand. She had by now ceased to struggle, and hung limp, muttering "My God." Her hair, close to his nose, had an unpleasant smell, like rancid bacon grease. She was very repulsive to him. Unfortunately he couldn't have made the same point with Billie-Jo, who was more feasible. However, you might say it was being made for him on the ground below. "Wonderful," he shouted down, and to himself, with even more gusto: "Old fellow, you may as well accept it: at last you've had your success."

There remained no reason why he should continue to take off his clothes, and much to be said against it. When she saw his trousers going back on, Grace asked numbly: "Now what?"

He signaled to the audience, and several of them, inspired by the splendid example their fellows were setting with Billie-Jo, came up the staris.

"I?" he answered. "I'm going home. I'm a married man."

He dressed quickly while the men negotiated with her, for rape, of course, was out of the question; he was happy they had not made that erroneous interpretation; these chaps, take them all in all, were the salt of the earth, and though his own tastes might vary from theirs, he felt no undue superiority over them. Sex is a poor area for one-upmanship, considering what we all have done or will yet do, not to mention unconsummated aspirations.

When Reinhart was once again in full street attire, he bade a jolly goodnight to all and went through the curtain into the front compartment. A premonition told him to spy around the corner of the door-flap before issuing through it to the exterior. He saw a squad of sinister-looking roustabouts advancing on the tent, led by Al the ticket taker, who was middle-aged but carried a piece of lead pipe, and followed by the three girls that had got away. These last had covered their nudity with chenille bathrobes, hems angelically dragging the ground and raising little clouds of dust.

Now Reinhart did briefly consider slipping out by another route. In some ways, victories are more taxing than failures, and he was very tired. At the thought of mounting still another attack he could only groan. Nevertheless, he would not tolerate the obscuring of the principles he had given so much to establish.

He marched out boldly, flashing a half dollar in the palm of one hand and waving the bill of sale for the Gigantic in the other.

"Jenkins of the County Vice Squad," he growled at Al. Then stowing away his fake badge and search warrant and thrusting out his belly, he said: "I'm running you in for flagrant immorality. And if you don't drop that pipe, I'll shove it down you throat."

Al let his weapon fall, punched the greyhound girl in the mouth, screaming: "You said he was a reformer," and wailed at Reinhart: "Wha do you guys want, my blood? I already paid off your partner when we come in yesterday, and since then we ain't grossed a hundred. Jesus, what a locality. Go on, take it all, take my shoes while you're at it. Who gives Al a break? Sock it inta Al, it's the national sport." He began to sob, his old jowls aquiver.

Miss Greyhound spat out a tooth, and said: "Al, we could—" Al's roundhouse knocked her flat.

"Here now," Reinhart remonstrated, "Brutality to women is prohibited by the laws of this county."

"Well, I got you there," said Al, grinning through his tears. "That happens to be my wife."

"I'll tell you what," Reinhard said. "I didn't know one of my boys had already been around. Callahan, probably—round-faced fella about five-ten with sandy hair?"

"Nah, tall fella, long-faced fella, called Dixon."

Reinhart nodded. "Yeah, Dixon." The sounds of merriment came from the tent behind them. "Don't worry so much: listen to how well the show's going."

"And you tole me he broke it up," said Al to his wife and caught her with a left hook just as she was rising on one knee.

"I don't care if you are married to her, that sort of thing makes me very uneasy," Reinhart admitted. "I wish you would quit it."

"Why don't you butt out, you sonofabitch?" the woman yelled at Reinhart.

Al would have kicked her had he not been blocked. He threw up his puffy fingers, which were yellow from cigarettes. "Listen to that. She ain't got no sense, officer. Don't hold it against me."

"I don't, said Reinhart. "It is clear that woman cares for you, Al, and I never question Love, but rather marvel at its existence in a world so full of other distractions." He then gave permission to carry on with the show, free of further harassment by Jenkins of the Vice Squad providing only that certain alterations, of which Al would be apprised by Billie-Jo and Grace, be maintained.

"You will make more money," Reinhart said. "Your customers will be satisfied, and not frustrated. And finally, though the entertainment will still err on the side of vulgarity, in the degree to which it makes public what under perfect conditions would be kept private—which charge of course can be brought against any art—it will no longer outrage Nature to anything like the old extent. Just remember, you never have to apologize for normality."

Saluting God and country, he made himself scarce.

Chapter 25

Reinhart had been sidetracked, but in a good cause. He had always wanted to strike a blow against that teasing. "Only in America," as a great man once said, "can you find a woman who looks like a whore, dresses like a whore, and acts like a whore, but who if you treat her like a whore will call a policeman." Reinhart had no faith that his reforms would last—he was opposed by the whole mystique of modern entertainment as well as the general sexual trend of *pis aller;* also, in this show he had been operating on the lowest level—but the principle had been stated. Despite Bee's advice he could not help being idealistic.

He went towards the roadhouse to fetch Homer, whose car was still parked in the lot but no longer by itself, the evening being well into the shank, the game afoot, and the area alight with pseudo carriage lanterns. He was twice almost run down by arriving customers, one vehicle carrying the sort of young marrieds who pledge at their nuptials never to become stodgy, and for the first year go out on the town every Thursday night; the other, a bald-headed joker with a kidney condition: he couldn't drink himself, but liked to see some life around him while he ate his chicken sandwich on whole wheat. Naturally Reinhart couldn't *know* these details, but the possibility that he might be absolutely wrong—that the couple were gloomy adulterers and the other fellow an alcoholic—made it all the more interesting to speculate.

Speaking of patrons, the door suddenly swung open and one came hurtling out upon the shoe of a brawny chap in a tuxedo, who cried:

"And *stay* out!" Carried on by momentum, the ejectee went some yards into the parking lot, clawing feebly at nothing, like a lobster en route to the boil; at last his borrowed energy ran dry and, spreading the eagle, he plunged to the earth, nose down.

As luck would have it, he fell directly in Reinhart's path. Otherwise the ex-corporal would have ignored him at all costs, there being little profit in commerce with a drunk, escpecially when one himself is sobering.

"Come on," said Reinhart, prodding him with a shoe, "you're in the roadway and might get run over."

The drunk put his hands beneath his chest and did a perfect push-up, one straight line from back-swell to heels—he did ten, in fact, up and down, before collapsing prone again.

"Do that, drunk or sober," he said, the words rattling out of the gravel against which his mouth was pressed, "you rotten mongrel, and then tell me I'm no gentleman."

"Hello, Blaine," said Reinhart, for by the light of the fake carriage lanterns he could mark that it was indeed his father-in-law, whom he had earlier seen at the bar as if in a vision.

Raven rolled over onto his back and, looking up with closed eyes, asked: "What's your school?"

"Dartmouth," said Reinhart to pacify him. "Where's your topcoat?"

The next moment the door opened again and the bouncer flung out the garment in question. Reinhart had turned to fetch it when Raven, having risen quietly to his knees, tackled him ferociously.

"Fumble!" he crowed. "Our ball." He clutched the wadded coat to his midsection and ran towards the highway, stepping high and carrying a fixed straight-arm for which he soon found a use: down went the bald-headed guy, who had just left his sedan. At the edge of the highway Raven turned left and circled back, crazy-legging along the line of parked cars. Reinhart was not nearly so nimble; he also felled the bald-headed chap, who was just arising, but by accident; and had to postpone his apology.

It became clear he would never catch his father-in-law by direct pursuit, Reinhart himself moving like a freight train, inexorable but slow. Nor was wearing down the quarry to his taste, for by that time scandal would long have outrun them.

So he stopped midway alongside a convertible and shouted: "Out of bounds! Your ball and ten to go."

Raven whined in protest, but at last he trudged, head down, back to the arbitrary line of scrimmage and surrendered his coat to Reinhart, who now represented the disinterested referee instead of Dartmouth.

"God, these field lights are poor," said Reinhart, pointing to one of the lanterns on a post nearby, and as Raven snapped his head in that direction in the resentful, too-quick reflex of the drunk, Reinhart threw the topcoat over his father-in-law, buttoned it as a strait-jacket, and carried him to the old blue Continental, whose location he had established during the chase. Raven uttered a few expletives deep within his swaddling clothes, then apparently passed out, his weight going sodden.

The key had been left in the ignition, so after tripping the device that moved the driver's seat back to accommodate his length, Reinhart started the motor and pulled out, leaving his plans behind and Homer to the mercies of roadhouse personnel.

Put a father-in-law before friends and before thyself, said the old maxim, probably Chinese, that Reinhart hereby honored, not to mention mere common decency. Reinhart really was a traditional person even though he habitually frequented innovators, and nobody could say he did not keep the faith, even when to do so hardly accorded with his own welfare. It would be much too late, by the time he got Raven home, to start out again for the river—these things are done only when the wind is up. Tomorrow he must take his medicine, and everyone would turn against him, no doubt including Genevieve. He drove towards total disaster, and yet whistled along with a popular tune that came over the radio, which oddly enough worked, though notes in the lower registers vibrated the whole car. Was he mad? No, if you can question your reason, you still have it; so says every expert in the field. He was simply trying to take life as it came, which always seems odd.

Meanwhile he twisted the tone-control back to treble, in cultural superiority to Raven, who was out of date in a preference for the bass notes; everybody nowadays was turning to treble, along with other harshnesses, no doubt in reaction to the mushiness of wartime.

After the first quarter mile he opened a button at the neck of the topcoat to give Raven air; and after the second he closed it again, on the principle that better the passenger suffocate than the driver be overcome; it had smelled as if they were closeted in a distillery. Booze could be a philosophy only to the unaesthetic. But it was poor satisfaction indeed to count his points against Raven: look at the slob—who actually couldn't be seen because of the topcoat hiding him. Reinhart opened it again, and also the windows, even if the night felt cool now that he was at last relatively static after a long day of almost continual motion. The incoming breeze blew back the covert-cloth lapel, revealing Raven's face in the glow of the oil-gauge: features of prime quality, lower lip petulant, evident infantilism, absence of doubt—the world was wrong but never Raven—*But, poor bastard,* it suddenly occurred to Reinhart, *he must be over forty.*

This was the sort of reflection that Reinhart felt gave him depth and perhaps compensated for some of his failures of judgment. At present, however, it served to mask his authentic feeling. Her father's chin reminded him of Genevieve and the resemblance made Reinhart jealous, causing him to doubt whether he was loved to the same degree as, say, Al the dirty-show operator. What appeared to be pity was thus actually a mean gloating at the likelihood of his outliving Raven by at least two decades.

He had some difficulty, when he reached town, in finding his in-law's house, for he had been there only twice before, by day; and by night the neighborhood was rather dangerous—to the soul, not the body; no lurking footpads, but a fluorescent nameplate at the mouth of every driveway, so that the headlights gave acclaim to a succession of misapplied apostrophes: "The Wilson's," "The J. Dominic Santangelo's," and the like. Raven's house, however, when discovered at the end of the block, had none such, and Reinhart felt a little twinge of pride.

His substitute dad jerked to life as they entered the drive. While Reinhart pulled on the parking brake and switched off the ignition, he was conscious of being watched by beady eyes, and prepared to defend himself. Consequently, when Raven put across his right hand, Reinhart captured it and squeezed hard.

"Sir," said Raven, wincing, "it is my pleasure to serve with you. Welcome aboard. . . . You have a mighty grip, as I have too, except you claimed the initiative."

"Are you all right now, Blaine?" asked Reinhart, letting him loose. "Because if you are, I'm leaving."

"Ah, we're on first-name terms?" Raven asked, widening his mean eyes. "I'm sorry, sir, you have the advantage on me. Are we acquainted? School, club, Corps, or before the bar?"

"Bar," said Reinhart. "To be specific, the Kit Kat Klub. I don't mind your forgetting that, but in view of the trouble I've just gone to in bringing you home, you might remember that I am your son-in-law."

Raven chuckled. "Excellent jest, my dear chap. You must be my guest soon at the officers' club. Have the darky seat you at my usual table if you arrive before me." He was shaken briefly by a drinker's cough deep in the gullet, then flung out the door and lurched across the lawn, making it to the first shrub and falling therein.

Forty-five minutes later, when Reinhart had reached his own home by putting one shoe ahead of the other *ad infinitum*—he had forgotten to take the money from his sock, and had a great blister to show for it—Genevieve answered the door in her pneumatic housecoat, across which he had to bend a considerable distance to find her mouth. She tasted of licorice.

He licked his lips and remarked genially: "I see you have already launched the attack on your constipation."

She shook her limp hair, and wouldn't have looked like much to anyone not related to her. "Yes, and I'm sightly nauseous. I forgot I never could stand licorish as a child. Mary Janes were what I liked, and those mothballs with an almond inside."

"Weren't they great?" said Reinhart, falling into both nostalgia and the leather chair and taking her, childish mother, onto his knee. "And do you recall those miniature pop bottles made of wax and filled with colored water, which you drank and then chewed the bottle like gum? . . . We're getting old, Gen, and though you may want someday to leave me, you will never be a virgin again."

"Carl, you can be quite asinine into the bargain," Gen replied, from which phrase he knew she had spent the afternoon reading. "I trust you've had a productive day. You reek of beer."

He deflected his mouth. "Business, I assure you. Did Claude ever call?"

"Hours ago. Carl, why did you also miss supper both last night and tonight?"

"It's too complicated at this juncture," said Reinhart; "and since I wasn't untrue to you, it really doesn't matter." He let her sink into the chair as he left it. "I'd better call him back. Darling, we may have to take a trip, even though you're not supposed to travel. But pregnant movie stars do it all the time without mishap, and so do the wives of prime ministers and other heads of state. You just have to keep calm. And think of the pioneers opening up the West in their covered wagons, along trails where comfort stations were unknown. Have we really degenerated so much since? Not if I know my Genevieve!"

While this malarkey still echoed through the vaulted living

379

room, he went to solarium telephone and literally dialed C-L-A-U-D-E—CLermont 2833.

"Bud, greetings and salutations!" shouted the boss before Reinhart had even identified himself. "If this ain't bud, get off the pipe, fella, because I ain't got time for no one else."

"Yeah, Claude," Reinhart admitted sheepishly. "O.K., let's have the worst."

"Where you been all day, bud? I hope it ain't with my enemies, because you won't be happy with 'em, guy. Lissen, you and me work together like ham and mustard. Ain't I always said one day I'd take my hat off to you? Well it's on the floor here right now—or was till the durn dog run off with it—*Hey! Get him, Louise, in the dining room!*—scuse me, bud, that pooch is a mind-reader rivaling the best to be found in the trained acts of two continents. I will maybe go on tour with him if you turn me down, but you won't, no sir, you would never do that to Claude Humbold who brought you up like a dad. . . . I just had your own daddy on the horn, bud, and he is proud as me. You recall just last spring when he begged me to take you on, I figured you was feeble-minded. I'm big enough to admit it bud, so don't throw it in my face."

Reinhart couldn't make head nor tail of this, so he stuck to his original assumption. "All I ask," he said, "is that you give Splendor a break. He had nothing to do with it, even though the excavation is near his house. It was all my idea." So long as he was going to get it in the neck anyway, Reinhart had decided to be noble.

"I'm way ahead of you," cried Claude. "Your friend already told me that himself." He went into a ridiculous imitation that sounded nothing like Splendor, who never—well, really he had once, and perhaps for tactical reasons had again: "Ohhh, Massa Claude, Massa Reinhart done blowed up duh whole West Side."

That's my friend, all right, said Reinhart to himself.

"Now I never had anything against a smoke, bud, and no man can say I gouged them on the rent all the years I have owned them crummy dwellings on Mohawk Street, but I call that typical: your typical coon never looks ahead like you and me. However, what I can't figure is how you knew I just negotiated, in the name of the town, a government loan to raze that district and erect a nice new development of reinforced concrete, with a swell blacktop parking lot out front where we'll paint white lines so the kids can play hopscotch and suchlike during the day when the cars are gone. I can't figure it, bud, because I kept it mighty durn quiet on account of the Senator's connection—nuff said, bud, these phones might be bugged."

"On the contrary," said Reinhart, from his coma of clairvoyance. "He's the only one who does look ahead. That's what is so sinister about him."

"I don't get your drift, bud, but whatever you say is jake with me, because I couldn't have got them dumps cleared of inhabitants all winter without blowing them up—which you did. I consider that remarkable timing, and want you to know a fella is already down the office relettering the door in the name of Bud Reinhart, Limited, followed by your name as chairman of the board. That's big stuff, guy. You can also keep the house and car, and I'm sending over a deep-freeze in the morning. Call my butcher for a deal on T-bones, bud; he flies to Texas once a week and collars his beef on the open range."

Reinhart closed his eyes and cleared his lungs; he was very tired, what with beatings, performances, and football games, but had saved strength to ask wryly: "Claude, I think I deserve to know. Do you have any intention of actually building this project?"

"Bud," said Claude, "to make a long story short, that rests like everything else in the hands of the Guy Upstaris, don't it? And now with your big hole, I figure it to be humanly impossible to do anything but wait till the earth settles; your snows are on the way, bud, already developing up in Western Canada, wherever that is; and your rains will come next, bringing you already up to the Fourth a July weekend, when everybody goes out to the highways and run one another down now that you can't blow yourself up with firecrackers any more. And so it goes to Thanksgiving, and you got turkey and fixings to stick your face in. In short, bud, I can give you every assurance that the situation will bear deep thought; and if Humbold Houses ever rises against the skyline, it will be a true triumph of man against nature." Claude cleared his throat. "That's all I would predict at this here time, bud, because already I can hear the scratching of some filthy spy tapping these wires. Just grateful it ain't you, bud."

"Claude," said Reinhart, "I wonder whether we might work out something for Splendor? I might even make that a condition of my own involvement. I'll tell you about that guy: I have never figured out whether I even like him. I sometimes suspect he has never told me the truth about anything. For example, he makes the most fantastic comments on his own family. He has been guilty of certain inexcusable failings. I fear his interest in power, and am suspicious of his attitude towards authority. Yet when all is said and done, Claude, I feel privileged to be associated with him. It might sound strange in view of the foregoing, but judging by the standards of dignity, exquisite manners, and moral vision—and meaning no offense to present company—Splendor is the only real gentleman I have ever known this side of the Atlantic."

"Bud," said Claude, "you can gas all day about the oddities of a nigger, without making a buck on the transaction. If they wasn't funny peculiar, then they wouldn't be niggers, if you get me. What would be the point? Personally, I like them and hope they keep it up. You'll never find a nigger who's a pacifist, bud, and that's good enough for me any old day.

"But speaking of your pal," he howled, "who you think's president of the new firm? So nobody can say there's prejudice in relocating our dark-skinned friends? Who I'm going to put, incidentally, up in Vetsville and run out them college types— no offense, bud, but I don't see they pull their weight. And I rely on you, as an ex-serviceman, to keep the Legion off my neck. Tell them they can have my present residence for a clubhouse. Me and the Mrs. are moving in one room over a groshery store. I ain't got no need for space, bud. Give me a phone and a Cad, and I'm happy: communication and transportation. You know my motto, fella: *Never knock democracy!* See ya tomorrow at the office."

Reinhart hung up, and was still in the same contemplative mood when he reached Genevieve.

She said firmly: "Carl, I have thought it over and decided to stay put, right here in my own house."

"Well then, that's that," said Reinhart, who was big enough of soul to let her think she had won the point, and small enough to add: "By the way, I spent some time with your father this evening."

"You see? I knew everything would turn out right when you came to understand him. That's generally true with everybody, Carl. Why, when I first saw you myself I though you were an awful jerk."

"It is true," Reinhart confessed philosophically, worming himself under her, "that I am generally underestimated." He yawned. "I think it has something to do with my facial expression. Perhaps I should squint a little—you know, narrow my eyes to look crafty. Or grow a mustache, like Claude's. What do you think?"

Gen applied herself to the problem, studying his features at a range of three inches, he holding his breath because of the beer.

"If you care to know my opinion," she said finally, "I would grin so as not to show my front teeth."

These books?
Fiction.
Keep telling
yourself that
as you read.